BURKE'S STEERAGE

BURKE'S STEERAGE

by Tom Burke

G. P. Putnam's Sons, New York

Copyright © 1965, 1966, 1967, 1968, 1969, 1970, 1971, 1972, 1973, 1974, 1975, 1976 by Tom Burke

SBN: 399–11662–1

Library of Congress Catalog
Card Number: 75–34992

PRINTED IN THE UNITED STATES OF AMERICA

For my parents and
Kim Stanley, John Dodds, and Vivian Vance

Acknowledgments

The material about Catherine Deneuve, Robert Redford, Federico Fellini, David Merrick and Lauren Bacall originally appeared in, the New York *Times.* The material about Julie Christie and Mia Farrow originally appeared in a somewhat different form in the same publication.

The material about Ryan O'Neal, Jon Voight, Truman Capote, Dennis Hopper, Malcolm McDowell, Geraldo Rivera, Pat Boone, Cathy Macauley, John Schlesinger and "Princess Leda's Castle in the Air" originally appeared in *Esquire* in a somewhat different form.

The material about Roman Polanski, David Carradine and Kris Kristofferson originally appeared in *Rolling Stone,* as did the material about Liza Minnelli and "The Violent Millennium," in a somewhat different form.

The material about Peter Fonda originally appeared in *Cosmopolitan,* as did the material about Cybill Shepherd, in a somewhat different form.

The material entitled "1966: When There Was Still Splendor in the Grass" originally appeared in a different form in *Gentlemen's Quarterly.*

The material about Jane Fonda originally appeared in *Holiday.*

CONTENTS

Introduction

It is said that Benjamin Guggenheim refused to believe that the *Titanic* was sinking until the water licked the soles of his alligator pumps. He had first-class passage, and in his ingenuous era, first-class passengers simply did not sink into the ocean. The people in steerage believed. Pity that Benjamin Guggenheim remained cloistered on the upper deck; if he'd ridden steerage, he'd have believed and could have saved himself by buying one of the lifeboats.

Aboard our present *Titanic,* outward bound, we all know perfectly well where the ship is going to end up. There aren't enough lifeboats, and almost everyone's traveling steerage. No time for swimming lessons; besides, the water, like the air, is packed with obstructions. No use attending survival class, the school burned down. No use sending distress signals; even if there were someone to hear, the line's out of order.

Lifeboats, though barely seaworthy, do exist, and are available to a few first-class passengers with the money to buy them and the wits to use them. Such people may pursue the last happiness by the last viable means: they may seal themselves inside climate-controlled Maseratis, fly privately to ecologically balanced private islands, avoiding such ultimate steerage as the Boeing 747. There are no harmful chemicals in the pâté at "21" or Le Bistro. Let the help electrocute itself in microwave ovens, abridge itself in trash compactors.

Even in Benjamin Guggenheim's time, even before the *Titanic*'s maiden voyage was violated by an icy protrudence, canny forward-thinking types—Elsa Maxwell, Lizzie Borden— perceived that we'd soon enter an age in which survival would become uppermost, and that the only assurance of it, eventually, would be via the new celebrity, or notoriety, being created at nickelodeons, on crystal sets and in modern newsprint. They also sensed the multiple benedictions of the new eminence once movies talked and the wireless added pictures—power undreamed of in all the eons, beyond anything imagined by any stage actor, even a Bernhardt or a Duse, or by anyone ever mentioned in a newspaper before Patricia Hearst's grandfather thought of syndicated columnists.

Fame looked like such a seaworthy lifeboat. There was no

way to understand, yet, that escaping steerage through media canonization would subject one to Guggenheim's undesirable fate, profound discomfort caused by unfamiliarity with truth. Some who'd fought up, via fame, to Deck A did see that the benevolent soft lighting in first-class obliterates too many realities, and tried to descend again into steerage, to examine things under bare bulbs. There are a few of these on the passenger list here, a few who've made it back down. Too often, though, the down staircase is permanently sealed.

So those who don't return below remain in the last lifeboat, the vessel of self-cherishing insulation. In which, of course, they will at least sink with a measure of grace, descending through days which, though clearly numbered, are symmetrical, harmonious, lived, as they are, in hybrid worlds. Which, if not braver or newer, are worlds that others many only ponder, and covet.

New York, 1976   —TOM BURKE

BURKE'S STEERAGE

1.

The Day of The Day of the Locust

THE WIND MACHINE IS IN THE SHOT AND IT IS NOT A PERI-OD WIND MACHINE. The first assistant director rasps that through his bullhorn down the resonant length of Stage 15, Paramount, Hollywood, and the other assistant directors, the special-effects and lighting men and the stunt coordinators converge upon John Schlesinger like flies on a crumb. Whispered consultations are held.

"Spray the fucking thing black," is Schlesinger's decision. A thousand artists, actors and technicians wait in freeze frame until this is done, until five glossy Panavision cameras, turning with the whisper of feeding insects, focus again on an old Mitchell camera shaped like a 1937 Cord, resting on an ancient camera crane with iron struts like the Eiffel Tower's, as it feigns the shooting of "The Battle of Waterloo," the climactic scene of *Waterloo,* the movie-within-the-movie of the novel *The Day of the Locust.* An asbestos stone farmhouse, set against an elaborate faked French-countryside backdrop, bursts once more into nonconsuming flame, cannons fire blanks, rented horses rear, and men dressed as soldiers charge up Mont St. Jean, a steep wood-and-canvas hill erected and dressed reverently all week like a Druid mound. The hill topples spectacularly in a complex mess of splintered scaffolding. Schlesinger grins, wickedly triumphant, not just because his shot has gone so well. In *The Day of the Locust,* the novel, Nathanael West meant the collapse of the *Waterloo* set as metaphor for the future collapse of Hollywood movies. He perceived, even in the thirties, when he wrote his books, that no other culture in all the aeons had invented movies because no other culture had so needed opulent, per-

15

petually replaceable illusions; that the illusions wouldn't work; that the industry that produced them would attract staggering multitudes of the psychotically vain and avaricious, the monumentally self-serving, who would finally destroy it. In Hollywood at this moment, no one is more aware of this, or more removed from it and amused by it than John Schlesinger.

For in what the current illusionists hopefully refer to as the New Now Hollywood, Schlesinger has never been and is not now either new or now. In spite of *Darling* and *Midnight Cowboy*, both of which made a good profit, and *Sunday, Bloody Sunday*, which didn't, but was vaguely assumed by movie people to be "quality product," meaning it was authoritatively discussed but largely unattended; in spite of Oscars and the delivery to audiences of Julie Christie, Jon Voight and Alan Bates (previously unknown and mostly unemployed), Schlesinger has missed, or avoided, becoming really fashionable and therefore readily bankable. People don't want to finance his movies. He is not invited to Bel Air brunches where film deals are conceived, he is not asked to Sue Mengers' parties, Bob Evans doesn't give little dinners for him. Joyce Haber doesn't know from him. Hef doesn't ask him up to the Playboy Mansion West. His name is mush upon the palates of the gas-station and parking-lot entrepreneurs who back films; it is chronically mispronounced, the "ger" enunciated not like the "G" in Gene Kelly, as is correct, but like the "G" in Gulf and Western.

Partly, the problem is physical: Schlesinger is forty-eight, and though he sometimes wears Bel Air circuit uniforms, suedes and leathers do not quite hang right if you rather resemble Santa without the hair. Those directors for whom little dinners *are* given—Peter Bogdanovich, Billy Friedkin, Francis Coppola, Sydney Pollack, the Pointer Sisters of contemporary film making—are not only the correct age, a sort of perpetual thirty-eight, and the correct size, also thirty-eight, but they make correct movies, appropriate products to represent our nation at foreign film festivals. Their work is regarded, in Hollywood, as intelligent without being intellectual, and sensual while remaining heterosexual, whereas Schlesinger's themes are held to be dank, anti-American, too thoughtful, and rather too kinkily British. "Of course nobody in Hollywood had actually read *The Day of the Locust*," a film producer, not with Paramount, asserts.

16

"You don't exactly see the book on Beverly Hills coffee tables. All they knew was that it was supposed to be Schlesinger's great Hollywood putdown. Except one big-studio PR man, I *swear* this is true, he said to me, very seriously, 'I hear Schlesinger wants to bank this English sci-fi, about bugs. . . .' "

All of which vastly entertains Jolly John. The shooting of the collapse of Mont St. Jean is supposed to last four days; everyone knows it will last seven because Schlesinger is notoriously painstaking and will not be hurried, not by anybody's budget. This is the first day, Monday: after the shooting of an early, brief battle sequence involving only a few extras, studio carpenters begin hammering moodily about the great hill's superstructure, rigging cables that will be tripped for the final collapse. The wait for the next take will be long, and Schlesinger pauses, a rarity, in someone else's canvas chair, because Marge Champion's son, who plays a French drummer boy, is doing homework in his. "Whether I am an A party guest or a B party guest is of supreme disinterest to me," he offers, when asked. His teeth are perfect, and appear real. "I categorically refuse to attend these bloody Hollywood parties where movie deals are done, movies either get made or they don't get made. I put together my own packages. I don't want some hostess saying, 'Listen, dear, be a good boy and read this script, it's written by a brilliant client of ours and of course he knows that dear so-and-so is dying to work with you.' What utter bullshit. *Too* comical. Oh well, I'm not fashionable at home either. Critics everywhere dislike me, the studio boys blanch at the sight of me. They read *Bloody Sunday* and said, 'Uh, do those two men *have* to kiss? Could they just be involved on the phone?' Jesus! One simply stands one's ground, and if you think they are dense in this country, go to England, where there is *no* film industry now whatsoever without American backing. The distribution and release patterns there are prehistoric: They sit around conference tables in Wardour Street and decide that if there is a bit of a queue outside *Bloody Sunday* in Leicester Square, then you distribute it as you would a James Bond. 'Well, this ought to go in university towns,' they say, and then release it when the students are on holiday. . . ."

A great clattering up on the mountain stills him; one repeats what Lindsay Anderson said of *Bloody Sunday* at a London cock-

tail party: "We have better dramas than that on the telly."
Schlesinger does something that he does, he smiles as if his jaws
were wired with steel and he was testing its tensile strength.
"Well, there's this sad lack of generosity, this hideous sour
bitchiness among British artists that I deplore, it's *so* boring. In
England, it matters very little whether you succeed or fail;
success is rather unfashionable, whereas here it counts for
everything, and in that sense I am *very* American. I am terrifically volatile and emotional and enthusiastic, and I want everyone around me to be so." Then, sweetly, "I really have no quar-
rel with Hollywood, quite the contrary: I'm mad for the place."

He's on his feet, speaking with satiric relish. "Where else
could Kathryn Kuhlman have become a great star? When I first
saw Hollywood, in 1967, I'd just read *Locust* and Jesus, how bizarre: West realized that *this* was America, this city, the dream
ended here! I'd come from London for the premiere of *Far
from the Madding Crowd,* which had been a disaster in New
York, and all the MGM brass met me at the LA airport looking
sepulchral—they ushered me down that concourse with those
incredible children's paintings as if to the grave; in the limousine they said, 'We've canceled the parties but we can't cancel
the premiere.' I paid no attention. I was already overwhelmed
with the garish quality of the city, the smog like an enchanted
mist, people gardening in the afternoon in nightdresses and
pajamas! Sprinkler systems with no one tending them, watering
grass, cement, finally watering water! Film sets spilling out into
the streets, Mayan cottages, Assyrian split-levels, what delightful zingyness! There are no seasons, it's always spring, even the
time of day is unimportant, the sun blesses everyone all the
time, it doesn't matter if you work, if you get out of bed, if you
shave. The first day here I drove past a cemetery and saw a
woman planting, on a grave, a plastic Christmas tree, in October!"

"Sir, excuse me," people are saying to him during this: without interrupting himself, with only nods and signs, he has approved changes in the placement of a tree on the mountain, in
the color of the French soldiers' muskets, in the drape of the
Scotch Greys' kilts. Polanski has this when he works, so does
Fellini—a curious ability to switch concentration from the trivial to the vital to the crucial fluidly, impartially.

18

" . . . and of course West saw that the movie stars who press buttons in their living rooms and a Cézanne ascends into the ceiling to reveal a screen for home showings, that they were boring and not representative, while the anonymous, the rootless, the derelicts who came here for the orange juice *were* the town. It's rather like Israel, where everyone came from somewhere else to find the promised land. Absolutely no reality, because there's no continuity: the sidewalks are empty, one sees only the heads of people in moving cages of metal and glass. Their eyes perpetually *price* things; all the houses are for sale, not actually to sell but to determine the worth of the place. Why not send your daughter into the streets to see how much she can raise? And of course there is no proportion, the cars are too large, the road signs too big to read. But my God, the faces! That first trip, in sixty-seven, I'd begun work with Waldo Salt on the *Midnight Cowboy* script, and some of the, uh, more far-out moments we used in it happened to me here, not in New York: the woman in the all-night diner who is on an acid trip, running the toy mouse over the little boy's face, I saw that on Sunset Strip! And West had seen all this too, when it was not at all 'in' to examine Hollywood so savagely. 'Few things are sadder than the truly monstrous,' that's the most important line in the novel. . . ."

A lady extra, costumed in musty thirties soigné, sidles up to create a pause. "Uh, Mr. Schlesinger, may I introduce you to somebody?" When he turns she offers a young man who smiles manically. "This is Jimmy Boyd."

He says, "Nice to meet you, John. I heard you've rented Michael Butler's house? You took it with all the paintings in it and everything? I looked at it, I was thinking of buying it. Wild house."

"Well, it's for sale," Schlesinger explains cordially. When the boy is gone, Schlesinger's PR man says, "He was a child star, John. He recorded a song called "I Saw Mommy Kissing Santa Claus." Schlesinger's grin is Hogarthian, as he makes another mental note.

On Tuesday morning, the ambience of Stage 15 is decidedly schizoid: four hundred extras have been dressed for the movie-within-the-movie to resemble English infantrymen, French

19

grenadiers, carpenters, gaffers, grips and key grips, script girls and assistant directors; they are indistinguishable from the real carpenters, gaffers, et cetera, as in a Pirandello play. Schlesinger is picking his way gingerly under the hill's scaffolding, holding large storyboards on which each shot of the collapse scene has been sketched in sequence. "Today I am totally paranoid," he announces cheerfully, gesturing at the hill's fragile-looking underbelly, its intricate framework of beams, poles, joists, laths, struts, buttresses and transverse beams, most of pine, others, the collapsible ones, of balsa wood soft as hard cheese. "I have no idea which of these cables sets off the collapse, so mind you don't touch them or the fucking thing comes down on our heads." Saying this, he trips on a cable, the timbers tremble, as do we all. "Two areas up above on the hill are rigged to fall through as soon as anybody steps on them, this morning a workman stepped on them and fell right through, nearly killed himself. We'll use five cameras simultaneously from every possible angle: above, underneath, two sides, long shots of the whole bloody mess. Here's the sequence, on these boards: we see the troops in combat, Napoleon's lieutenant killed, lots of blood and smoke, and the old camera on the crane filming it, so we know we're on a movie set; carpenters are still hammering at the top of the hill so we know the set's not finished. Then an overzealous assistant director—here, in this sketch, with the plus fours and the megaphone—he shouts at the camera, 'Keep rolling,' and orders the soldiers to follow him up the hill. He falls through first, then the soldiers, this middle section goes, finally the whole mountain crashes down. We can't redo the last big collapse without days of rebuilding so it's *got* to be right on the first take. Too many variables, it's in the lap of the gods," and satirically he crosses himself.

A circling camera crane, not the antique one, misses decapitating him by six inches. Ignoring it, he turns to confer with the Coordinator of the Stunt Men, a weird youth with dilated eyes and a military demeanor who addresses Schlesinger thus: Yes, SIR, the men will be ready when you are, SIR, the horses will rear on command, SIR. And he salutes, or nearly. The older of the men to whom he refers wait for the first take engaged in cards and cigarette smoking, like the older dress extras, who came to LA probably in the fifties, looking like the time's con-

20

cept of a leading man, seeing themselves as such. Realistic, they did not necessarily expect to be movie stars, but rather feature players, doing the sorts of roles done then by Macdonald Carey, failing to understand that that sort of acting required more skill than stars ever needed. There wasn't any work for them. They decided to adjust to the career of a lesser feature player, meanwhile working in movies as extras. Finally they resigned themselves to being members-in-good-standing of the Screen Extras Guild, to being paid union scale for standing around in backgrounds. Simulating a certain unembittered pride, they continue to pay each year for the inclusion of their pictures and credits in casting guides. "Well, I have walked, run, skated, swum, rowed, sailed, played deck tennis and badminton in a hundred seventeen films," a large man whose hair is tinted with Great Day explains. "I have appeared with, oh Jesus, Doris Day, Lucy Ball, Loretta Young, Bob Stack, Nat Wood, Bob Cummings, Bob Taylor," the list is very long. He supports three children by two marriages and spends weekends transporting the kids to their various mothers, just like the stars do. He resides among the moribund palms of North Hollywood, the San Fernando Valley's most depressed and depressing area, in the shadow of the Hollywood sign, which smiles down on freeway cloverleaves through a disenchanted mist of mauve smog. "Now, next week I go to read for a small *speaking* part in *Chopper One*. . . . "

Of course the principals of *Locust* do not mingle with the extras, preferring to remain behind the doors of their dressing rooms until called; neither do the bit players, those with lines, willingly mingle with extras. Prominent among the battle scene's bit players is a Steve McQueen type in tight white Napoleonic britches who portrays the doomed French lieutenant. When not needed, which is usually, he occupies, rather provocatively, any empty canvas chair, though he never presumes to sit in Schlesinger's. He has silently rehearsed his only line, "Vive l'Empereur." When the scene is shot, he will first be seen rehearsing the line, coached by the bit player who plays the overzealous assistant director; then he will shout the line as a Panavision camera records the old camera supposedly recording his death. At the moment, he rehearses the rehearsal, coached by a real a.d. Watching, a knowing assistant from the costuming department observes, sotto voce, "They hired him because he can't say 'Vive l'Empereur' right. Isn't that going to be a marvelous touch?" Then, "He forgot to put on his Jockey shorts this morning, didn't he? There are a number of people on this set who wouldn't mind being the French lieutenant's woman."

It happens that Schlesinger does the lieutenant's bit first; it is rather overacted, the line is spoken incorrectly. Beaming approval, Schlesinger gets what he wants in two brief takes and thanks the lieutenant warmly.

"Well done," says the costume assistant in an aside, imitating George Sanders praising Marilyn Monroe's fawning on the producer in *All About Eve*. "I can see your career rising in the east, like the sun."

William Castle, who directed a couple of Joan Crawford films, is making a guest appearance in the bit part of the director of the movie-within-the-movie. He idles happily on the edge of the activity, in plus fours and high boots. One asks him about *The Day of the Locust,* the novel. "Loved it, wonderful book," he asserts absently. It seems best not to quiz him further, and anyway, he changes, the subject: "I started out acting, and so did John. . . ."

WATCH YOUR BACKS, PLEASE, COMING THROUGH. Castle does not hear and is jostled by a workman rolling a large light. Approaching, Schlesinger tells him, "Almost ready, God help us everyone," and he makes fainting motions.

"Ah, but John, I see you smiling, you're enjoying it, confess," Castle demands obsequiously.

"This *is* rather fun, the point at which you are besieged with doubts and must conceal them."

"I just hope I can direct for you again sometime," Castle persists. A look of what may be overwhelming contempt passes behind Schlesinger's eyes, but he replies, kindly, "Next time I'll be in one of yours."

HIT THE CHICKEN COOPS, someone commands, aiming his bullhorn upward at great banks of lights in chicken-wire cages a hundred feet above, on the sound-stage ceiling. PLACES. ALL FIVE CAMERAS ROLLING, CUED BY THE NUMBERS: ONE, TWO, THREE. . . . Explosions, bagpipes, dying screams; the old camera crane rises through the smoke like a dinosaur's neck.

22

French soldiers retreat toward the hill. Backing upward toward his destiny, the assistant a.d. screams through his megaphone, "Keep rolling, come on, you schmucks, follow me!"

CUT. The hill does not collapse. The ersatz assistant a.d. is castigated by the real assistant a.d. "Wally, you missed your mark, you're supposed to back to your mark by six count. No, that's not the fucking mark, *that's* the fucking mark!"

Unruffled, Schlesinger turns from this confrontation; his smile is only slightly steely. "Come sit in my dressing room, they'll have to re-rehearse the movements, my assistant can handle it." You can feel him, here, rechanneling his concentration: now he will concentrate on being interviewed. "This is perhaps the third time I have sat down in here," he remarks, closing the door, pouring coffee. "Thank God we are working indoors, on a sound stage, where at least the weather and light can be controlled, because this is the most difficult sequence I have ever had to face. Did you see those *faces,* among the extras—the few we picked off the streets, I mean. Evenings, I take walks with an assistant, we spot someone who looks interesting, and I have the assistant do the dirty work: he approaches and asks if they'd like to be in a movie, and of couse in this town nearly everyone says yes. Many ask, 'What channel will it be on?' Others think of it as their big break. They never give up, really. . . ."

It strikes you about here that Schlesinger somewhat stage-manages his sessions with the press, channeling conversation toward certain areas of the work so that others are neglected—for instance the *Locust* script, which supposedly has gone through six rewrites and is still being altered. Asked about this, he does not blink or scowl, neither does he exactly answer. "We began with one hundred twenty-odd white pages of script, revisions were done on yellow, blue, pink, and there is not a single white page left. You understand that we have been some six *years* on this project. A producer—*not* Jerry Hellman, who produced *Midnight Cowboy* and is now our producer—sent me the novel. I loved its possibilities; it was about people who preferred dreams to dreams coming true, which I think is what all my films are about. Lovely, except that no one, but *no* one wanted ed to back it. 'Too dicey, too chancey,' they said, 'no starring roles,' you know how they talk. 'Reader reports say it's pessimistic, a downer,' and I would shout, 'Do not tell me about reader reports, what do *you* think?' Of course they do *not* think. Then *Cowboy* became a huge success and suddenly Warner Brothers called and asked what I'd like to do for them and I told them *Locust.* They actually optioned it and we commenced a series of those horrific movie-deal lunches. A Warner's man would say, 'Uh, we see it as a twelve-week picture.' I'd say, 'How can you see it as *anything*, we don't have a fucking *script* yet!' Waldo Salt was on his second rewrite and we were still nowhere near satisfied, and at this Warners party in London the head of their literary department came up to me and said, 'I *do* hope that one day you'll find something you'd like to do for us.' As I was in the *middle* of doing something for them I decided we were dealing with madmen and that I'd pull out. Instead I came back here, worked with Waldo on the third draft, delivered it, Warners announced they were thrilled. Then silence. In Hollywood, people would ring up and say, 'Terribly sorry to hear the news.' *What* news? 'That your movie's off.' Usually, they'd heard it from agents, all of whom *thrive* on disaster. Well from that day to this I have never heard another word from Warners. We finally contacted a lawyer of theirs who said, 'Oh, they decided to drop it.' Bloody rude, considering all those we're-thrilled-you're-thrilled meetings. Rudeness, though, is the nature of the beast."

Except at Paramount, this year anyway. Schlesinger called Jerry Hellman who called Peter Bart, a Paramount executive, who then called Frank Yablans, the president. Yablans had read the book. From that moment, everyone was very encouraging and helpful, even Natalie Wood, who lent Schlesinger her house to use during the final negotiations. "Oh, I did have to attend a couple of those poolside discussions at the Bel-Air Hotel, and at one point I flew to New York and acted out the entire end of the picture for Yablans in his office, but since then, we haven't heard a negative word from anyone. They've given us total freedom. . . ."

Lovely. But about the script. Why all the rewrites, if, as has been intimated, the screenplay closely follows the novel? In it, a young artist, name of Tod, has come from Yale to Hollywood to take a dull job as a set designer at National Films and a room at the San Berdoo Arms, a shabby haven for misfits, losers and dress extras, while he completes his painting *The Burning of Los Angeles,* in which these pariahs set the city afire during a riot that resembles Fascist outbreaks of the thirties. His San Berdoo neighbors include Harry Greener, a grotesque failed vaudevillian, and Harry's daughter Faye, an extra with aspirations to stardom, whose affectations are "so completely artificial that to be with her was like being backstage during an amateurish, ridiculous play." Harry dies; Faye moves in with Homer Simpson, a retired bookkeeper whose dreams are suppressed even in his sleep, and who has come West for the good life. Faye cons him and leaves him. Desolate, he murders a dreadful child actor who's been tormenting him; the crowd at a movie premiere sees this and tears him apart in front of Grauman's Chinese Theatre. Tod, watching, sees in his mind his painting completed: "The burning city, a great bonfire of architectural styles." In the foreground, "the mob carrying baseball bats and torches . . . the people who come to California to die; the cultists of all sorts, economic as well as religious, the wave, airplane, funeral and preview watchers—all those poor devils who can only be stirred by the promise of miracles and then only to violence . . . a great united front of screwballs and screwboxes to purify the land. No longer bored, they sang and danced joyously in the red light of the flames."

Before the film of *The Great Gatsby* was launched on East Egg Bay, Paramount flacks never tired of pointing out that Scott Fitzgerald and Nathanael West had been great friends, had died on practically the same day, and had written the only two "acknowledged classics" about Hollywood, *The Last Tycoon* and *The Day of the Locust,* as if these associations lent credence and respectability to West, the black sheep, and proved that if one bit of popular literary Americana could be turned into a profitable film, so could another obscure one. After *Gatsby's* release, this line of reasoning was abruptly dropped and an alternative one sought without success. Suddenly, no one speaks of *Gatsby,* except obliquely: the West novel, it is maintained, deals with "real" people, implying that Fitzgerald failed the studio fifty years previous by writing characters who are too gossamer and ephemeral. The West project, promises Jerry Hellman, will be "more than wardrobe and romanticism."

Assuming it's got a workable script. Asked again about this,

Schlesinger grimaces, remarks that he does not like discussing specifics of a screenplay before the finished film is available, and returns briskly to Mont St. Jean, having neatly tapped the ball into Waldo Salt's court.

"Such a beautiful literary conceit, West's," Salt is saying, "Hollywood a sargasso sea where no dream is ever completely lost." He is a gentle bearded man with a mild antic laugh and a manner that suggests apology, even here on the set of his film. "First of all, the screen is . . . an overwhelming *presence*." This he has whispered, awed. "It completely engulfs you, you can put a book down, plays have intermissions, TV has commercials, but there is no escape from the screen once you sit down in the theatre. So there's no time in a screenplay for introspection, for intellectual confrontation. The job here was to find specific visual ways to exaggerate what West analyzed in prose—the consuming need of these people for beauty, romance, illusion. Faye Greener, for instance: she wants to be a star, yet the reality of that would destroy her, it would shatter her fantasy of what a movie star is. In the film we see her consuming ice cream and candy like a greedy infant, like . . . a pig. She cannot face an adult reality, no one in the story can. In the cockfight scene, the dwarf takes his dying bird in his arms and puts the head into his mouth, to give the bird breath, life— my God, the need that expresses visually, the need for identification, self-assertion! Uh, this is very difficult to verbalize. . . ."

Allowing a journalist to read the shooting script of a film is, to those involved, like trusting a satanic priest with a piece of the true cross. Sometimes, though, these precious documents are carelessly left about on a set. One finds the *Locust* scenario eventually, near an actor's empty canvas chair, and retires with it behind a wind machine. Salt is right, a screenplay cannot be explained; yet somehow he has managed in his to open up the action, spilling it out onto the scorched, shabby Hollywood streets. The self-cherishing illusions of his characters—they are now somehow more Salt's than West's—are so fierce and complete that they create, on the page, a continuing tension of their own.

But then the script is crossly retrieved by its owner and the wind machine is wheeled away, to blow cannon smoke again up

26

the mountain behind the stunt men. A half dozen of them and the a.d. fall through the lower part of the hill successfully this time, and without injury; the first and least spectacular of the collapse shots is thus completed, and it is six o'clock, time to wrap it up for the day, the week; the big collapse must wait until Monday.

A great rush of relieved laughter rises toward the darkening chicken coops. The stunt men dust one another off in mutual congratulation and join the extras in the long paycheck lines. The vast exit doors slide open and slam. In the parking lot outside, an exhaust cloud forms like the cannon smoke. Executives guide their leased Mercedes through the side gates onto Melrose Avenue; the great ornamental gate with the wrought-iron "Paramount" crowning it is closed now, but one remembers when Norma Desmond drove through it to meet De Mille in *Sunset Boulevard*. One leaves by the long way, driving through the deserted sets, all oppressively silent, as if waiting for the shooting of a sci-fi story in which humankind is extinct. The sun is still hot, there are daytime ghosts: presences move at upper windows when one looks away.

Outside on Melrose Avenue, dozens of dress extras, ordinary now in street clothes, wait for buses, sharing the benches with the elderly. West had known them: "People who come to California to die. . . . All their lives they had slaved at some kind of dull labor . . . saving their pennies and dreaming of the leisure that would be theirs when they had enough. Finally that day came. . . . Where else should they go but California, the land of sunshine and oranges? Once there, they discover that sunshine isn't enough. . . . Their boredom becomes more and more terrible. They realize that they've been tricked and burn with resentment. . . . Nothing can ever be violent enough to make taut their slack minds and bodies. They have been cheated and betrayed. They have slaved and saved for nothing."

That night, Schlesinger is coerced by his associates into giving a little impromptu party. He has stayed late on the lot and then been gathered up by certain assistants from sets and costumes, and somehow this group has acquired the military stunt coordinator, and they've all converged upon the sitting room of

27

his house. They lounge rather than sit: there are no chairs, but instead great Moroccan pillows, poufs and chaises of eccentric fabric. The ceilings are canopied, expensively. Some present are quite stoned, though not Schlesinger: he takes some of the wine, not much, but smokes not at all. He listens rather than talks. Clearly he is not a raconteur or much of a social creature. "He isn't at all an intellectual, you know," his publicity man has said the day before on the set. "He's simply a film maker, a storyteller. They're the best directors. They carry the whole story in their heads, and simply tell it." Oh.

The strange stunt coordinator, flying high, rises and sniffs ceremonially from an amyl nitrite inhaler. "To *you*, SIR," and he raises his wineglass and passes the inhaler. Two or three people sniff at it politely. "We are going to give you the best goddamn spectacular collapse you could possibly want, SIR. Until then, SIR, there is no way I could honor you higher than this." And he disrobes quickly, completely, and executes an arabesque through the open patio doors, into the lighted pool. Schlesinger laughs as fully as anyone, but briefly; minutes later, on the way to the bathroom, one observes him in the study at the rear of the house, standing over the *Waterloo* storyboards spread out on a long table, rearranging them intently like solitaire cards.

Now the pool is deserted; the underwater lights bounce on the surface, still mottled by the stunt man's plunge. Schlesinger wanders out alone and sits with a wineglass, to watch not the lights of Beverly Hills miles below but the refracted pool light. A sprinkler, automatically activated, waters both the grass and the pool water, and he nods at it, pleased. ". . . Sprinklers watering water."

He refuses a cigarette. "The first thing that Ruth Gordon ever said to me was . . . that first trip I made here, with *Madding Crowd*, at the first party, the first person I met was Ruth Gordon. And the first thing she said to me was, 'I read your movie's reviews. Well, dear, this'll teach you to leave those fucking classics alone.'"

But his laugh is metallic. "So here I am doing another fucking classic. But this one, I think we have it right; I *think*. No, I'm sure. It's just that at this stage, almost the finish, the arse end, my paranoia is Herculean. I loathe watching the rushes, it all looks dreadful to me, it's still raw fodder until I get it into the cutting room. My first plan was to make it *look* like a thirties film, but that's wrong: the characters and situations are extreme, savage, I realized that they must be made realistic, contemporary. The production's colors, though, are very monochromatic—muted, lots of browns, creams, beiges, dark blues, bottle greens, like a coloroto section of an old newspaper. . . ."

One asks point-blank why he is a director, interrupting gently. Startled, he considers, as though the question were not a simple one. Then, "When I was young, I was a disaster. At everything. I was a constant source of disappointment to my father because I didn't do anything that a good little middle-class British Jewish boy should do. I could not ride a bike until I was eleven, I was terrified of . . . physical involvement, loathed sports. I was good at all the wrong things: painting, music, photography. I was an excellent *magician*, for God's sake! But I felt compelled to play the game, to try to be good at games, and later to join the army, to be keen on being an officer, which I never became. I did become very ill, though for some reason nobody believed it. I was put in this great disused mill in the north of England, and on Christmas Eve I was moved to a military hospital, only it was actually a padded cell in the local insane asylum. I was fed milk through a dropper thing: extraordinary Christmas Eve. Then back to the disused mill. One day, the p.t. sergeant came up to my bed and said, ON YOUR FEET. I looked up at him and suddenly said, I CANNOT AND WILL NOT GET ON MY FEET. He was speechless. It was a moment of enormous transition for me. I kind of wept, for joy, because I somehow knew that I would never again play their game. We became great friends, that sergeant and I."

Pause. "That moment, when I said that I would never again be like anyone else, that I would value individuality above all, that was when I began to become a director. I suddenly understood a sense of authority. Later I became an actor, but not for long because I knew that a director can*not* be concerned with just one role, one element; he must use every piece of himself, every piece of his experience, observation, knowledge—and everybody else's, too, he must pick everybody's brains; I loved that idea! I worked first in television, for the BBC, which expected their directors to shoot their films and deliver them up

29

for someone else to edit and dub and I flatly refused that, I told them *I* would edit. I became a real pain in the ass about it, but I won. A director can*not* be mucked about by anyone, ever. He must fucking well hang in there because he has the total picture, the total concept, no one else."

How nice to have won. This makes him frown and he gets up quickly. "No, because you never quite win. You always could have been better. That's quite American of me, isn't it? I could never retire. You want to continue to do what is not expected of you." Sitting again, he adds, oddly, "I . . . loathe being totally alone, to me it is the most frightening thing, I'm very bad at it. I've always shared my home, wherever it is, with . . . close friends. I don't necessarily mean lovers. There are other sorts of friends with whom one can share very closely. For some reason, I don't know why, great success is intolerable alone, unbearable, much, much worse, somehow, than failure. . . ."

A call from the house interrupts him, he seems glad of it; in the living-room light he looks weary and old. But on the set Monday, he is as usual, concentrated, kinetic, fascinated with a somewhat rare sight: when he is ready to begin the great-collapse shot, the stunt coordinator blows a whistle, like the start of a race, and all the stunt men scurry forward. EACH MAN, the coordinator announces, WILL BUILD WHAT HE WANTS TO BUILD, AND WHEN HE IS SATISFIED, HE WILL LET ME KNOW. They rush under the scaffolding, where stacks of old mattresses, slabs of cardboard, quilting and pillowing await, and with these, under the hill, they erect mounds with which to break their falls.

ALL SPECTATORS BACK BEHIND THE WIND MACHINES. CUE THE BAGPIPES. ALL CAMERAS BY THE NUMBERS. When the grenadiers reach the hilltop, the master switches are finally thrown, the cables released, and with a shudder the mountain disintegrates. Billowing dust, then utter silence. The spectators applaud perfunctorily, but somehow it has been anticlimactic.

"Yes, of course," Schlesinger says when this is mentioned, turning from a gaggle of congratulatory assistants. "Because nobody got hurt. All week, they were waiting for blood. It wasn't violent enough for them, finally." And he grins, in his way. Hollywood has collapsed, as West predicted.

2.

Julie Christie: Still Far from the Madding Crowd

JULIE CHRISTIE will do certain selected interviews. This news Metro-Goldwyn-Mayer dispenses like Selznick announcing he'd found somebody to play Scarlett. *There is a new Julie Christie,* the MGM flacks assert, and cite as admissible evidence her actual live appearance at their New York premiere of John Schlesinger's *Far from the Madding Crowd,* where the girl who'd spent the two years since her *Darling* Oscar disdaining premieres, kliegs, writers, and MGM flacks stepped from her limousine like Shirley Temple Black campaigning, and posed; then progressed leisurely, languidly into the Capitol Theater lobby, proffering sunny, vapid statements into network microphones and punching her costar, Terence Stamp, playfully for photographers. Of course the fact that *Madding Crowd* is a film in serious, expensive trouble, even before its endless opening credits, printed on a portentous "Hardy Country" sky, has nothing to do with her abrupt embracement of The People.

One is supposed to have lunch with her alone the next day, but somehow that doesn't quite work out. Photographers are waiting coiled in the restaurant foyer, columnists do febrile little four-question interviews. She answers them at amazing smiling length. The reserved table turns out to be set for four, at least two of which places are occupied by her MGM entourage, which does not quite dare to address her directly.

"Will Julie want a drink before lunch?"

"Does she usually drink before lunch?"

"Uh, Julie, what would you like to drink before lunch?"

"What did she say? I think she said milk."

"Yes, Julie wants a glass of milk."

"Waiter, five Bloody Marys and one very large milk."

Once, you spy a dolphin's smile sliding across her incredible, curiously dour face; and the next day, when she answers the door of the big West Side apartment where she's a guest for her New York stay, she is already laughing. "That must have been *very* jolly for you, that lunch," she offers, loping, as she does, in black boots, into a fashionably Spartan living room, falling into a lounge beside a coffee table laid with silver tea service and milk in a Sealtest carton. "I thought you'd like to be alone today," and she blesses the quiet apartment with her cigarette; whether she's aware of one's firm request of MGM for one hour of privacy with her is unclear. "I know, I sent 'em up shamelessly yesterday, the studio oafs, but I couldn't help it. I do find this brouhaha hilarious. I'll tell you, in part their idiot publicity's true, I *have* come into the world a bit, I'm not minding the public part of this business quite as I did. It's the old cliché, if you're doing it, laugh with it, and I'm trying to. For me, one way's to send 'em up, yesterday I had to or I'd have screamed their bloody heads off."

Which is rather what she did when she read *Madding Crowd*'s reviews. "Christ, the critics seemed to have expected another *Darling!* Didn't they ever read the Hardy novel? Why the bloody hell should I *ever* remake *Darling*? I don't see the point of anything unless there's adventure in it, growth; Hardy heroines are acting dreams, I *loved* Bathsheba Everdine, so what if the film's a melodrama? Oh yes, something else idiotic in the papers, this thing about the '*Darling* team,' as though I'm somehow shackled forever to John Schlesinger and Freddy Raphael, what utter bullshit. Look, I'm aware I owe all this to John, to him spotting me and chancing an inexperienced girl in the complex *Darling* role, then risking that I could switch, become Bathsheba Everdine, and sustain her through a long movie. And he directs so gently, so quietly, he's so organized, so *humorous*. He conveys confidence, I have days without a trace of it. When we shot the scene in which Bathsheba addresses all the farm laborers, I suddenly stood up in front of them, I could not speak. John strolled up and whispered, 'What's the trouble today, love, is it your period, or what?' There was something so ludicrous about that, such a trivial question in the midst of all the seriousness, it untangled my knots. I was tied in knots be-

32

cause, as I whispered back to John, 'All of them staring at me up here, and they're all so *good*. John, am I good enough?'"

Contemplative inhale, exhale. "Anyway, one's certainly indebted to Schlesinger, but I'm not a joiner of teams. I am simply an actress employed by him to do a job, it's decidedly not a binding partnership. No ruts for me, luv. End of subject." Resolutely, she pours tea, the cigarette hanging from her wide mouth. Watching it's easy to see her as Diana, *Darling*'s heroine, an early beauty, pampered and unique even as a child. A darling. It would be idiotic to ask her about it, it's so plain; besides, she's suddenly abstracted, staring out at Central Park's bare trees. "You're never out of sight of cars, are you? In New York, I mean. Even in that park. I don't drive, because I can't pass the bloody driving test. Cars frighten me, also mobs of people. Did it ever strike anyone who calls me aloof that, faced with a crowd like that premiere mob, one's in *physical danger*? I'm terrified of that. That some nut would want to. . . ."

"Change the subject," she orders.

Okay: What about the Julie Christie the press has already so painstakingly reported? Her casual, rambling Kensington flat, decorated with a huge camp Union Jack, and dozens of her "mates"—comfortable sincere friends far from the madding film crowd. Frown. She's bought a house now. In Fulham. Just a house, Georgian, no time to decorate it. "Mates?" Scoff, silence. "Everyone meets new people along the way. Don't you?" Her mood has altered sharply; something troubled, confounded has surfaced, like ice floes in the winter Hudson. "I never seem to have time anymore, I'm endlessly required to be 'Julie Christie.' There *is* no 'Julie Christie.' She's a commodity, an autograph-writing machine you kick if it doesn't work, a lie created by press agents. I suppose you'll ask now if I'm living with Don Bessant. The artist. Everyone does. Well, if y'like a chap terribly, y'want t'be with 'im all the time, don'tcha? If I were just a shop girl living with a man, nobody'd give a bloody hell."

The shop-girl inflection is evidently meant to lighten the mood, the dim November afternoon room. It doesn't. One suggests that often she sounds as though she were trying to convince herself of what she says.

"I can't help that." She doesn't like it, either.

"You've said you don't believe in marriage."

"I've been misquoted a lot! I believe very much in marriage, when its timing is right. Just now, the demands on my time are too great. I've thought about giving up my profession to get married, and six months or so ago, I might have. But I've accepted a reality: that I am an actress. That acting's terribly important to me, whether I like it or not. I care about it now. Call it ambition if you like. I'm ambitious for roles that are right for me, and I'll keep on being. There, you may now write a story about a driven, grasping, ambitious professional." Gargoyle smile.

She's told reporters she worries about becoming a bitch; unless that too has been misquoted. "No, that's accurate. I don't worry about it anymore though. Acknowledging it in the beginning, as I did, worrying about it initially—that solved half the problem right there."

This time, she doesn't smile.

3.

The Restoration of Roman Polanski

MACABRE, unseemly: not Polanski himself so much as his presence two winters ago at the premiere of *Macbeth,* his first movie since the slaughter of his pregnant wife at the hands of Manson & Company. You have resolved not to allow the specters of Sharon & Jay & Abigail & Voyteck & Charlie to hover over the proceedings like the glum tabloid Eumenides created by the press at the time of the murder, nor to expect that Polanski should make this, his first large public appearance since the crime in August, 1969, an occasion to skulk in wearing black and looking inaccessible; still, the ambience in the then-new Playboy Playhouse, Manhattan, is jarring. Down in row one is little Roman, in a blood-colored velvet suit, chattering with Hugh Hefner, who has, incredibly, served, from his dark tower in Chicago, as *Macbeth's* producer. The screen before them is covered with the pastel heads of decapitated rabbits. After the celebrity audience has rubbernecked at the diminutive, legendary director, the rabbit heads dissolve to the portentous *Macbeth* titles, which dissolve to a curious movie relentlessly bloody, which dissolves to a garish, Hogarthian gala atop the Playboy Club up the street, featuring the usual Bunnies like Breughel barmaids, medieval crowns of sculptured ice on the buffet tables and Polanski grinning demonically for the flash cameras of *Women's Wear.*

Why do you distinctly mistrust him that night? Because his handshake is too firm and his smile like something dipped in instant silver cleaner? Because *Macbeth* is being hyped like the Playmate of the Year? Because you wonder why, after brilliant work on films conjured from his own obviously unique vision—

Knife in the Water, Cul-de-Sac, the impeccable *Repulsion*—he would have bothered with *Macbeth* at all, unless in the cause of some silly classics jerk-off? Because, for a recent piece in *Esquire* by his friend Ken Tynan, he posed satirically for the photographer with a butcher knife? No matter, except that when you are asked to write about him, you have only these sour memories, and the knowledge that he is back in LA making his first large movie since *Macbeth,* a large, expensive, movie star-sounding project, something with the commercial smell of Sydney Pollack or Peter Bogdanovich. You have no way of knowing then that this picture, called, oddly, *Chinatown,* will be so perfect a suspense piece and so perfectly a satire of one that it could put Hitchcock out to pasture forever in regional college film-night nostalgia orgies; that watching it, you will be convinced that only Polanski could have made *Gatsby* exciting or *The Exorcist* intelligent; that the man himself, this Polish troll, this cunning urchin, will turn out, through his egomania, his arrogance, his grace, his bluntness, his brilliance, to alter your focuses and perceptions irrevocably. "That bastard," a compatriot of his whispers one night at his house, watching him cross a room exuding charm, "that son-of-a-bitch. I would die for him."

The preliminaries to meeting him are infuriating: a mound of unheeded messages left with his polite but French houseboy, finally the master's voice, weary, impersonal, somehow challenging, British inflections pockmarked with something harsh and Germanic. He does not like interviews, he allows, and doesn't do any. Okay, let's forget it. No, no, come round Sunday, this invitation extended as if to the IRS. One arrives purposely late, after a late night, in dark glasses, with scotch and various stimulants still staining the vocal cords. Beyond the gate, electronically and otherwise locked, awaits an aspect like that which confronted Margaret O'Brien when she found the right door in *The Secret Garden:* huge carnivorous plants, a deafening waterfall feeding a kidney pool, a house glassy and transparent as a terrarium, with an oppressive view of the enchanted mauve mist of Beverly Hills smog, all the property of Dinah Shore's former husband George Montgomery, "Actor and furniture maker" of the the televised Johnson Wax commercials. The house's lessee stands resplendent like a small, athletic sunburst in the living room's merciless light, tensed as if

36

for first serve, effortlessly deep-breathing. He is known to hate cigarettes. One lights one.

"I am awake since nine, I like to take cold showers mornings," he offers, bounding around the room finding an ashtray, gesturing to the houseboy for coffee. "Ice cold, terrible of course, but half-hour later you feel terrific!" He speaks in a sort of emphatic shorthand, with extra consonants. "I go to fly in an hour, I take flying lessons. I want to go fly last evening, the weather is perfect in Hollywood, but at airport a great bank of grayish stuff is rolling upon me." Conversationally you remark that that's probably smog, expecting if anything, a nod, but he considers sharply. "No! What causes sudden changes of weather is flow of air, constant moving of it, change of temperature within it which is called, in meteorology, *fronts!* Cold front comes under warm front, great lift occurs . . . clouds, crystallization into ice!" There is in this something ingenuous and amazed and at the same time something professorial, a more than casual interest in being right. For the moment you miss the wicked ironies under these explanations of his, which burgeon unexpectedly from chance remarks, fragments of thought, like lush plants growing from seedlings in speeded-up photography. A half-hour later I ask something about actors who work from instinct and again he starts: "But none of us are born with instinct! We're born only with certain capacity to develop instinct, some to develop their imaginations, others only their muscles! This is not enough realized! That all peoples on this planet through all the ages, there were never two born exactly alike, every cell of my organism is different from yours, only certain basic things are genetic, all newborn babies will move its arm away if you burn it, will suck at the breast if you put one in its mouth, and do things only necessary for survival. Instinct, which is something which tells you by the tone of your wife's voice that she has been fucking other man, that is not born, that is accumulated experience. . . ."

Though these extraordinary monologues may spin on indefinitely, they can be instantly terminated. He watches your face carefully whenever he talks and if he detects the slightest flicker of restlessness near your eyes or mouth, he will change the subject with great purpose, with an almost physical will, like a nervous keno dealer.

37

There is also this: that he watches intently when *you* talk, for what you may be, may be concealing or secretly intent upon; this is not to ingratiate, though clearly he is capable of calculated niceness. Ignoring his coffee, he suddenly wants to know about writing, why one does it. "Is writing not a certain special kind of verbal memory? Is it not a lot like film editing? By arranging order of words in sentence, you arrange a meaning? In *Chinatown,* for example, I just realize that by changing a hand gesture of one very minor character—it takes four frames and there are thirty-six frames per *second*—we change whole meaning of scene. Changing series of shots in scene can also destroy picture, an example there is my *The Fearless Vampire Killers,* made in Europe, but a man called Gene Gutowski was producer and he convinced me he should be in charge for the final cut for the U.S. because he knows U.S. audience. Okay, I trust him, and he takes my movie away, cuts twenty minutes from it, redubs it and changes music around, then adds a little cartoon at the beginning to explain what it's about because now, after the cuts, nobody understands it any more! My version has played almost constantly in Europe since it opens, seven years! His version, which plays here, is a disaster, I tell you, it made more money in Formosa than it's ever made in U.S. and Canada put together! They show it here all the time on television, I get the shakes, it is so bad, but it is out of my control. So, does this happen to you as writer? Is this cutting done at *Rolling Stone*?" Never, one explains; well hardly ever. He isn't listening.

"I learn from that, on this one Bob and I have complete approval of final cut." He means Robert Evans, goad of Paramount, head of its production; while Evans was largely responsible for *Love Story, Rosemary's Baby* and *The Great Gatsby,* Polanski's *Chinatown* is the first Paramount movie he has produced entirely on his own. "Evans, lemme tell you, is no fool: Public thinks of him simply as good-looking former husband of Ali McGraw and so on, but there would have been no *Rosemary's Baby* without him. Look, when you are making a picture, you are continually under *attack*—from your stars, crew and studio with its financial statements. I am publicly called by many of these a megalomaniac and they are absolutely right, you *must* be one to make a good film! Because *you* must believe at all times that your decisions are utterly right—even when they are

38

wrong. There is one reason why you do a film at all: to make happen in cinema a vision, a concept, which is totally yours, only in your mind, no one else's, it is cinema of one human being, *I* am the only one who perceives my vision! I am known as an expensive perfectionist; truth is, sometimes a certain scene is not quite within your vision correctly yet, but you dunno why, so you must do fifty takes of it to find out. Okay, the moneymen do not comprehend this. And here you need a man like Evans, who does. The other corporate big boys, they dunno what *Rosemary's Baby* was about at all, they think it is some cockamamie thing like *The Exorcist* or something, they are screaming at Evans, 'Make him work fast, throw the fucking little Polack out!' We have a big meeting, I blow, I tell 'em, 'Okay, I *know* how to shoot your way, like TV, ten pages a day, I finish your fucking movie in three days!' They nod happily and Evans gets up, and I swear, he was putting his job then on the line, he tells them, 'This is just jacking off, Roman, go back to the set and do just what you've been doing, making a good movie.' You dunno the guts that took him then, and he has totally preserved me from such bullshit on *Chinatown.* . . ."

Yes, yes; so what's this *Chinatown* about? He's been up and down half a dozen times in half an hour, rearranging bits of George Montgomery's shiny handiwork, adjusting minutely the soft complaint of James Taylor from invisible speakers, and this question does not settle him. "*Very* difficult to say. Having just spent six weeks rewriting Bob Towne's script with him. I am too close to trees to see forest, is that it, in English? This won't help you, but it is about a private detective, played by Jack Nicholson, a flashy character working in LA in the thirties in matrimonial cases, and against his will he gets involved in a criminal case, a gigantic swindle in the city's water supply, you see there is this huge *drought*. Anyway, that isn't the mystery at all: There is this very enigmatic woman, Faye Dunaway, and a young girl, and her father, and Faye's husband, and in *them* is the real mystery, only you don't know that, *nothing* is as it appears!" Delighted laugh, an arpeggio. "That's the plot. Why I make it? Why of course, for money!" This is almost unbearably funny to him. "Yes, yes! You don't believe me but it is the truth. That, and that I want to do every genre of film—horror, Western, detective, and this is my latter! Listen, I have less money

39

than anybody knows, for two reasons: First, I have always done in films what I wanted to do, which is very expensive; to make cinema money you must make concessions and I have never done that. I have simple life principle: that money serves to buy pleasures, satisfy desires, and my number one pleasure and desire has always been filmmaking! So I purchase my pleasure with *unearned* money, you unnerstand? I could have never done *Cul-de-Sac,* which is, by the way, my best, the most cinematic of all, if I'd asked 'em for alotta bread. So I never develop a caring for business, I have never thought to set up things like percentage-of-profits for myself, I made nothing on *Rosemary's Baby* and the fucker made millions! Okay, I begin to notice all these people around me making fortunes and now I think there is nothing wrong with me having one, and I'll know how to spend it, don't you worry. There is the other reason I have nothing, I live *very* well. I would *loathe* to be caught dead with alotta money in the bank! Understand: I would now like to buy a small plane, but though I want this, I would still not make trash films. Though I am whore, I am whore with principle. *Chinatown* is commercial but artistic, and now I must go fly."

First there are rapid consultations with the houseboy, and with the phone, which now complains from various extensions all over the house, and with Eva, an incredible-looking girl with an accent like his who lives somewhere on the house's lower level and studies acting with Lee Strasberg, at Roman's recommendation. Something reminds him of a joke but he can't get it right. As if playing Chopin, he chooses numbers on the living room's touch-tone extension and discusses, without complete success, the joke with Mike Nichols in Connecticut.

". . . It is this British TV game show, and the riddle is: What is two feet long, a foot wide and ebony colored? And this old English type like Sybil Thorndike asks, 'Could the answer be nigger cock?' " The telling dissatisfies him; at the door he says, "Listen, you and me, we do not yet entirely communicate. No? You come tomorrow to watch me shoot the picture. Listen, the movie publicity men, they bring in this article by you from *Esquire* about Ryan O'Neal and say, 'Do *not* have him.' So I read it, and you are the only one I am having. Okay?"

The narrow steep driveway he takes in his leased Mercedes at literally close to fifty, smiling—yet there is still in his eyes the thing you have noted all morning, an extreme vulnerability to pain and an equal determination not to reveal it. You assume at work he will play the Tartar, and the atmosphere at his location shooting the next day is sinister, though not because of him: It is a cold nighttime on Hope Street in downtown LA where he must complete a short, extremely difficult sequence and the only one in *Chinatown* that actually takes place in Chinatown. By sundown the street is already crammed with light and equipment trucks; an old tea warehouse covered with gold Chinese letters like mutant insects, David Yee Mee Loo's Cocktail Bar and the Fing Loy Café are rendered older by the cruel movie lights and the lines of the gentle 1937 cars brought downtown for the scene by Paramount drivers. Dozens of crewmen, assistants, extras and mute Orientals, gaping skeptically from behind police lines, wait more or less in freeze-frame for the endless setting of the lights; there is a kinetic energy, a feeling of participants waiting for the start of some bizarre satanic ceremony, a street fair in hell, a party inside the eye of a hurricane that is indigenous to big, location movie-shootings. Chilled air steams on the huge hot lights; from this steam Polanski materializes, smaller in the exaggerated scale of the equipment, adolescent in jeans, a long sweater, a short old corduroy jacket. A dozen supplicating technical people hurry behind his odd, slightly pigeon-toed, slightly hunched gait. "You will be cold," is his greeting. "Gets very cold here, I will get you a big coat." And he actually does, somebody's parka sails through the gloom like half a ghost.

And he is gone with John Alonzo, his cameraman. The end of the movie must be shot tonight: One of the main characters must be shot, murdered driving away in a gargantuan old yellow 12-cylinder Packard convertible, and Roman and his cameraman and crew bustle around it now like midgets inspecting a buttercup-colored Sherman tank. "No, John, no, blood on windshield is not right, blood on the bullet holes, must be much more, try again, spray more, Mr. Propman!"

"Yes, Mr. Director." He does this sort of vaudevillian exchange constantly with the crew, most of whom are clearly devoted to him. But before the scene in the bloody car, the street scene leading to it must be finished, a complex one involving Nicholson, John Huston and Perry Lopez who plays another

41

detective. Huston fluffs a line, Roman is impeccably courteous to the old man; he fluffs a second time and there is a large, friendly laugh from the boy-director. "Now come on, John, we got it right yesterday, come we try again!" In the pronounced tension, his English is blurring slightly. "Awful good, that time, but what I really want . . ." And he does what he does, working, his finger strokes his forehead as he strides briskly away twenty feet, considering; he apparently requires this brief physical separateness to think. "Okay, now this is important—Jack is to move only to this spot, I want it marked, where's the man with the chalk? Come on, I'm asking for a simple chalk mark, where's everyone? Aw shit!" His working method, filmmaking as a team sport with him as cheerful coach, has disintegrated momentarily and he is abruptly unboyish. "I want the mark now! Actors, you must prepare before scene, maintain the internal rage we need here! I want you not wandering off telling stupid anecdotes, I don't tell you this again!"

Dead silence, total efficiency. In one more perfect take he gets what he wants. "Veddy good, beaudiful!" The lighting must be changed again and he motions to me to come inside his trailer, where an unfinished chess game and pieces of the script wait on the table beside the hot coffee. "Do actors have brains?" he says, pouring, not really asking a question. "There is no answer to that, no rules. Some, like Olivier, are very intellectual, others, like Brando, are organic. Jack! You see how he gets angry in a scene? Unbelievably scary! He cannot stop, he goes into a kind of fit, you dunno whether he is acting any more! He is one distinct acting school, almost opposite to Stanislavsky: You build anger by getting it physically, pounding tables, people, it comes not mentally but by inducing it in your body, *with* your body, take *that,* you motherfucker," and he pounds the Formica counter until the trailer shakes. "Unnerstand? Your glands, endocrine or whatever, they start secreting substances, the blood races. It can be very hard on you physically, it is hard on Jack, but what wonderful results! And frightening: When I direct Catherine Deneuve in *Repulsion,* after a week I really started worrying, because I see a complete change in her personality, she was becoming the mad girl of the story, literally, she could not, at night, return to her own self. Suppose you pretend for a month to have a limp; you will be unable in one day to stop limping, and it's the same thing. Now I worry about Dunaway, I have never known an actress to take work as seriously as she does. I tell you, she is a maniac. She spends ten hours learning lines, five on preparation, three on makeup, there is finally no time left for her to sleep! The thirties, I tell her, was period when women used lots of powder, I wants lots of powder, so she spends two hours applying it and then we have what we call a false start—begin a take and cut after few seconds—and she disappears to redo powder! And her Blistex! It is used on lips to prevent cracking, her Blistex has become a legend!

"In a scene, she will raise a drinking glass at a different moment in each take, imagining that I can somehow splice this all together in the cutting room, and of course if you tried that it would come out looking like fruit salad. Perry Lopez, tonight by mistake he calls Jack 'Lou,' *his* character's name, and instantly breaks the take, which was a wonderful one; I could easily have post-synced this error, but now the take is ruined. You *must*, as director, forgive them, I suppose: He is so right for his part, and Dunaway, though clearly insane she has *exactly* the quality of mystery, the unexplainable. . . ."

Edgy now, he essays the trailer door, checking without on the technical progression. "She is quite easily insulted, Faye: If she is guest in my home, I say, 'Faye, please sit over here,' but on a set, there is *no time*! A surgeon doesn't say, 'Scalpel, please,' and when I'm working I say, 'Sit here!' And she is most wounded. Actors! I detest having to analyze my intentions for them, I don't *want* to think why I do a scene so-and-so way, and they will demand to know, and I must give answers, so I have to start looking for answers and this is not good for me, I don't always know or want to know my reasons. My God, when painting, you don't think before each brush stroke! When I question what you call my instincts, I fail, not just in cinema but in life. Dunaway will sometimes give impossible readings, and when you start fussing with them, it goes on literally forever, and one can't afford that time! Jesus, the understanding an actor has for his part should be, I maintain, enough motivation for reading lines properly. Just say it this way, Faye! And she bursts into hysteria!"

He picks methodically at his wristwatch, as if this would speed time, the delays outside. "I learn something interesting making this film: Always before, when I'm telling a story cinematically, there isn't special need to follow the thread every instant; you abandon it from time to time, you set up something intriguing for viewer, then you veer from it, then come back, but in this type movie, this detective-suspense genre, this thriller, you are *not allowed* to do so! You must stay with story every moment, which is to me simplistic, but it pays off. Think of good detective books you've read! Why do you love them, why is Raymond Chandler so terrific? Because he won't let you rest! Maybe the best scene in *Chinatown* is one where finally Jack lies down to go to sleep—and here again is Nicholson's genius, here would be such a temptation to act for the camera, which he never does, only for his internal self—anyway, he's in bed and finally we are going to get a breather, and the telephone starts, and keeps on and on. He doesn't touch it for minutes yet you *know* he's going to have to! It's that moment when, as kid, you are into a detective book and mother is calling you to table, and you call, 'One more moment, one more page!'"

From outside there's a call for him and he is gone instantly. The monstrous yellow car waits, still not properly bloodied. "Where is chair for Mr. Huston to sit? Get one!" Sitting, Huston falls flat, Roman singlehandedly rights him. "Where is Faye?" Still in her trailer, it turns out; portable electric heaters are being arranged around her chair. "Ain't hot enough for her out here," a crewman offers malevolently, aiming the heat lamps like ray guns. Bob Evans has arrived for the important scene; abruptly Dunaway materializes in costume and powder and jokes sotto voce with her producer. "Evans, you bastard," she says loudly, laughing, punching him; ignoring them, Roman hops into the driver's seat of the Packard, distressed. "Blood is still wrong!" He smears it about with his fingers, then flicks it on with a paint brush. "No; wipe it off, it isn't real, try other color, this one looks like puke." There's blood all over the car seat now, on crewmen, on Roman. "Let's try that little thing," he suggests, and a tiny cannonlike device is produced, which explodes, with a minuscule blast, gore against the windshield like blood from an exploded skull. "Yes, *yes*, more! It looks like shot-out brains! Wunnerful!"

Nearby a swarthy Oriental, his small eyes feverish with mercantile wisdom, complains to one of the a.d.s that people can't

44

get through the police barriers to his "social club" down at the end of the street. "I got my job, you got yours," he insists, not inscrutably Eastern. "We all gotta eat, am I right?"

Saturday Roman goes to fly; one goes instead to see Evans, whose Beverly Hills place is properly spectacular, though one sees little of it; you're shown through the oval entrance hall by David, the British houseboy, right out past the oval pool to a sort of poolhouse-game-lounging room—the tennis court is through the far door—where, at a fine antique oval table, Evans, tanned in tennis shorts sits with Warren Beatty and Jack Nicholson. Clearly, they've known each other well a long time; there's an easy, ironical camaraderie between them. Somebody puts down *Gatsby*. "Don't blame me for it," Evans says, laughing. "David Merrick produced it." He tells Beatty he didn't like *McCabe and Mrs. Miller* because they couldn't hear the soundtrack. Like that. A model Evans had known has recently overdosed; her picture has been in *Vogue*, and he wants Warren to look through the issue and guess who she is, a test he fails. Nicholson, not customarily garrulous, is obviously proud of *Chinatown*; when Evans and Beatty wander outside to talk to a couple of *Vogue*-type women taking the sun by the pool, one asks him how he rates his performance in it. "One of the three best," he says quickly. "Maybe *the* best. There is no director alive with Roman's genius. What I'd like is to work with him again, soonest. . . ."

This is what Evans wants too; when he comes back and the others go out to the pool, he settles with his brown legs stretched. He is concentrated when he talks, like Polanski, more edited, more precise. When questioned he says, "I was sitting with Bob Towne a few years ago in Dominique's restaurant telling him I wanted to do, produce a good man-woman story, because I was looking for something for my then-wife Ali. He said he and Nicholson were working on something called *Chinatown*, right away I loved the title. I don't know why. I said what's it about; he said I don't have that yet, just this idea. It's got nothing to do with Chinatown except that this woman in it, she is almost Oriental, something about her you never grasp; *she's* like Chinatown. Well, Bob was busted at this time, really broke, I gave him some money to develop the story, but Paramount wasn't paying him much and he had to take other assignments and the script was a long time coming, about sixteen months actually. I'd done *Rosemary's Baby* with Roman and he was the only person I wanted to give it to. We'd gotten very close. He is *not* an easy person, as I suppose you know now—very difficult to crack, but once you do, there is no man and no filmmaker like him. We've gone through a helluvalot together. Jesus, my marriage; and the post-funeral of Sharon was here at this house, meaning that everybody came back here afterward. Roman stayed here with me then for a good while; it was a horrendous time. Later I told him that the first picture I produced on my own I wanted him to direct, and he wanted to do a literary property, to adapt a book, like *Rosemary's Baby*. That script *was* Roman's, and we wanted to try the same procedure again. I sent him a number of things that weren't right. "I'm not equipped to do that," he would always reply, but as soon as *Chinatown* was in rough draft I made him come over here; this was last April. He loved it. He started working like hell with Bob Towne, so did I; the picture now follows the script almost literally to the word. That's how Roman is, gets the script dead right and is then very meticulous with it. I don't mean that *Chinatown* reads as well as it plays, but neither, believe me, did *Rosemary's Baby*; he adds that indefinable, inexplicable thing of his. Not with ease. God, the *bitter* fights we all had finishing the writing. One night we were in here with the whole thing spread on the floor, yelling at each other; Roman walks out, 'I will stay here no longer!' It has *not* been a passive set. He's tough as hell with actors no matter what impression he gives you; it must be what *he* wants—that's strength in a director and I *love* strength. His nature is *high* tension, if you don't know how to take that, with him you're finished; if you do, my God, you've got everything. You've got *the* original. Who else could you honestly say that about?"

He has the next one for Roman, "and he's getting his ass back here from Europe *early* in the fall to do it. A book by Bill Goldman called *The Marathon Man*, he'll be working with Goldman writing the script. Me, too, maybe." Oh? "I would *love* to write. *Love* it. Did it as a young man. Right now, there is literally not time or freedom. In my present position, I can only get a movie made once every eighteen months because when you're head of studio production, you are involved in every fucking picture and every fucking one has *large* problems. And you're responsible. Budgets! I'll tell you something, with Polanski I don't worry; I happen to know he is going to come in *under* the shooting schedule, the number of days the studio allows him to work. As opposed to the past, as opposed to a few other recent nightmares I've had to worry about."

Meaning *Gatsby?* His teeth, against the tan, are as if just scrubbed with Pearl Drops. "I think if I'd produced it I could have done something, but David Merrick produced it." What about Merrick's recent interviews, venomous against Paramount, and Evans in particular? "Apparently he was uptight because he thought *I* was getting credit as producer, which I was not and was trying to deny at every opportunity. Eighty percent of what he said in print was lies, I don't want to go into it. The result of the picture proves his movie-producing talent. Look, I could fill your paper with stuff about Merrick and *Gatsby*, but why? I would rather . . . um, remain a gentleman by not commenting." And he repeats his satiric grin, squinting into the sun, which is blessing him now through the glass.

One has been too easy on Roman and allowed him to postpone the discussion of his wife too long. He's said, "We'll talk about it, not today, it's too nice out," and so on. Now the picture's finished, soon he'll be leaving for Spoleto to direct the opera *Lulu*; there can be no more reprieves and he knows it. But you get to his house to find, first, that a dinner is planned, that one of his girls is coming to eat, a young blonde named Tish, the sort he prefers: fresh, pretty, healthy, studentish, almost totally uninterested in filmmaking and movie-starring; and second, that his father has arrived from Poland for a visit and will eat with us, too. Over the food, turbot served invisibly by the houseboy, Roman conducts a lively conversation in English, and Polish for his father, an old gentleman with long gray hair who smiles perpetually and almost never speaks. In English Roman tells the story of what has become "the famous meeting," a dramatic gathering demanded by Faye Dunaway to air her profound grievances against her director. "You have, I guarantee, never seen such certifiable proof of craziness. Working with Faye, I might eventually have actually questioned my own methods had I not known that she has had the same confrontations with *all* her directors, and gained the reputation as a gigantic pain-in-the-ass. I finally tell her this, she screams, '*Who said that, Preminger? He is an asshole anyway!*' One day last week she flatly refused to give the reading I required and walked off the set and then comes famous meeting, within an enormous mahogany conference room at Paramount, with Bob Evans exhausted and trying to stay awake at one end of big table, and her agent unsure of where to sit because his position might indicate misbalanced loyalties, and Faye wild-eyed, and me, running in from editing in my old clothes looking at my watch!" This memory especially delights him. "Dunaway starts screaming instantly, I would not even repeat for print what she called me. After twenty minutes or so of this, I remark, 'But Faye, you must understand, you are not completely normal. For example, the hair business.' And she stands and sobs, 'YES, YES, HOW ABOUT THAT GODDAMN HAIR!' She meant, there had been a close-shot of Jack's face over her shoulder and one strand of her hair was sticking out, it was back-lit and looked awful, I said, 'Hold it,' stepped to her and quickly not *pulled*, merely *plucked* at one inch of the hair careful not to hurt her and she went crazy. I did not know she had a hair fetish. So at meeting she screams, 'YES, YOU DO NOT DO SUCH THINGS TO PEOPLE!' So noisy poor Bob Evans woke up."

His laughter gets him up from the table, moves him around it. "You must picture all this! These are the things I love about Hollywood, this total improbability, this playing of endless children's games in an intellectual Sahara, a seductive place in which glorious child-toys called movies are made! I want to work much more with Evans, with Jack, I think I am ready to move back here, to buy a house, sell my London place, become one of them! Delightful insanity!"

When the phone calls him from the table, his father says to Tish, with a wry smile, "I am seventy. Soon, I think, I'm invited upstairs." She misunderstands. "You're invited, um, to a party?" "Upstairs," he repeats, gesturing gracefully toward the ceiling beams. When Roman comes back, sensing something, he spends most of dessert talking Polish. After it, he and Tish go into his big bedroom, with the enormous rented Sony TV-taping outfit on which he recorded endless cassette hours of Kathryn Kuhlman and Cal Worthington Dodge commercials, which fascinate him.

"That call," he offers, "from Spoleto, I must go soon, you been? Oh, it's wunnerful, this festival, no money but a marvelous, supercilious, gay, snobbish atmosphere, very much fun. No such exact thing could come about in America! Interesting: Years ago this school in Paris granted me some kind of stipend to go there. I was unheard of, saw plays, concerts, but knew no one and was totally alone. Next time I go was two years ago, and three places I am *very* big, don't ask why, are Germany, Brazil and Italy, so they all recognize me in Spoleto, and bow and flirt. I thrive on my popularity as if it were physical nourishment! *Very* amusing! I don't mean it is all the time: It can often be a terrible drag, you can do nothing but it is publicly known. Question: Was I happier now, or when I was unrecognized? I try to figure this, because I am in truth mixture of introvert and opposite. To come to a party when I was unknown, it was sickening, I felt always totally superfluous, that I was somehow an intruder. No more. It *is* very nice, when very rarely in a gathering anybody asks, 'What do you do?' You unnerstand? Very convenient."

Tish is not fascinated with this subject, and with gestures and grand-opera delivery he tells of not quite the first time he got laid, "But I *was* very, *very* young and naïve, this was in Vienna, I had made only short films but knew this mad Viennese promoter who took me out one night with a man whom I call 'The King of Laundry,' as he controlled all laundromats of Salzburg. We go to nightclub which was once ornate old opera house, the dancing girls were available, and at the end of evening the King of Laundry makes arrangements for me and I find myself with tall girl upstairs in one of the old theater boxes, the drapes of it drawn, the orchestra still playing below. She orders champagne, then washes herself with it, then washes *me* with it! Incredible! She then applies to me a rubber. And afterwards, I will never forget this visual detail, she drops used rubber into the ice of champagne bucket! And abruptly, the King of Laundry comes in, draws open the drapes so that all could see, and begins throw money, great wads of it, large bills, in an elegant, slow shower, down to the performing musicians. . . ."

Tish leaves not long after that. He knows he cannot remain the raconteur now; that he is supposed to start remembering. "Let's go downstairs to the office," he suggests, not happily, and we do, to sit in the plain chamber with a desk where he and Towne worked on *Chinatown*. We start with his childhood, which he describes in a subdued, almost militaristic way. Born, Paris, August, 1933; father a Polish Jew employed by a recording company. Three years later they move home to Cracow. Early recollection: the Nazis constructing a concrete wall across the end of his street, to seal off the ghetto. Next year, both parents vanished into Auschwitz. "I then go to live in the country," he offers, "I was eight." He means that he escaped from the ghetto—he does not want to go into how—to a farm outside the city belonging to friends of friends of his father's, devout Catholics who did not instill in him awe of Mother Church. He slept in "a sort of garret, on hay," sharing his bed with all manner of parasitic insects. In the fields one day, German soldiers started shooting at him; this was only the first attempt on his life. When Cracow was liberated, the only bomb of the last German air raid of the war blew him through a bathroom door. His mother never returned from Auschwitz, but his father did, and remarried, and helped Roman to find a room of his own in the city and start in art school. "Then, an unbelievable thing happened: I was absorbed with bicycle-racing, and I met this guy, slightly older, he said, 'I'll sell you a racing bike very cheap,' and told me to meet him next day at this German bunker near the park. He said the bike was inside, it was pitch dark in there; I step in, he was behind, he hit me with a rock he had rolled in a newspaper, five times, very hard. When I woke up, my money and watch were gone, blood was pouring over my face into my eyes, to this day when I get under a shower and the water starts, I can feel that blood. I stagger out of bunker, a woman asks me what's wrong, I push her away, leaving a bloody hand print on her coat, which I also still see. . . ."

He still has five harsh little scars under the hair on his skull; the story he has actually somewhat enjoyed recalling, the fact that he was a bit later almost a Polish child-acting star does not seem to impress him. "Yeh, I was fascinated with radio when a little boy, built a crystal set, there was a children's program on the radio and they invited kids down to see it, I could hardly wait. I told them the actors were too stiff and showed I could do it better and they engaged me." He was also in a hit play in Cracow, and though he still acts—he is briefly and spectacularly in *Chinatown*—what he wanted was a power over the work far

50

beyond that available to actors. "My big thrill as kid was going in cinema, they played American films with subtitles in Cracow during the occupation. When they sealed off the ghetto we couldn't go, but the Nazis would show newsreels on a screen in a marketplace just outside the wall and I found a place to see, through the barbed wire. Of course all they showed was German army victories, but even that fascinated me, and as soon as I get out of the ghetto, I work selling papers to go to films. They were very cheap; Germans wanted people to go. Poles considered it very unpatriotic to do so, you would see written on walls, 'Only Pigs Go to Cinema,' but I didn't care, fuck it. Politics bore me even then, very mediocre people always enter politics."

He thought they'd keep him out of the famous State Film School at Lodz, however. "This was fifties, Communists had taken over Poland, my father was running small plastics company, this was considered by the Party to be 'private initiative,' very bad, that stuff mattered a lot when trying to get into the school but somehow I made it. Soviet Union was very interested in film as Lenin luckily had said that among all the arts, cinema was most important to Communist State, and at the time, Lodz was undoubtedly best film school in world. Wonderful practical training in camera operating, editing, optics, even still photography, which is most important if you wantta understand cinematography. The course was five years, each year you made your own film, first a short documentary, in final year a diploma film which could run up to twenty minutes. Mine was named *When Angels Fall*, a fantasy about an old woman who is attendant in public toilet, ran five minutes too long and naturally was over budget. We were shown an unbelievable number of films, all sorts, there were fierce schools-within-the-school. Older students were into Social Realism and devoted to *Potemkin*, others devoted to *The Bicycle Thief*, young kids like me worshiped *Citizen Kane*. There were savage arguments, I also bear scar from one of those. Does this occur now in American film schools? It should, 'cause from this you get strong, specific goals of what movie should be: It was from all that arguing and thinking that it first occur to me, movie is thing which must have a distinct dramatic and visual *shape*—a thing almost tangible which can be touched, felt, like piece of sculpture. . . ."

His frown is apologetic: He knows this isn't what he's supposed to be talking about. "You are forcing me to become a man of words, which I am not," he asserts, and laughs, without humor, at what he has said. "But I don't think you grasp importance of what I've said: Without that training I would never have made *Knife in the Water*—which was great accomplishment because you had to get your film money from the government, and they didn't want me to make this, they rejected it again and again, finally they give me a tiny budget, which I exceeded. Why I was intent upon it, I don't know. Gerard Brach, who wrote it with me, also *Repulsion* and *Cul de Sac*, we had nothing really for it but verbal concepts. I knew I wanted to do film in Poland's lake country; I knew I wish to do picture with only four people in it and *nobody* in background, no extras. When we start, I have nothing more in mind than a scene in which there are two men in sailboat and one falls in water. Why? Don't know, except I am fascinated early by mood, atmosphere, people reacting to some heightened situation such as terror."

The word stops him. Abruptly he grabs the phone and makes a prolonged, apparently unnecessary call. When he hangs up, you can feel him reinforcing a practiced discipline within himself. He folds his hands quietly; the emotion is left to you. "So ask me questions if you want to know something," he directs, not cruelly, not warmly. "Meeting Sharon? When I hired her for *Fearless Vampire Killers*, of course. We get married in 1968. By summer of '69, she was very pregnant and I was very busy, working on film script in London, it seemed best she go home to house we rented in LA and I stay on and finish film and get to LA soon as I could. Every day we talk on the phone; when it rings, one day, I thought it was her. It was my agent, in LA. He is crying. My reaction first, naturally, is no reaction, stunned disbelief, I suppose you call it. Friends came to me quickly, I think we went out for long walk, they called a doctor who gave me something, a shot, I sleep. Then I take plane to LA. You must understand, there is much which now I can't recall, which I've blocked out of recollection. After the funeral, I stayed on in LA because I had the ludicrous notion that finding the murderer would somehow ease my grief. I worked very close to the police for long time, who I've got to tell you, were quite human and wonderful, I had no idea that cops could be like this. Sharon's parents worked with them, too; yes, I'm still in touch with the Tates, naturally. What a question! I don't think this is known: that just before the police found Manson and all of them, I offered a reward, $20,000, for public information leading to arrest of killers. It wasn't collected, no. As soon as police discover Manson, I get the hell out of LA immediately, I could take no more, there was no more point to staying. I had begun then to accept Sharon's death, which I'd really never done before, which is really all that matters to me about it at all anymore, that she is gone. The worst started: I went to Switzerland and tried to ski and become very jet-set, the idea of work was impossible. Everybody kept saying to me, get to work immediately. Idiotic. Only Stanley Kubrick understood, he told me, 'You cannot and must not work now.'"

It is clear that he wishes to get up, pace the room, break it up perhaps, but he remains quietly seated and purposefully motionless. "See, I attempted for a while there, before starting *Macbeth*, to become a hedonist, as the papers had said we all were. Jesus, I hated the press for a long time after it, because, I swear this, although I already well knew how press exaggerates, especially in sensational matters, I *could not believe* what was printed about Sharon! My God, 'The Sharon Tate Orgies.' Interviews given by people whom Sharon and I had never met! I swear, I could not find one word of truth in any story printed about us anywhere, and I would not and could not lie about this fact! If there had been anything to any of that shit, I would admit it to you now. My God, it was, is, unbelievable. The murder was all a horrible mistake, you know, Manson's people were after somebody else entirely, who'd been renting the house before us! What was actually going on there was this: Gibby Folger and Voyteck were staying in the house with Sharon to keep her company, we'd agreed on this, they were good friends, the place was big and it seemed a good idea since she was eight and half months pregnant. Gibby was working very hard as social worker, getting up at dawn every day to go work in Watts and studying speed-reading at night. I was planning a film involving dolphins—like *Day of the Dolphin*—and Voyteck wanted very much to work in movies and was devoting lots of time to research on dolphins for me. Jay Sebring was another friend who came up often but never stayed one night all night at the house. I was dying to finish work and get there; the last time I talked to Sharon, only hours before murder, I told her I'd get there the following Monday even if work *wasn't* finished. Things had been so perfect between us: We'd had some nice times in that LA house, Sharon would cook dinner for friends and after we'd all sit outside and look at the sky, the constellations, and talk about everything. Just quiet, pleasant evenings. Sharon and I would make plans, we had a wonderful future extensively mapped. . . ."

Still he sits perfectly calm, though his eyes are such that it is uncomfortable to meet them. In a little while, you go home.

Countless hours now he has been locked up in a close, sunless Paramount editing room with Sam O'Steen, a fortyish, bearded, congenial film editor who did *Rosemary's Baby* and most of Mike Nichols' films and is considered in Hollywood, and by Roman, to be the best in the trade. Polanski is at his best with him, ingenuous again, vigorous, verbal and very feisty, as is O'Steen. They are nearly done, except for details, tiny moments of *Chinatown* narrative.

"We play that shot on Curley, for the line," Roman says to Sam, as if this were taken for granted, knowing full well it isn't.

"Can't do it, Roman, Jack overlaps him every take."

They are shouting over the projection machine, which plays over and over a six-second sequence.

"I bet you there is room, Sam, listen to me once!"

"I already know what you're going to say."

"No, no, no, we do *not* understand each other, do it exactly as you did it this morning, except you use—"

"Can't."

"Lemme finish! Do same, except you add bit in front of cut and play her line off screen!"

"Then how do I get a pick up?"

"Aw Shit!"

It is all very friendly, this. O'Steen enjoys it and proceeds to edit as he was going to anyway. Roman strides happily around. "See what I told you, that it's like writing? The vital use of one word! We have here an important scene that doesn't play well with a certain line that is vital. A few frames and we are days on it! You have a work of art or a fuck-up, depending on what is accomplished in this room! The same shots here, in different

54

order, it's a different movie. Sam is superb, we argue all day, I go home, sleep on it, wake up and think, 'Shit, Sam was right again!' I realize here, the hardest thing of this picture was having two people just sit and talk. Jack and Faye are having iced tea, nothing visual is happening, you are powerless as director, you try everything and know that whatever you do, it will simply look fake, like you're trying to jazz it up, and this is amateurish. Experience teaches you stuff like that; also, to leave in little mistakes, which young directors fear. We have scene in which Jack attempts to light cigarette and lighter doesn't work. Good, he had sense *not* to break the take, to just keep struggling with it, finally giving up, and what you've got there is something small, funny, wonderfully visual which you could never have planned."

He beckons me to the outer office, very excited. "Listen, you want to see the movie tomorrow?" This is whispered. "I want you to, and listen, don't tell nobody, we have to do it in big secret as they would shit here at studio did they think I show it now to anybody, *anybody*, especially the press, but you gotta see it, so I arrange it in secrecy!"

One has the sense, the next day, of gaining entrance to Paramount by deception; one parks unobtrusively and follows his phoned directions to the screening room. Still, he whispers. "Music is not in yet, there's a couple of sound flubs I must still overdub, but watch it, watch it! I cannot stay, I have . . . an appointment." He grins to himself; clearly he's perceived that his presence would be a distraction.

He is right, anything would be. One has had to urinate when the projectionist had begun the movie, and it is not possible to get up and go out and do it; the pain is preferable to missing something, and, finally, worth it.

After the end, one pees; the picture has been so scary that even being alone in the men's room is sinister. Polanski, not surprisingly, is waiting outside, and seems more overjoyed when you explain about not being able to get up during the showing than anything else you say about his work. "Terrific, wunnerful, wunnerful," and he jogs to the waiting Mercedes. "I know you tell me the truth! So I *do* it, huh? I really do it! An audience movie! See why I want to show it to you? You like her, you see why I am tough with her? Because I got it! Because she is worth all the trouble! You see now why I wish to do my detective story, why I do this genre? I will do all of them! Listen, every man thinks, 'I want to have fucked black girl, Chinese girl, Japanese!' A gay guy thinks, 'I would like to fuck a chimney sweep!'" Giggling wildly, he is starting the car. "Why chimney sweep? Oh, that is old joke, about guy who has fucked everybody, every possible combination, and he is asked, 'You ever fuck a nigger?' He thinks. 'No,' he replies, 'but I once fuck a chimney sweep!'

And he roars off the Paramount lot laughing, as though the cumbersome auto were the means to an unexplored asteroid.

4.

Catherine Deneuve: Belle de Jour
Comes Across

SHE idolizes Garbo, and is closely convoyed at all times by her producer, director and hairdresser. The PR men sheepishly explain to a legion of supplicating interviewers that she does not talk on her free time, nor in her hotel, nor during the difficult days of making her first film in America, *The April Fools*, nor when her hair is in curlers. Thus journalistic appetites are properly whetted, and Catherine Deneuve, suddenly the most valuable French loan since the Louvre sent over the Mona Lisa, is hotly pursued all over the New York shooting location route, only to be glimpsed hurrying into limousines or through the windows of her locked dressing room trailer. But finally, if you agree to speed to a nighttime filming at Kennedy airport, and promise not to be rude about her illegitimate son by Roger Vadim, her dissolving marriage to photographer David Bailey, or the car-crash death in June, 1967, of her actress-sister, Françoise Dorleac, then you triumph where others have succumbed. She comes to your table in the TWA terminal restaurant, in blue bell-bottoms and pink shirt, flanked by the producer, director and hairdresser, who eye you suspiciously, before retreating to a nearby table to set up watch.

"Oh, I feel so terrible, so lousy," she exclaims, flopping down and tossing her incredible hair. "My head hurts, my throat aches. In this picture I must speak English, and there are so many words still so hard for me. And here you have air conditioning, which I loathe. I would rather perspire, it is so cold. Oh, *Simone!*"

She calls across in French to the hairdresser, whose face crumples sympathetically. It is clear that Simone feels her charge to be the victim of American inanity; in Europe, after all, Deneuve graces the covers of magazines without having to talk.

"Now you must ask me new, good questions. You are going to ask me about *Belle de Jour*? Two things that you must *not* ask are, if it is the girl's fantasy, and what was in the little box. Because this is my best performance and it will be best remembered of all my films here, and people will ask each other for the rest of their lives if she dreams these things or does them, and no one will know. I *will* tell you that the girl really works in the brothel, and really has a gangster-lover, and that her husband was really shot. But no more! Luis Buñuel, the director, is a genius. His method is to explain nothing. He talks very little with the actors, and this is good. Here, actors think too much about why a character does this or that. Such involvement is not needed. Buñuel is very *sympathique*, but does not explain. I will not tell you what was inside the box because I do not know! Because Buñuel would never tell me!"

Laughing delightedly, she tells the hovering waiter to bring onion soup and a vodka. When he shakes his head, because there is no onion soup, Simone, sensing difficulty, hurries over to offer her sandwich as a substitute. The maître d' intervenes, promising to find the ingredients and prepare the soup with his own hands.

"So. Fine. I will have my soup. People here believe my success is due to Vadim, and that is not so. I owe it all to my darling Jacques Demy. I love him, and I love his wife. Before *Umbrellas of Cherbourg*, I did not take acting seriously. I grew up in Paris and both my parents were once in the theater, and my older sister, Françoise, was beautiful and talented and got into films, but I did not care to. But she asks them to test me for one of her pictures and they hire me. Vadim saw me and tried to build me into a sex symbol. Then Jacques put me in the *Umbrellas*. I know that I am very pretty, but Jacques make me feel that I am beautiful. He sees, too, that I am sensitive. He made me learn to act, to love acting for the first time, and to *believe* what I act. And, oh, what fun we had, working in Cherbourg, all living together in a hotel. We eat together and laugh. We were— swinging, flying! In *The Young Girls of Rochefort*, Jacques made me learn to dance, and we don't dance so well as Americans. But four years ago, at Cannes, I win the award for *Umbrellas* when I am only twenty years old!"

The soup is brought, but she ignores it, and plays with the ice in the vodka glass. She is pleased that she became the darling of the *nouvelle vague* in France, that she was chosen by such serious filmmakers as Philippe de Broca and Agnes Varda and that she will soon work for Truffaut in *La Sirène de Mississippi*. But with *Repulsion* she proved conclusively that there is range and stature beneath the golden Botticelli façade and, after that, tragic roles ceased to seem quite so challenging. It is not without significance that she has chosen to make her American debut as a rich, exquisitely dressed woman in *The April Fools,* an expensive bit of fluff with co-stars Jack Lemmon. Asked what actresses, besides Garbo, she admires, she answers: Carole Lombard and Marilyn Monroe.

"No, I will not make another *Repulsion*, though I am good in it, and Polanski is brilliant. He works by talking a great deal to the actors and analyzing emotions, yet he did not wish me to think about why the girl in the film was crazy. He did not wish the audience to wonder either. She was one of those dirty jokes of nature, without reason or point. Nor did I feel that I must know what made her crazy to play her. Polanski put in the photograph of her as a child to show us that she was always sick. A freak. Roman will use nine, ten cameras, and shoot from every possible angle. We rehearse only two scenes, when I kill the man with the candle holder, and when I stab the man with the razor. The rehearsal is for the cameras. I am able to discard the emotion completely the moment we finish. You must never become so involved that you bring the role away from work with you. I stab the man again and again, he suffers horribly, there is blood everywhere. Then we finish, and right away we all laugh, and wipe off the blood, and go and eat lunch together!"

She downed the vodka in a gulp and frowned. "The hardest thing in film acting is not to play a crazy woman. It is to walk across a room with no pockets in your dress, and still make the audience believe."

"You've said very little about Vadim's methods."

"What about Vadim? He is—talented. He directs with talk.

59

But now I must go and have my hair combed and put on my costume for the scene. If you will stay a while, then perhaps we will talk more, later. . . ."

Later, much later: 2 A.M. in the terminal lobby, Deneuve has played scenes with Lemmon and Peter Lawford, and, when a break is called, has eluded newly arrived reporters and vanished behind the locked door of TWA's Ambassador lounge. Seated in this neuterized, *Space Odyssey* retreat, attended by Simone, she looks up and blinks eyes now circled with pale blue smudges of fatigue.

"Okay, I will talk more, but softly, because we just have the doctor to spray my throat, it hurts so. What is your—zodiac? Birth sign? Mine is Libra, which means justice, and so I will be just and talk. Yes, I guard myself from journalists. I will not see them because you know, I really care nothing for this being a 'film star.' I have no ambition for publicity. I hate those who become hard and wish always to be written about. I am too cool. I don't give a damn. I tell you how clever I am: In my hotel in New York, I could have a big suite, like the big house they have rented for me in Hollywood. But I ask only for one room. Why? Because, with a suite, you cannot get rid of people so easy. With a room, you don't even have to let them come in. I hate parties. In Paris, I have a few friends to dinner. I have just bought a chateau in the country, and I tell no one where it is. My Paris flat is in the Trocadero. I tell that because already everyone knows. I must guard my time with my life, or I will have no life."

Pause. Simone has apparently dozed off. And now, once more, about Vadim? Very well: the son, Christian, is nearly five. His father and mother are not bad friends; in fact, Jane Fonda, Vadim's wife, is like a sister to Deneuve. The star and her director did not marry because "at the time, I did not believe in marriage. That is all. And I don't give a damn what is said about it!"

Not long after she bore Vadim's son, she apparently altered her stand on wedlock, for she married posh fashion photographer David Bailey, in a somewhat bizarre ceremony in London. She wore black, the bridegroom wore a blue sweater, and Mick Jagger was best man. This year, she left her husband and the international gossips have been swapping stories about Bradley's alliance with American model Penelope Tree; yet when *Vogue* wanted Deneuve in a fashion layout, she told them she would agree to pose for only two photographers—Richard Avedon or David Bailey. Reminded of all this, she only nods, and smiles enigmatically, and says, "I have no plan to divorce David. And I have no new romance. Is that enough?"

Almost. One has read a great deal, too, about her relationship with her sister—that they competed and quarreled, but that in spite of feuds, Deneuve has never really recovered from the news of the frightful flaming car accident. When this is mentioned, the tired eyes are suddenly wet, and angry, and it is clear that if there was ever conflict, the memory of it has been dissolved by the tragedy.

"I think you must be very insensitive to bring this matter up!" she says with an anguish that has nothing to do with fatigue, sore throats or air-conditioned air.

Then she was silent, and sat with closed eyes until it was time to have her hair combed again, and go back downstairs to do exterior shots with Peter Lawford. Lights had been reset outside the terminal's revolving doors. Most of the airline's traffic-jammed passengers had dispersed by then, and there was no audience but the chauffeurs of the limousines hired by the film company, who dozed in the front seats of black Cadillacs lined up at the curb, tail to grille, like the sections of a dragon with its nose pointed west, toward California.

5.

Do Not Smoke Skippy Peanut Butter

Dear Miss Macauley: My name is Herbie and I am being held in the Bronx House of Detention for a crime I did not really commit. Life is lonely, Cathy, in the House of Detention, but they let us read the papers and I have seen a great many articles about you being a hippie even though you have millions of dollars and come from a fine society family, and about your wearing hippie "gear" and doing your thing, as they say, no matter what society people think. I really admire that, Cathy. Except that I did my thing and look where it got me. Anyway, I am not asking for money or help. I just want a pen pal, as they say. I know you are popular and busy, but if you could take a minute and answer, I. . . . (December 5, 1968)

MARVELOUS, Herbie. Keep those cards and letters coming in, as they say. But about that answer: You see, your prospective pen pal, Cathleen Macauley, the columnists' "richest hippie" (can a rich girl, Herbie, be a hippie?), the twenty-two-year-old debutante who inherited the twenty-eight-room apartment where she does not live, *is* a soul sister and would like to write you, but her life has become terribly complex. Take this morning: The doorman of the building on East Sixty-sixth Street, where she does live, has made a number of darting little sorties into the crosstown traffic to find her a taxi; and she has come out to wait on the sidewalk, rather than in the lobby, where she would be inconspicuous, because the neighborhood has not yet seen the outfit she is wearing—yards of soiled black velvet trailing down around the ankles of her square-heeled black boots ("my step-on-your-boyfriend's-face boots"), a black velvet jacket with leg-o'-mutton sleeves, a tall black witch's hat, an old fence chain around her hips hung with huge rusty dungeon keys, and red false eyelashes. She carries, besides a dozen or so letters like yours, an envelope stuffed with her press clippings, a bunch of plastic violets, and a black velvet muff containing a Russian blue cat named Nicki. Brisk matrons in Peck & Peck stop dead at the sight of her; delivery boys grin and grimace and make curious clucking sounds; traffic slows to a crawl. And at precisely the right moment she reaches into a pocket of her skirt and extracts, with a flourish, a popper (known in the Bronx as a snapper), an ampul of amyl nitrite, the stimulant meant for persons stricken with angina pectoris. She crushes the little mesh-wrapped glass cylinder between her fingers, drops it into a custom-made gold basket-weave inhaler, holds it to her nose and sniffs deeply. The frantic doorman has pounced upon a vacant cab, but she is flying on amyl now, and as she drags her skirt, the muff, the clippings, the cat and her mail into the back seat, some of the letters fall into the gutter. Yours may be among them; the doorman may or may not retrieve it. Who can say?

"Wow," she exclaims softly. "Oh, *wow. Where is my head?*" The driver turns, and she holds out the inhaler to him. "You want a sniff, man? No, I guess you don't. Okay, take us to 960 Fifth." As he watches in the rearview mirror, she leans back and closes her red-lashed lids. With her straggly yellow bangs and long, slim, pointed nose she resembles an anteater with an eye infection.

"So I brought along some of my fan letters, and some of my clips. Oh, wow. Like, why do the papers have to print my *address*, for Christ's sake? It was in that article about Jackie, uh, Onassis and me both making the *Social Register* again this year, even though everybody thought we'd be dropped. They didn't print *her* address! Now the letters come from everywhere—from guys in prison, for God's sake, from brokers who want to handle my money, movie studios who want me to screen-test, from schlemiels with systems to beat roulette. I get dirty mail from sex fiends, which is sometimes groovy reading, and letters from heads in Vietnam, who write to say that everybody over there, *everybody*, man, is on grass. I guess I should answer the ones from Vietnam. I guess it's my duty. But shee-et, man! I haven't got time. Like, why *me*? Why do they write to *me*?"

Of course she knows why, as do we all: Cathy Macauley is a celebrity. One tries to count the actual number of words printed about her since the press discovered her a year and a half ago, and gives up, because there are too many thousands. Suzy Knickerbocker devotes entire columns to the "sugar-sweet" little heiress. She is described, inevitably, as "the Now Girl," "the Golden Girl"—sweet little Cathy with skin as clear as Karo syrup and hair as sunny as Mazola margarine, and the controlling interest in Karo, Mazola, Hellmann's mayonnaise, Skippy peanut butter, and all the expendables made by the Corn Products Company. In *Look* the picture-story was titled "Kooky Cathy Macauley" and headed "She's Nutty! She's Rich! She's New York's Nuttiest Rich Kid!" ("It sounded like a goddamn *candy bar*," says the Golden Girl.) Marylin Bender began a New York *Times* feature about her with "Everyone's talking about Cathy Macauley." When she went to the Met opening wearing old black pants, a red vest covered with bits of mirror, and a five-and-dime store's cat leash around her neck, there was her picture in *Women's Wear Daily* on the same page with the Mayor, Maria Callas, Ethel Scull, Mrs. Charles Revson and Mrs. Charles Wrightsman, except that while they were all properly dressed, she looked like she had spent the day sleeping in Tompkins Square. When a film company wanted to stage a Beautiful People party to introduce Catherine Deneuve to New York, they asked her to be hostess, although she had never met Catherine Deneuve. She arrived in sheepskin chaps and a white vest with nothing under it, and got her picture taken more often than the movie star did. ("I told the dum-dum photographers *I* was Catherine Deneuve, and they believed me.") She has talked on all the talk shows and appeared as the celebrity date on the big Saturday night version of *Dating Game*. ("Here she is, folks, the little girl with the great big twenty-eight-room apartment. . . .")

So the question is not why Vietnam heads and swinging convicts write to her, but why they should have heard of her at all. Twenty-eight rooms are enough to get one on *Dating Game*, but they do not explain a year and a half of intense notoriety. Neither does money; neither does the *Social Register*. She was totally obscure before late December, 1967, when she gave her first party. Suzy and the rest reported it breathlessly, but never seem to explain why they continue to write about her, for since then she has given only one other party, and has not posed nude, worked for charity, acted, designed, married, hired a press agent, or really done much of anything, newsworthy or otherwise. Weird clothes do not explain her fame; Marylin Bender tired to interpret her as Baby Jane Holzer's successor, ignoring the fact that 1964's girl of the year was, besides a successful model and underground film star, a fashion celebrity, whose name columnists could count on linking to Courrèges, St. Laurent, Chanel, et al. The fashion press, which includes "society" columnists and reporters, will lionize you according to your labels; it recoils in horror from such names as Salvation Army and Tepee Town, where most of Macauley's ensembles originate. So, the more one thinks of it, the more one wonders, why?

"Why?" she echoes, in her curious blend of private-school hot potato and St. Mark's Place slur. "God, *I* dunno.. I really have no idea. I'm certainly nothing like Jane Holzer. I mean, she had an interesting look for her time. But she's, like, twenty-seven or twenty-eight, isn't she? And, like, *couturier-oriented.* Ughkk. Okay, here we are, the legendary pad. . . ."

We are bowed into 960 Fifth by two elderly impassive doormen in clean white gloves, and greeted in the apartment's huge paneled foyer by Blanche, the Scotch maid. When she has eyed the little mistress of Manderley satirically, and vanished into the servants' wing, we move over Aubusson carpets and Carrara marble floors, beneath massive dusty Waterford crystal chandeliers, past Trumeau mirrors, Gainsboroughs and signed Chippendale wallpaper on a brief, desultory tour of about half the twenty-eight rooms. During it, the Golden Girl explains indifferently that she won't live here because the place is creepy; that it was the home of her maternal grandmother, Mrs. George S. Mahana, wife of one of Corn Products' founders; that grandmother hated publicity but loved to play baccarat at Monte Carlo; that her parents, who also hate publicity, don't live together, and that her mother is staying here at the moment but prefers the Washington house; that grandmother would never open the drapes because the sun might fade the rugs, and now the estate's trustees feel the same way; that the trustees should drop dead; that she longs to rip down the curtains and *let the sunshine in, man*; that the pantry contains enough priceless china to serve a twenty-course meal to one hundred people, but that all they ever ate off here were big white plates that looked as if they came from Woolworth's; that she thinks the solid gold and marble johns, the fourposter beds and the claw-and-ball feet on the massive cast-iron hotel stoves in the enormous kitchen are, well, groovy in their way, but that everything is so *old*, man, and that the only room that doesn't *creak* is the library, so let's go in there and talk.

"Sit, man, relax." She drops to the library floor, stretches out, and watches Nicki claw at the Aubusson. "See the little holes in the paneling? My grandfather—he died when I was little—used to say there were worms in there. Grandmother would come in and we would be listening to the walls to hear the worms crawling. That freaked her out. You want something to drink? I'll ring for Blanche."

She reaches up, yanks at a bell cord, bums a cigarette and lights it impatiently.

"You want my autobiography? My father used to be in the State Department, but he never did much that I know of. We moved a lot: Washington, London, Paris, Washington again, Indonesia. I never made any friends. I was a fat brat and shy as hell. I had these tutors and English nannies. One of them I tried to strangle with a coat hanger. Then they put me in Foxcroft. Oh, *wow*. A sick place, man. They make you sleep on porches and drill and wear Confederate uniforms. So about four of us used to print this underground newspaper with the truth in it. Like, we were sure that these two teachers were dikes. We listened at their door at night. We never exactly said it in print, but I got bounced out. I made 'em mail me my diploma, though. I really made a stink about. . . ."

Blanche has entered very quietly. "Oh, could we have, like, some Cokes or something?"

"But, Cathy, your mother will be home soon. Aren't you and the young man going to have tea with her?"

"Huh? No, no. We gotta split. Forget the Cokes."

When Blanche has retreated, she takes out another popper, breaks it, inhales, offers it, and lies back on the floor smiling. "So. *Wow.* So anyway, then I had a schlemiely coming-out party in Washington. Then I went to Sarah Lawrence, but all they'd taught me at Foxcroft was marching, so I didn't know how to study. And there was the matter of these four guys from Yale who came over to see me. They had been tripping and had these fencing foils with them, and when they couldn't find me they fenced the Dean of Admissions onto the top of her desk. I got blamed. Good-bye, Sarah Lawrence. The family wasn't too pleased and wouldn't give me any bread, so I took a pad in the Village, on Gay Street—I got kidded a lot about that—and worked as a waitress in the Café Feenjon, and as a go-go dancer in this dive in Union City, New Jersey. No, I'm not putting you on, man. It was good money, which I needed. Then one night there was this drunken brawl and the manager told me to get my clothes on and get out fast, because the fuzz was arriving and I was underage. There I was on the Hudson Tube, half-dressed. . . ."

She gets up suddenly, goes to a window, pulls the heavy drapes apart, thinks about it, and yanks them closed again. "Come on, man, let's split. I don't want to run into my mother. She's nice, but she doesn't care for my . . . image. Hey, *Blanche! We're splitting now!*"

From far down a hall there is a small sound of acknowledgment. Waiting for the elevator, Cathy is silent and distracted; one notices for the first time the little puzzled crease between her eyebrows, and the furrows that run from the ends of her nostrils to the corners of her mouth, surprising because they should belong to a much older face.

"Look, uh, let's go down to this friend of mine's photography studio and talk there. Peter Strongwater's studio. You know him? He does a lot of rock-group pictures and fashion stuff. See, I can't groove here. This place bugs me. When I inherited it, I was going to put an ad in *The Village Voice* and *The East Village Other* saying, 'You, too, can live on Fifth Avenue for one hundred dollars.' The maintenance here is twelve hundred a month. I figured I could get, like, twelve groovy people to share the rent. Sort of an uptown Group Image pad. You can imagine how the trustees reacted to that, not to mention my mother."

As we walk through the lobby, between the smiling doormen, she says loudly, "Oh, yeah—tonight, Peter and I are going to this orgy. You wanna come?"

Between the interview at Peter's studio and the evening's entertainment, one attempts, without success, to organize two hours of further conversation into a pattern which will explain the Macauley phenomenon. Item: She eats Skippy peanut-butter sandwiches, and a mixture of raw kidney, egg yolk, Mazola oil, vitamin powder and canned mackerel meant to be fed to cats. Item: She pays—or rather, the estate pays—an analyst fifty dollars an hour four times a week to try to discover "the cause of my kinkiness." So far, nothing much has come of these sessions, she says, except a new wing for the shrink's summer house. Item: Doris Duke is her godmother.

Item: The Beautiful People are decidedly not amused by her weird attire. At Effie Chew's sedate Newport wedding, she arrived late in a fringed Indian tunic, scout boots, and a beaded headband; Auchinclosses, Vanderbilts and Cushings stared malevolently. At the Mortimers' in Tuxedo Park, at the Drexels' in Hobe Sound, at Sam Le Tulle's Sutton Square town house, ladies in Mainbocher are just sitting down to the first course when in comes a ravaged child in a Merlin-the-Magician cape, or trailing dungeon keys, or as Hiawatha in drag. "They still ask me because they think it's a phase. Little do they know I've just begun."

Item: She *does* care about clothes—not high fashion, but "a look." The look is hard to define. She worked in one of Alexander's boutiques for a couple of months, but found their ideas square and the hours inconvenient. Now she would like to have a boutique of her own. She often tells people she has one, even though she doesn't. (To a cabdriver: "Yeh, it's, uh, on top of this bank building on Third Avenue and, uh, Fifty-fifth. On the top floor. The roof. There are these long colored streamers hanging down from it. Haven't you noticed them?") She is trying to find backing for the boutique, because she cannot afford the venture herself; in fact, the phrase "I cannot afford" runs through her monologues like a leaden thread. Most of her money, she explains sullenly, is in trust; her two apartments and her answering service and some of her clothes are paid for by the estate, and she is not exactly strapped for ready cash, but the bulk of her vast fortune will remain tempting and untouchable for several more years. She would like to set up some sort of colony near an ocean where groovy people could live without financial annoyance. A boyfriend has explained the plight of

69

the American Indian to her; she realizes how desperately the various tribes need bread, man. But "I cannot afford. . . ."

Item: She says that she has no unusual sexual hangups.

Dear Cathy: Though I do not know you, I am writing to ask you a favor. Not for money. All I really crave, Cathy, is for a pretty girl to turn me over her knee and whip me very hard. That's all. I hope you will not think I am some kind of sex freak or weirdo. And, Cathy, if you can't oblige, would you have any girl friends who. . . . (January 11, 1969)

On East Sixty-sixth Street at nine-thirty—we are to meet there and proceed to the orgy—her apartment door is open. Inside the Rolling Stones wail, *Good-bye, Ru-by Tuesday*, at maximum volume.

"Is that you? Come in, man. I'm in the bedroom. I'm not ready yet and Peter's late. You're getting an exclusive here. I mean, I've never let a reporter see this place before. Go on in the living room, see if you can find somewhere to sit."

One cannot. There are no chairs in the living room. In fact there is no furniture at all, except a small Parsons table in the exact center of the large room, and it is occupied by Nicki and her other three cats. On one wall there is a huge canvas, defaced by two curious brown marks—her painting phase. In a corner, there is a No Parking sign, the kind mounted on a concrete base. At first glance, there seems to be a carpet, but it turns out to be a blend of weeks of soot, old newspapers, shed cat hair and spilled Kitty Litter. In the foyer, where there are bookshelves, masses of *Eye, Status* and the *Los Angeles Free Press* cascade down onto the tops of the portable stereo speakers on the floor.

"So what do you think of it?" she asks from the bedroom door.

"Well . . . at least the Collier Brothers stacked the papers."

"The who? I know I've gotta get it organized someday, and cop some furniture. The super even offered to help me clean, free of charge. You think the living room is bad, look in here."

The only thing in the bedroom is a sort of pad strewn with sheets the color of cigarette ash and a dirty leopard print cover.

"You think you're ready for the kitchen?" Beyond the kitch-

70

en door, usually chained shut with a cat's leash, are several bags of old garbage and a sink full to the rim with what appears to be pus.

"*Cathy?*"

Peter Strongwater crunches through the Kitty Litter to join us. He is tall, and his hair is very long; his features, though amiable, seem to run together, as if he had once partially melted. He wears a blue velvet Mr. Fish suit and, inevitably, Gucci loafers.

"Cathy, are you ready?" He inspects her ensemble: motorcycle boots, a leather jacket and skirt ("which I stole, well, borrowed, actually, from Ohrbach's") and a number of heavy chains.

"I think you need something else. Aren't you going to wear the fall?"

"Nicki pissed on it."

"Well, I think you *need* the fall."

"Peter, I *just told you*, the cat. . . ."

"All right, *all right!*"

"Je-*sus*, Peter!"

And we are off.

The apartment is enormous. Moroccan, strobe-lit, reeking of hashish. Long glass windows look out at the reservoir in Central Park, and from this height and angle—or is it the drugged air?—the water seems boundless, the way the sea looks from the Carmel cliffs. Dozens of guests, some of them instantly recognizable, recline on gold crushed-velvet chaises and huge ottomans, smoking, or eating lobster Thermidor. Peter Strongwater quickly loses himself in the crowd. The Golden Girl makes no effort to find the host; her eyes glaze over with marvelous indifference and she makes odd, casual frugging movements to *Magical Mystery Tour* crashing at a million decibels through Klipschorn speakers.

"Cathy!" It is one of the columns' favorite bachelors. "Cathy, I'm stoned. Zonked. You want a poke of hash?"

"Later."

"Cathy Macauley? Hi." The woman wears black beads and smokes from a tiny jeweled pipe.

"Oh, yeh—hi."

"Darling, I haven't seen you since Newport. When you wore that marvelous little Indian costume to the wedding. So original."

"Yeh. *Ciao.*" And the Golden Girl turns her back.

"Cathy, dear, we want you to come for cocktails. . . .

It is a Beautiful Young Couple. When they have moved on in search of the hash pipe, she frowns and briefly sticks out her tongue.

"Uh, you don't care if I don't introduce you, do you? Because most of them are schlemiels anyway. *Shee-et!* I can feel this turning into a drag. I mean, take the music—these cats think The Beatles are where it's all at. They don't know Dylan or Jimi Hendrix. They don't know from real dirty, funky blues, like Johnny Winter plays. Wow! That *beautiful* cross-eyed albino! They've never heard of him. They play whatever record *Vogue* says people are talking about. I'm serious. This 'Beautiful People' bag is so incredibly boring. They are all so unbelievably up tight and so *effing* insecure!"

We find an ottoman; she bums a cigarette. "You see, man, the public actually believes they have fun. Nobody on the outside of this has any conception of the insecurity of these people. The women *and* the men. Of course over half the men are fags. Like the two that asked me for drinks—he's having an affair with his own *brother-in-law*, for God's sake! And they come to a thing like this and spend all night pretending to each other that they're straight. My village friends, they don't have to pretend. A guy is gay, so what? If he has a good head, so what? But up here, baby, it's all play-acting. The women all hate each other, so having a fag to talk to is like having a girl friend. Actually, the fags can be groovy, but the straight ones—Christ! They all have to prove themselves with you immediately, and then they tell you they won't respect you if you sleep with somebody else. Victorian, man! *Schlemiels!* Like, haven't they heard? Sex is supposed to be *fun.* The women haven't heard either. They *might* be beautiful if somebody taught them how to relax, let loose, groove. So limited, man. They limit themselves. They can't, like, go to the Village, just groove on people. They have to go out with men from their 'class,' with short hair and *business* contacts. What especially cracks me up are the rich Jewish girls. So they happen to be Jewish. So who cares? But they spend fortunes going to the Waspiest schools they can find in order to marry Waspy Wall Street types and make it in uptight, insecure, Waspy New York society! Or they do it like Susan Stein did, by going to England, where nobody cares what Americans are, as long as they've got bread. Susan managed to meet all the lords and duchesses and then gave big parties for them when they came over here. Much worse than Susan is Caterine Milinaire, the most insufferable snob God ever created. Whenever she can get away with it, she introduces herself as the Duke of Bedford's daughter, she's not even related to him, her mother just happened to marry him. Dig this: Prince Egon Furstenberg actually told me, very solemnly, he's no longer using the 'Prince.' That's his idea of being democratic. He goes to everything, I truly think he'd attend the opening of a grave if he thought that's where the rest of them were going."

She squints through the blue-gray smoke at a member of one of America's great industrial families. "Now dig her. All that money—*real* bread—and all the clothes in the world and *no* imagination. A stick. Made of stone. All these chicks have *got* to have their couturière labels or they have hysteria attacks. Even in Hobe Sound, which is supposed to be a resort, they've got to have their Lilly Pulitzer jeans! I know, man. I've seen it. And the hippies! The ones that papers call hippies. That, man, is the saddest scene of all!"

Someone has changed the record. She sings with the new side—"We were talking—about the space between us all"—as if she has lost her train of thought. She has not.

"What is a hippie, man? What does it mean? To be free, right? Free inside. Well, *Women's Wear* thinks you're a hippie if you *work*, and go to parties like this, and treat your fag designer like an equal, and take him to the country with you, and have him make you harem pants out of curtain fabric. Hippies! These girls have all the freedom of a constipated provincial concierge. They're dead—the walking dead. The frugging dead! And frigid, man. *All frigid.* What the Beautiful People really need—and I wish them well with this—is a good screw. A *good* screw!"

But that, she observes, getting up, is not about to happen here.

"Peter. *Peter.* Come over here. . . . Look, man, this is a drag."

"You're telling me? I heard that, last time, at least *something* or other was going on in the bedrooms."

It is decided they will meet David Bailey and Penelope Tree, who are at another party downtown.

"We better thank him or something," Peter remarks.

"For *this*? Some orgy. Up his."

In the hash haze above Fifth Avenue, the Golden Girl's fame has suddenly seemed explainable, and one forfeits the downtown affair for a private orgy of reviewing notes, tapes and press clips. Of the latter, none dates before December 22, 1967, as though Cathy Macauley had been born, or issued, like a press release, on that morning. Two nights before, she gave a little dance at 960 Fifth. At this time, she knew not one Beautiful Person, yet nearly three hundred of them showed up, including Senators Javits and Pell, Carter and Amanda Burden, Gian Carlo Menotti, Katherine Houghton, Count and Countess Pecci Blunt, Fords, Vanderbilts, Auchinclosses and Woodwards. Huntington Hartford crashed. To meet a girl no one had ever heard of. All the papers came, and called it the party of the year. Given by Cathy Macauley. Cathy *who?*

One or two guests did not know who. A couple of summers before, they had met but not noticed the Golden Girl, who was not then Golden, in Spoleto, Italy, where she was spending the season in pursuit of the arts with her friend Pam Drexel. At that time she was still fat and painfully shy, an eminently forgettable, taciturn teeny-bopper, but it got around that she was in the *Social Register* and so the fringes of the jet set—designers, and others whose projects often require financial aid—made inquiries. They discovered she was the granddaughter of that incredibly rich American woman named Mahana who spent *her* summers playing for huge stakes at the casino in Monte. "Then they, like, nodded and smiled. But that was all."

All, until September of 1967, when Mrs. George S. Mahana died quietly, and Beni Montresor, a sometime designer of opera sets and children's books and a frequent party-goer, stopped up to offer his condolences and remark how much the old mausoleum needed a party to liven it up. "Yeh, well, why

74

don't I have something?" said the now-heiress. Her idea was to invite some of her Village crowd and perhaps rent a jukebox. But Beni had a different conception of the evening. In fact, he took over all the arrangements, particularly the guest list. His hostess, who was working at Alexander's then, did not know exactly who was coming, but earnestly wrote the department store's phone number under the RSVP on the invitations. It was, after all, where she could be reached. Everyone involved thought that rather a camp, with the exception of Alexander's, who had to send couriers all over the store every ten minutes for Cathy to tell her somebody named Woodward wanted her on the phone.

So Beni Montresor received old friends and made lots of new ones, and Cathy Macauley made the papers. And loved it. And wanted more. Enter Peter Strongwater, who became to her what Justin de Villeneuve is to Twiggy. "Yeh, he was my Pygmalion," the Golden Girl admits easily. "Peter is rich, but not social. He comes from this very rich Jewish family. He's a buddy to me. Not a boyfriend. I really trust him. And he just told me to do my thing."

Not quite. Peter Strongwater was older (twenty-six) and wiser than Galatea. And though he hadn't been a photographer long ("I decided to be one after seeing *Blow-Up*"), he'd been around enough to realize that the press had been feverishly creating fashion celebrities for almost ten years now, ever since Eugenia Sheppard and *Women's Wear* evolved the formula. He also knew that the press is restive. How about tossing them an entirely new image? Be the first in your neighborhood to spit in the face of haute couture! Give them dungeon keys and cat-leash necklaces!

Of course it worked only because Cathy Macauley was already rich, social and initially publicized. But the timing was perfect. The papers loved it. A rich rebel! Even *Women's Wear* masochistically succumbed. Peter Strongwater had created a new kind of celebrity—the Anti-Fashionable. The Thrift-Shop Socialite. The Un-Beautiful Person. Peck & Peck's bad girl.

"But you know, man," she says thoughtfully at the end of the tape. "I'm not going to keep this up if it doesn't lead somewhere. I mean, I want publicity now because I want to do something constructive with it. It's useful, right? Like, I told you about my boutique. It's easier to get backing if you're . . . *known*, right? Also, I am thinking seriously about acting. I studied for a couple of months at Herbert Berghof's. And acting is such a tough racket that if I'm *known* to begin with. . . . Anyway, it better pay off soon, because these parties are all so *schlemiely*. Like this thing tomorrow night. The Nine O'Clocks. Oh, wow. . . ."

Dear Miss Macauley: I was a garbage man until I was stricken with cancer of the tongue and neck. Removal of part of my jaw makes it difficult for me to eat my baby foods. I cannot work, or buy food for my wife and six children. We barely have enough to buy my baby foods. If you could spare a few moments from your partying to send a check to. . . . (November 26, 1968)

The Nine O'Clocks. If you are invited to be a member, you send a check to the governing board, and if you are approved, you get to attend the three annual dances. Proceeds are not donated to further cancer or any other research; no one pretends that the money is used for anything but the champagne, the capon, and the rental of the hall. All the old-guard aristocracy turns out for the Nine O'Clocks. It is very refreshing for them, three times a year, not to have to pretend.

Though supper is supposed to be served at nine o'clock sharp, the Golden Girl is not ready to leave at nine, nor is she dressed. And Peter Strongwater is hungry. The cats prowl nervously, listening to threats and counterthreats and Peter's furious announcements of the late hour. It is nearly ten when the Macauley party reaches the foyer of the Rainbow Room.

"Well, it's okay after all," says Peter sotto voce. "A lot of them still haven't gone in to eat. The receiving line is probably bottlenecked."

Wendy Vanderbilt, in regal white satin, nods; Mrs. Winston "Cee-Zee" Guest, in pink Mainbocher, smiles. The Golden Girl, who has had a popper in the elevator, nods *and* smiles at both. A woman in crystal beads stops dead at the sight of her evening's costume: a jeweled suede bib with nothing underneath it, lent to her by her designer-friend Giorgio di Sant' Angelo, a black leather slit skirt and black patent leather hip boots. Her fall is not the same color as her hair; her eyes, penciled in black and gold, look like restless poisonous insects. Around one leather thigh she has wound a long, fat, gold-mesh snake.

"Cathy, dear. Well, *really*, dear. I mean, this is *not* a Mardi Gras party!"

The Golden Girl raises her golden inhaler in a sort of salute, rather the way Bette Davis saluted George Sanders with the scallion in *All About Eve*, and sticks it resolutely into her right nostril.

"Cathy," Peter whispers, "will you please *cool it* with these little popper numbers you are doing?"

And it is time for the grand entrance. We wait until all the Nine O'Clocks are seated at the Rainbow Room tables. On the bandstand, Meyer Davis conducts a jaunty, mindless arrangement of gems from *Cabaret*. In the circular dancing area, decorated with three tall trees hung with what appears to be gilded Spanish moss, an elderly couple fox-trots, but they do not interfere with the Golden Girl's choreography. She pauses until all of them—Mrs. Guest, and Jane Pickens Langley, and Merle Oberon Pagliai, and young Prince Egon Fuerstenberg and the Vanderbilt girls and Justine Cushing and all of them—turn to look. Then she steps onto the dance floor.

"Hey, man, it revolves!" she shouts to Peter. And she is right: The floor, the trees, the elderly couple, and the Golden Girl are all turning slowly clockwise. She raises her inhaler and sniffs ostentatiously.

"Shee-et, man! It really revolves!"

But it is a drag. Meyer Davis is a drag, so is the food, so are the people. And we really must run anyway, for there is a little dinner for Giorgio di Sant' Angelo being held at that very moment over at the Spanish Pavilion, attended by the fashion crowd: Marisol, Mica Ertegun, Eleanor Lambert, and, of course, Giorgio's business manager and close friend, Michael Foley. Giorgio, in black velvet and chains, looks surprisingly like Kay Thompson. Though he pays ample homage to the Golden Girl, she is not pleased.

"Peter, this is just more bull. Let's go back to the Rainbow Room."

But Peter is conferring with Ethel Scull. Cathy sighs and bums another cigarette. A slender young man with gone-to-seed-dandelion hair, rings made of colored yarn and a cigarette holder—no, it is the way he holds the cigarette—runs up to her table.

"Ohhhh," he says in a sort of muted scream, "it's the sugar heiress!"

"Corn," snarls the Golden Girl. "Corn. At least get it right, dummy."

"Were you over at that Rainbow Room thing? Was it *ghastly?* But listen, I hear a rock group is supposed to come in later. So would you want to go back? I mean, can I go back *with* you? Oh, marvelous, let's go now, because this is a disaster. I'll go get us somebody's car to use."

He scampers off to borrow one of the limousines waiting in the rain.

"You know him? His father's very big in the music world. I can't stand him. Did you hear that crap? 'Sugar heiress.' He wouldn't be talking to me except for that. Oh, wow. The insecure little snob."

She grimaces and gets up.

"But he's sort of . . . campy. And I have this idea: If I can get him to help me, maybe we can find the controls of that revolving floor up there. And make it go faster. Very fast. Wouldn't that be a gas?"

And she was gone, without saying good-bye, as is her habit.

The next morning, the papers all noted her presence at the Nine O'Clocks, and her outfit, but there was no mention of the floor going faster. Apparently she didn't find the controls.

6.

The Sweeter Options of Truman Capote

IT is to be expected that he will be small, but as he marches up the steps to the terrace of the Southampton restaurant, looking like a ruined Puck, he is startling. Though Truman Capote is not a dwarf, nor a hydrocephalic, his head does appear to have been left underwater too long, and his body seems out of proportion to ordinary surroundings, as if he moved continually through the room in the fun house where the furniture is larger than life-size. One assumes that his manner and conversation, some special depth in his pale eyes, will compensate for his physique with a particular wisdom, or humor. This is not the case. He behaves with the distracted, vaguely labored courtesy of persons who have been interviewed too often, to whom no questions can really be amusing or challenging, whose demeanors are perpetually embroidered with intricate little floral arrangements of boredom and weary endurance.

"Now, where shall we SIT?" he begins, gliding by the excited headwaiter like a catboat overtaking a Chris-Craft. "Over here, yes, HERE, I don't think anybody else is sitting here. Oh, we don't need their silly menu, all those elaborate dishes, let's have HAMBURGERS, I love them, don't you? Well, now; is your chair comfortable? Was the train ride ghastly? Oh, for GOD'S sake, put that notebook right back in your pocket, that's not FUN, that ruins the spontaneity. I can't talk if you're going to do THAT. Make things up if you can't remember, I couldn't care less. Is that pretty girl a waitress? Oh, miss, we'll have HAMBURGERS, without potatoes."

The girl smiles as if auditioning for him, a smile he does not return. When quoting him, writers tend to indicate that he speaks in italics, but this seems incorrect. What he does is speak in capital letters, sometimes for emphasis, often at random. The curious speech pattern really has nothing to do with the voice itself, which is not the result of a cleft palate or a harelip, and could not accurately be described as lisp.

"Now, WHY," he is saying, "does that fellow keep WATCH-ING me? I don't come here often, I don't know him." Across the room, the headwaiter waits, every pore coiled like a spring, but the question is redundant. Arriving early, I have asked the man for Mr. Capote's table, and he has responded with a surprised smile followed by a patronizing smirk. Imagine, supposing Mr. Capote would need to make a reservation! If Truman Capote wants to eat here, the smirk implies, then, naturally, regular patrons will be expelled to make room. Though the place requires gentlemen to wear a coat and tie, even at lunch, it will not matter if Truman Capote comes in—as he does—in washed-out chinos, little soiled tennis sneakers and a polo shirt with a missing button.

In the fifties, when funky clothes were not yet thought clever, Capote showed up at a Metropolitan Opera opening night in pretty much the same costume. He was admitted then, too, because he was already as well known, and just as rich, as the singers booked for the evening. About ten years before, when he was twenty-one, his story, *A Tree of Night*, appeared in *Harper's Bazaar* and caused a great sensation. What caused even more of a sensation was its author. While his contemporaries were still being photographed clutching pipes, or confronting bulls in Pamplona, Capote was depicted languishing on settees beneath varieties of Dixie foliage like a tiny blond Theda Bara. One of these notorious photos was used on the jacket of his first novel, *Other Voices, Other Rooms*. In 1948, when it came out, there were very few best-sellers about ghostly transvestites who seduce adolescent boys, and the book made a fortune. It was also well reviewed. As time passed, a number of sterner critics refused to take seriously a writer so obsessed with characters such as Miss Sook Faulk, the sort of woman whom a Northerner suspects was not so much recorded by Southern writing as created by it, and with persons whose ultimate tragedy was that they had never seen snow; but that didn't make the slightest difference to the author. In *New Faces of 1952,* Ronny Graham lounged in a hammock, tenderly spraying spittle onto the footlights during a Capote-esque monologue, and the audience roared with instant recognition. Little Truman had somehow become both rich and a major celebrity, if not exactly a literary one.

Neither has his legend been very much based on his later works, which have included the script for *Beat the Devil,* in collaboration with John Huston, the dramatization of his novel *The Grass Harp* and the script and lyrics for *House of Flowers* (with Harold Arlen). The prose has ranged from *Breakfast at Tiffany's* through *In Cold Blood.* Whether or not you consider that a range depends on whether you consider *In Cold Blood* something more than a stylish piece of research masquerading as "a nonfiction novel." Actually, many of Capote's fans didn't consider it at all, because they don't read. He had already reached so many millions by means of television and other somewhat bizarre public appearances that he had become idolized, as actors are, by countless persons who never go to movies. His image was self-created; he even had the sense to refine and improve it. By the early sixties, he had discarded or hidden away his little tennis shoes; no longer did he loll about in hammocks. Abruptly, his feet were shod in alligator, his torso wrapped in vicuña. Priceless watches and heavy antique jewelry circled his tiny wrists. He made friends with the columnists, who began reporting at stultifying length the progression of this manicured gnome, morris-dancing over a shimmering landscape hand in hand with Babe Paley, Gloria Vanderbilt, the Bennett Cerfs, the Carter Burdens, Countess This, Marquesa That, and yes, Them, the sisters. Does Mailer possess all seven private telephone numbers of Mrs. Jackie? Are Breslin's palms smooth enough to hold the hands of Princess Lee?

Well, then; why, exactly, does this archetype of style confront someone who is going to write about him clad in this surprising mufti? Perhaps he is exercising an unsuspected option—self-imposed austerity, an elaborate poor-mouthism, the sort instigated by Gloria Vanderbilt two years ago when, stepping off a plane from Europe via the back door, she told a reporter she always flew tourist these days, that it seemed in keeping with the dark times, that first class was, actually, well, rather parvenu.

I ask if he usually has hamburgers for lunch. "Oh, I don't even eat LUNCH very often, not when I'm out here. I don't eat breakfast either. No, of COURSE I don't keep a cook out here, I live very SIMPLY. This is where I WORK. Are you finished, do you want coffee?" Often, he will become impatient in the middle of his own sentence, and he does so now. "Well, then, come on, come see my studio. . . ."

It is actually several miles away, in Bridgehampton. I have not noticed him park, and so his car is another revelation: a liver-colored station wagon, a Buick, dusty, incredibly cluttered inside. Besides papers, books, and unopened mail, the rear seat contains Maggie, an English bulldog who resembles Elsa Maxwell. She is slavering ecstatically at her master's approach.

"Well, MAGGIE-KINS, MAGGIE-FACE!" he says, getting in, and offers a number of similar endearments until we are under way. "Maggie is still a little GIRL, only a year, I had another, CHARLIE, who succumbed to old age. Just push that junk off the seat. I keep a nice XK-E in Palm Springs, and I had one out here, until the accident last fall." It seems that he was driving an XK-E convertible, top down, when Maggie spied an interesting dog near the road. When she tried to leap out, he turned to hold her, and wrapped the car around a tree. A woman found him unconscious in the wreck and rushed him to Southampton Hospital. Though she didn't recognize him, the nurses in emergency did. Nobody asked to see his Blue Cross card. Dr. William C. T. Gaynor, healer of people who summer in large Long Island houses, was rushed to his bedside. The crash left what its victim describes as "THIS AWFUL BIG HOLE in my forehead," but the scar was rendered almost invisible by the noted Dr. Norman Orentreich, who pioneered hair transplanting, and is, with the possible exception of Christiaan Barnard, the world's most expensive medic.

"And I DON'T have any hospitalization insurance at ALL," says Truman, concluding the story. "I guess that's silly of me." He is smiling, ever so slyly. How much, then, did Maggie's impetuousness eventually cost him? "Oh, thousands, I suppose, I don't really know. I mean, I don't get DISCOUNTS. My money is managed, by a wonderful lawyer, by my publisher. I suppose I have LOTS. I don't really think about MONEY very much, do you? I've always had enough, at different times in my life, to do what I wanted at THAT particular time. When I needed more, I worked and GOT more. Writing is a very practical thing, a business, like any other. But then, you should know that, shouldn't you?"

He taps the accelerator with his toe, as if to insert a little ex-clamation point. Capote drives with vigor and a certain brava-do. A few minutes out of Southampton—this has reminded him of his accident—we have rounded a corner, hit a stretch of broken pavement and a soft shoulder, and spun sideways, near-ly over the edge of a steep drop. Maggie has shrieked. "Now, now, MAGGIE-KINS!" The car has been righted expertly and we have hurtled on with hardly a pause; the driver hasn't even blanched. "No, I never been afraid a DRIVIN'," he has said, reading the line as Miss Sook might, using the Gaylord Ravenal inflection to reassure. "Oh, I could have a DRIVER, but I love driving myself. When you can afford a chauffeur, that's when you don't want one. I always drive from New York out to my house in Palm Springs, me and MAGGIE-FACE, don't we, Maggie? And I stay in motels, I love motels. There are, oh, only two DECENT hotels in the United States. In London, you have the CONNAUGHT, in PARIS the Ritz, in Rome the Excelsior; I wouldn't stay anywhere else in those places, but then, I don't stay in hotels much abroad, because I am always somebody's GUEST. In America, there is the Bel-Air and the BOSTON Ritz, and NO others. So I stay in MO-tels, which are terribly sexy. You know: just get some ice in the little BUCKET and turn on the color TV set and. . . ." He completes the sentence with an odd noise, a sort of snort. "Now what if I had a chauffeur, driving me across the country, in and out of motels? Don't you see? There would be NO privacy! No freedom! There is so much freedom, traveling alone, you know, staying where nobody KNOWS you. . . ."

The studio is a small gray frame cottage, apparently the an-nex of another, larger gray frame cottage. Only the latter is called "the cottage." It looks occupied, but Capote doesn't ex-plain. Isolated, even from the sea, both buildings protrude from the flat dunes like halfhearted burial mounds. There is no wall, no gate, no hedge, no mailbox; mail is picked up in town. Neither is the studio door locked, but then the place would scarcely tempt an enterprising burglar. Its kitchen is uninteresting, the bedrooms Spartan, the living room a two-storied affair, walled on one side with screened windows that overlook the sand and some low dusty bushes. A circular iron stairway leads up to a wide balcony, or gallery. Everything seems to be covered with a harsh dark blue lacquer—floors, walls, the staircase, a huge wicker fan chair. To the north, a white brick fireplace separates twin bookcases, overflowing. On the balcony, a long wall plastered with pictures of the author: a snapshot of a child in a Buster Brown suit, an Avedon photo, a remarkable Van Vechten photo (the Theda Bara look), portraits from the covers of *Newsweek* and *Saturday Review.* Upstairs, downstairs, there are . . . talismans, of a sort of lady's gold dancing slipper containing an arrangement of dried weeds; a number of whimsical glass paperweights; small things made of crystal, china, polished metal; butterflies with mother-of-pearl wings. Truman has explained that he is writing a new book, a very long novel called *Answered Prayers* ("Saint Theresa said there are more tears from ANSWERED prayers than unanswered ones," he murmurs enigmatically), yet the work table is clear, except for a scarred Olivetti.

"My papers are all packed because I'm going to SWITZERLAND in a few days. Maybe I'll finish the book there. I have several of these little OLIVETTIS. I can't stand electric typewriters. You find them easier? Well, I HATE how they hum, and jump around. I write my first drafts in longhand, on big PADS. Then I do all the typing myself, because I rewrite and polish as I type. I've never had a secretary, or even a typist, heavens no!"

The luxury of labor one isn't forced to do. Yet why not make the mechanics of work simpler, if you can afford to? He considers this, as if he had not really thought it out before. "I THINK . . . that I like the time I work to be difficult. I have to do it all myself. Satisfaction? Habit, perhaps, I don't know, but I have always worked the same way. I suppose I have to be free of everything except the work, even little luxuries, because luxuries can become complicated. Now, SUPPOSE your electric machine burns out a CELL, or whatever they burn out. Then you have to stop to have it fixed, don't you? Simple machines don't interrupt you. I write as a rule from, oh, nine to noon, and then stop for ERRANDS. I like doing them myself, dull things, mail, groceries. There's only a cleaning woman out HERE, who comes in every other day, and I have about the same arrangement in SWITZERLAND. Well, then, about four o'clock, I write again and keep on till six. I do eat DINNER. It seems there is somehow always somebody around to get my dinner. Out here, well, Jack Dunphy, the writer and translator, do you know his work? No? Oh, he's awfully good, we've been friends for years and YEARS, and Jack stays up there in the COTTAGE, and I always have dinner with him, he's a WUN-NERFUL cook!"

He is sidling along the front of the bookcases. "Have you read that?" The book is Lillian Hellman's *An Unfinished Woman*. "No, I did NOT care for it, so much UNsaid, I mean, WAS she a Communist or not? I read constantly, sometimes a book a day. Did you get through THAT, or THAT? I just couldn't." Major works by half a dozen of his peers are dismissed with the flick of an index finger. "Did you ever read *Myra Breckinridge*? Who WERE those people in that movie, weren't they despicable? Except poor Mae West, I wanted to jump up and drag her off the screen, and say, 'NO, dear, you mustn't do this to yourself!' Well, you can say THIS about the novel, it's the only thing of Gore Vidal's I can possibly IMAGINE reading all the way through. Now, here's something WUNNERFUL. . . ."

On tiptoes, he extracts a copy of Willa Cather's *A Lost Lady*. "Oh, if you haven't read it, take this copy. YES, you must."

I thank him. There is something oddly disturbing in the way he offers the gift: casually, eyes averted. The presentation is followed by a pause, a curious one; he seems distracted, or awaiting something. Then he shrugs, businesslike. "Now, let's drive over and see Gloria Vanderbilt, and I have to pick up the MAIL, and. . . ." In the car, he does not use the air conditioning, though the day has turned deadly hot. Maggie drools over his shoulder. Once, at a stoplight, he fans her with his hand. Gloria Vanderbilt's great Southampton house is deserted except for a governess with tired eyes, and we hurry on. "I wish you could have MET Gloria," he says, burning rubber on the driveway, "she is FUN. I don't really mix with this Southampton crowd, though, because once you start, it never stops and you don't get any writing done, but I like Gloria." There is a definite implication that, for one who travels so securely with giants, Long Island summer society would be equivalent to spending a weekend at the Boatel in Fire Island Pines. "Oh, hell, now I'm down HERE and forgot something I had to do in Bridgehampton. Too much to do before Switzerland. I have to do it all myself, I've tried to delegate the authority, or whatever you say, and I could, but I worry when I do. A compulsion. When I grew up I was poor and always had to take care of everything myself, and I wonder if that isn't something that's impossible to escape from? Now, I spend UNCOUNTABLE sums to keep all my houses open, and have lawyers to see to details about them, and still, there is this WELTER of little things I have to do myself." I ask what; he stares blandly ahead. "The CHALET over in Switzerland isn't sumptuous. On the other hand, my Palm Springs place is NOT exactly a shack! I entertain a lot there, and have a full-time housekeeper, who cooks, and I give NICE big dinner parties, but I actually WRITE there. The only place I can NEVER write is New York. So many phone calls, and the ambience is wrong. I don't see how anyone can. Now, how do you MANAGE it?"

I ask if he minds flying very much, or begins to get anxious about it just prior to doing it. "No, no, I never think about it. That REMINDS me, I lost my ticket to Switzerland, do you think the airlines people will trust me?" One is not fool enough to answer. "The only thing I ever really MIND about planes is the people who want to come up from the tourist section, you know, and talk to me. If the seat next to me happens to be vacant, it's TERRIBLE, because somebody always sits down." Then why not purchase the other seat as well, and pile lots of things on it? "Hmmm. Never thought of THAT. Oh, well, no, it wouldn't really do any good, they'd just come and PERCH on the armrest, you know, or lean OVER and go right on talking. You can't really be rude. Even if you are, they DON'T understand."

After the post office, we head for the railway station, so that I may catch the late-afternoon train to Manhattan. Truman tells a rather intricate story about a homosexual friend, a story apparently meant to amuse. The heat has become unbearable; I point to an air-conditioning vent on the dashboard and ask if it is working. "I suppose it is, it was the LAST time I tried it." He flicks a switch, but doesn't roll up the windows. "So, ANYWAY,

86

what he SAID to this boy was. . . ." During a pause between anecdotes, I ask if Gloria Vanderbilt has been a friend for very long.

"Who? Oh, GLORIA. Yes, for ages, she and her husband WYATT Cooper, lovely people. They would do ANYTHING for me." Could that be said of many of his friends? "Well, take LEE . . . Radziwill." A limousine drives silently through the pause, first name to last. "Lee is a GOOD soul, a BUDDY. She is not exactly what you would call BRILLIANTLY witty, but she is very shrewd, VERY perceptive. Lee is both CANDID and COZY. I like those qualities in a buddy. I can go to a party with Lee and then afterward, we go home and sit down on the floor in front of the fire, and she can DISSECT what went on, the machinations, the people, with such delicious SHREWDNESS. But she is warm, too, like the fire."

At the station, he remains in the car with the motor running while I buy a ticket. I ask if I may visit him in his New York apartment. He agrees, not enthusiastically. "Oh, call me in the city Wednesday. Now, MAGGIE, say good-bye to Tom. Tom, say good-bye to MAGGIE. . . ."

The train is passing under the myriad trestles of Queens before it occurs to me that, during the long silence following the giving of the book, I was expected to ask Capote to write some sentiment in it. Or, at the very least, to request an autograph in the frontispiece.

Why anyone noted for a sense of style would choose to live in the United Nations Plaza is very puzzling. The building, utterly styleless, resembles an upended celluloid florist's box, the kind in which long-stem roses were delivered in movies of the Thirties. Though few of its cooperative apartments sell for less than a couple of hundred thousand, and though its tenants have included the Robert F. Kennedys, Mrs. Philip L. Graham (owner of *Newsweek* and the Washington *Post*) and the Johnny Carsons, the lobby, the elevators, the corridors might have been imagined by Mies van der Rohe during delirium tremens. When I ask Capote if the tight security controls lured him—one must be cleared by several very tense doormen—he laughs airily, and makes a moue.

"Good heavens, no." He stares a moment, his eyes narrowed.

87

"Maybe YOU worry about that, I never do. I've been ROBBED, oh, I don't know how many times. Once in Palm Springs, or was it twice? I guess I've got some insurance. I never do anything else special about it, beyond locking my doors at night. Yes, I suppose YOU do concern yourself with that sort of thing." Though his speech seems more constricted in the city, less given to sudden, erratic emphases, he still answers certain questions as if performing a tiny playlet, like a television commercial: mild surprise progresses to amused boredom, and the final curtain falls upon a challenging little query. "I did have this big HOUSE, you know, over in Brooklyn Heights, for years and years, but so many things go wrong with big old houses, and it took me just as long to fix my toilet as it would take you. A big tip doesn't make the SLIGHTEST difference anymore. So I wanted to move somewhere that I knew those things would be minimal. Don't mention The Dakota to ME! It's got all the things wrong that old houses have. Creaky elevators and BAD hot water. Here, the water always works, and you have the GARAGE man to take you car away and wash it, and the DESK captain receives people, and the PACKAGE room gets your big mail, and the VALET service cleans your clothes. They do a wonderful job, the valet service. Of COURSE they're expensive, it's ALL dreadfully expensive, but you're not going to ask me how much, because I don't know or care."

Again, the tiny pinched smile. I notice that his hands are trembling, that he seems vaguely unsteady as if he had spent a weekend cruising rough waters in a small boat, and had not yet adjusted to dry land, and I recall a remark of his, made in Bridgehampton. Asked, after our near auto accident, if he ever experienced any sort of fear, if he felt himself to be as tough beneath the façade as his publicity implies, he had replied, "I don't know about TOUGH, but I don't have any fear. No, and I never have had any." He had squinted far ahead of us, down the dirt road, and added, "But I do have anxieties. Yes, anxieties. . . ." Then he had interrupted himself to point out and explain some local landmark, and there was traffic to negotiate, and he never finished his sentence. His shaking hands recall this. Perhaps the stern guards at the UN Plaza entrance provide a kind of reassurance that he would not care to explain, or admit, to a stranger. One can imagine him alone in a large house in Brooklyn Heights, vulnerable as the Clutter family of *In Cold Blood*. Did he ever see himself that way, or dream it?

"What a weird question, of course not, don't you want to look around?" He is wearing a blue Dunhill's blazer. Dunhill's, he has explained, comes up and measures him for three or four suits and jackets every year; they never wear out, and so he has dozens. "Of course, a lot of my things are packed, or put away, because I'm leaving, but there's still a lot left around here to see. Now, if we're interrupted by the phone or something, you mustn't mind, because I'm still preparing for the trip. AND I have to lunch this afternoon with Kay GRAHAM, and there's a party up at Bennett Cerf's country place tomorrow, I'll probably stay overnight. Oh, and I have to go to the airport tomorrow morning, to meet an old FRIEND." When I ask who, he says, "Now, to go to the AIRPORT, I don't drive myself, I hire a car and chauffeur. That's a TERRIBLE drive out there, so depressing. See my view? It's even better than my Brooklyn view." The south wall, all glass, faces the United Nations and the gray East River. Though the living room is long, the dining room is square and cramped, the ceilings too low, the air too centrally air-conditioned, neither dry nor damp, nor comfortable, hotel-room air. The furniture, individual, fanciful, seems forlorn in rooms so unreceptive to it.

"Now, here is my wisteria-tree Tiffany lamp." He has taken on the role of curator. "Isn't it wonderful? And there are my RATS, my Chinese RATS." In the center of the round dinner table three exquisite ceramics, rat-size, face one another, straining upward toward an invisible bit of food. Apparently they are a matched group, but it turns out that two were purchased at different auctions in Europe, and the third was "a gift from LEE Radziwill, who had seen my other rats here, of course, and then spotted THAT one by chance at a New York auction, and came running up here with it in a state of HIGH HYSTERIA! Now, come see my MOSQUE windows.

In the living room, above a Regency sofa, two arched stained-glass windows hang like twin paintings against the wall, subdued, not giving onto light or a view. "They're from a real MOSQUE, the SHAH gave 'em to me."

"The Shah?"

He looks genuinely puzzled. "Yes, the Shah of IRAN. There

is only ONE Shah, you know. Oh, before I forget, I MUST call Dr. Orentreich, who fixed the hole in my head? I have this, uh, GROWTH on my big TOE, and I want him to remove it." He disappears down a hall, is heard dialing in a bedroom. "Doctor? How ARE ya?" The door shuts. There are only two other phones in the apartment, a plain black one, lightless, button-less, and a standard white wall phone in the kitchen. Capote uses no answering services whatsoever. Still, jotted on the wall beside the kitchen extension is a number, and beside it the word "Kennedy." The kitchen contains a wall oven, a dishwash-er, and a jar of honey from the Greek islands. The furniture in the living room, though expensive, is of an odd size, scaled down, like the furniture in rich people's children's playhouses a century ago. Tables, desks, all flat surfaces are covered with trinkets, paperweights, tiny porcelain boxes, little gold-framed photos of the author, and by what could only be called "pus-sycats," made of china. In the portrait of Capote by René Bouché, which hangs over the window seat, the subject is posed in a furry black suit, his head tilted sharply in mock or real ar-rogance, his wrist anchored by a heavy. gold bracelet, both wrists tenuously attached to his hips, palms extended, like little wings, as if he were about to soar up and out of the canvas. The pillows on the window seat are covered in cotton leopard skin.

"Dr. ORENTREICH is impossible to see, you know," Tru-man announces, returning from the call. "You have to make an appointment months in advance. But I got one for this AF-TERNOON, at two-thirty, imagine that!" He skips to the Re-gency sofa and sits in the exact center of it, crosses his legs, ad-justs his tinted glasses, plucks briefly at one of the tiny light hairs that grow from the bridge of his nose. "Don't you miss seeing MAGGIE here? She's going to stay the summer out at the cottage, with Jack. I'm so glad Jack is out there, because maintaining these FOUR houses can be so tiresome, and that's one off my mind for the moment. I suppose that this is my MAIN indulgence, my notion of luxury: to change my setting several times a year. You see, each house is a SETTING, an ex-tension of me. I keep things I love in each. People, things. Some of my paperweights are in Switzerland, one of them cost nearly three THOUSAND dollars. It is nice to be able to spend that much on a paperweight. But I have so that I can walk into any of them and it looks like I had just stepped out for the mail. Here, the building service takes care of the place for me. In Switzerland—oh, it's a darling little chalet, you must come and see it—I have a caretaker. And in Palm SPRINGS, I have BOTH a friend who looks in, who has been looking in for about the last six years, he's very responsible, like Jack, and also my wonderful housekeeper, Myrtle. Myrtle BENNETT. I've had HER five years. She was once a dancer at the Cotton Club in Harlem, isn't that delicious?"

Newspapers have printed that he will open a sort of manpower business in partnership with Myrtle Bennett, a service to make the lives of certain privileged persons even more privileged, by providing servants to open and close houses, clean, sit with babies or poodles, furnish food and waiters for any sort of party from an intimate alfresco lunch to a sit-down dinner for hundreds. But only those who are invited may avail themselves of the service, and they must pay an initial $250 membership fee; labor and supplies are extra, on a job basis. "A VERY old FRIEND who lives out there is also a partner. We'll start just in Palm Springs, and then, if it works OUT, we'll expand." But isn't this a kind of franchising of Truman Capote, rather like Johnny Carson sponsoring a string of drive-in restaurants called "Here's Johnny"? The question, worded more tactfully than that, still annoys him. "I think that it's a very NICE sort of thing," he murmurs, miffed. "And it's really just for MYR-TLE."

Impatiently, he consults his watch, then sees me looking at it and says, "Beautiful, isn't it? What it is is an 1890 WATCH, from Cartier. The papers get things wrong, they say I wear Patek Philippe watches, but I get ALL my jewelry at Cartier. I like 'em there, they're accommodating. I pick out gifts for friends myself, always, and I just go over to Cartier. I suppose there's a certain FREEDOM in just being able to do that whenever you want to." The watch seems to fascinate him, and he is silent a long time. "That's what you have been trying to find out, isn't it? How I make everything work nicely for myself? Well, the answer is that life is not especially NICE no matter who you are or how clever. But I just said my own little key word, which is freedom. Freedom is what you learn NOT to bother with—in my case, so many things, no wife, no family, houses withOUT

91

cooks, servants, complications. And that really leaves me MORE time, OCEANS more, to see all my friends, to entertain them. To give them the ATTENTION that friendship deserves."

Insouciant pause. He recrosses his legs. But isn't he usually someone's guest, in the course of attending to these friendships? And how much freedom is to be enjoyed by one so beholden? "Oh, MY friends always make me feel perfectly casual. I don't even feel like a GUEST with them anymore. I'm . . . one of their families. My close friends, anyway." Who are these, exactly? "Oh, well, CLOSE? Besides LEE, there's, oh, Gloria and Bennett and Phyllis—Cerf—and, let's see, Babe PALEY and Cee Zee Guest and Bunny MELLON and the Gianni Agnellis. I'm going to stay on the Agnellis' YACHT for a couple of weeks soon, and Lee will come too. The Agnellis are marvelous, witty people, and they have the world's only hydrofoil YACHT. They would do ANYTHING for me. Now, you can call any of those people, and ask them what they think of me, for your research."

I explain that I would find that a little ludicrous, as ludicrous as calling up his enemies. He laughs, nods. "Well, they're all charming anyway. Now, THERE'S a sort of option I've exercised. I mean—well, I'd never have met such people, you see— wealthy, famous—if I hadn't WORKED very hard and become famous myself."

A vision of him hangs in the air between us, like his words: Truman, cavorting through the halls of the court, delighting the Princess with his quick little vaudeville turns. Canny Truman, dashing from Carson to Cavett, tending his public image, delighting his public, because mass audiences, not honed paragraphs, equal fame, which equals not riches, but access to the very rich, and their special implements of isolation. Gibraltar may crumble, but how pleasant, how comforting, that the sound will be drowned out by the hum of hydrofoil engines.

". . . must go, I'll be late," he is saying. "What if I can't find a taxi?" As he gathers his things, searches for his house keys, he makes conversation by talking about movies. "There were several I wanted to see in the city, now I won't have time. I love them, but did you see *Easy Rider*? I just did, finally, it was out in Bridgehampton. Well, what a FAKE! I come from the South, and I have traveled through the South, oh, countless times, and people are very GENTLE down there. Very HOSPITABLE!" His face flushes, he seems genuinely incensed. "They would NEVER treat anybody the way they treated those boys in that movie, even if the boys did have long HAIR. If the boys behaved themselves, they'd be welcomed!" I explain that I have traveled through the South recently, with fairly long hair, and had behaved myself, and still found no welcome mat, even though I was not on a motorcycle, but he is nearly out the door, not listening. "Poor Kay GRAHAM, I'm LATE, she's sitting alone waiting for me in La Grenouille. Do you like that restaurant? I go a lot. Oh? You've never BEEN?"

In the lobby, the attendants bow and scrape, muttering "Mr. Capote" over and over, like a litany with a single supplication. When he turns his back, they exchange fisheyed looks. Outside, a garageman calls, in an odd, high, obsequious voice, "Your car is washed, Mr. Capote." A cab stops grudgingly; he grabs open the door with surprising force. His hands are still shaking. He is long gone when I remember that I did not ask him again about the nature of his anxieties.

7.

Jane Fonda as Prerevolutionary Wife and Mother

ROGER VADIM aims his Arriflex out the window of the Malibu house at his wife, who sits motionless on the beach beyond the sundeck. All he can see of her is the back of her lemon-colored beach coat and floppy hat, but the camera hums on and on. He does not actually fondle the Arriflex, or talk to it, but he holds it as if it were animate, and sometimes his lips move soundlessly.

Three minutes pass, four. There is no movement anywhere, unless you count Vadim's lips and the gentle surf, and no sound but the camera's. In the distance Jane Fonda rises slowly, holding her baby daughter. She walks up the beach to the house as Vadim films her approach, her entrance, and finally the hand held out to me, the Fonda smile.

"This is Vanessa," she says in a businesslike way, placing the baby on the couch with elaborate care, looking away from her only when she must. "She's named for Vanessa Redgrave. God, what a talent! I used to think that nobody was better than Kim Stanley, but now, I don't know."

Vadim has moved to the other side of the room, still filming. She does not look toward him, but is totally aware of his presence. As she talks about the baby ("She'll be bilingual, because I speak only English to her, and Vadim speaks only French"), and the baby's horoscope, which has already been cast ("They said she may be a noted courtesan, but I'm not worried"), one ponders the contrast between the woman on the sofa and the Jane Fonda of the wide screen. She seems dainty, decidedly underweight, apparently flat-chested. The intelligent blue eyes are clear, but circled with pale blue smudges of fatigue, and the rich blond mane has been exchanged for a cursory brown bob. Of course the movie she is making, *They Shoot Horses, Don't They?* is a grim drama of Depression dance marathons; but the change in her is more profound than anything required by a film role, as if she had abruptly decided to erase the Jane Fonda image that began nine years and fifteen pictures ago with the buxom cheerleader of *Tall Story,* and reached its zenith, or nadir, with *Barbarella,* the third vapid voluptuary she has played under Vadim's direction.

"Uh, don't pay too much attention to the way I look," she says abruptly. "It's Saturday. And I'm not talking like myself, either." She laughs the quick, apologetic laugh that surfaces perpetually. "I mean, the girl in the picture I'm doing is uneducated, tough, bitter, cynical, and right now, I'm talking like her. Talking bad, using a lotta bad English, et cetera and so forth. I let it happen. It's part of the way I prepare for a role." Vadim has turned off his Arriflex and sits at a desk, scribbling intently on a legal pad. "And it's the toughest thing I've had to do, *ever.* I mean, this girl is a born loser, and knows it."

Like *Barbarella?* "Look, there are a lotta people who hate *Barbarella,* and a lotta people who've seen it eight times. I happen to like it. I'm sure as hell not ashamed of it. I'd never have done it on my own, but Vadim said it could be a new kind of campy, crazy science fiction. Well, the style was totally foreign to us, and it could have been a hundred times more pulled together, we know that. Still, it's a groovy picture. You know, I *have* done a *couple* of movies that used me, my brains, my acting, but boy, do just one *Barbarella* and you're instantly branded as some sort of goddamn *Space Odyssey* sex goddess. Even before I finished it, I realized that the next part *had* to be a complete switch. When it got around that I was doing *Horses,* and that I wanted to cut my hair for it, you know what people said? 'Jane, *dahling,* you're out of your mind, *don't cut your hair!*' I thought, oh wow, so that's what I've become—a lotta goddamn blond hair!"

I ask why her movie career's been so checkered, and the answer leads her into a meandering autobiography, back to the first film and beyond, to the days when as an adolescent girl she and her little brother Peter, who was also her best friend, gathered eggs, rode burros and milked cows on their parents' farm.

Except that the farm was really a Brentwood estate disguised to look like a New England homestead, and that the farmer was really Henry Fonda, and that the farmer's wife was a society beauty named Frances Seymour Brokaw who committed suicide when her daughter was twelve. Though Jane will discuss her childhood, her career, her shortcomings with a certain engaging irony, she sets her curiously puckered lips when her mother is mentioned.

"I don't talk about that anymore. The best way to do an interview is to lie, but I don't lie. I tell the truth or I don't discuss. Since I've been with Vadim, it doesn't matter what I say to writers. They always imply that we live in some kind of weird, perpetual orgy. Good God, we don't even go to Denise Minnelli's, much less to orgies. And we don't go in for the Hollywood jazz. I mean, people just drop in here. Peter, Dennis Hopper—they've just made a terrific movie together, I just saw the rough cut, it's called *Easy Rider*—Christian Marquand, Roman Polanski, John Phillip Law. It's very loose—I mean, casual—down here on the beach. If I don't feel like talking, I just go upstairs and read. We had Simone Signoret over the other night, and Roy Lichtenstein, and we screened *Nude Restaurant* and *Flesh*. This is an orgy? Well, I don't care what's printed about that, but I do care when members of my family are hurt by what I say."

There was a time, too, when reporters were flying back and forth between Jane and Henry Fonda, collecting bitter quotes from both camps. She resented a childhood spent wishing she was a boy, so that she could be "like Dad," called him distant, aloof. He called her "disrespectful." Today, mention his name and her eyes widen in awe.

"You see, he is *apparently* a very simple man. My stepmother Susan—she's his fourth wife—once said, 'He should have been a librarian in Omaha.' I know what she means, because that is how he seems. But he is actually a very complex man with *torturous* drives. God, is he an artist!"

She had always panicked at the idea of being judged as her father's daughter, and to avoid it, went to Vassar, Paris, art school and a piano teacher, in that order. "I'd worked out about fifty good reasons for not going on the stage. The truth was that I had no self-confidence, man, none. In those days, I didn't even believe I *looked* good."

But she believed she could act. In 1959 she began studying with Lee Strasberg at Actors Studio. Of course he firmly agreed. So did Joshua Logan, her godfather and an old family friend, who directed her in both her first Broadway play, *There Was a Little Girl* (it flopped, but the New York drama critics voted her Most Promising New Actress of 1959–60), and her first movie, *Tall Story.*

"And if I was lousy in that, well, I didn't contribute much to it. Even then I hated the idea of playing healthy American types. I mean, my *father* played them. Besides, what do you do with a role when it's so goddamned insipid to begin with? Sandy Dennis can make a part like that multidimensional, I can't. The key to my whole career was, I wanted to work. Besides, I've never had that much faith in my own judgment about roles. I mean, *I* wanted to do *In the Cool of the Day,* and it was *not* one of the screen's major achievements. And *Any Wednesday*—bad, man, bad. But there have been scenes in some real bombs—for instance, *The Chapman Report*—that I am proud of. And yes, *Hurry Sundown* was lousy, but I did a scene in that, toward the end, which was a completely new color for me, something I could store away in my, uh, cubbyhole of colors and pull out later when I needed it."

Abruptly, she stops, studies me for a moment, and says, very clearly and firmly, "Of course I've done my best work with Vadim. I have a special fondness for *La Curée.* What was it called in English? Yeh, *The Game Is Over.* It was not a perfect movie, and neither was the first one I did for him, *La Ronde.* But I learned more from Vadim about ridding myself of phony mannerisms and bad acting habits than from anyone else. *Anyone.* For years, I've been *showing* emotions. Vadim taught me how to let them happen."

Isn't Lee Strasberg supposed to teach that? "Oh, of course Lee helped me immeasurably. But Vadim has been my best teacher."

I ask why she refers to him by his last name, the way Calpurnia referred to Caesar. She laughs. "It's *not* his last name, it's one of his first names. He's actually Russian, his last name is Plemiannikov. I am Mrs. Plemiannikov." And she repeats the name again, smiling to herself.

She reclines, the baby asleep in her lap; she strokes the glass

98

of Chablis the housekeeper's brought, examines the sullen Pacific. One asks what she's thinking about. Her house, she says, in St. Ouen Marchefroy, near Paris. It is their real home, and she misses it. "I *had* to live in the country—so I found this 1830 farm house, gutted it, and rebuilt it myself. There weren't any trees, so I had full-grown ones brought out from Paris. It was wild. Every morning, you watched these lines of trees advancing up the road, like Birnam wood coming to Dunsinane. I groove there. I grow our vegetables, we've got nine dogs, and a myna bird that barks like the dogs. Terrific place for kids to grow up. It's flat, looks like Nebraska or Kansas. I cook there, I—" Pause, wry grin. "Oh, hell, *that's* not the kinda thing you want to hear about, is it?"

How should she be described to someone who's never met her or seen her movies? She puts her fingers to her lips, the way her father does.

"Wow. I'm gonna need a cigarette to answer that." I light one and hand it to her, she inhales deeply and coughs. "Okay. You mean with no holds barred. Okay. 'She is terribly intelligent. Subtle. Sensual.' I can't honestly say 'beautiful'—make it 'attractive'. Uh, 'People think she's easy to figure. She isn't.' Okay? Interesting, that I said 'intelligent' first. I worry about it. To me, real intelligence is, uh, the capacity for synthesis, and I'm unable to grasp the total picture. If I had a choice of talents, I would be a historian-philosopher, like Toynbee. Now, Vadim can look at things that way. He thinks, I brood—about a lotta things. I wish I were more . . . generous. I wish I were crazier. Yeh, crazier! I mean, I simply cannot groove until errands are done, calls made, letters written, and I loathe writing letters. I am constantly making *lists*. I envy people who can just say *screw it all*. Vadim can. He knows how to relax. I can't even take a vacation unless I've worked two solid years beforehand. Not Vadim."

Once more, her husband has picked up his Arriflex and is aiming it at her. "You know," Jane says solemnly, "I couldn't stand Vadim at first." Instantly, the camera stops whirring. "I kid you not. I was eighteen when I first went to Paris, and I heard things about him that'd curl your hair. That he was sadistic, vicious, cynical, perverted, that he was a manipulator of women, et cetera and so forth. When I met him, he was with his

99

second wife, Annette Stroyberg. Then he came to Hollywood and asked me to meet him for a drink, to talk about doing a picture. I went, but I was terrified. Like, I thought he was gonna rape me right there in the Polo Lounge. But he was terribly quiet and polite. I thought, 'Boy, what a clever act.' Four years later, he wanted to talk to me about another movie. Okay, I'm older, and I think, 'Christ, I never gave the guy a chance.' This time—well, I was absolutely floored. He was the *antithesis* of what I'd been told. I found a shyness, a—"

She turns to him with a faintly anxious smile, but he has gone back to his desk again. Why they were married in Las Vegas? She looks down at her baby, explains that she was making a movie at the time, and it seemed the easiest. "Because it takes like five minutes. We rented a plane, and Peter came and played his guitar during the ceremony, it was wild. We forgot the ring. I *still* don't have a goddamn ring! Afterward, we gambled all night and went to the show at the Dunes, which was a strip tease version of the French Revolution. Perfect! It was all terrifically funny! I'd been living very happily with Vadim without a marriage license, and I didn't see why we should get one, except for the sake of convention, which I don't give a damn about. But one of Vadim's children was staying with us, going to school out here, and as Vadim said, if you make such a point of *not* getting married, you're putting more emphasis on it than if you do."

"Which of the children was here?"

Tiny pause. "Uh, Natalie, Annette Stroyberg's child. I know all Vadim's women. I like Annette. I like Bardot."

And Catherine Deneuve? Vadim is the father of her son, though they never found any reason at all for going through with the ceremony. "I *especially* like Catherine. I had Vanessa in the same hospital room that she had *her* baby, isn't that wild? Her little boy comes to visit us, too, often at the same time Natalie's here. It's marvelous, having all the children together. I don't believe in sacrificing a career for a child, though. I was an actress before I was a mother, and the identity I found as an actress is desperately important to me. Oh, I do feel about two hundred times more pulled together since I met Vadim, but if I had not had that identity to begin with, it might not have

100

worked out at all. I'm certain that, profoundly, I *still* have no confidence. Really, that's no bull. If a situation begins badly, if I feel I'm being boring, or that I don't look good, man, I *crumble*. I want to hide, but the old ego won't let you. So you go onto a stage, or a screen, and hide behind the mask of a character. You're safe, but people are still looking at you. My father is like that. It has *got* to be the prime motivation of every actor. That, and a certain exhibitionism."

How much is exhibitionism in her case? Hearing the word a second time, Vadim rises, steps quickly over, smiling.

"When you ask this question," he says softly, "do you ask in a moral sense? In this country, you are all so Puritan, so prude. You worry so much about showing the body. All actors are exhibitionists. I know, for I was an actor. It sometimes seems that the only good reviews I ever had were as an actor."

Jane laughs, too heartily.

"But I suffered agonies as an actor, for I am *not* an exhibitionist. A voyeur, perhaps, but not an exhibitionist."

"Vadim, I don't think he means in a physical sense. He means, do I need attention?"

"*Ah.* Yes. Well, you exhibit yourself as a kind of—experiment. You would not need to do this if you knew, really, who you are. But you do not quite, and so you make tests, as in chemistry, to find out."

Jane's eyes dilate. "Yes! Wow! Yeh, you're absolutely right! I never realized that until this moment—that I do in life exactly what I do when I act! I go through this extroverted, exhibitionistic period—talking like the character, and so on—as an experiment."

They beam at one another. And exhibitionism in a purely physical sense? The smiles fade.

"I'm not a physical exhibitionist," Jane says firmly. Has she read David Slavitt's novel, *The Exhibitionist,* whose heroine is said to be very like her? No, she does not read trash. "Nudity, in movies, it's certainly not something I get any kicks from. I agree with Vadim about it. In each picture, it was necessary to the text, to achieve the proper dramatic effect."

But the current film's meant to erase the memory of that particular dramatic effect. What about Vadim's next scenario? "We

101

won't know about that until it's written, will we? But I trust his judgment. I'll do what the script calls for."

She looks at her husband loyally, gets up, stretches. "I've got to fix Vanessa's bottle soon. You want to walk on the beach first?"

As we exit, Vadim starts the Arriflex again.

8.

Peter Fonda Saves Himself

"THIS is my survival kit, man," Peter Fonda is saying, stretching his six feet of tanned bones on the aft deck of his eighty-foot, two-masted ketch, his nut-colored face further blessed by the Malibu sun. He is grinning, showing all his unblemished, prominent front teeth; Bugs Bunny with good bones. "This is my ark. We're about three years from the hard edge of total collapse. Ecological disaster. Mass panic. I don't intend to stay around for that. The day the smog clouds settle down and don't lift again, the day they come after us with guns, the men from Sphincter Control—that day, my lad, I shall set sail in this vessel." He glances over to see if you enjoy his word-choice; seeing that you do he nods and grins again. "I'm going to take my lady and my children and split. Circumnavigate the globe. We'll survive a little longer that way. It'll cost a great deal of bread. I'm against being obsessed with money, *not* against money itself. You've got to think of bread like a game, like Monopoly. Money means personal survival to me, and I'm for that. Survival is intelligent."

So much for the notion that Peter Fonda shares the selfless radicalism of his older sister, Jane of the Barricades, who has stated publicly about one hundred and fifty times that she is giving away most of her worldly goods. As for her brother's intelligence, his IQ is 160, and it shows. Sometimes, though, you have to listen closely to catch his hardheadedness amid the wordy cul-de-sacs.

". . . And on different parts of this voyage, I'm going to have my friends join us, ride along for a while. Larry Hagman, his wife and kids, Bill Heyward, my partner, his kids." And

Dennis Hopper? Peter doesn't say anything, but he stops grinning.

Actually, Peter grins a lot. He is grinning when we meet the day before in his office, a shabby cottage in a graveled yard on a seedy street in depleted West Hollywood. Inside, the walls swim in psychedelic Technicolor. The three girls who work for Peter and his Pando Company are hip in the mild, cheerful way of Southern California and are done up in romantic ensembles from Sunset Strip boutiques. Behind their desks stands a watchful photo cutout of the boss—blown up beyond life-size—dressed not as *East Rider*'s Captain America but as he usually is: jeans, Western boots, a bleached denim workshirt. Upstairs there's a sort of alcove, curtained in Indian print, containing one Indian-print mattress and Peter Fonda himself, who is, at the moment, communicating with the big world via a bleached, buttoned phone.

"That was the FBI," he explains delightedly when he hangs up. "They want to know what I know about Angela Davis. I told them, 'Man, I don't even *know* Angela Davis.' When there's trouble, they call Fonda first. The Los Angeles sheriff's helicopters still circle over my house—they've been doing that for five years, watching through their telephoto lenses, trying to catch me freaking out on acid or something. What do you want to talk about, Tom? My time is completely yours. What do you want to do? I know something we could do you'd really like. Come on, let's boogie over to the water." In ten seconds we're downstairs and into his car, and he's waving to Mary, his personal secretary, who's waving some unsigned checks at his back.

So far this isn't the Peter Fonda you've expected, especially when you're already well acquainted with Dennis Hopper, the flamboyant scene-maker and scene-stealer, the florid self-named genius. This is the son and brother of opulent superstars, product of private schools, Manhattan mansions, and Beverly Hills estates, survivor of one of the most spectacularly troubled adolescences since Leopold's and Loeb's: shot himself in the stomach at age ten, six months after his mother had committed suicide in a mental hospital; at fifteen, an alcoholic, at thirty-two, a counter-culture Hercules. And what is he doing at the moment, this zero-cool Captain America? He is bouncing happily along the San Diego Freeway in a lumpy black vehicle—part large jeep, part small tank—looking like a prep-school junior with his first driver's license.

"That's New Mexico mud," Peter explains proudly, pointing at the floorboard, rummaging around under the seat as he drives. Finally, he pulls out a mud-caked, black-bound film script of *The Hired Hand,* a Universal movie in which he has just directed himself in the leading role: "Made the whole thing down near Taos. It's a very simple Western, a classical Western." Did he give a lot of thought to the film with which he'd follow *Easy Rider?* "Nope. I suppose I should have, but I'm honestly not career-minded in that way, Tom. I can't think like that. Well, with *Easy Rider* I *did* realize that bike movies made money, but I would *not* have made just *any* bike movie *just* to make money. Now, the cat who wrote *The Hired Hand,* a Scottish cat named Alan Sharpe, he knows the Old West like he grew up in it. I knew I wanted to do the movie the first time I read it. Then I read it five more times to be *sure* it was good. Beautiful flick—it'll blow your mind."

For a moment he whistles and hums to himself, smiling, watching me out of the corner of his eye. When he's sure my attention isn't on the traffic or the scenery, he remarks, as if to the air, "Uh, I better call the office. I think one of those checks *had* to be signed today." Like a small boy with a new fire engine he has kept in the toy chest until just the right dramatic moment, he produces a telephone receiver from under the dashboard, presses a button. "This is New Mexico 8749J," he says into the mouthpiece, his eyes bright. "Hello, Mary? Peter. About that payment to. . . ." He is still watching me, straining his peripheral vision. When he hangs up, he explains that his isn't a car phone but a private-band radio licensed in New Mexico. "I don't know what it costs exactly. My company pays for it. I really do need it, Tom, I travel around so much. I'm very into toys, but this isn't just a plaything."

So what if it is? Peter can afford F.A.O. Schwartz. During the next few years, his eighteen percent of the gross of *Easy Rider* will probably net him somewhere between $2 and $3 million. And the *Easy Rider* bonanza has rendered him bankable at studios like Universal, which gave Dennis Hopper upward of a million to make his second picture, *The Last Movie,* and just as willingly entrusted the same sum to Peter to go and do his solo thing. Peter handles the idea of solvency well—he was born to it, after all—but there are still these little wisps of guilt, this overexplaining. Riches just don't mix with the counterculture hero's image, and he knows it: "This young cat came down to the boat right after I bought it. He looked it all over, then said, 'Oh, man, you really bought yourself a big materialistic trip here. That's pretty weird.' I said, 'Man, do you know how much a good two-hundred-acre farm costs? What it takes to run one? Well, I'm on the same gig as the man who leaves the city for a farm. Now, you'd say the guy who buys the farm is really being a natural man, right? If I'd bought a ranch, like Hopper just did, that'd be okay with you, right? Well, this is *my* ranch. I'm a Pisces . . . I'm going back to the sea. And, uh, I don't have The Man flying over my head in helicopters out on the ocean. And I don't have to pay land taxes.'"

We've pulled up at the marina. Peter leads the way down a pier between small cabin cruisers and then large yachts ("That one there's a narco's boat," he says with amusement) until we reach his stupendous vessel, the biggest in the harbor. "Meet my first mate," he says, introducing a bright, friendly college dropout named Ted who wants to take us below to point out some trouble that has developed in the auxiliary engine. But first, Peter wants to watch my reactions to the boat's interior. Next to the main salon, replete with big couches and nautical maps and a ship-to-shore phone, there's a galley that deserves a more exalted name: wall ovens, teak cabinets, even a paneled breakfast nook. Beyond the galley are three Bel-Air Hotel bedrooms with elaborate baths and glass-enclosed showers. And the engine room is larger than most apartment kitchens. In twenty minutes, Peter has solved the engine difficulty.

"I, uh, studied engines," Peter says diffidently. We've stepped back up on deck, and he is examining the rich woods of the mast. "I bought plastic models of engines, took them apart, put them together." But can a man fix serious breakdowns by fiddling with plastic models? "I, uh, sort of sense those things. I've always loved machinery. I can get high on it. Let me tell you how everything changed when I first dropped acid, Tom. That was five years ago. What it did for me was—well, for in-

106

stance, I used to *collect* machines. I once had a Jaguar XKE, a Facel Vega, a Mercedes 300 SL Gullwing, two bikes, a Buick Riviera, a big station wagon, and a couple of others, *all at the same time.* Can you believe it? Well, I first smoked grass, oh, eight years ago. I was afraid of it, but I told Susan, my lady, that I'd smoked it lots of times. She tried it, too, and all she did was cough, but I got really *stoned.* I was laughing, then freezing, then hungry, than paranoid. I didn't turn on again for two years, but I thought about it a lot. I was drinking then, too, drinking a lot . . . I *had* to have a drink. I was still super uptight straight. *A registered Republican!* Can you believe that, Tom? I wore suits. Thought my old lady ought to have a fur coat. I was emulating . . . what?"

His father, maybe? "Maybe. He'd been presented to me as *perfect.* Then this friend laid some acid on me in 1965. Wow! Heavy changes, Tom. I used to worry about *relating* to my father, my sister, my Aunt Harriet in Omaha, who mostly raised me. Then all of a sudden I was just *grooving* on everything that had previously worried me. I'd kicked the past! I looked at my house . . . I'd never really seen it as it was. A few days before, I'd cut down these beautiful trees, four huge sycamores. Do you know why? *Because they were dropping leaves on my cars!* My God, I had killed those magnificent, fine living things. I went and stared at those automobiles and said, out loud, 'If you wanted to go riding now, you would *not* be able to decide which fucking car to drive!' Sold every one of them within two weeks. No, I don't drop acid anymore. Now I get high on sailing. And hash. And Heineken's.

Smile, anxious pause. "But I *earned* this boat, Tom. I wanted a boat so much I almost completed a deal with American International to make three movies if they'd buy me a big boat. They even went and *bought* one! Then I thought about the crap I'd have to act in for them. I said no and opted for *Easy Rider* instead. Well, I *deserve* to be sitting here on top of all this teakwood. Right? Right."

Lovingly, Peter touches the deck, the brass hardware, the nylon ropes that soar up to the mast: "The guy who built this ship paid a million for it. That was ten years ago . . . it's now worth more than that, but he was ill and wanted to sell quick, and I got it for a quarter mil. Now Hopper, with *his Easy Rider* money, he

107

bought this ranch near Taos for two hundred thou, and said, 'Man, what a bargain!' I figure he was ripped off on that deal by about a hundred thousand. Wow. I don't understand that Dennis. I guess I never did. He *sued* me, you know that? He thought he was owed more of the *Easy Rider* profits than he was getting. Actually, he dropped the suit—temporarily. But not until he served me with a summons. Do you know how that hurt me, Tom? Do you know how I felt?"

Peter gets up and bounds below, returning with two Heineken's and a little pipe. "Beer? Smoke?" He can't find a match, pats all his pockets impatiently; the subject of Dennis Hopper has chilled and subdued him. They met, these two men of antithetic, yet intertwining backgrounds, in Jane Fonda's apartment in New York in August, 1961. Dennis, who had grown up in colorless circumstances amid the wheat of western Kansas, was that day marrying Brooke Hayward, daughter of Leland Hayward, the Broadway producer who has since died, and the wedding was taking place at Jane's apartment. Henry Fonda had once been married to Brooke's late mother, actress Margaret Sullavan, and Peter himself had been in love with Brooke's sister, Bridget, who committed suicide in 1960. If Peter and Dennis weren't blood kin, they did at least seem connected by divorces and deaths.

"We weren't exactly buddies the moment we met," Peter says, squinting ironically. "It took me a while to get into Dennis' head." But they did have something in common: their failure. Dennis, still aping the rebelliousness of his dead friend James Dean, was considered nearly unemployable by the movie establishment. As for Peter, he had made three forgettable pictures preacid and *The Wild Ones* and *The Trip* posttripping, and had earned very little money, a terrible press, and a worse personal reputation. Nobody wanted to hire him except the mavens at American International, whose previous efforts had included *How to Stuff a Wild Bikini* and who were chiefly interested in exploiting the image of Peter Fonda astride a Harley-Davidson, as per the popular poster that became a favorite of erotic paperback shops and groupies of various sexes.

Then three o'clock one morning in 1967 Peter, who was stoned on wine and Seconal, called Dennis "because he was the only cat I knew freaky enough to dig what I was saying" and explained his movie idea: "The modern Western—two cats just riding across the country on choppers instead of horses, and they don't care where they're going . . . they're free. And then two duck poachers kill them off because they don't like long hair. The Captain America thing came later."

Was that Dennis's idea? Sad grin: "He's now saying it was. Me, I'd rather not get into who thought of what. I assumed we were above that kind of pettiness." Anyway, the possibilities of the picture left Dennis speechless for the first time in his life, but the next day, they both started outlining the script. Nobody would back them, a fact that now has had the moguls of many studios privately kicking themselves, for *Easy Rider,* eventually distributed by Columbia Pictures, turned out to be the movie that would revolutionize the industry, introduce the era of the earnest, low-budget, high-profit, ode-to-the-road show, and make its stars, previously unemployable eccentrics, instantly indispensable to the Woodstock Nation.

"Cult hero?" Peter says, "One reason I took all those acid trips was to break down that kind of ego. I'm a success, fine— that means I can make the kind of movies I want to make. Direct them, act in them. *That's* my motivation, Tom. I couldn't became a John Wayne-type 'star,' the idea's abhorrent to me. No, I wouldn't enjoy being an idol, no way. Hopper enjoys attention more than I do.

Thoughtful clearing of throat. "On our picture, I was the producer, and that didn't read too well with Dennis, having to relate to me as boss, even though he was the director. You know how he thinks: the director is God. And I accepted that. But in the flick *I* was the romantic figure, Dennis the buffoon—*that was how Dennis wanted the script to be.* Well, Hopper considers himself a pretty romantic guy too, and after the flick came out and this cult-hero thing happened with me, it bugs him. He doesn't like his image. See? See what this star thing can do to the people around you? They don't relate the same. Cats I've known for years—their whole attitude is subtly different now. I really object to that, Tom."

Surprisingly, during this monologue Peter has turned into a young Henry Fonda: the expressions, the eyes, particularly the voice. Writers keep insisting he resembles his sister; he never does, but his father often passes through him, fades, returns.

Clearly, Peter isn't aware of the transformation, which has nothing to do with the subject he happens to be discussing. Actually, he doesn't want to talk much about Henry Fonda, nor about his sister. He likes Jane—digs her, as he puts it. He would like to make pornographic movies with her, he will say, half joking. "Jane's really sincere about the trip she's on now. Naturally there's got to be a big change in this country. I just don't agree with how she wants to accomplish it." As for his father, "We communicate better than we used to. I think he's even smoked grass. At least I heard he did. But we don't talk about it."

But these topics—his relatives, his friends—do not make Peter comfortable. The subject of Jack Nicholson and his prize-winning job in *Easy Rider* doesn't seem a particularly pregnant one, either: "Jack is, umm, one of our best actors. And in our film he was—uh, good. Audiences identified easily with him because he was the innocent, the good guy. I didn't *want* them to identify with my character. Why should they admire or copy a dope pusher? The best performance in the picture was . . . Dennis'. Brilliant, man, and he was directing himself, that's no mean task."

Peter's directing himself now, too. How does he feel about doing it? "Scared, man. But wait'll you see the result. I'm so proud of it, Tom! You know, I'm going to set up a screening of the rough cut for you tomorrow morning. Never done that for a writer before. But I feel I trust you. Hey, you wanta hear about the next one? It's going to be about how we've screwed up the environment—physically *and* mentally. My children, Tom, they get sick when the smog levels are high. *I* get sick! Then there's spiritual pollution. Black people have been misused, but armed revolt is no solution."

Carefully, he crumples his beer cans and sets them aside; he doesn't even toss his finished cigarette into the water below us. "I mean, the militant blacks are behaving like all reactionaries, they're acting *against,* not working *for,* something. It's wrong to think in terms of black identity, white identity. Man, what we *must* get with is *human* identity! These black cats who're solidifying the black community, they're doing the same number whites did—a black version of it. As long as people think of themselves as some color, we're finished, nobody's brain is black

110

or white! But all these years of tradition. It isn't improving, it's getting worse, and time is running out. . . ."

Abruptly he's silent; his mood alters, late afternoons, he tires, withdraws, broods. But the next morning, when he picks me up at my hotel, he's wide awake, although it's early. He's refreshed, eager, and as we sit in the dim screening room at Universal City waiting for the projectionist to run *The Hired Hand,* he talks exuberantly: "Now, this is what I call a *classical* Western, Tom, about a cowboy who's been on the road seven years—that's the part I play. I have these two buddies riding with me, and the younger one gets shot, and I shoot the murderer, but I don't kill him. I'm really fed up with the road life, and I go home to the wife and little girl I deserted. And my wife doesn't really *want* me back. Then in the mail I receive a finger belonging to my older buddy—his little finger—and I know the murderer is holding him hostage because he really wants *me.* So I'm faced with this terrible decision. And I make the wrong choice: I go to help my friend. And get killed. I'm saying, here, that when you've been on the road too long, you can't settle down again, you can't go home again, things change. People want the good old days back, but they're gone. The movie's allegorical: In the beginning, the first thing we see is the sun—the light, God—and a cowboy emerging from the river where he's bathing—man emerging from water—and he staggers up on the sand and falls on his ass. In other words, man is created and falls on his ass, which is exactly what mankind *has* done. Man had an obligation, and he made the wrong choices and failed."

When the film's over, we don't say much. Clearly, he's very proud of it. When we reach the boat again, he is humming, hovering on the edge of a laugh. Comically, he shakes hands with the crew Ted has assembled for the day's sail. After numerous preliminary rope tricks, we edge out of the little harbor, all eighty feet of us, and turn north toward the distant, slate-colored water off Malibu. The Heineken's and hash are accompanied by Three Dog Night screaming from the boat's elaborate stereo. At the helm stands Peter, the wind filling his workshirt as it does the sails, pressing his ginger-ale beard against his cheekbones. He is of another time and place, a seaman out of Conrad or Melville. Obviously he is secure in this

111

role of Ahab or Noah, there is something of gallantry about him, on the monotonous Pacific, something heroic, honorable, perhaps even noble.

When we dock, he heads through the pastel Los Angeles twilight up to Coldwater Canyon. "I called Susan, she's making us some supper. I feel good when I'm going home to my lady. Does she like the boat? She's afraid to take the children on it, they could fall off so easily. . . ."

The house—small, glass-walled—is on Lime Orchard Road, almost hidden by trees. It's flanked by a huge tennis court littered with candy-colored toys and a swimming pool full of leafy water. In the living room, beneath two mammoth *Easy Rider* posters, an oversized mattress covered in Indian print contains Bridget, ten, who looks exactly like Jane Fonda, and Justin, six, the image of Peter. Both children are naked; they dress to go to school and when it's chilly or when they feel like it. Peter's wife, a striking gentle girl with fine, chocolate hair and distant eyes— he married her ten years ago, when he was in a Broadway play and she was studying at Sarah Lawrence—comes in smiling, murmuring phrases of welcome, carrying a beef ragout and fresh green salad. We sit on cushions and eat from a low table carefully set with white dishes and candles. Peter looks at Susan most of the time, nodding, smiling, sometimes with great wonder, as though he had just met her. She converses politely, and one feels comfortable with her; but there is something half-removed in her manner, semidetached. She is very much alive, but where, in what time? Though she is keenly aware of her husband's presence, she almost never looks at him.

Later I go into the kitchen, where she is talking softly to the children as she washes the dishes. It is hard to know what to say to her. I tell her how much I like the house. "Yes," she says, her eyes on the soapsuds. "I've gotten so I hate to leave it. I hate to leave even to take the children to school." Later I repeat her remark to Peter. He says, "That's true, she stays home. I try to get her to go out—anywhere, wherever she wants. You know, she can have anything she wants, Tom. She doesn't . . . *want* anything. She's strange to me." He is shaking his head sadly, and you're struck by the contrast between his public and private self. With the boat crew (who, like almost everyone else, defers slightly to him and falls abruptly silent even when he clears his throat), he is benevolently dominant, graceful, assured. But

112

without such an audience he sometimes falters and moves about restively, awkwardly, as if he were not sure of the firmness of the floor.

We've sat a long time out by the pool after dinner, and now Peter is driving me back to the hotel, but he seems to want to go on talking and so comes up to my room. In the elevator, two matrons in fur stoles appraise him. Too timid to acknowledge their excitement, they instead compliment his shirt, a bright-striped number he had changed into before dinner. Peter smiles, thanks them, bows slightly—and the ladies giggle. But once inside the room, he's distracted again. Beer is ordered from room service; abruptly he resumes the conversation, as if there had been no break.

"I don't know what I'd do without my lady, Tom. She's my life, she and Justin and Bridget." Why should he have to do without them? "Think . . . what's happened to me in the last year is difficult for Susan. She's proud of my success, I know that. But I've had to be away from home so much. And all the publicity. Susan's a private person, and she doesn't like this invasion of our privacy. And her needs come first with me! Hell, Tom, I think I could, uh, meet any girl I wanted to." In Paris, on an *Easy Rider* promotional tour, he did meet the model Veruschka. More than once: "She was pretty interested, Tom. There's nobody in the world for me except Susan, but sometimes I can't *talk* to her. I mean, I talk, but I don't get through. I beg her to argue, yell. She never does.

"That's what I mean in *The Hired Hand,* about things changing. You can't go home. Things changed for me. Dennis, I love the guy like a brother, and I'm baffled by him. Why the man now suddenly has a desire to hurt me is beyond my comprehension. One of the great things I've done in my thirty-odd years was *Easy Rider.* The *greatest* thing, of course, was the children. And I chose movie-making as my art because it's a *communal* art, many people creating something together, like a mass orgy but on a higher level. And, Tom, I accomplished that picture *with the help of my friends.* What saddens me now is to see, uh, several of the people involved in it trying to cop total credit. It's like making love with somebody and afterward one of you saying, 'Wow, look what *I* just did!' "

Pained silence, one's cue to change the subject, and I mention something that struck me watching *The Hired Hand:* that Peter has an onscreen demeanor which at times is almost Christ-like. He misinterprets the statement. "I'm *not* Christ, Tom. I couldn't even make it as Francis of Assisi!" Quick laugh: "'No more drinking, lad, no more drugs,no more wenching!'" His St. Francis is curiously Irish. "Seriously, I don't want to lead anybody. You know something? If Christ came back, we'd blow it again, because humanity just isn't together enough. That's really what I was saying at the end of *Easy Rider,* with the line, 'We blew it.' I meant the entire world. *People* blew it. These cats that go around shouting, 'Power to the people.' The people have *had* the power, and they blew it! And I'm not copping some Barry Goldwater slogan here, I truly believe it. We're destroying ourselves, and there's probably *no* way out anymore. It isn't just America. The Japanese, for instance, are flushing millions of gallons of oil from huge tankers into the ocean every year. So someday the oceans will become cesspools, the forests will go, so will our oxygen, and there's *no way* to prevent this happening because you cannot prevent human greed. We're too *human* to save ourselves. I think of humanity, Tom, as retarded. And I include myself, naturally. I have to.

"So what's left? One thing: the individual. I say, 'Power to the individual!' Right now, you're not in a country, a state, you're not sitting on a square yard of somebody's property: you are *inside yourself!* The kingdom of the body! I have hope and pride only in *my life,* Tom. My life is my art. I mean, I *am.* I have faith only in those two words."

Then he yawns. "I think I'm going down and sleep on the boat tonight. Sometimes I sleep better down there. Ted doesn't always stay aboard. Somebody ought to be watching that boat."

He gets up, stretches. "My sister, when I talk to her like I'm talking now, she says, 'You shouldn't say those things, they're so negative.' I counter that by saying, 'If I told people that humanity can be saved, they'd just nod and go on wondering who was going to do it. If I say we're doomed and nothing can save us, maybe they'll get angry enough to try to prove me wrong.' Maybe."

He leaves, smiling slightly, en route to his ark.

114

9.

Dennis Hopper Saves the Movies

THE room in the hotel in the Andes is small and green; air hangs in it dense as moss, because Dennis Hopper prefers to keep his drapes drawn, especially at night. He has been living in the room for almost two months, while directing himself in the starring role of a movie that he conceived and wrote (with a scenarist, but it's Dennis' show, fade-in to fade-out), and wanted to make in Mexico, and then decided to make in Peru because the Mexican government had seen *Easy Rider* and told him that, if he came there to work, all the actors would have to wear shoes, and censorship is one of the myriad fascistic ploys which Dennis intends battling to the death. Three of the room's walls are hung with paintings he has bought in South America, depressing studies of saints with watery walleyes and masochistic demeanors. Dennis looks at them often as he talks, glancing up from one of the twin beds as if consulting them. The other bed is occupied by his roommate, Pilar, a lovely Peruvian girl with applebutter skin and hair the color and length that Dennis' used to be, before he cut it off for his new film. Pilar neither speaks nor understands English, but listens to him intently, watching with mild, diffusive concern as he sniffs cocaine from a tiny silver scoop, a dollhouse teaspoon, and talks about his next movie. Not his current move, the one he is making in Peru, which is called *The Last Movie,* but the movie he and Peter Fonda are planning to make immediately after it, which is called *Second Chance.*

"*If* Peter straightens up," he is saying, and he doesn't smile when he says it. One waits, having noticed that it is inadvisable to ask him direct questions about Peter Fonda. When one does, suddenly his cigarettes or the distant mountains or the details of the coke scoop become intensely interesting to him. One must be satisfied with enigmatic bits of information dropped by minuscule pinches into rambling monologues, the way Hollywood acid freaks drop grains of strychnine into bowls of sunshine punch, to heighten the trip. "And what it will be about is, going from LA to New York with Peter several years ago, the year the Pope was there, and how we tried to raise money for *this* movie. And, uh, these people turning us down. These big producers who didn't like the sound of the picture. And that's one thing the picture will do, man—give me a chance to *show* these frivolous men, man, who laughed at us then. We were asking Carter Burden, man, we were asking Huntington Hartford, we asked George Plimpton, man, these cats who could have written the bread off their undershirts; everybody Peter knew, and everybody I knew, and I was very well-married at the time. And, uh, seeing a pigeon with a broken wing in the snow; and watching helicopters land on the, uh, Pan Am Building; and sitting in the Russian Tea Room with this civil rights activist who told us that black power is in, that it's all over for whitey, man; and Peter's father's limousine dropping Bobby Walker and me at this church, and us trying to get into the church on acid, and everything is covered with black crepe because the Pope has just left."

He stops as if the film ends there, but after a short emphatic sniff from the spoon he continues in his soft, reedy tenor, the voice of a Midwestern undergraduate. With all his hair and his moustache gone, and his eyes drug-bright, he almost looks like one. "And going to the Cloisters, and seeing there the copy of the Mérode Altarpiece, this painting of Mary in a Flemish kitchen and Joseph in his workshop making a rattrap to catch the devil. See, it was painted in 1425 by this man by the name of Robert Campin, who was known as the Master of Flémalle. Robert Campin was the first painter ever to use oils seriously. He thought that artists should control all the communications in the country; and, uh, there was this unpopular war going on at the time involving the artists' guilds, and it stopped all communications. Then, uh, Robert Campin took over, in a sort of bloodless coup. And what he did was, he saved art, man. He gave art a second chance."

116

For the first time in perhaps an hour, he glances over at Pilar. She has fallen asleep, and he seems mildly annoyed. "And, and the way the picture *begins,* man, Peter and I are, uh, driving out to the airport in LA to start the trip, and, uh, I'm saying, 'We've gotta save the movie industry, man. *We* gotta save it, or it's all over for the movies!' And that's what the picture is about. Do you dig, man? For fifteen years, I had been telling the movie studios it was all over for them. 'You are dying, man,' I shouted, and they laughed at me! I, I sat in a chair, and, uh, watched a fly dying on the wall. And I thought, if I could just help that fly find an air current, that led to a window. . . ."

His angular face is vivid in the bedside lamp, and he is deadly serious. When Dennis talks about movies, he is always deadly serious, and he talks about them incessantly. Often, he refers to them as motion pictures; seldom, if ever, does he use the word "flick." No matter what you ask him, somehow the answer spins effortlessly, like film through a modern projector, back to his obsession. "My work, man, is my life," he will say, very earnestly. "I have no other life now. You want to understand me, then you have to understand my goals."

Okay; except that a couple of years ago, his goals seemed slightly less complex. Yes, he perceived that the movie industry was in trouble; so did the movie industry, and most of the moviegoing public. People *weren't* going, at least not to expensive spectacles. Salvaging the American cinema is a praiseworthy goal; it is also a goal which, if achieved, means that Dennis will go on working. At any rate, he set out to prove himself in the cleverest way possible: By making a picture for $350,000 that would appeal to the then not-quite-realized youth market. As things stand, his effort, which was based on an idea that occurred to Peter Fonda at three A.M. after a night of blowing pot and playing the guitar, will gross during the next few years between $70,000,000 (Dennis' estimate) and $30,000,000 (a recent trade-paper estimate). And with *Easy Rider's* incredible success has come, besides money and fame ("irrelevant, man"), and future employment, a new self-image: Hopper, transformed from savior manqué to savior bona fide. The transformation is so recent that Dennis has not yet recognized it. There is no arrogance in it, actually; it is almost pitiably sincere, and, if one respects Dennis' unquestioned talent, somewhat worrisome. Cynics have written that *Easy Rider's* principal message was that when persons with long hair travel in open vehicles, they ought to do so in groups larger than two; nevertheless, the picture did make a simple, persuasive statement about the perils of further escalating America's great life-style war, and it spoke directly to the kids who buy all the tickets. Dennis' next two projects are very significantly different: Both movies are *about* movies, or rather, movies about how Dennis feels about movies, a subject of consuming interest to movie-industry people, most of whom, unfortunately, manage to get into movies free.

On location, one is advised not to bother reading the scenario of *The Last Movie* because, "Well, you have to see it." This is oddly disturbing, when you consider that Dennis Hopper demonstrated remarkable ability as a director in a first film that could easily be explained in a simple sentence or two, and it becomes even more disturbing after one talks to the large cast that Dennis has brought to Peru from Hollywood and New York. All the actors are his personal friends—he refuses to work with people he does not know well—and all exhibit profound and obviously genuine respect for him as a director, writer, actor and visionary, and yet not one can explain exactly what his movie is about. Then you read the script and you understand why. The first thing one sees on the screen is leader numbers, reeling off backward, 9-8-7-6-5, etc., so that you know you are watching A Film. Then one sees, within The Film, another film, a big Hollywood Western being made in a small Peruvian Indian village. There is the real village, and the fake, movieset village; when the Hollywood company finishes and departs, it leaves the movie-set village erect in the real village, and the real villagers, who have observed all the fake gunfights, fistfights and shootings, begin to make *another* film, a pretend film. Except that *their* fights and shootings are real. They construct elaborate symbolic cameras, microphone booms and light reflectors from sticks and flowers, and carry these in quasi-religious ceremonies; they desert their church, and their priest, and carry the statues from the altar of the real church to the altar of the movie-set church. They force a dissolute cowboy stuntman named Kansas—Dennis plays this role—who has taken the pratfalls for the Hollywood star in the Hollywood film,

118

to act out the star's role in their ersatz film. Or rather, their pretend version of the Hollywood film. Kansas isn't in very good shape to begin with (he drinks), and at the end they threaten him so fiercely that he dies (via slow motion, flashforwards, flash-backwards, etc.) of fright. Or a heart attack. Perhaps. The end isn't really finalized yet. It may be that in the last sequence of *The Last Movie,* Dennis Hopper—not the character he plays—gets up, after death, and jeers at the camera. To indicate that what we have watched is a film about a film. Or rather, a film about *several* films. Or a film about Dennis Hopper making a film about several real and imagined films. Perhaps.

Riding in the red Ford truck from Cuzco, where the hotel is, to Chinchero, the real Indian village where all this is being accomplished, I ask Dennis if he has read the plays of Luigi Pirandello, especially *Six Characters in Search of an Author.* Well, he knows of them of course. "I never read much, man, I don't like reading. I've read maybe seven, eight books in my life. I don't want to read about experiences, I want to have them; you know, go out in the street, man, get it *on."* It is just past dawn, but he is wide-awake, eager to get to work, and he drives with abandon. The truck will appear in the picture, and on its side is lettered, "KANSAS—Hollywood, Calif.—Broken Bones But Rarin' To Go!" Dennis is also dressed as Kansas, as he has been during every waking moment since his arrival in Peru: rancid Levi's, stovepipe boots, rancid work shirt, scruffy Stetson. He holds a bottle of Peruvian beer, and a cigarette. In his shirt pocket are several joints which he rolled before leaving, but may not smoke until nightfall. "I swear, man, I get so wrapped up in the work that some days I actually *forget* to *turn on."* Beside him is the beautiful silent Pilar, staring moodily out at the dirt road, at brown Indians on muddy hillsides herding testy, foolish-looking llamas, at the occasional brown cluster of roadside huts, and at the highest Andes, jutting too abruptly and independently, back-lot peaks painted on expertly stretched canvas.

"Dig those mountains, man. Far out. The Indians have seen flying saucers land up there." The subject of the film, and its meaning, is introduced. Dennis takes a long, thoughtful swig from the beer bottle and wipes his mouth on his sleeve. "Well, it deals with, uh, several levels of reality. Symbolism, mysticism and realism. And that is what life is to me: an inseparable combination of those three elements. Like, when you really get into the *I Ching*, man. Whew! I mean, man, there aren't any accidents."

Yes, but the picture?

"Well, first, man, I want to make the audience believe; I want to build a reality for them. Then, toward the end, I start breaking down that reality. So that it, uh, deals with the *nature* of reality. I don't know whether I'm going to die or not at the end, but at the *very* end you'll see lots of cuts of old movies, like W. C. Fields and Mae West and so on. Universal, which put up the money, they've got a fantastic old film library, man. I can do anything I want with it. Then the film jerks and cuts and tears, and you see the leader numbers again, so that, uh, it doesn't matter if Kansas dies or not, it's the *film* that dies."

Pilar has made a small noise; there is a starved dog sleeping in the road in front of us. Dennis tromps the brakes with such vigor that we nearly hurtle over the mile drop to our left. The dog regards the truck's bumper with feverish indifference, rises with difficulty and limps away. "And it's about, uh, your responsibilities when you make movies," Dennis says, shifting gears impatiently, "because in the next few years, well, I believe—I *know*—that motion pictures are going to evolve, from adolescence into full-blown maturity. With subliminal cutting, for instance, it's going to be possible to make Adolf Hitler into a sympathetic character. Show him burning Jews and cut in with tiny flashes of, say, a mother and a baby, and the audience is going to come out saying, 'Gee, what a sympathetic guy!' So the film maker has got a *responsibility*, man! When I was first trying to get this done, they asked, 'Does it have any sex and violence?' Well, right now, we're communicating to the *world* with our movies, and is *that* really what we want to communicate? I know that when I was a kid, I believed that those bullets up on the screen were real, that those cats were *dying* up there! I remember when Elvis Presley came to Hollywood for his first picture, we met, and he told me he was worried because the script called for him to hit Debra Paget. And he said to me, 'Man, I never hit a woman before.' Now, he believed that movie fights were real, and that movie bullets were real, and when I explained that

120

they weren't, he got *very* pissed off at me! And Elvis was *twenty-one years old* at the time! That proved to me the influence of motion pictures. The form is now fifty years old, we're in the same period as the artists were right after the, uh, Flemish Renaissance! Fifty years later, man, came the Italian Renaissance; and, man, film makers should be making Sistine Chapels now! Michelangelo and da Vinci, they didn't dig working for that Establishment Pope, but they didn't get negative about it, they tried to do something that was a little uplifting. Not dirty, not violent! And *that's* what it's about, man!"

He smiles politely, awaiting the next question. Perhaps it is the altitude, which renders everyone but Peruvians perpetually light-headed, or the sun's ultraviolet rays, excessive at this height; but for the moment, one has no further questions, and joins Pilar in her steady blank forward gaze. The truck is nearly vertical now, in pure ascent, and Dennis shifts gears again. "Arrunngh, arrunghhunngh," he says happily, making engine noises. One breathes deeply and tries to recall the specifics of the scenario: a man brutally shot down (in the opening), Indians killing one another with bare fists, an Indian with his throat cut, dying sheep with slashed, gaping throats, a whore beaten slowly unconscious, a whorehouse orgy, a man beaten and tortured by the mob, his hands broken methodically by boot heels, his blood, his death by fright. The question is not fashionable, but one asks it: in what way, exactly, can any film make much of a statement against sex and violence by dwelling on both for much of its running time?

Square, a square query. Dennis stares ahead at the road, still smiling. "Well, what can I say, man? I mean—see the movie."

We go around with that a few more times. "Can't tell much from the script," he asserts. I ask why, considering that the script is very complete, and that he seems to be following it closely. "Well, I, uh, improvise." But the script is followed? "Sure, scene by scene. Still, I believe in taking the moment, going with it, moment-to-moment reality, the little miracles that happen every day. A dog wanders into the shot when I die, it's beautiful, how do you explain it?" He laughs. "That there are a lotta stray dogs in Peru? Okay, but to me it's like little miracles. That's what Fellini does: makes the most of the unplanned moment. Except the big difference between Fellini and me is that I

121

make movies in eight weeks, and he makes movies in eight months." Again he laughs, quite modestly. "As if that were the only difference. But man, I never met a director in my life who gave a shit about keeping to to the schedule, or staying under the budget, and I care, man, I really care."

In this case, as Dennis is quick to point out, his concern is not particularly lofty. It's a simple matter of dollars and cents, specifically the $850,000 to $1,000,000 which Universal has given him, on the strength of the *Easy Rider* bonanza, to go do his thing, make a movie, any movie. Dennis has demanded and been granted complete control, total autonomy, as long as he stays within the budget. "But, listen, man, once I exceed that $850,000 mark, they start taking points away from me. I'm being paid *nothing* to do this picture—well, $500 a week, but what's that? Instead of a salary, I'm retaining fifty percent of the movie's profits. And by the time I exceed the million-dollar line, I could, contractually, lose *all* my fifty points, and end up working for nothing. I don't care about that. Far worse is that if I spend too much, they have a right to send *another director* down here!" He is suddenly very excited, very pale, and barely looks at the road. "Well, that's not gonna happen, man! No way! This is my picture, nobody else is *gonna* get it!"

Pilar raises her gentle hands to her ears; he glances at her, and laughs his high, embarrassed giggle, a sound he often makes in tense situations. "Wow! *Whew!* But that's me, man, I really get involved. We're already about three days behind schedule. The rain up here. But if I get everything done today that I've planned, we'll be back *on* schedule by sunset. . . ."

By sunset, he is. If one invested money in movies on the strength of the director's diligence, one would readily lay out at least a couple of hundred thousand after a morning on the set of a Hopper picture, especially this one. The logistics are remarkably difficult. Chinchero's town square is actually a series of dusty or muddy circles around a weathered statue of some forgotten Spanish war hero, shadowed by the mountains and by the only impressive building, the inevitable church. Most of the area's few thousand Indians gather here every day before sunrise, even before Dennis arrives, and stay until dusk, breast-feeding their children, kicking their bony dogs, and watching the actors with a certain bemused, almost cynical curiosity.

When needed, a handful of the men are recruited to carry lights and equipment; for this, they receive the equivalent of a little more than a dollar a day, and the Indians who serve as extras—some shots require hundreds—receive a little less. What they don't get in currency, however, Dennis makes up for with courtesy. He is elaborately kind to them, even when they are uncooperative, or bored, or purposely obtuse, which they often are, and has taken the trouble to learn a bit of Quechua, their obscure complicated language. To his actresses—there are four important female roles in *The Last Movie*—he is firm, but courtly. He addresses them as "man," but treats them with boyish, almost bashful respect, as though they were plain girls at a prom with whom no one else bothered to dance.

With the males, he is quite another Dennis, all blusters and cursing, a hip Otto Preminger. One or two faulty takes he endures with businesslike calm. "Cut!" he says quietly; then, gently, caressingly, to the actor, "Listen, man, now what did I tell you about this shot? Huh, man? Now, please, man. You know we're a little behind. Okay?" He turns to the watching crowd. "May I have quiet, please? Okay: action—roll it, please."

But the next "Cut!" he spits out like a profanity, and in two long strides he is facing his actor, sculptured nose to sculptured nose.

"Now, you listen to me, man—"

"Wait a minute, Dennis," the actor begins.

"Wait a minute for *me*, man! For *me!* I'll tell you one more time, if you elaborate on *anything* in this shot, we are dead! Just do what we rehearsed, Mr. Actors Studio, or I'll cut off your cocaine supply. Now, GET IT TOGETHER!"

The actor turns very pale. The next take is perfect. Dennis must immediately go into a sequence in which he directs himself and a girl in a highly emotional scene. He glances nervously at his watch, then runs over to his actor, embraces him, and whispers something at which they both roar with laughter.

"Vince," Dennis yells at his assistant, "have we got time, man, for this scene before lunch?"

"Only fifteen minutes, Dennis."

"Well, let's go with it anyway, man."

Of course the shot takes half an hour. Not even the dour grips and electricians seem to mind, proof of what may be Den-

nis' most notable gift, the executive *machismo*. If somebody protests the brutal schedule, he does not shout; but he appears so
profoundly injured at this lack of team spirit, so genuinely
crestfallen, that it is simpler, if one believes in him, to shut up
and overwork. On his set, it is impossible to hear, or to over-
hear, one word said against him by anyone. Reporters assigned
to *The Last Movie* are constantly being drawn aside by the actors, and even the crew, for whispered recommendations. "He's
a genius," a lighting man keeps saying. "He *feels,* deeper than
other men. I love this guy. I'm not queer, but I swear, I love this
guy, I almost love him *physically.*"

On the other hand, every decision, from the smallest to the
most complicated, must revert to Dennis. The picture does
have a producer, a distracted, taciturn man named Paul Lewis,
but apparently he is only a figurehead. "Universal," says Dennis, "made the deal with *me, I* make the rules, man, I mean, *I*
hired my own *producer.*" One of a movie producer's functions,
in the course of a routine movie, is to schedule interviews, and
the singular despotic situation of *The Last Movie* does not make
the journalist's lot easier, partly because it is virtually impossible
to see Dennis alone. One assumes, early on, that this is the fault
of the twelve-hour-a-day six-day workweek; then one notices
that when he *is* available, a friend always happens to be present,
too; and that when questions shift from a professional to a personal level, Dennis and his friend swiftly shift them back again,
to movies. Lunches on location become impromptu press conferences, in which the various reporters vie, in a subtly choreographed assault, for the strategic places closest to the director.
But Dennis makes it clear that lunch break is a time for light
conversation, eating, and midday joint-smoking; and anyway,
these little group sessions are pretty much dominated by the
writer from *Rolling Stone,* a very tall adolescent with opulent jet-
black Jesus locks and navel-length beard, who has just
"bopped" (his word) in from "Kesey's far-out ranch, man, up in
Oregon," with one pair of jeans, a tape recorder and a great,
great deal of enthusiasm, and who almost literally snaps at Dennis' heels, his eyes dilated with the sheer ecstasy of being next to
a Noted Film Maker. And so luncheon repartee deals mainly
with Kesey's ranch, Kesey's bust, Kesey's bus, Jagger's concert,
Jagger's rap, and the far-out, spaced-out, mind-blowing mountains, about which one has to get back and tell one's old lady.

("Man, what a right-on place for a commune!") And the Revolution, stateside. And movies, of course. Kenneth Anger! Haskell Wexler! Peter Bogdanovich! The juxtaposing of images! Antonion*ioni!* FARR OUUT!

The older reporters—their median age, alas, is thirty-two—exchange despairing looks, and the more aggressive attempt to interrupt, but it is no use. Obviously, Dennis likes and trusts this boy, and addresses most of his remarks to him, even answers to questions asked by others. One gets the idea—possibly misguided—that Dennis Hopper is a man to whom trust comes with utmost difficulty, and who, in the end, trusts only strangers, and the very young.

He calls the customary, "Cut, print it!" Within five minutes, the evening rains begin, turning the road home into a blur of reddish slime, but he is exhilarated. The day has been completely successful, and there has been another pleasant development. For some time, it seems, the mayor of Chinchero and the district governor have been vying with the local priest for the goodwill of the Indians and *The Last Movie* has finally brought this condition to a head. Several officials have drawn Dennis aside, during the afternoon, to explain that his offer to leave his movie set there in the town intact, when the work is over—the way it happens in his script—so that the people may use the building materials to advantage, has inspired the whole community. The priest will no longer be so powerful; the people will now look to the mayor and the governor for leadership. They will build a new school. Or, as Dennis puts it, "They're gonna get their town together, man, they're gonna break with that priest, stand on their own. It's going to be gorgeous, man!"

We are stuck in the fifth mud rut in perhaps a mile, and he guns the truck's engine, holding in his right hand both a Winston and a joint. "The ancestors of those Indians, they built this land, laid stone on stone, independence was their tradition." An actor friend, whom he has brought along for the ride, says, "Right, man! This movie, man, has shown them the way to revolution! Like, *Easy Rider* exposed one kind of imperialism, and this flick puts down another. Wow! Holy shit! Nobody ever thought they'd make it in Cuba, right? And they did, man, they did!"

I ask Dennis how much he knew of Peruvian politics before

125

he arrived. "Well, really nothing, man. Not much. I just sort of
. . . fell in, you know?"

(Days later, at a dinner party in Lima, a Peruvian movie director who spent a year making the only studious, full-length
documentary film about his country, smiled quietly at the reports from Chinchero. "I have great respect for Dennis," he
says in Spanish, "I visited him there, you know, on his location.
He has much talent, he is a fine boy. But . . . he doesn't seem
to realize that the Indians are not affected by these little political power plays. They will always revere their priest, as they
have for centuries. The Incas had their sun god, the Indians
have their Church. Build a new school, they will not go. What
need do they have for reading and writing, when they have, as
always, their cattle, their crops? A movie coming to their town;
it makes no difference to them, once it is gone. Build cameras of
sticks, play at film making?" He laughs softly. "No, of course
not. It is something that would only occur to a leisure class. But
that is not a criticism of the movie Dennis is making. I think he
can make gold from straw. He has his own—hmm—his own vision.")

It has taken three hours to make the muddy trip back to Cuzco, and Dennis is plainly exhausted; still, he welcomes a few of
his closest friends, all male, to his room to smoke, sniff, and
drink beer and Pisco, the Peruvian brandy. They are all dressed
like Dennis, who is dressed like Kansas; cowboy boots are
propped on the bed's edges, ten-gallon hats pushed back on
brows, or tilted forward for a sinister effect. Everyone has
known everyone else for years, there is an ambience of shared
experience. Then what is wrong? Why does one sense the same
curiously formalized, subtly wooden group demeanor one has
sensed before in these midnight gatherings? Why should one
perceive here these little wisps of distrust? Everyone looks at
ease; the conversation is spontaneous, desultory.

"What a far-out day, man! Whew! Those Indians—outasight
cats, man."

"I want to buy a ranch down here, man, bring the old lady
down. Few head a cattle, some stallions. Far out."

"You wanta fetch your ax, man, play us a tune?"

"Naw, that's too heavy, man. . . ."

126

Ax, one has learned, means guitar. It is not fetched, because they are yawning, getting up, stretching, heading for the bunkhouse. The Marlboro men. That's it, of course. They must convince one another of these curious, bogus identities, and they are about as believable as the wranglers in cigarette commercials. There is no self-parody here, they move and speak as if born to the saddle; yet among them are two actors who have appeared extensively on Broadway and television, and spent most of their lives in casting offices, or bars like Joe Allen's. A third, an unknown musician named Kris Kristofferson who's composing the film's score, was, one discovers, a Rhodes scholar. And then, of course, there is Dennis, movie actor since *Rebel Without a Cause,* Shakespearean actor before that, painter, sculptor, photographer (his pictures have appeared in *Vogue*), early collector of Rauschenberg and Jasper Johns, friend of Jean vanden Heuvel, early defender Miles Davis, former husband of the daughter of Broadway producer Leland Hayward, student of the Flemish and Italian Renaissances.

When they are gone, and we are abruptly alone (except, of course, for Pilar, who is dozing on her bed), I again try some nitty-gritty questions. Dennis, in a diversionary tactic, decides to order up some more beer, but before he can get to the phone, I ask about his marriage. "Well, uh . . . well, Brooke was all right, man. Her mother died of an overdose of barbiturates, you know? She was Margaret Sullavan, who was once very big in films and on Broadway and her father was originally her mother's agent, and I think that when her father branched out and became a producer, the marriage broke up. When he became independent. The same thing happened to us. When I was leaving to make *Easy Rider,* Brooke said, 'You are going after fool's gold,' and that didn't read very well with me. We've got a great little baby daughter, who I don't see too often, because I'm away working so much. After I cut my hair off, I sent it to my daughter, because I wanted her to have it. I, uh, sent it to her in an old Polaroid box I had. . . ."

Pause. Dennis yawns, studies the bedspread. I ask about his childhood, and, surprisingly, he sits up, stimulated, and begins talking about Kansas—Dodge City, Kansas, where he was born in 1936. "In movies about Dodge City, man, they always put in big mountains, but there aren't any, just wheat fields stretching to the horizon." When his father left to fight World War II, he went to live with his grandparents, on their farm near Garden City, "where *In Cold Blood* happened, they made the picture there, too." Summers, he helped with the wheat harvest, "and I'm going to make a picture about that, man—the harvest trains that start in Oklahoma and follow the crops, same families every year, great long lines of combines and trucks moving across that flat horizon. They're beautiful, simple, trusting people, man, those Okies, somebody should do a film about them." Winters *and* summers, he spent every Saturday in the local movie house. "I'd walk into town with my grandmother, she had her apron full of eggs, and when she sold the eggs, we'd take the money and go to see Gene Autry, or Smiley Burnette, or Roy Rogers. Then all the next week, I'd live that movie, man! Those dark movie theatres in Kansas, Saturday afternoons, that was big news to me!"

When he was fourteen, the family moved to San Diego. "The reason I'm creative," he says, with elaborate irony, "is that when I first saw mountains, I was seriously disillusioned." (Pause; he has told this story before, and has the timing worked out.) "The mountains in my head were much bigger, and the ocean—why, hell, I thought, 'that's the same horizon line as in my wheat field.'" High school bored him. "I thought, I already know more than most of these kids. Why should I study other people's ideas, when I can find everything out just by using my ears and eyes? It was an ego trip, but when I look back, I'm glad. I was right, man. A lot of college graduates put art on too high a pedestal, they can think, but they can no longer create. They should learn to think through their *senses,* man."

He was shy, he says, but felt compelled to enter debating contests, which he usually won. His seventeenth summer, he apprenticed at the La Jolla Playhouse, then run by the actress Dorothy McGuire and her husband, John Swope. With his high-school diploma, he received a scholarship to the National Shakespeare Festival at San Diego's Old Globe Theatre, and when he played in *Twelfth Night* and *The Merchant of Venice,* the Swopes came to watch, told him to go to Hollywood, and gave him introductory letters, which no one read. He delivered phone books, stole milk from porches, "and, you know, just generally sort of hustled." It is the familiar actor's litany: a television walk-on, a ten-line part, a ten-minute part, and offers from three movie studios. At Columbia, the legendary Harry ("King") Cohn wanted to sign him, but added, "We'll have to send you to acting school, to take that Shakespeare out of you." Dennis told Cohn to "go screw yourself," and instantly became an *enfant terrible:* He was banned from Columbia, and so was his newly acquired agent. But Warner Brothers hired him, and cast him in *Rebel Without a Cause,* which was to alter his life totally. James Dean, the picture's star, has been dead fifteen years, but Dennis still talks of him constantly, almost as much as he talks of movies. He has instigated a James Dean memorial mass in Peru, though he obviously has little love for Catholicism; and the sign on the saloon of his movie set reads, "Jimmy's."

"I had seen *East of Eden,* man," he is saying, almost in a whisper, "and then in the commissary at Warners, somebody told me, 'That's Jimmy Dean,' and I didn't believe it. Here was this grubby guy in tennis sneakers, an old turtleneck and glasses, sitting with a cup of coffee, pouring sugar into it, and watching the sugar dissolve. Spoon after spoon he'd pour, always watching it, till the cup was full of sugar. We were introduced, and he didn't even turn around, he didn't say hello. That's how he was, man. Honest. If he didn't feel like talking to you, he just didn't. Then I got to know him, during *Rebel,* and we found we were so much alike, man, both from farms, this early loneliness, unable to communicate at home, having to . . . create, to justify our lives. He was the most creative person I ever knew, and he was twenty years ahead of his time. Man, Jimmy and I were into peyote and grass when it was still, like, something you couldn't even mention to your closest buddies."

He is silent a moment, obviously moved by these memories. The cocaine and the spoon are on the bedside table, and he toys with the bottle, but doesn't open it. "Jimmy wanted to direct, too, man. He wouldn't take anything from the studios, wouldn't let them rust his machinery. That's why he was almost fired during *Giant.* He was his own man, man. When he was killed in the car crash, and this guy came to tell me, I hit the guy in the mouth. I said, 'Don't you ever put me on like that again, man!'

"I couldn't get things together for a long time after that. . . ."

In his grief, Dennis began his own rebellion against the studio moguls. He had studied with Lee Strasberg, but most of his directors just didn't cotton to Method acting. Dennis started refusing to approach roles any other way, and it got around that he was unemployable, even in television. "For three years, man, I didn't work at all. I stayed home and painted, and cried a lot." During this period, he married Brooke Hayward. The wedding reception was held in Jane Fonda's apartment in New York, and Peter Fonda attended. "And then one night, back in LA Peter called and asked me to come up, because he wanted to talk about writing a movie. . . ."

Dennis owns seven percent of the gross of *Easy Rider*. "Peter's got twelve percent. He, uh, managed to get five points from me." This is said without any malice, but he doesn't elaborate. "Peter behaved beautifully down here, man. I mean, better than he behaved on *Easy Rider*. I only needed him briefly at the beginning, he doesn't have a big part. But he was beautiful, about things like showing up on time, and not crying about where he was, and not complaining about whether he had lunch or not, and not calling off shooting just because he hadn't eaten. Almost everybody has been beautiful, man. I mean, we had sort of a bad start: Thirty-eight of them came down together on a plane from LA. I was already here. So what do they do? As soon as the 'No Smoking' sign is off, a goodly number of joints are lit simultaneously. They turned on two stewardesses before they got to Lima. No, listen, man, this is not funny! An international flight! I mean, I expect people to be cool! I carry *nothing* across international borders! I'm paranoiac enough without making that scene!"

Then where did he get his present supply? Cocaine is purchasable in Peru but, generally, marijuana isn't, and I have noticed that on his director's chair on the set, someone has drawn, under the DENNIS HOPPER, a little sun and written, "Take Sunshine!!" He smiles, somewhat patronizingly. "The coke and grass I bought in Lima, took me two weeks to get it together. But I'm not into acid that much, it never really changed my head. Peyote did; I took peyote fifteen years ago, man. Acid was like an afterthought, a synthetic. I mean, *I'd* had the *real* thing, the *flower*. I don't *have* to have coke or pot, but I feel pretty uncomfortable without some grass around, it's like an old friend. Wow, man! How absurd, that our government makes its, uh, intellectuals feel like criminals with this big taboo system. *I* don't find it kicks to be illegal, man! I've been smoking grass for seventeen years; does it affect *my* functioning? Have *I* stopped working?"

He is rolling a joint now, looking very agitated. "The FBI heard about that scene on the plane, man, and now there is an investigation going on, and I will probably be busted the minute I set foot back in the States. Wow. *Whew!* I don't care for myself, man, but I've got to edit this *picture* when I get back. I mean, this could affect the *picture!* And even before I get *out* of Peru, there could, well, be a bust, with all the *ding-a-lings* running around loose. . . ."

The ding-a-lings are various young ladies (the *Rolling Stone* reporter refers to them as "our groupies") who are not officially attached to *The Last Movie,* nor indeed to much of anything, except the central tables in the hotel bar, and to Dennis, not necessarily in that order. They have followed the company south, by mysterious means, from various points in the States, for the sole purpose of being in constant earshot of, and eye contact with, the guru of the new maverick directors. Dennis, always the gentleman, is loath to gossip about them, though he will admit, under pressure, to being intimately involved (in the pre-Pilar days) with more than one, especially a slim brunette who is said to carry a pistol, which, if it exists, may or may not be loaded. At first, they were not a problem: Dennis apparently assumed that after the romance of South America had browned around the edges, they would all disappear together on one of the dawn flights out of Cuzco, but this has not been the case. Nobody has left, and nobody has permanent rooms, and if there's a plaintive little knock on your door at two A.M. you can be pretty sure it isn't the housemaid bringing the clean towels. Afternoons, the girls drink Coca-Cola with the somewhat sinister-looking local representatives of Peru's markedly anti-American, anti-pothead government, and it is this indiscreet socializing which irks Dennis most.

". . . For all I know, man, they're telling the chief of police, between sessions, about how the hotel is full of junkies. I have been heavily questioned by the authorities here, more than once. Like, *hey,* man!" He sniffs angrily from the spoon. "All I

131

need is *another* bust, anywhere. I was already busted in LA driving on the Strip at midnight, and they stop me only because my hair was somewhat long, and I was driving an old car. They said I'd thrown a roach out of the car, which I had *not*. Well, I did have this roach in my *pocket*. Then, in court, they produce as evidence not *my* roach, which was wrapped in *white* paper, but somebody else's roach, which was wrapped in *black* paper. How ludicrous, man! It was dark, they couldn't have even *seen* a *black* roach!"

He breaks off, looking a bit confused, glances up at the paintings, then continues about women. (Pilar seems to be listening again; perhaps she understands more English than she lets on.) The story is very complex, involving an East Coast chick, a West Coast chick, and Dennis' seemingly murky relationships with both, and still another girl, a non-actress whom he felt would have been perfect for one of the film's leads, "the part of the whore, man, because all her important scenes are with Kansas—with me—and I *knew* the chick, man, inside and outside. The reason I only use friends in movies is that I *have* to understand an actor's personal psychology. Well, I know all the guys here, but when this chick and I had this little disagreement, and she, uh, decided not to come with us, I had to find another actress in a hurry, and ended up bringing this stranger. Well, I mean, I have *tried* to get to know her, but she's *married*. Rather standoffish. Also, she seemed to prefer Kristofferson's company. And hey, man, she may turn out to be the only weak thing in the movie! I must *communicate*, man, with my actors! I *hate* verbal acting!"

I remind him that we were talking about girls, not acting; he appears annoyed, but begins a long, convoluted story of a girl he was living with, and a second girl who wanted to move in, too. A third girl friend he drops in on unexpectedly, only to find a stranger (male) inscribing her thighs with quotations from *The Little Prince*. ("No, I didn't yell at her, man, I didn't like to interfere, I mean, the chick was drunk, and I hate scenes, I really hate scenes.") In the course of another romance, however, his patience is too sorely tried, and he kicks in a door, drags a girl by her hair from the apartment of a neighbor (male), and is stabbed through the thigh with a steak knife. Police pop in and out like Keystone Kops; at one point, five of

132

them invade Dennis' apartment with drawn guns, in search of one or more of the above cast ("Thank *God* I happened to be out of dope at the time"). Girls come looking for Dennis, and if he isn't at home, they become instantly involved with whoever is, male or female.

He is not attempting to amuse with these tales, which sound at times as though he were narrating a serious autobiographical film, and at others as though he were soberly explaining a risqué version of an "Archie" comic book. He is sitting on the edge of the bed, his head in his hands; when he looks up, he is smiling but very sadly. "See, man? My private life is a *tragedy.* I think one of the songs Kristofferson wrote for this picture says it pretty well." He clears his throat, and recites, rather than sings, the lyric:

> He's a poet, he's a picker,
> He's a prophet, he's a pusher,
> He's a pilgrim and a preacher, and
> A problem when he's stoned.
>
> He's a walking contradiction,
> Partly truth and partly fiction.
> Taking every wrong direction
> On his lonely way back home.

Long, suitable silence. Dennis' eyes are wet. "Hey, man," he says at last, "I just realized, you're asking me all these personal things, don't ask them, they're nothing, that's not me, my work is me. Or, why don't you ask me something explosive, like about the Chicago Seven? I mean, if those guys were actually *convicted,* then can you imagine what's going to happen to *me,* if the government decides my actors were offensive, smoking on that airplane? And what could happen to the *movie?"*

It seems best to return to personal questions, and I ask about the money he is making. "Money isn't a reality. Hey, man, listen to my schedule for the rest of my life: three months to write a movie, two months to get it ready, two months to shoot it, a year to edit it. Then: three months to write, two to get ready . . . dig? *That's* me, *that's* my life! And *no* vacations, until I'm firmly established! Listen, everybody in Hollywood is saying that *Easy*

133

Rider was a mistake, and that I'm an undisciplined kook! Well, an undisciplined kook doesn't make *Easy Rider* in *seven weeks!* I am *not* a paranoid, I'm just protecting myself, man, against an industry that couldn't care less about me! When Michelangelo was lying on his back, painting that ceiling, did the Pope give a shit about his welfare? All they care about in Hollywood is that the ceiling—the movie—makes bread. And the only reason *I* care about that is, it will allow me to make *another* profitable movie. Otherwise, success is meaningless. It all goes back to Kipling's *If,* one of my favorite numbers; it says something like, you can treat triumph and disaster the same, because they're both impostors. Which they are. All that matters to me is. . . ."

Very soon, one says goodnight and returns to one's room, and goes to bed, still wakeful. It is nearly dawn, the likely hour for ponderous thoughts. About movies, and the difficulties that come with success within the American movie industry, no matter who's controlling it. And about the ceilings of chapels: how the Sistine ceiling might have turned out if Michelangelo hadn't had the Pope lurking down there under the scaffolds, hampering his freedom, feeding him discipline.

Important considerations, without a doubt. One suddenly sleeps.

10.

Ryan O'Neal, The Sheik of Malibu

RYAN O'NEAL'S surgical scar is a bloated purple worm stretching four-and-one-half inches up the spine from the waist of his Levi shorts, or rather, his traditional Levi's which have been hacked off at the thigh as if impatiently on a hot day with a penknife, and which now hang randomly on hips expressive as those of Douglas Fairbanks. The scar, one might say, is the only imperfect thing about Ryan O'Neal. In Hollywood now, if there is a nuclear equivalent of Doug, picaresque demigod, it's not recalcitrant young Fonda, nor phlegmatic Beatty, nor sobersides Voight, nor Newman of the Democratic politics and the stolid wife, nor Redford, who, for God's sake, lives in *Idaho*. No, it is this man, prancing down the Malibu surf line from his beach house, his third-world Pickfair, seeming as he prances to convert the very energy of the sun into a buffed-brass light of his own, as if by alchemy, or special effects. "Heyaaaeeae!" he calls, as if to astound the very air. He shadowboxes, he pauses to feel the triceps of his arms. His teeth never required corrective therapy, there were never irregularities in his nose or jaw to subdue. He was delivered by Caesarean section, thereby avoiding the often-disfiguring journey through the birth canal. It is the curious prerogative of movie-industry people's children that they be born properly photogenic.

"I am *convinced*," he is saying as he jogs south, leaving straight-pointed footprints, the way the Indians once did, "I absolutely *know* that the great pornographic box-office bonanza hasn't yet been made, and it can be, I mean, I go into a movie theatre now, and, man, *Arraughar!*" His gleeful italics visibly startle some children on the beach who have been quietly de-

135

stroying a sand castle. "I see it *all* going on! Now *waaitaminute!* I remember when you looked at that in some kid's garage and, 'Shh, I hear Mom coming,' and now it is absolutely out on the *streets,* okay, wheee, *open house!*" He jumps forward as if to hit a volleyball; to a dark-blonde girl who has been running methodically toward us and now passes, he says, gently, "Hey-goyeh, baby, right on!" Without breaking her stride, she slides her eyes left and smiles winningly, as if for a close-up. "That lady runs two, three miles every day, man, she's taking care of that body! Beautiful! In the porn film I'm going to use only totally beautiful bodies, I mean, this movie can do twenty million, and you give everybody in it a piece because you work with your lovers, your friends, your kids, with *volunteeers.* . . ."

Like them, the couple we are now approaching, who stand on the beach, giggling together: his wife, professionally called Leigh Taylor-Young, and his press agent, whose name is Steve Jaffe. The woman, aggressively healthy, almost *zaftig,* Diana hunting, is perhaps twenty-eight or nine, yet, facing Ryan, moves in her cotton smock like a romantic post-adolescent, the sort of girl who takes her horse with her to college. In her presence, her husband suggests a horny varsity halfback fated to die early in some war. Jaffe, grinning sleepily as if recalling a pubescent dream, plays Jughead to his client's Archie, and is known in Hollywood as a new counterculture flack, funky-fuzzy.

"Hiunmanumn," Jaffe remarks in Ryan's direction, as if awake, but Ryan is distracted by the faculty-blender sound of something overhead, an advancing helicopter which contains, incredibly, a man leaning out its side, as in old film chases, holding an Arriflex aimed at the group on the beach. "Look at that!" Ryan makes harsh gestures skyward. "It's *Ron Galella,* hi Ron, hiya mother! No, what it really is is the state thing, the Parks Commission, right!" Leigh Taylor-Young nods, concerned. "They got a law, there has to be more public easements onto this beach, terrific, the public gets down here and it's Santa Monica Saturday night, beer cans through the windows and people shooting guns at one another. Look, the f——ing photographers are here already, hanging from the pilings, last Sunday *he* was actually here lunging at me, *Ron Galella!* Leigh and I were out tossing the Frisbee and three of them materialize with their cameras, and under those pictures will be printed, 'Ryan and Leigh look happy but there's terror under the smiles.' Or they'll take a shot of me with Barbra and it's 'Has Ryan left his faith for Judaism?' *What* faith? So totally asshole inaccurate, and I have had to put up with this for seven f——ing years, since the start of *Peyton Place*. They suppose, truly, that there's some sort of perpetual orgy occurring down here."

This is rather what the public assumes about Ryan, smelling it out from the Sunday-supplement features—sexuality, like patchouli. You see them lined up Sundays on the Pacific Coast Highway, in unwashed economy cars, staring. Somewhere behind those Malibu walls, the bodies recline. The men at the wheels of the cars seem especially disgruntled and hard-eyed. "There's something in Ryan that challenges males," asserts Lee Grant, the actress who played Stella Chernak to his Rodney Harrington in *Peyton Place*. "He was always jockeying for position with the crew, the director, half-kidding, but under the shiny surface terribly anxious and troubled about it. They were, let's face it, jealous of him, and they would pick on him in subtle ways, especially in front of women. Who, unanimously, loved him. Watch him on a movie set sometime."

On the set of *What's Up, Doc?*, inside stage seventeen, Warner's, Burbank, a flattened Hilton Hotel, corridors with no rooms beyond the doors, rooms without corridors, he is standing around slue-foot waiting for a take in a challenging costume, tux pants and a bow tie; his chest appears smeared with Nivea, like the breast of a roasted turkey. The waiting crew apparently ignores him. He smells not of patchouli but of Dial soap. "Know what happened to me recently?" he begins, having first introduced himself. "I was driving rather high and highway patrol stops me for speeding, and I said, 'Hey, fellas,' facing them, 'hey, *"Love means never having to say you're sorry!"* Right, fellas?' Forget it, they were not amused. I once spent fifty-two days in the Lincoln Heights jail, a pesthole, downtown LA, for simple battery, I'd hit this guy, in jail all we talked about was balling, and my cell mate, this Spanish fellow, he said, quietly, 'Man, *I* balled Barbara Graham.' What, what? 'Yeh, the chick they gassed for murder, I was working in the San Quentin morgue when they brought her in from the gas chamber,

137

and I was alone with her.' You dig that? *Barbara Graham was dead at the time!"*

Here, Barbra Streisand slides her thin arm into his. She is wearing a white bathrobe. They cuff one another a bit. Ryan explains that they have been studying *It Pays to Increase Your Word Power.* "Well, I have something in my, this, whatdoyoucallit," Barbra asserts elegantly, pointing to the corner of her left eye.

"Tear duct, dummy, *tear duct."* She belts him matter-of-factly. Warner's public-relations people glance at one another distracted, having overheard. *Barbra has something in her eye.* Shortly, she is convoyed out the sound-stage door to a warmed-up limousine containing what looks like a nurse. Entering the car, she smiles back satirically at Ryan, making a moue. He laughs into the Cadillac's exhaust. "Too much, right? Great! Funny turned-on chick. You heard about her smoking onstage at Vegas? She will do anything!" Pause, he sneezes. "That's my car over there, the little Mini Cooper, fun to drive, one night I was speeding on the entrance to the San Diego Freeway. . . ."

When one first arrives at Ryan O'Neal's beach house—months before the day of the jogging—the entrance appears portentous like the gate that Margaret O'Brien had to open in *The Secret Garden,* behind which everything changed from black-and-white to Technicolor. Beyond Ryan's gate there is also a garden, but gray and desultory, like the Pacific. The young man who answers the bell—it turns out that he also answers the phones when they ring—is Technicolored in a sense, vividly freckled. He too wears hacked-off Levi's, and explains that his name is Greg, smiling, with California teeth. The house one follows him into suggests the interior of a redwood tree; a wall of glass seems to enlarge the ocean, as did Elizabeth Taylor's windows in *The Sandpiper.* Another boy, resembling Ryan or Greg, is bouncing around the pool table, under the green work light, with the master of the house; they are saying loudly to one another, "Hey, hey," and "Thatawaytogo," as if playing a larger outdoor game. A girl, slim, cinnamon-colored, wanders through the opened glass doors from the beach. "Hey, hey!" Ryan is defeated, at pool, a moment he does not accept pleasantly. Pale, very bright-eyed, he steps behind the bar, around which the others gather, chastened, sitting on the barstools, while he regains the moment, first by demonstrating an ancient stone pipe he has bought, then by pouring Chablis, by providing matches, by tapping the glass fishbowl home of Wayne, a tarantula the size of a coiled snake, by retelling the story of the night Bill Holden threw his Oscar into the Bay of Naples. He appears feverish, excited, as if he tended always, when facing an audience, to run a temperature consistently higher than normal, like a dog's. There seems something cold, sardonic about his delivery. In a way, it is reminiscent of Phyllis Diller's. "Get this, are you ready? I have this leather bag, right? Well, I need it to carry things. Okay, I'm going to the Troubadour, where they have the rock groups, and I'm alone on the corner of Santa Monica Boulevard, waiting for the light to change, and this Rolls pulls up and this woman in it says, *'Hiiii, I'm Toni Holt!'*" He waits for the laughter. "This gossip-column chick, too much, she's looking around to see if I'm hiding somebody behind a lamppost; that I would be out alone, that is not within her scheme of reality. So I said, *Hiiii, Toni,* and sort of swung the bag, sort of flounced it across the street, and she is *staring,* man! Terrific! But the next day, on this TV show she has, she said, "What giiirl was Ryan hiding?' Shit! I thought she'd ask, *'Has Ryan gone gay?'* I mean, *that* would have been fun. . . ."

The air is now somewhat blue, James Taylor is singing through the speakers; the waves look higher, about to break through the glass and across the rustic floor. Greg, it has been explained, is an aspiring artist, sponsored currently by Ryan; he assembles collages from magazine cutouts, quite painstaking concepts, such as a jet airliner flying through the dim upper reaches of a cathedral. In one of Greg's works, greatly enlarged and hung beyond the pool table, a giant king cobra stands erect above a calm seascape, and now the snake seems to extend itself into the room. Ryan moves, slow and stately, out onto the deck, to recline precariously on its narrow rail. The cinnamon girl stands over him, stroking his chest hair, whispering; the boys drift outside, attentive, though not appearing to be. These people do not wear dark glasses in the sun, nor do they squint; no one here has ever had pimples on his back. It is an atmosphere in which *blondness* is important: If one comes here shielded by smoked glasses, wrapped in unnecessary clothes, not beautiful,

139

then one is an emissary from a gray, anxious, motivated world, an enemy of symmetry, radiance, physicality, opponent of hedonism, and is gently, circumspectly mocked. One's needs are seen to with great elaborateness; certain dubious smiles are exchanged. It is like being in a house with a reputation for ghosts, in which things move insultingly just as one turns away from them.

"Hey, man, gladaseeya, hey!" It is a month later, and the day of the jogging, the ambience has changed, mellowed. Greg is still answering the gate bell, he has apparently not changed clothes since the fall; inside, the same pool game is going on, but Leigh Taylor-Young has joined the ensemble, and there is something in her manner that is kind and reliable. Ryan's various business representatives have warned well in advance that he doesn't talk about Leigh, or about his first wife, or about his children by this first wife, either publicly or privately. Neither will his wives talk about him, and the kids aren't old enough. When he was twenty-one, he married an actress named Joanna Moore, who was twenty-three at the time. They had a son and a daughter named, oddly, Griffin and Tatum. The divorce was bristingly reported by sob sisters: In court, Ryan asserted that the mother of his children wasn't prepared to function as such, but Joanna Moore won the custody suit (with the understanding that custody could go to Ryan sometime in the future) and Ryan married Leigh Taylor-Young, whom he'd met at work—she replaced Mia Farrow in *Peyton Place*—twenty-two hours after the divorce was final. If he didn't see much of his older children at the time (he has since been given custody), neither, it turns out, is he in constant touch with Patrick, his youngest. Leigh has the boy with her at the place she bought a year ago in New Mexico; she is only visiting today at Malibu. They separated about the time that Ryan began working with Barbra Streisand on *What's Up, Doc?* ("But you know it's just how those people all operate," says a California writer, "they just sort of date around. And Leigh always had her outside interests, maybe even before he did." Lee Grant remarks, wistfully, "Ryan and Leigh, well, they're both too beautiful to be mated. They look alike. I see him with Barbra, or her with maybe Omar Sharif, but together they're looking into a mirror, it's incredibly narcissistic.") No

matter what the nature of his marriage, the recent one, Ryan has not denied himself friends: Streisand was reported displeased when actress Peggy Lipton arrived at the *What's Up, Doc?* location shooting in San Francisco. Leigh, meanwhile, had supposedly become quite friendly with Tom Stern, who used to be married to Samantha Eggar. Finger snap! Peggy goes home, Barbra goes out with Milos Forman, Ryan goes out with Barbara Parkins, Leigh goes out with a New Mexican, Galella snaps, Rona writes. *Photoplay* declares, "Mrs. Ryan O'Neal: *'I Have to Beg My Husband for Love.'*"

"So you wanta walk on the beach?" Ryan O'Neal has said, replacing his pool cue. "Aw, take off those boots, man, feel the sand on your flesh." To his friends he waves, and we are out into the sun. "Guess how many episodes of *Peyton Place* I did, you ready? *Five hundred and fourteen!* My principal function in the script was to get everybody pregnant. The show was my big break, right? Listen man, you do television, and in this town you are s——. Films don't want you, and in TV you ask, 'How do you want this scene?' and they say, 'Thursday.' You think anybody but Ali MacGraw really wanted me in *Love Story?* Man, they were testing waiters from Nate 'n' Al's Delicatessen! I got twenty thousand for it and I'll never get another cent and the mother's going to outgross *The Sound of Music.* Look, I know this business, I grew up in it, it's *all* I f——ing know! I never finished high school. When I was a senior this series, *The Vikings,* was shooting and I went and got a job as a stunt man, broke several limbs and caught fire twice and never went back to class, man, I was into acting. See, we lived everywhere: my dad's name is Charlie O'Neal, he's a movie writer and a great Irishman, my mother was an actress and, get this, had a terrible auto accident right down that road out there exactly forty years ago, *the night before her screen test for King Vidor!* So she had us instead of a career, me and my brother Kevin. We moved where pictures were shooting. I went to school in, get this, London, Munich, Switzerland, New York, and five in California, including University High which we all drifted in and out of. There are *dozens* of us, industry kids: Liza, Beau Bridges, Peter and Jane, Jim Mitchum. My best friends in high school were Johnny Weismuller, Jr., and Joe Amsler, the guy who tried to

141

kidnap Frank Sinatra, Jr. He is now my stand-in. We are shell-shocked, battle-weary, and all of us f——ing *stuck* in this!"

He's stopped dead on the sand, he appears to be trembling. "Weird! If my dad was working, we'd move out of the San Fernando Valley up to Pacific Palisades; things got rocky, we're back in the Valley. You moved with the money, by age twelve I could pack all my possessions neatly in half an hour! This was *not* a normal childhood, we did *not* turn out to be ordinary people, which is why we're all actors. Who wants to watch *ordinariness?* You came down here to the beach from Beverly Hills and Bel Air, this was the action, too *much* action, we actually believed in following the sun, the next wave, this was the Southern California existence, except we didn't have marijuana then to level us, we did it on beer and cheap wine, which makes you mean, you fight all the time. My dad was always showing up in police stations, in an overcoat over his pajamas, to bail me out. Man, it was a corrupt life down here; and *shallow.*"

We're opposite the house again; Leigh is sitting on the sand below the deck, as if waiting. "Hey, Leigh, we gonna have some lunch?" She smiles and gets up. "And wait, listen, please send Patrick out here with something to, you know." He draws on an invisible cigarette; presently Patrick, who's four, hurries across the sand, a long stumbling run that ends against Ryan's leg. He says, "Hey, Dad!" The little features are not his parents' but the expression is alert, his long hair is perfectly blond, his teeth are flawless. He is naked. Ryan boxes with him joyfully. "Patrick, would you like to walk along with us awhile?" The running girl has overtaken and passed us again. Ryan says, "Leigh does that too, runs a couple of miles every day, so *healthy.* I love four-wall handball, used to box, but now, with this back. . . . All of a sudden, three discs in my spine went *Krupeghff! Did you know that Jeff Chandler died from the operation I had?* This was my first surgery, you had any yet? Well, man, half hour out of it and I was *screaming* for morphine! Then I lay there for days and thought: all my life, go, go, push, punch the clock and pick the cotton, and now, I am finally in this strategically perfect position, and I know what I want: juice, power, bread!" Pause. "And to *act well,* I have got good serious performances in me, I. . . ." The statement seems to have embarrassed him, and he grabs the child to his chest.

142

"Right, Patrick? Hey, I want Patrick in our porn movie too. Get this: Yesterday he was watching Leigh and me kissing in the bathroom and he got excited. Yeh!" This had been stage-whispered. "He wouldn't let me see. I said, 'What you got there, Patrick?' and he ran away, *he knew what it was!* Isn't that great, it's such a great feeling, sexuality! Arousement! So healthy, and God gave it to us and we've suppressed it for so long, our parents put it down, man, Lenny Bruce used to put me uptight, man, talking about jacking off to a mixed audience. Now, wow, kids are getting it on and women are loosening up, getting gay, 'cause that's what they always wanted but it was so ugly for them, they had to wear combat boots and tattoos and break their noses. Kids are getting sex education is schools, we'll end venereal disease this way, I see *great* things happening. . . ."

Patrick's pounding his father's shoulder, laughing at the words.

"Cary Grant's a fine comedian," Peter Bogdanovich is saying; "so is Ryan O'Neal." Peter is standing just outside his office suite at Warner's, gingerly facing the sun in an attempt to alter a perniciously anemic complexion which he acquired while sitting for twenty-two of his thirty-two years in dark theaters and projection rooms. Although Peter has rarely seen daylight, he has seen and apparently memorized more than six thousand old movies, one of which, *Bringing Up Baby,* he imagines he has remade in *What's Up, Doc?* "Peter's great at the Cary Grant-type style himself," Ryan has explained, "the bewilderment, the double takes. He gave me every movement, the line readings, showed me exactly what he wanted. Man, he acted out Barbra's part for her too, even told her how to sing! Barbra Streisand, this great singer, Peter is *showing* her!" Affirming this now, Peter squints warily, as is his wont, through pear-shaped tinted shades, his one third-world prop; his hair is modestly cut, like Lon McCallister's in *Scudda Hoo! Scudda Hay!* He prefers chinos and canvas shoes such as those worn by Cliff Robertson in *PT 109.* Ryan and Barbra, he asserts, approached his movie with attitudes of impeccable creativity and complete professionalism; yes, yes, would he comment on why he's so absorbed in reproducing a kind of film and directorial style older than he is? Grimace, glower, squint. Because he's a traditionalist. "There's been a whole evolving tradition in American movies. I'm very involved in preserving it."

But not much, apparently, with preserving Ryan O'Neal who does Cary Grant probably as well as any young actor could without caricaturizing, but who probably shouldn't be doing Cary Grant at all. His career is still vulnerable: with *Love Story,* his potential for serious work was noted; subsequent to the Bogdanovich effort, he has made another light comedy, a form he may be too intense, under the shiny façade, ever to play properly, and will follow it with the *new* Bogdanovich, an imitation of a Howard Hawks Western. Maybe he's not yet prepared to perform, say, *Lenny,* though his skepticism and timing might serve the role well, but he's hardly ready to be retired by *any* film maker into the pastures of cute.

Ryan doesn't see it that way, or, if he does, he's not acknowledging it; when he talks of *What's Up, Doc?,* though, he's oddly edgy. "Pauline Kael in *The New Yorker,* she was *very* uptight because in the picture we had a little fun at the end with the line, 'Love means never having to say you're sorry.' Said I was dumping on *Love Story.* Big deal. Look, *Love Story* isn't a very good picture, I have no special loyalty to it. *I* think I was a whole lot better in *What's Up, Doc?* I like Peter's work, why shouldn't I do comedy?" Pause. "And after *Love Story,* man, I was *not* sent a whole lot of serious scripts, period." Suddenly he brightens: "Look, you're gonna like the new one, *The Thief Who Came To Dinner,* I play this cat burglar, man, I love active roles, doing my own stunts, know who I'd love to play? *Douglas Fairbanks!* Now, he married, what was her name?" Jaffe, the press agent, who's wandered out to sit on the sand with us, replies, "Huh?"

"She was queen of the movies."

"Barrymore?" Jaffe says.

"That's a *he. Queen* of the movies?" Large laugh.

"*Ethel* Barrymore?" Jaffe suggests, exhaling, passing.

"No, man, she was America's sweetheart!"

"Man, I'm not into that. America's. . . ."

"Well, it was Mary Pickford, dummy." Jaffe gets up and wanders inside. ". . . Hollywood then was very sexy, they sniffed coke a lot, were very sensuous and promiscuous, they took care of their bodies! Fairbanks and Pickford, man, they were the perfect couple: both stars of equal magnitude, both totally—beautiful. When they went to get on trains, thousands came to the station, there were riots to see these two *unique* people. That's how they made contact with their fans." Pause; sadly, "I'll never make contact like that. Why, those people were *kings!* Jack Warner? Listen, Leigh had costume fittings at his old studio. I went with her, there was a box of his memorabilia stored in wardrobe, I stole some of it! There were these pictures of him taken with his son. Warner always looked the same while the kid grew bigger and increasingly terrified! I asked the wardrobe lady what happened to him, she said, 'Jack made him a producer but one day he drove on the lot and the guard said, "Sorry, can't let you in, orders from your dad."' *Banned from his own father's lot!* Yeh, Warner gave the cruncher to his own son, man! Do you know what a son is? This Patrick here, he is my ego trip! You can make a son into anything!" Patrick, who's been dozing, wakes. "You are going to be a heavyweight champion," Ryan explains to him. "Or maybe President."

Patrick says, "No, Dad, *you* are!"

Tuesday Weld is thinking. After a very long while she says, softly, into the phone, "Ryan, hmmmm, Ryan is a, hmm, puppy dog disguised as Clark Gable disguised as a German shepherd." No, she can't elaborate on that. "When did I meet Ryan? Hmmmmmmm. A hundred years ago." One doesn't call up any more of his friends after that.

"Now this is the normal way to hold it, but hell, if you like it better that way, between your fingers, well that's how the real hustlers do it." The others have disappeared, perhaps into bedrooms, and Ryan is instructing me in pool, patriarchally. He fires upon the ball, misses his shot, curses vehemently. "The mother. You want some wine?" He's at the bar, pouring. "I get tired, my back, and I've got to go out to dinner tonight, friend of Leigh's. I dunno: I have trouble getting it together to go out anymore, I don't mean to people's houses so much, but they print I go to the Whisky, which is bull, I go maybe once a year. I do *not* like going into public, and it's an ego trip, but I can't help it. Barbra said, 'I have this great fear of being killed! That somebody out there really hates my guts and wants me dead.' Hell, if they shoot at the Pope, an actor hasn't got a chance. Outside, these guys come up to me for autographs, guys with nineteen-inch necks and flags on their windshields, the guy has *not* got a lot of love for rich decadent movie stars, and he says, 'I wanta autograph for my wife over there.' Challengingly! And if I say no, which I'll do if they're mean enough, I gotta fight him, this big guy!" He does a little self-deprecating shuffle-off-to-Buffalo. "*Sooo,* I usually get that pen working. . . .

"Hey, man, hey, hey," he is suddenly shouting; the room has darkened, there's only the green hanging light, and his younger brother has seemed to descend upon us, as if on wires, like Peter Pan. "Hey, Kevin!" They double-shake hands, shouting. Kevin is a replica of his brother, with longer hair and something noisy, flushed, expectant about him, as though his temperature was even higher than a dog's. He is followed by a thin, totally silent organic blonde who sits for the remainder of the scenario at the bar. Ryan and Kevin box, and then soon Kevin is morris-dancing around the pool table, trying to get a game going. Abruptly, Ryan looks white and haggard. "Come on, come on," he says hoarsely, and we're into the master bedroom, and he's in the bathroom adjoining it. "Look at this, I still gotta use it." It's a special toilet seat, raised above normal height by about two feet of metal base. "This is because it hurts to sit down." He closes the door, after a while comes out wearing a cerulean terry robe: he folds himself onto the big bed. "Here, light this, you need a match? Jesus, I was in London for this *Love Story* command performance, and this writer from *Life* followed me everywhere, I could not even get *laid.* The story then appears, titled *A Very Brash Young Man,* about fifty words in which it's starlet time, I look like an asshole, and look, I am *not* an asshole, I have worked very hard *not* to be an asshole!" The idea that *Life* readers might think of him so unsettles him mightily. "Man, the world is mad, spinning! Did you know Sharon Tate? That is a story of today's Hollywood! She was an angel, so gentle, so . . . healthy. Did you know that her father, this square Army colonel, retired after the murder, grew a beard, dressed as a hippie, went out and mingled in the hip scene, to get information? Jay Sebring used to cut my hair. Roman's a friend of mine, so is Bill Tennant, who was his agent and who identified

146

the bodies, and his wife Sandy was Sharon's best friend, she still visits the grave twice a week. And *communicates* with Sharon. Roman said to her, 'You take the car,' this 1954 white Rolls he had had shipped here for Sharon's birthday. But the car's in probate, because Sharon's estate isn't settled yet. And the house owners sued Roman Polanski for diminishing the resale value of the house! That's the Hollywood tag to that story! And in Washington we have these very uptight people who are *just* as crazy. And powerful, that is real juice up there!" He pounds the bed. "And very *old*. The head of the FBI was nearly *eighty* when he died. Once this man was after Dillinger and Mad Dog Coll and at the end the best he could do was a couple of priests and a nun! And Nixon, this man with the shaking jowls representing us in China? Man, couldn't they have sent John Lindsay and *said* he was Nixon? Right?" A very high laugh, like an arpeggio. "And this great-looking guy gets off the plane in Peking, looking *stoned*! Know where I met John? At Michael Butler's house! What a funky place to meet the Mayor! I dunno, though, maybe it's not yet time for the first turned-on President. . . ."

From the bathroom, Patrick is calling, "Dad, please wipe me." Ryan shouts genially, "Patrick, you're old enough to do that yourself, I hate that job," but he goes to his son and comes back holding him. The boy is naked, as usual. "Listen, I try to do something about the country," Ryan says, as if continuing an interrupted sentence, "I send checks to things, but I don't go to rallies much, actors have this edge because they're famous and I don't approve of that. Jane Fonda, though, I admire her, she *means* it." He's settled on the bed again. He shakes his head twice, as if inserting quotation marks. "I think the black people, man, are really gonna take it, take it all, and I hope, when they do, they don't kill us, that they let us hang around, teach us to dance, let us drive for 'em. They could use us as long-distance runners. . . ."

Jaffe had asked him to attend an Angela Davis benefit concert; now he repeats that he doesn't go out much. "Hell, I don't like crowds, and I don't like airports; those men in airports now with crew cuts and gray suits, those expressionless robots, they're supposedly searching for bombs and guns, but they are also busting whoever they can for dope. Dig this, you'll like this:

147

I'm going New York to Rome, right, me and Kevin and two friends, one of whom's got a lid of grass in his pocket. At the airport they say, "Mr. O'Neal, into the VIP lounge, please,' and who's in there but *Judy Agnew!* I even got to say hello to her! Anyway, they board her, then say, 'Mr. O'Neal, will you and your party go on now please.' Big deal, I'm a celebrity, we get to go ahead of the two hundred others on the line, and the feds bust my friend! Right! For the grass, pulled him out of the line, eventually it cost him $35,000 to get his record clean, which he wanted. The tag is, if I hadn't been me, we'd have been on the line, seen the search occurring up ahead, and dumped the stuff somehow, or at least hid it well. So that's the big advantage *I* have, man." He's pounding the mattress again. "Well, I have got this advantage, I can now make a lotta bread, and these days you need *buying* money, who knows when any of us'll have to do some buying?" His expression is changing rapidly, pleased to disgruntled, like Walk and Don't Walk signs in triple time. "Listen: soon you'll be able to buy a video tape recorder for less than five hundred. So all of 'em out there will get hip to this great pastime! So they do their *own* movies; you, too, can be a film maker, they get the kids on camera like they used to give 'em ballet lessons, and they make *their own movie stars, without leaving the house!* Listen, I don't like this, I want actors to be a se-lect hip few, respected like samurai!" He leaps up, very excited. "And, and on tape, dig, they *do balling!* Sex, man! 'Hey, you wanna see my wife and me balling, and can we watch you and Margaret doing it?' Except they never *actually* watch each other, *only on video tape!*

"Well, then, I've got to make my porn picture quick, before one of *them* does! See, you get friends, volunteers, some great-looking people you happen to pick up hitchhiking, and every-body gets together, gets high together, gets to know each other, gets it *very* loose, we choose partners! A visual trip! And we'll discuss what's vulgarity, 'cause we don't want it vulgar. And we'll make all the bodies look great, put Nivea all over them. Because, the trip is, during the balling sequences, you wear a mask. Everybody wears a mask! And you design your own mask! I kinda like the idea, for myself, of a stocking. . . ."

His wife enters, smiling whimsically; she has changed into a fine black dress and boots. "Yeh, I know, I have to drag ass," he says to her gently.

When he comes out to the bar, where everybody else is waiting, he's wearing his U.S. flag shirt, and he's frowning. "Five years of marriage," he says abruptly, quietly, to no one in particular. "Know what that means? Fifteen f——ing gifts, between us: one anniversary, two birthdays every f——ing year." His wife smiles uncertainly. Ryan starts another sentence, but his brother is bounding around in front of him, chattering, and we all move outside, through the dim garden to the garage, where the O'Neals enter Ryan's new car, a long, low, graceful Citroën Maserati SM, opulently appointed within, as private railroad cars were, and watch as they pull effortlessly out the drive and into the fast traffic lane, beyond the line of ordinary, straining vehicles.

11.

Whatever Cybill Wants . . .

CYBILL SHEPHERD, a buttercream that someone's pinched to test its center, squats Indian-fashion on the creamy rug, smiling at the Hollywood apartment, which is decorated in Sunset Strip Renaissance: Randy gold cherubs hold the lamps. She is describing a dream, not the one that's come true—top model at eighteen, movie star at twenty-one—but the puzzling one she had last night. "Ryan O'Neal was in it," she is saying in her light, nasal voice, from which most traces of her native Memphis have been carefully pruned, "and Peter, of course." She means her Goldwyn, director Peter Bogdanovich, who cast her without a screen test or an audition as Jacy Farrow, the lovely, icy teenage bitch in his *The Last Picture Show,* and whose apartment this is. No one's acknowledged, yet, that Cybill and Peter live together; not Cybill, nor Peter, nor Polly Pratt, Peter's wife and designer of his movies. "And Polly was in the dream, it was terrible." Her laugh is oddly heavy, insouciant, matronly. "I seemed to be lying down, in a garbage dump, and this pickup truck was backing toward me, and the truck was full of tons of something, something loose, that was about to be dumped on me. Rocks? But the things were red, like apples. Also, there was a swimming pool, an indoor pool. . . ."

Like the one in *The Last Picture Show* beside which Cybill, who said when she signed for the film that she'd not do a nude scene, did her nude scene? "No, not like that. I have no idea what it means." Then she smiles, enigmatically, which is not surprising: Cybill Shepherd is nothing if not an enigma, a contradiction. Consider just her looks: You'd suppose, from all those cover pictures and Cover Girl commercials, that her fa-

151

çade is flawless, yet her eyes are too widely spaced and her face and nose seem curiously flat, as if they had been gently pressed by a large adult hand while she was still an infant, before the bones of the skull had hardened; at the same time, there is about her a sort of kinetic aura, color it amber-gold. Or take the more prosaic facts of her life: She was a star high-school athlete, but flunked gym. She had never acted at all before the Bogdanovich movie, yet managed in it to convey a rich sense of a youthful, early-fifties bitch, and she was an infant in the fifties. Or take her manner: remote, removed, indifferent, as though while speaking of one thing her mind were on another, something private, a private joke.

"Um, you see, I had this wonderful modeling career, and I was in no hurry to rush into movies." She's facing the windows and the relentless Los Angeles sun, but she's not blinking. "And I'd talked to so many girls who'd had these *incredible* experiences in their first films, who'd gotten involved in some dumb pornographic exploitation thing, and so when my model agency said that Peter Bogdanovich was interested in seeing me for a movie, I was very blasé. I told him right off that if I did the part, I wouldn't take off my clothes. Peter said okay, but by the time we got to the nude swimming scene we'd already shot most of the picture, and I relied on him totally. As an *artist,* I mean, I knew by then that he wouldn't misuse my nudity. He made me very responsive, very *pliable.*" She hesitates, regretting the word. "Peter's very strong, he likes to show actors their movements, but I couldn't mimic him, so instead we just talked about the feeling of a scene. Oh, I hated Jacy Farrow, but I think that everybody's got many identities, personalities, and you use those when you act. I *think.* People think of Jacy as the town whore, but I, uh, didn't feel it that way, I felt she must be very innocent in her destructiveness. And Peter, well, he made me so comfortable that I actually *enjoyed* the nude scene, it gave me the chance to prove something I really believe, that there's nothing dirty in nakedness." Pause; again, the odd laugh.

From there, she segues into a description of Anarene, Texas, where *The Last Picture Show* was made, deflecting personal questions like a volleyball player. Peter Bogdanovich has already made it clear that he intends to keep rather mum about what he refers to as "Cybill's and my relationship," and Polly

Pratt won't comment on it either, perhaps because a New York *Times* article about Peter made all of them appear loose-lipped. ("You know my moment of greatest jealousy?" Mrs. Bogdanovich told the *Times,* "When I learned that Peter had taken Cybill to see *Seven Chances,* a great-old Buster Keaton movie.") The agency people and photographers who worked with Cybill when she modeled predate her Bogdanovich alliance, but they, too, seem exceptionally guarded when speaking of her, and their remarks are all similarly vapid: "Beautiful girl . . . extraordinary eyes . . . we're, uh, all proud of her success." (One photographer remarks, after a long, thoughtful silence, "*I* don't think Cybill's like the girl in the movie." Then others do? "Oh, I didn't mean *that.*") Eventually, by chance, one meets a person acquainted with all parties, who says, hesitantly, "Look, Cybill's pleasant enough, in an impersonal way. She's very young. She's also far more ambitious than she lets on. I do think the connection between Cybill and Peter was instantaneous and very sexy. They couldn't help themselves, though you wonder what somebody of his sophistication could see in her, beyond the physical. You can imagine the effect it had on his wife; they'd been together something like ten years, they've got two children. Let me put it this way: I think it disturbed *Peter,* and *Polly,* enormously."

"I always felt a desire *not* to fulfill what people expected of me, or expected me to be, knowhatimean?" Cybill is saying. She's gone into the kitchen for some grapes and a cup of tea, and now picks an errant grape seed from her blue jeans. She's barefoot, her toes are vaguely prehensile. The blouse she's wearing is paisley, but it isn't demure. "I mean, did you ever meet somebody you'd been intrigued by from afar—I'm thinking of Joe Namath—and then find that you could have predicted every word he said? I have a horror of that, of being predictable. I was always sort of a rebel." In Memphis' East High School, she was a basketball and swimming star, earned medals in track, and set a district record for the long jump; that was the year she failed gym and got bumped from the cheerleading squad. "I was a smart aleck," she says of this matter-of-factly, "and a total nincompoop in some ways. I remember my parents giving my brother and sister and me a record player for Christmas with a record of Elvis Presley singing 'You Ain't Nothin' But a Hound Dog,' and Elvis became my ideal, my hero. I knew nothing about classical music or art. I ran track instead of studying dancing." She was, it turns out, president of her high-school sorority and was voted the most attractive girl in her class, "but I was never really popular. No, I don't know why. Too defiant? I had this boyfriend who played rock and looked like Mick Jagger, and even had long hair, which was an unbelievable thing to have in Memphis five years ago."

During her Jagger phase, a cousin talked her into entering the Miss Teenage Memphis Contest, and she won. Cybill calls this "one of the great experiences of my life." She's girlish, speaking of it. "They had the finals on a local TV station, I even got into the Miss Teenage America contest." Which she didn't win, but the Stewart modeling agency in New York spotted her and persuaded her to enter CBS-TV's Model of the Year Pageant. "I think I looked rather like Dracula's daughter at the time," Cybill asserts, modestly, "but *Seventeen* did a model-of-the-year article and ran my picture on the cover, and the agency asked me to come to New York, and guaranteed me twenty-five thousand dollars in modeling fees my first year of work, and found an apartment for me, everything. I jumped at it! I'd never thought of modeling, but I'd dreamed for ages of getting out of Memphis. My dad, who's smart, *he* got out, my folks got divorced and my dad broke away from this dreary uptight atmosphere of Memphis and went to St. Louis and *never* came back, and if you ever had to live in Memphis, you'd know why. The hypocrisy: To French-kiss a boy, that's a sin! Sexuality starts in your cradle, babies are very sensitive to touch, but in Memphis, you're physically and mentally frustrated from birth. Show the slightest interest in sex and you get slapped! Sex is dirty! The homes there, they were *too* clean, it's the old obsession with housewife cleanliness. I think sexual frustration causes a *lot* of the violence in this society, there's too much repression. In the South, especially, women are conditioned to be modest, soft and submissive, and that was never for me; women, men, everybody should just got out and *do* what they want, whether it's writing, or painting, or sex, or just being *free*. You know?"

154

Just being free was hardly the point, for Cybill; neither was her modeling success. For a while it sufficed, her $75-an-hour fee, seeing herself on the cover of major fashion magazines, being taken to major discotheques by major Manhattan bachelors. A year or so, and she was spending evenings behind horn-rimmed glasses majoring in English lit. at New York University, "because I realized that I had never had any real intellectual curiosity." Did Peter Bogdanovich have anything to do with that realization? Annoyance flickers around her eyes at the question, but she says, evenly, "No, the total *mindlessness* of modeling depressed me, I thought, 'These girls all say they're going to study someday and they never do, and the secret must be to *do* it.'" Pause, then, sharply, "People think all models are imbeciles, and I resented it! Even the photographers and stylists, who should know better, talked to each other as if you weren't there at all. A reporter who interviewed me came in with this incredible list of *names* that I was supposed to identify for him! Can you believe it? He'd say Jackson Pollock and Aaron Copland and I was supposed to say who they were. Incredibly insulting, and dumb."

She rubs her temples, then laughs, to regain the detachment that is, one sees, her way of handling strangers who might pose a threat, such as writers. "You want something to eat? Yes, I'm into healthy foods, and at the same time I'm subject to terrible fits of eating junk. I think being stoned is very interesting, it's a higher level of consciousness. I have a younger brother, and that generation, it seems so unenthusiastic, so intolerant of tradition: great music, great art, the past—kids cheat themselves out of a huge amount of experience by saying, 'The past is dead, I can't relate to it.'"

You wonder if, before Bogdanovich, she used phrases like "intolerant of tradition." In the silence, she yawns, hugely, a question is required to wake her. What's it like to move through life knowing you look a lot better than almost everyone around you? She frowns and strolls the room, digs her toes into the meringue of the rug. "I've, uh, given this a lot of thought. You've got to have a lot of narcissism to model, and when I realized that, I didn't like it. Then I saw that when you're on a magazine cover, you represent perfection to millions of people; that people, women, think if they don't look this way, like me, they're unattractive! I mean, sex is a very narcissistic thing, too. To enjoy it you've got to feel like . . . a *peacock*. Really beautiful. Frigidity comes from feeling unattractive, and I hate that my picture would make anybody feel that. When I did TV commercials, I saw that millions of people would buy what I'm advertising, maybe poor people who don't need it and can't afford it, and I'm using *my* face, *my* body to sell it to them. That really got to me, but I couldn't make myself give up the money I earned doing it, the freedom that money gives you. I'd try to think, Well, but that image in the commercial, it really hasn't anything to do with . . . *me*. I don't know, maybe I just sold out once too often."

But she yawns again, and bites once at a fingernail. "Sometimes I think I ought to have the courage to hold a press conference and say that Cover Girl Makeup rots your skin off."

Right. Back to the question. How about a beauty's day-to-day encounters? "People discriminate against you. When I first came to Hollywood and went to parties with Peter, I felt incredibly intimidated, even though I was with him. People acted very surprised that I could *talk*. Knowhatimean? People always told me, 'You've got it made,' that's untrue, looks create problems. Like, because I look nice, people get very competitive, and if you fall into it, competing, you lose, uh . . . your center, your personal truth. Everything a person does has got to feel true inside. Peter taught me those things. He. . . ."

Yes, yes? This yawn she stifles perfunctorily. "I can't put into words my feelings about Peter, and even if I did, it would be edited, or changed, or printed, um, out of context. Distorted. That always happens."

Oh.

"I can't put into words," Peter is saying, "how I feel about the girl. She had no experience before my film, but her instincts for the role were superb." Markedly restive, discussing Cybill, he will smile suddenly, thinking of her, like a lepidopterist considering a rare specimen. "Jacy Farrow is like a butterfly, flitting from flower to flower, but she's a victim as much as she's a bitch. People characterize the thing between Cybill and me as the old director-star bit, they're reviewing that instead of my movies. I think my, um, affection for Cybill is evident in the way I direct

156

her, it's all there on the screen. Yeh, it's true, I saw her on the cover of *Glamor,* we'd never met, but I instantly said to myself, 'That's Jacy!' I really didn't know just how Jacy should be played until we talked. I had to direct her in the role very little. No, she didn't mind, that I cast her just by, um, observing her. . . ."

She laughs a last time. "No, of *course* I didn't mind that." She's assembling her things to leave for a dance class. "I, uh, respected Peter's talent too much to mind." Her exit, the aggressive gait, the swinging dance bag, is media-oriented, a commercial in which the saleswoman herself is the product.

12.

Mia Farrow: Rosemary's Baby in Person

BIOGRAPH STUDIOS, in the drabber reaches of the
Bronx, haven't been repainted since D.W. Griffith made *The
New York Hat* there in 1912, but it's New York's last large movie
facility, and sorely needed by *John and Mary,* as one of the picture's stars, Dustin Hoffman, is in a Broadway play while he's
shooting. The other star, Mia Farrow, is not on Broadway, and
is not happy about Biograph, New York, the script, or the
shade of buttercup that 20th Century-Fox has painted her Biograph dressing room, although she spends all her spare time
staring at it, behind a locked door. Mia has been described as "a
black moonchild" (Dali) and "an airborne colleen" *(Time).* But
long after Dustin's talked amiably about his new film, Mia has
not talked at all, though her secretary has been persistently consulted. When one is finally introduced, Mia only remarks that
she likes to check all quotes in all stories written about her, an
idea which strikes one as not markedly airborne.

When she is mentioned to Dustin Hoffman, he smiles at his
unpainted dressing room like a garboyle. "She's, um, actually
all right. I guess. Except that she talks alot about meditation. I
tend to avoid those conversations."

After a week more of waiting, Mia's secretary grudgingly ar-
ranges for her to answer questions during her evening trip
home from Biograph to Manhattan. Shortly after six, she
emerges from her dressing room and hurries past me down the
stairs to her limousine, the secretary in hot pursuit. The
chauffeur is holding the door of the Cadillac open for her; she
turns, apparently amazed to see that I, too, expect to enter the
car.

"Oh. Uh, *you're* coming with us?" She is not pleased, but we all get in and the driver heads south. I begin with a simple question about the picture, which is not answered, because she has spied something of interest out the car window.

"Oh, uh, wait," she says softly to the driver. "Uh, we'll have to go back."

"You want to go back to the studio?"

"No, uh, just back a little way. Just around the block." She turns to me. "I saw, uh, a wishing star. In the sky. And I don't pass up a wishing star."

Without comment, the chauffeur maneuvers the enormous automobile around a tight corner, then another, and stops. Mia Farrow gets out and disappears into the dark Bronx street.

"Haven't you ever done that?" the secretary asks nervously. "Wished on the first star in the sky?"

We wait. It does not seem likely I am going to find out what she wished, but when she finally returns, and we start again, I ask. I am right: I am not to find out. Then would she want to explain why she chose to do this picture? "Uh, because . . . I had a commitment. With Fox, for a picture. And, uh . . . I saw *Bullitt*. Peter Yates, our director, he, uh, directed that."

Pause. How had *Bullitt* influenced her decision? "Uh . . . I liked it." Could she say something about how she approached the role of Mary? Uh, no. Could she say something about how she approaches any role? No, she couldn't. Does she feel that Peter Yates' rehearsals before shooting are helpful? Uh, she guesses so. Did Roman Polanski rehearse *Rosemary's Baby,* or if not, how did he work? Silence.

"Uh, we did some blocking. Then, uh, we got tired, and started to play, because Roman had this machine, a home television taping machine, so we were all on home television and that was fun. John Cassavetes and me and Roman, we made all kinds of silly television commercials. That was fun. . . ."

She laughs abruptly, a curious, rich "ah-HAH-ha-ha" sound, the way Ann Sheridan used to laugh. I ask about Dustin Hoffman, which seems to fan some dim spark, but only faintly.

"Dustin is, uh, instantly, totally, honestly there. But . . . no, we don't talk about acting. We just talk. He tells me little stories. Or, like today, we read from one of the books on the set. A book of facts. We read about, uh, the man who swallowed the

160

most things. Of anybody who'd ever swallowed things. He swallowed, uh, three rosaries, uh, seventeen religious medals, three pairs of tweezers, three pairs of toenail clippers, twenty-seven something-or-others, uh. . . ."

At the end of this weird litany, we are both silent. The car arrives at her building overlooking the East River and I am invited in. During a further half-hour in the apartment, a temporary home furnished mainly with carpets from India, I detect the following: that meditation is good ("You travel to the source of thought and reach, uh, the absolute, not table, chair, work, pencils, talk, but just to *be*"), and that she has bought a house on Martha's Vineyard ("It will be my all-the-time place, there will be chickens and goats, my brother and his wife Susan will come and we will build a barn and their children will run free in the woods and we will grow vegetables and Susan will weave, on her loom, out under the trees in summer"). Watching her sitting cross-legged on the floor, you feel suddenly that you are tête-à-tête with the lunatic child of *Secret Ceremony*. Then it occurs to you that she is not really a lunatic child, a black moonchild, or a child at all, but a twenty-three-year-old woman, a seasoned actress, the divorced wife of Frank Sinatra, and a big star who has agreed to be interviewed, has been asked several reasonable questions about her work, has apparently cared enough about her public image to check past quotes, and has said to at least one previous reporter that she doesn't like having quotes "made up" for her.

Her point is well-taken. One is glad to oblige.

13.

Conversations with, um, Jon Voight

JON VOIGHT has just said something coarse, startling the crew of his new movie and causing attendant journalists to scratch intently on their note pads. He is about to be lowered over the edge of a thousand-foot precipice in Rabun County, northern Georgia, a cliff which, in the script, he has just climbed, but there's a delay: The steel cable which is going to support him is visible; all you're supposed to see holding him up is an old-looking rope. The man hired to deal with such exigencies steps to the cliff edge and sprays the cable with neutral paint; at the same time, the man hired to make sure that the other end of the cable is tied to a tree hurries to recheck his knot. Abruptly grinning, Jon points to the knot man.

"I hope he knows what he's doing," Jon calls, "because if there's any doubt, we better tie the fucking thing around his balls."

When movie stars say funny things on the set, the crew often overreacts, but this is a special case: Jon Voight almost never says anything funny on the set, certainly nothing involving bawdy words. In public, he spurns the trivial, the venal, the obscene, preferring to appear about as comfortable, within the milieu of film making, as a Salvation Army major at St. Tropez. The condition of movie stardom, its awesome prerogative, is, he tells reporters, fraught with obligations unknown to, say, a CPA, a priest, and people like him for that. Everybody likes him, though careful research reveals that almost nobody knows him very well. What they like—or respect, affectionately—besides his aura of diffidence and self-effacement is his talent. Take Joe Buck in *Midnight Cowboy*, they will say; could Red-

163

ford, McQueen, Newman, or, yes, even Nicholson have so deftly set aside his own personality and conjured up a fresh, separate one, making Joe Buck, who was basically an egocentric cretin and all-around horse's ass, appear somehow significant, and, *and at the same time,* have accomplished what Redford, McQueen, Newman are adept at, projecting themselves? That's what it's all about, they will add, concluding the eulogy, clearly unaware that Jon, had he overheard, would blanch, furious. "I *am* into the, um, creating of characters more than a lot of actors," he will allow, not pleasantly, his face no longer resembling that of a Campbell Kid who has dieted. "I would say that, hmm, Dusty Hoffman and I are really after finding people within ourselves who look different than we look, sound different, are psychologically differentiated, but the rest of it is bullshit. That doesn't make me *better.* This really tees me off, this business of one thing being *better* than another, or best, *the* best. This is one of the poisons of our current thinking, this matter of making *comparisons* between. . . ."

His sentence bends through deepening channels, like the river beneath the cliff they hung him over, and remains, as Jon did most of that Georgia afternoon, cliff-hanging; yet one is loath to interrupt, because he just speaks stolidly on if you do, and because his delivery is so painstaking and contemplative that interruptions seem gauche, like giggling at high mass. Besides, it is nearly impossible to get him to start talking at all, something one has discovered months before, in Hollywood. Various studio people must first be phoned and phoned again, his personal manager must run an eligibility check; and finally, Jon himself comes to see you for a sort of penultimate clearance session, an interview about being interviewed. If he decides in your favor, you also discover that he can sometimes be, if not wildly jocose, at least mildly satirical about certain facets of his image: his teetotaling, his insistence upon spartan furnished apartments, plain businesslike automobiles, functional washable clothing; about his disdain of cigarette smoking and drug taking, and the fact that he has never been to The Factory or Le Club. But mention his profession, his position, and the curious furrow between his eyebrows deepens, making sharp demands upon the pixie expression he likes to assume. A silence, a grimace; he explains that he does not really approve of interviews, their concept is invalid, they attempt to define, and defining is synonymous with comparing, an actor should be defined only by his work, and besides, he really doesn't have the time to sit here talking. In Hollywood, the problem was that he'd just finished a movie, *The All-American Boy,* and actually he'd been thinking about renting a camper tomorrow and taking this girl he knows on a trip. In Georgia, he explains early on that he's really been working too concentratedly to talk. And, um, there's this girl, not the same girl, the camping-trip girl, a different girl.

One arrives there, in the mountains northeast of Atlanta, at the same time the girl does, when the movie is nearly finished. The New York office of Warner Brothers, who is paying for it, has pointed out in a series of tense, jocular phone calls that, actually, journalists are barred from the location during the first part of the shooting schedule, because Jon is working too strenuously to bear distractions, also it's downright physically dangerous there: Cottonmouth moccasins abound in north Georgia rivers. The reason that Georgia and rivers are involved is because the project is the movie version of Dixie poet James Dickey's first novel, *Deliverance,* which concerns four Atlanta men, suburbanites, whose canoe outing in the mountains becomes a nightmare of homosexual rape, killing and murderous revenge. "They're still down in the river," the gracious Warner's executive keeps saying, "I mean, yes, shooting river scenes, if you could possibly wait until about a week from Tuesday . . . interior shots then, no snakes . . . I'm *certain* Jon will talk." But he doesn't sound certain.

Neither does Jon. There he is, as promised, reclining on a table in the emergency room of the Clayton hospital, a cinder-block structure shaped like a pauper's coffin, attended by the picture's director, John Boorman, a young Britisher previously responsible for *Point-Blank* and *Leo the Last,* and by a real local doctor who's playing the doctor in the movie. During a break, the unit publicist advances tremulously and returns triumphant, leading the star. Jon appears to have aged ten years, but perhaps it is the hair, dulled from its natural white blond, the color of a pine floor just washed with lye, to a mouse brown, and the newly grown moustache. He shakes hands distractedly, tries a smile, frowns portentously. He's not sure, not sure at all that he's going to have much time. Rehearsals. Conferences. Long shooting day. Excessive fatigue. "And look, my, um, girl just got in from LA. Only been with her a few months. She's, um, pretty demanding of my off-hours. Knowhatimean?" The publicist's eyes dilate in panic. "Well, maybe . . . let's see, lunchtime. Maybe a dinner. . . ."

It's impossible to comprehend much about the mystique of Jon's working procedure from the emergency-room sequence, which seems to involve only one line spoken by the doctor, and to require of Jon nothing more than lying prone and looking dazed. Ten minutes to lunch break, the publicist introduces a girl of about twenty who is very sanpaku—in fact, an inordinate amount of veinless white shows beneath the lampblack pupils—and almost intimidatingly beautiful, in the way of California girls who never, not even in adolescence, had acne. Her hair is ironed. Her name is Marcheline. Someone asks her how was LA and she says, joyous, incredulous, "Oh, I visited my parents, and I found out something: that I don't have anything to say to them anymore. I mean, *they* aren't my family now. *Jon* is my family now." Then she sits down serenely, every pore concentrated on the emergency-room door; but when it's time to eat, Jon is markedly preoccupied, and says nothing to her, or to anyone, until the equally silent local man hired to drive him has deposited us at the Clayton Hotel, a block away, where a cafeteria-style meal is to be served to the cast, the crew and a few thousand luminous, malevolent flies.

"Well, Marcheline, I guess you're going to have to suffer through some interviewing here," Jon says soberly after he has found a table for three and disposed of our trays.

"Oh, I really shouldn't be here while you're doing it," she announces with adoration. Jon makes a small patriarchal movement, indicating that she should keep her seat. "Well, but I don't ever want to intrude on your working life. I mean . . . well, I won't make a sound."

And she does not, though she never takes her eyes from his face. One is ready with a question; during the Hollywood session, when one has tried some casual conversation, he has suddenly exclaimed, "Let's get on with it, I'm not just marking time here." But surprisingly, he begins by asking my reaction to the screenplay. It's fine, I reply, because it is the book; because

166

Dickey, in adapting his own novel for the screen, did not elaborate upon his initial achievement, a small, completely satisfying suspense story that read pretty much like a good scenario in the first place; because he did not, for instance, attempt to expand the four central characters who somehow need to be pallid for us to believe what they do and what happens to them. Jon listens carefully, nodding, until the bit about the characters, which seems to disturb him in some way. The brow-furrow appears, as though someone had touched a dull blade to his lower forehead. Apparently he starts to say something, thinks better of it, and says instead that he hadn't much liked the script his first time through it. "It seemed to be that the effect depended on, uh, unprovoked and unnecessary violence. And you know how I feel about *that*. I want *definitely* to think that the films I'm in attempt to make people more compassionate or understanding, that they champion the concept of human dignity, the human potential, that they make a *contribution*. Anyway, the second time I read it, I saw something important about this guy I play, the guy who saves the others when they're really hung up in the river. All his life he has ducked responsibility, then it's suddenly thrust upon him, and he *must* change. So the movie is saying that life without commitment is not, um, living."

He brushes at the flies that are expressing interest in his plate of chicken and dumplings, and continues in that vein for some time. One has heard it before—to him, Joe Buck is a Quixote done in by materialism—and so it's simpler not to intervene with the suggestion that his role in the Dickey story is simply that of a man extremely eager to edge out of a tight corner alive. Jon's got to think of these men he plays as somehow ennobled; it hasn't seemed to affect the quality of his performances, perhaps it is what makes the performances unique. Better to let him speak his piece and then try another approach: When he's decided on a role, what next?

"Ummm. Well, I *have* begun by looking for physical things that will lead me to a character, but that's not always the best way of. . . . I mean, with *Cowboy*, I started looking for Joe Buck's walk. John Schlesinger and I, we knew what we wanted was a kind of swagger, but . . . well, we'd *talked* about every aspect of Joe, and I had *thought*, and gotten a walk, and a voice, but man, I was still nowhere. And it was time to start shooting the movie. Did some short scenes, like when he goes to the laundromat, and the bit in the pawnshop, and I thought, well, I can fake through this, but I was *scared.* I thought, 'My God, they're all trusting me, an unknown, in this huge role, and I'm going to let them down.' You know?"

And he breaks off, reliving this terrible, doubtful moment. Marcheline waits; the flies seem suspended in a freeze-frame. "And you know how it did finally come to me? The character?" We all wait again. "Well, we went to Texas for some location work, and I happened to talk to this nice country boy there, we'll call him Billy Joe, and I asked him what he wanted out of life, and he said, 'Well, suh, I want a li'l farm. And a coupla kids. An' I believe I'll get 'em.' See? It was the way he said, 'Well, suh' and 'Yessuh' and . . . his faith. *He believed that he knew exactly who he was!* And it struck me that the essence of Joe Buck is that he doesn't know who he is, but must at all times appear to himself that he does. Seewhatimean? Y'know? He is doing everything society told him to do, and still it all goes wrong for him. See? And once I could think like that, it all fell into place, I could respond like Joe in any given situation, and . . . do you see that? Do you understand?"

Not really, but one nods: Understanding is so obviously necessary to him. Smiling, he bends to his meal. Marcheline sighs and comments on the food, assuming that the interview is over. One asks if she is interested in acting.

"Do you mean for *me?* Oh, *no!*" Her teeth are ridiculously perfect. "I mean, that's Jon's profession. I'm just interested in being with him. I just want to travel wherever Jon has to travel. So that we don't *ever* have to be apart." Most of this is addressed to him; perhaps it is only the food, or the heat, or the flies which account for his tense silence, the taut flickering movements beneath his moustache.

Marcheline waits quietly in the sweltering hospital corridor the whole afternoon; that is about as close as any of us can get to the action, which takes place in a small room, and involves another short, virtually lineless scene, this one with Jon's costar, Burt Reynolds, more renowned in Georgia even than Jon as a result of a television series called *Dan August.* Reynolds lies in a hospital bed for this sequence; between the endless takes, Jon engages in urgent whispered conferences with his director; Reynolds relaxes in bed, smoking, examining the ceiling. There's a question about Jon's costume, his makeup; quietly he explains to the staff members involved why he should be wearing a certain belt here, why his hair would be mussed. "Uh, I wouldn't have had a comb, I'd have lost it in the river. Right?" Everyone murmurs and nods. The makeup man sprays something and returns to his chair, yawning. One begins to notice the subtle physical changes Jon has wrought to achieve his character: The walk is slightly but distinctly different from his own, less coordinated, less athletic, the arm movements somehow tentative; and he seems to maintain this demeanor when not before the camera. During breaks, when not consulting with Boorman, he stands alone, clearly unapproachable, his eyes wide, even manic. Moving lights and props, the crew gingerly avoids him. Once, late in the day, he ambles, as if in pain, to Marcheline and necks with her briefly.

He's said, without enthusiasm, that we'll talk again during dinner, but when the day's wrap is called he hurries in rigid silence to his car and one has to enlist the publicist's aid. "Well, he has to watch rushes, and. . . . I'll try to get you together with him about nine, can you wait that long to eat?" Because Jon has said that he hates unnecessary public appearances, it is assumed that the meal will take place in his house on the grounds of the Kingwood Inn and Country Club, an expensive golfing resort outside Clayton that Warner's has partially commandeered for the stars, director and visiting dignitaries. The Inn is more presentable than accommodations in the town, whose buildings are of the style of contemporary rural architecture based on the principle that all shade trees within a mile radius must be removed before foundations are dug—the result is a series of angular brick structures identical to the Clutter house of *In Cold Blood,* their perpetually drawn Venetian blinds seeming to conceal things sour and unspeakable. The Inn offers, besides rooms equipped with what may be the only air-conditioners in the county, several large cottages with kitchens. One imagines Marcheline unobtrusively serving a ragout; but no, surprisingly, Jon wants to eat in the Inn's dining room, and arrives there only a half-hour late, wearing, even more surprisingly, a neat brown summer suit with a Norfolk jacket, and an expensive blue sport shirt. As we move to our table, the feather-cut magenta heads of all the lady patrons—Atlanta golf widows, their husbands are, presumably, still on the course—swing slowly, like radar scanners. Anticipating this, Jon has assumed his public deportment, a small smile of dignified acknowledgment. He requests of the enthralled teen-age girl who takes our order a dry martini.

"Well, *sometimes* I have a drink," he says ironically when she has gone away. "*Sometimes* I dress up." Though he is attempting congeniality, there is, as there always is with him, some mood beneath this mood, something wary, impatient, harsh; so, even before he has ordered his roast beef and salad, grinning gallantly for the little waitress, one has gotten to business, by remarking on the agility with which he has seemed to hold, that afternoon, a particular moment through the weary traditional film-making progression from long shot to two-shot to close-up to reaction shot, a feat not easily accomplished by actors who've spent years in front of movie cameras. The prospect of discussing this pleases him: recklessly, he downs the whole martini.

"I think the trick, Tom, is to not think about it at all." His reading is confident, he has tilted his chair back and studies the tablecloth leisurely, as if the answer were easily decipherable in its pattern. "The trick is *life*—how you get *life* in front of a camera, and *keep* getting it, no matter what the shot is, no matter how many takes you've done. You've prepared, you've found the, um, mysterious thing that allows you to think like the character. You have changed your walk, your accouterments, you're ready. And they yell, 'Mr. Voight, on the set please!' At that instant, you clear your mind of everything, you *forget* all that preparation completely and go out there and *live*. Now, there are lots of days when you just don't feel like acting, you feel sloppy, tired, mean, but you gotta act. Well, that is when you're going to most need that, um, computer in your head, it's far more capable than your, um, consciousness. And if you do, it can be those very days that you do the best job. Jesus Christ, I really *did* it this morning, pulled the son of a bitch out of my loins! You know?"

Though he is laughing, he watches the reaction to this closely. "Knowhatimean? All the greats had that—Bogart, Tracy. Had *life*, which shot it is doesn't matter. Well, a lotta actors do say they really like acting in close-up best, but that's because close-ups come last, and they don't hit their peak until the last take. Me, I don't think of it that way, I just try to tell the story no matter where the camera is. Of course, there are actors who are terrific in close-up because they *love* that camera." Here he grins wickedly. "Dirk Bogarde—great in close-ups, he loves that camera, man, loves to talk for it and move for it. Hmm? No, I wouldn't say that's true for me. I *would* say that I have some sort of, um, instinct for the camera, for movie-acting. I've thought about that. It comes from my childhood. See, there was this show I was in, in junior high—"

One has wanted to interrupt for some time—perhaps, finally, it is sadistic to ask persons engaged in such a curious, self-cherishing profession ever to try to explain it—but now one breaks in legitimately, because he has already described his childhood and adolescence, during that long Hollywood afternoon, in minute detail, *twice*. There are two versions of it, one charmed, one somber; in the former, which he is fondest of and usually gives to the press, his father is the dashing but kindly golf pro of the Sunningdale Golf Club in Westchester County and his cheerful mother supervises the club's pool because she enjoys it, they don't really need the extra money. Then there is Jon's grandfather, who lives with the family, and whom he is especially fond of recalling, thus:

"In Czechoslovakia, where he came from, he'd worked in the coal mines, so he really loved his job here, working for the Yonkers Parkway Commission, tending the flowers and trees in parks. Greep even built the park benches himself, he could build a really sweet little chair, a funny chair, because you were never quite sure it wouldn't collapse when you sat on it. When he played with me, it was like actors improvising, we always did different characters, my father did that with me too. Then we'd roll on the floor laughing. It was truly creative playing, it *had* to have affected me positively. I, uh, would recommend that every kid play with my father a couple of days. Dad was also very distinguished, a sort of combination of John Barrymore and Cary Grant, y'know? His laughter, that was really a delightful sound. . . ."

In this version, the Voights seem to have spent half the year

171

preparing for Dickensian Christmases; puppies were hurried into the house in grown-ups' overcoat pockets, and Jon and his two brothers each got the same generous gift so no one would feel slighted. No one ever did. In high school, "teachers always took a special interest in me, I was considered to be this very promising artist, I wanted to play football more than anything, but the coach didn't want me to get banged up. I had this strong leadership ability, does that sound like an odd thing to say about yourself? I mean, there was the leader of the bad-guy jocks, like that, and I sort of led, the, uh, bright people who were doing things. You know? But I was also very friendly with the football crowd."

Though he improvised an old German roué in a school musical ("I just automatically veered toward character work, you know?"), he never thought of acting for money and, at Catholic University, majored in scene design and art. But people kept asking him to be in shows, not design them, and after college there was summer stock, and study with Sanford Meisner, goad of the Neighborhood Playhouse. By then he was hooked, and he didn't have to do much pavement pounding. Richard Rodgers hired him to replace the boy who saves the family and the girl in *The Sound of Music,* and shortly thereafter he was given the juvenile role in the off-Broadway revival of *A View from the Bridge.* Which led pretty directly to the lead in *That Summer— That Fall* on Broadway, to guest spots on television, and to an important part in an ultimately unimportant movie called *Out of It.* Then an actor friend sent him a book he hadn't read, had barely heard of, about this rube stud hustler. . . .

Did his family want him to become an actor? "Uh, no, but they're good, liberal people, they let me go my way." Before his first job, had he gone hungry, the way actors are supposed to do? "To tell you the truth, no. I could always have money from home if I needed it. I was . . . comfortable." Then almost nothing in his experience had prepared him to comprehend Joe Buck? The question troubles him—has he sounded too bland?—and after a few moments of tense considering, he murmurs that well, there *were* things. For instance, the trauma of Catholicism. "My God, the guilt it leaves you with, the sexual hang-ups! Um, of course I survived those pretty well, but . . . Catholicism is sick, you can't survive it completely." And the family: No, it wasn't that idyllic. The women of the

172

household were disappointed, bitterly, because the men underachieved. Why did Jon's father not become the golf star they'd thought he'd be? Why did Greep go complacently to work in the parks when he could have made something of himself? "See, I, um, *did* understand failure. I, um, grew up with this idea that I *must* win, it was up to me, a responsibility . . . my, um, earliest memory involved anxiety and some vague sense of failing . . . pressures were enormous . . . never really survived that. So I knew how Joe Buck felt!" This compulsiveness about winning, he adds, accounted for the breakup of his marriage to actress Lauri Peters—they met while they were in *The Sound of Music* and divorced five years later—and for the collapse of his two-year live-in arrangement with Jennifer Salt, who was Crazy Annie in *Midnight Cowboy.* "I . . . always had this clear idea of what I had to do. Any safe, permanent situation seems to oppose it. And I, um, never could stand the idea of opposition. I mean *that* kind. . . ."

Pause; he frowns. Possibly he has said more than he had intended. "But then, that stuff is negative, and I believe that talent—um, acting—is a positive thing. I think there's more point to what happened that first time I stepped onto a stage, in junior high. It was like—riding a wave, the wind, some natural element! I was totally energized, completely alive! I remember coming off-stage and consciously recording the fact that I did *not* know precisely what it was I'd done so well. That's important, because it's exactly what makes you good on film. Spontaneity." Significant pause. "And in that first little show, you see, I'd written my own part, made up my own dialogue, edited, rewrote. The director was a friend, he let me experiment, let me go with it, *become* it."

This last does turn out to be important, though not until later. "Got to get home," Jon says abruptly, folding his napkin, signing the check. As he leaves, all the radar scanners tilt upward again, but this time he isn't smiling. "Um, see you," he adds at the door. We're going to talk tomorrow, of course? "Well, I . . . got a rough day . . . might not be free." Here, the publicist materializes—possibly he has observed our meal from behind the plastic flowers—and Jon utilizes his entrance to accomplish a quick exit.

"Got some footage for you to watch," the publicist says, as if amazed: It is usual to try to keep writers from looking at unfinished movies by any diversionary tactic, including free drinks, free drugs, sex, cash. But what is shown in the darkened Kingwood suite being used as a projection room is about fifteen versions of Jon and another actor in a brief river sequence. One thing about it is notable: There's a significant dramatic speech of Jon's that doesn't seem to be in the final shooting script.

Asking James Dickey about recent changes in his scenario should be simple enough, because he is very accessible. In Clayton, unless you play golf in the dark, there's really nothing to do but sit in the Kingwood bar, a room got up to resemble a London pub by an unenthusiastic decorator. As usual, Dickey heads one of its long tables, surrounded by his wife, Maxine, a large, gentle woman with a perpetually ironic look; her mother, who is also called Maxine and has pleasant puffy eyes and an air of being permanently on a retired teachers' club tour; his two teen-age sons; and several lesser film-company people. One is first struck by how exceptionally quiet his family is; then one notices that when Dickey is present, no one else ever bothers to talk. A tall man in his late forties, with the odd melted look of someone who is drawing heavily upon interest accrued during youthful years of playing sports, Dickey does invite others to speak; or rather, smiling with earnest beneficence, he presents queries, then provides the answers himself. He is best caught at the morning meal which often includes martinis and/or Heineken beer; after a long congenial day, his questions do not even end with question marks, and joining his table is somewhat like signing up for a contemporary-novel seminar in which just one book is discussed.

"How y'all *doin'*," he says when I sit down, the smile glazed, sugar on a stale cake. "You gettin' everythang you want outa Mr. Voight! You findin' him pleasant! You enjoyin' y'self with him! A very . . . *alert* young man, don't y'think? This is gonna be a wunnerful film, very suspenseful, very *meanin'ful*. Like the book. You found the book very meanin'ful. *My* fav'rite charactuh in the book is. . . ." But he is being petitioned by someone on his left who has evidently asked him about other American writers. Dickey turns, ponders. "Wal, a course Updike does have a certain talent, but lacks *original'ty*. He's jus' nevuh gonna

174

be orig'nul. Joyce Carol Oates? Oh, she is one a these female intellectuals, we have so many of 'em, don't we, these ov'ly intense American intellectu'l *females,* such as Mary McCarthy. This sort of writin' is so unsavuh'bly negative. Updike, too: unsavuh'bly negative. Think how any a these writers might describe a lovely yaung woman enterin' one a those New Yawk *cawktail* parties they all attend. The young lady might be beautifully dressed, and what these writers would describe is the tiny run in her stockin'. I prefuh to observe her grace an' beauty! In *Deliverance,* I—"

When he pauses to raise his glass, one remarks that the view of mankind in *Deliverance* may be one of the glummest in recent memory. It doesn't stop him for a moment. Turning to the publicist, who has just joined us, he says, "Now, just what kinda promotional plan y'all makin' for the movie? What we wanta do is create an atmospheah in which people at *cawktail* parties gonna be sayin' to each othuh, 'You ain't seen it yet? Well, you bettuh do so *quick,* y'all ain't gonna *believe* it!' I mean, c'mon, let's all get rich from this project, ain't that right?"

There is no way to command his attention except by literally plucking at the sleeve of his golf shirt. *"Yessuh?* You ain't hardly gonna be able t'*help* writin' well about this pictuh, ain't that right? Y'gonna find your story jus' writes *itself!"* It is like trying to explore a sunken ship without breathing equipment, but one eventually transmits a couple of questions about changes in the script. Their effect is startling. Dickey turns full away from the others, his expression blurred.

"They a'not *my* changes," he says softly. "An' we'h gonna have to *see* about some a these changes, these additions, yessuh. They are unnecessary an' perhaps harmful." Including the new speech in the sequence I've just watched? "Yessuh. It is sentimental, extraneous. We're gonna have to *see* about that speech. *That's* not what my story is about."

Though he goes soon after that, his family and the publicist trailing protectively, the other movie people remain, drinking Jack Daniels, and one of them reveals a circumstance of the film's progress definitely not reported in the Warner's press releases: that Dickey had not been present during much of the shooting because the director asked him to leave. How was this accomplished? "Why, Boorman just said, 'Jim, I want you to

175

leave.' That simply and that quietly." The author, it is stated, did not react to this either simply or quietly, but did eventually depart. Now he's back, and may resume what caused the initial rhubarb: commenting on the takes, suggesting, objecting. "He wouldn't go 'til he heard it from the actors, too." And did he? "Damn right he did. Of course, they were gentle with him, tactful. But they were the ones he was bugging!" Voight in particular? Silence. "Man, Dickey bugged everybody!"

It's the next afternoon that Jon's to be lowered over the cliff. A lunch tent has been set up near the site, but we take plates of cold chicken back behind it to the dressing-room trailers and sit on the steps of his. Clayton's sky has turned the color of wet rocks; the clear sky of Jon's eyes has also darkened inexplicably, and he chews as if to destroy some palpable nuisance. In this mood—it seems to come upon him without reason, quick as a mountain shower—he has, months before, segued abruptly from casual reminiscence into an interminable, convoluted discourse upon the spoiled fruits of materialism and warlike aggressions; upon the human capacity for courage and grace; upon his own disdain of money. "I don't think of money as being anybody's, it's just something dirty that's passed back and forth. Y'know?" Not that he quite intends giving it all his away, like St. Francis, or Jane Fonda. He does admit to having helped a certain impoverished California family, but is adamant about keeping the details of his philanthropy a secret, to preserve its sincerity. "And sometimes I am *sickened* when I think of how much is spent on making movies while people, um, starve, and hospitals fill up and education disintegrates. Well, it's not my job to figure that out, I'm no good at finances, but *somebody* should. Knowhatimean? I do know that movies, to justify themselves, must attempt to expand the spirit, to uplift." Et cetera. During one of the two other long interviews he has ever granted, he did decry the fate of Abbie Hoffman and company in the courtrooms of the Windy City ("They're not lunatics, they're sane, and some of them might even be saints"), but now, when asked about radicalism, he grows vague, and deals out doughy generalities like an elderly solitaire player. An activist movie star, after all, will surely alienate some portion of his audience, and an alienated audience is not an easily uplifted audience.

So, when proselytizing seems imminent in the sudden tortured brow, it is best to fire a brief, innocuous question, such as how does he feel about having to be suspended from such a height by a slender cable? *"Sure* I'm scared of doing the shot, sure," he says, eating too fast, "but you have to do your own stunts these days, can't fake 'em, who'd believe, y'know?" Occasionally, his words and inflection smack lightly of Broadway and Forty-fifth. "But it's not destroying me, knowhatimean? I feel so secure now, in this film, I don't even mind the danger. A lot of that has to do with John Boorman. He's reassuring. Fine director. Good cat." In what way reassuring? "Well, it's . . . communication. Being able to. Before I signed for this, I met with him, had some long talks. I told him how I saw this guy I'm playing, he understood *immediately.* I felt a real rapport between us. One way to survive within this crazy industry is to find directors who are simpatico." John Schlesinger, he adds, is another, and so is Paul Williams, who gave him his first role in *Out of It* and then, after the Joe Buck bonanza, directed *The Revolutionary* for him, which Jon staunchly defends in spite of its failure to communicate much of anything to its audiences. "I mean, I was doing good work there, I had a character. Paul and I conceived the whole thing pretty much together. Then he kind of gave me a free rein." On the other hand, he is very concerned about *The All-American Boy,* because the rapport he had with Charles Eastman, who wrote and directed it, seemed to dissolve as the movie progressed. "I don't know, Charlie seemed . . . intimidated by my ideas. They seemed to threaten him in some way. He withdrew from me, y'know?" Beyond that, he won't discuss the problem for publication (neither, one finds later, will Eastman), and is reticent about Mike Nichols and the *Catch-22* experience. "Um, Mike had his own very strong vision of what the picture should be. I don't like how it turned out, I do *not* like my, um, contribution to it. God, I was aching to say, 'Mike, listen, I can make Milo Minderbender into somebody really spectacular, funny, sensational!" He wasn't interested in that. Mike hired me to play Jon Voight, you know? Whoever *he* may be. God, that infuriates me! I want to grab directors who say, 'Uh, just go out there and be yourself!'" This he illustrated with a strangling gesture and a maniacal expression. "I want to shout at them, 'Wait, I can give you something totally different from me and one million percent better. Lemme *show* you!'"

Evidently he has reflected upon this further during the afternoon, because he picks up a thread of it immediately, that evening, as if there had been no break. Pleased, the publicist reports before sundown that Jon would like me to come over to the house; that Jon will have an hour or so, that later Jon and Marcheline are going to have dinner in the club's dining room. There's a bottle of rosé on the living-room coffee table; Marcheline can be heard in the bedroom, humming.

"I thought of something important about my acting," he begins, then stops, choosing words. The wine is uncorked, there are two paper cups beside the bottle; finally I pour, since he does not, but he seems not to notice. "I just realized this, it probably goes back to *A View from the Bridge*. First thing I thought when I got the part in that was, Jesus, I'm totally wrong for this. This guy should be a young colt, goofy, spontaneous, and that's not me. *Then* I thought, 'Wait, I have just *described* to myself what I must do, as an actor, with the role!' Do you see? And it has been just the same with every part, Joe Buck, all of 'em: I approach them almost, um, negatively, with a very strong sense of inadequacy. *I* can't do the role, so I've got to find *another* guy who *can*. Seewhatimean? But I dunno, it *is* negative thinking. . . ."

So what, if it works? "Yeh, I guess . . . now Ed, whom I'm playing in this, I was also scared of. The guy's supposed to be a soft-living suburbanite with a safe desk job, the right wife and number of kids, he's forty-five, potbellied. And who's gonna believe me as that man? *Then:* I began to see Ed smoking a pipe. And wearing an old hat that he goes fishing in, you know? Then I thought a lot about this Southern guy I'd met, who's very slow and ponderous in his speech, very elaborate and civilized. He'd look at the river we're going to explore and say, 'Wal, we will have t'check ouah motivations heah, discover what processes are evidencin' themselves t'us.' See? A guy pulls a gun on him, he would drawl, 'Well, now what is it that you *requiah* of

178

us?' I mean, who in hell would say that to a goddamn killer, y'know?"

Who indeed? Not the character in the *Deliverance* script. One doesn't mention that, however; he's still talking: "And this guy—my role—he's a good golfer, charming, everybody's good-time Charlie, but basically he is empty, uncommitted, and, deep down, he *knows* that! Then I decided that it was really *Ed* who gets the four men together for the canoe trip. I, um, sort of gave him all the weight. And when his friend, who is *really* a simple, average man, dies on the trip, his sense of responsibility is . . . *crushing.* He must face what he is! We, uh, did a lot of improvising along those lines during rehearsals; then, if I was unsure of a moment, a scene, I would write my own version of that scene. And we did end up using a good part of that material. Yeh, I put in lines on every damn page. Boorman had to approve, of course, but generally he liked what I came up with. *I* like it, some of it is really valuable stuff. Um, I didn't do it *just* to change lines, only to focus my character clearly. When I . . . when we cut speeches it was because they were wrong, or unactable: Dickey's a writer but not a film maker. Of course, his speeches are there in spirit, as part of the, um, subtext."

But doesn't this really amount to having written a new script, or at least to the telling of a story quite opposed to Dickey's? If there must be a point to *Deliverance,* and to Jon's character, isn't it exactly the reverse, the man's growing and ultimate callousness? The question is not ecstatically received. "I'll tell you something: I don't think that, philosophically, I agree with Dickey. What he's saying is that the guy who kills to survive is the good guy. And I just don't believe that. I can't sanction that outlook. I mean . . . I can't believe that's really what the goddamn book is about! It's about. . . ."

A sort of mottled rash, raspberry colored, has appeared at his throat, about his neck. One waits; he doesn't seem to be going to finish his sentence. What about Dickey's requested exodus? Another silence. "He had to be asked to leave. How would *you* feel? You're the actor, and there is the writer looking over your shoulder all day saying, 'Well, suh, that's not the moment I wrote,' or even, 'Well, suh, *today* you did pretty good work.'" He has done Dickey like the sheriff in the Dodge commercial.

179

"Man, suppose I looked over *his* fucking shoulder while he wrote his fucking book? It was worse than the goddamn proud father at the Little League game, rooting so hard his kid can't hit the ball! Christ! I mean, man, I'm working a fuckin' twelve hours a day at absolute one-hundred-percent capacity, I don't want somebody even saying that I was okay, because I was *not* okay, I was giving the *best I've got!* Accept that, or take it and . . . Certain things in his script would have been pure *asshole-ism* to attempt! Just goddamn *literary!* And Dickey is there worrying over every fucking moment, and it is not good for me to be so exposed to negatives that I, um, can't come up with a positive contribution. We're trying to make a human document. And if some moment or other doesn't get Dickey a good review from Pauline Kael or somebody, well, I can't give a fuck about that."

Remembering the wine, he takes a long swallow from one of the paper cups, adding, unexpectedly, that he had nevertheless enjoyed conversing with Dickey about things other than the picture, that the man's "viewpoint, poetically, was always intriguing." One does not ask what this may mean. "And his, uh, feelings about . . . ecology. Very strong, very personal." And of course, we'll all have to wait and see the completed film to judge its effectiveness. The publicist has entered, as if tiptoeing, during the last several sentences, and has listened, nodding at suitable intervals, and now seizes a pause to ask did we know it's nearly eleven? Marcheline appears and comes to Jon's side, smiling as she might at a clearing sky, or a miracle. They prepare to leave for dinner at the Kingwood. Though the dining room has a strict, widely posted rule against serving anything to anyone after ten P.M., there seems little general doubt that they will eat.

14.

Malcolm McDowell: A Clockwork Top Banana

VERY Pinteresque, this limeade cricket pitch, the polleny trees, the ghostly stately home. Isn't that Julie Christie, strolling enigmatically on the far lawn? No, but that's inscrutable Malcolm McDowell, in ice-cream cricket whites, caught in freeze-frame in a classic batting stance, like a commemorative statue. Except that there is, as always, the antic, the satirical in his demeanor, a small mad smile belonging to, what? The protagonist of an animated cartoon. Facing him, behind the thrower, forbidding and blue-jawed, not at all antic, is his team's captain, Harold Pinter. "Harold, he takes 'is cricket verrrry seriously," Malcolm has explained with a Pinter scowl, and this play is crucial. All cricket matches appear to be performed by deaf-mutes; now, even the wind in the park is intimidated, as the star prepares to hit. Not that his teammates, who are mostly unknown entertainers, think of him as a star: not even during tea break do they in any way acknowledge him as the only young actor to be knighted by the counterculture since Dustin Hoffman did *The Graduate*. As suffering Dusty suited the sixties, Malcolm suits the frivolous seventies: He doesn't anguish, he mocks, he is more pertinent today even than Jagger, and so it is now his face, or rather, the ashen Breughel mask of *Clockwork's* Alex, in derby and false eyelashes, which sends up the straights from the chests of T-shirts and from patches sewn with abandon at crotch and backside. Witnessing his portrayal of the dashing Kubrickian ogre, *Time* gasped, inevitably, "superstar," but that is not a word used in Britain, at least not by British actors to describe other British actors, so here, at cricket, he is just folks, another teammate, and this condition actually does seem to suit him well. In fact, it's why he *likes* England. Contrast him here, loose, cheerful, kinetic, with the Malcolm McDowell of the Manhattan and Hollywood *Clockwork* promotional tour: phlegmatic, pale like a Midlander suspicious of the sun and never colored by it, glumly sneezing, gruffly giving offense. American reporters and television emcees, accustomed to interviewing the actor who has evolved a separate personality for the media on the often correct assumption that it will be more ingratiating than his own, are not prepared for one who presents at least as blunt and unembellished a self as any actor is probably capable of, and who deals flat-edged questions onto their dog-eared ones like new tarot cards. "Madam, you've got two hours to find out," he has snapped when some sob sister has asked what is really a Malcolm McDowell. "Why should I do your bloody work for you?" Lemony smile. In his meringue-colored Pierre suite, a blessing provided by Warner Brothers, he lights the afternoon's fortieth Rothmans of Pall Mall, asserting that New York has eighty-eight rapes a day, and that's what *A Clockwork Orange* is about, the fact that man has not progressed one inch morally since the Greeks, a theory which grievously wounds the skittish liberal readership of the Sunday New York *Times*. Though discreet, publicly, about Stanley Kubrick, you get the idea that he's not ecstatic over the director's domination of even the film's ads: "I mean, y'don't exactly ever *see* any other name, do ya?" And America punctures his psyche; and New York weather sucks.

But here, back on the sceptered isle, he is greened and jolly, often sportive, like the joyous, lumbering Labrador retriever which Kubrick gave him, and which he named Alex, and which is at this moment bounding across the lawn from the sidelines toward the cricket pitch, intent upon an offense never before committed in England, even by beasts, the interference with a cricket match. Consigned to spectators, Alex's leash has been neglected; Malcolm pretends not to notice his approach, but he alters his stance slightly, as he does when anticipating some delightful bit of everyday chaos, a little surprise to send someone up, as he puts it. He is, himself, adept at the send-up: When I arrive in England, he is absorbed in a movie called *O Lucky Man*, his first since *Clockwork* stardom, and Warner Brothers, which is going to release it, is being unusually protective. Mal-

182

colm, you know how cooperative he is but, ah, he's terribly tied up, maybe Tuesday lunch. One is hardly into one's hotel room, though, when a phone operator announces, aroused, "Mr. Albert *Finney* is calling." Followed by a male voice in a piece of mimicry so expert you actually recall what Albert Finney sounds like. ". . . Finney here, thought I'd just welcome you to England, do you like that hotel?" Followed by a large McDowell guffaw. "You'll get good service now!" But these days, wouldn't his own name get even better service? "Naw, 'at's a very toffee-nosed place y'r at, they don't go to X-rated cinema. Come for a drink, I've got the day off, I'm just over by Princess Margaret." Later, gesturing toward Kensington Palace, he remarks, "Never met 'er. Kubrick wants me to take off a day's shooting next week for some film-festival award, an' during *Clockwork* shooting I actually did get invited up there t'the Palace for luncheon, an' Stanley says, 'Aw, Malc, I don't wanta shut down the whole unit a day just for *her!*'"

He's come to the door of his tiny house at the end of a trim, sunny Kensington cul-de-sac wearing a warm-weather version of what he always wears: expensive, modest dark slacks, a pressed shirt, a cashmere sweater, boots that aspire to look like shoes. Civilized is how he presents himself; civilized, too, is his home, once the studio of a minor Victorian portrait painter, with its high, cast-iron ceiling and single arched window. The room is beige, the furniture the best from contemporary Scandinavia; downstairs, beyond the bedrooms and the small neat study, is a walled garden planted with one sycamore taller than the house. "Had the place a few years, it needed total repair," he explains soberly, looking at the sycamore through the big window, "and I've watched that tree grow and search up out of the dimness for the light, and that has been very important to me." Pause, wicked grin. "Symbolic, d'y'think?" Then, in his parody-Mayfair, "What will you drink, old man, I've some very *interesting* Chablis."

"How's New York, more rapes?" We're sitting now, he in his new Eames chair, "bought the bleedin' stool to go with it," there's the accustomed demon's humor in his curious popeyes, the dented hare's nose, the mouth like a bracket; Ariel rendered by Bosch. Politely he inquires about American things, but he is coiled, awaiting a reasonable pause; then he's striding the room, eagerly fitting tape spools onto his deck, so that we may listen to the rock score which Alan Price, once of The Animals, has composed for *O Lucky Man*. For Malcolm, this is not simply a next picture, nor his reunion with Lindsay Anderson, whom he regards as director and mentor rather the way Peter Bogdanovich regards John Ford, or Moses regarded God. The movie was actually Malcolm's own idea. It isn't often that a twenty-nine-year-old veteran of four pictures brings a complete idea for a feature film starring himself to a legendary director and gets the film made, even if he is a star, but Malcolm has accomplished that. He has a way of accomplishing things, it's called cheerfully not losing. He intended to write the scenario himself, and came to Lindsay with some finished scenes; gently, Lindsay steered him to David Sherwin, who did the script for *If. . . .* Then all three of them worked on the final treatment, which is . . . peculiar. On paper, *O Lucky Man* is interesting and peculiar. To fully understand the story and its originator, it is necessary first to consider Leeds, a north England city the color of dirty cotton, where mining dusts the windowsills and the cement cottages are chewed by corrosive air as if by unspeakable insects.

Clearly, Malcolm doesn't much like considering it; questioned about the past, he is, suddenly, cryptic. There's not much to say about his birthplace, really, or his family. His father owned a public house, for a time. Malcolm worked in it, serving, for a time. Silence. Then he remarks, oddly, "I approve of the British class system, because if you're born workin' class, as I was, you've bloody got somethin' t'fight out of, an' I don't mind a fight." After school, of which his recollections are also vague, he got a job as a coffee salesman, "Had to drive all over Manchester peddlin' coffee from an awful truck, from insane asylum to hotel to nuclear power station, which y'couldn't tell one from another, it was horrendous." Moreover, his girl friend kept disappearing inexplicably every Friday night, "an' Friday was payday, so I thought she was seein' another man." It turned out that she was taking acting lessons: "She thought I'd laugh at her. I said, 'No, take me with you to class.'" The teacher was a Mrs. Ackerley, "this dear old lady who talked endlessly about her days in silent pictures. I decided to study with her privately at home, I found her totally absorbing." The girl of the story is forgotten, his weird eyes are enormous, his tone is abruptly wistful; invoking this kind elder, rosy and vague in a yellowed factory-town parlor, he has become the untutored young coal miner in *The Corn Is Green.* "I knew nothing then, had read nothing, Joyce, Fitzgerald, they were but names to me, but I'd played some Shakespeare in school, and the idea of turning myself into someone else, on a stage, that seemed utterly easy. Mrs. Ackerley, she was a parent figure, no, that's too Jungian, she was a light, a star to follow, she corrected my Yorkshire accent, she seemed to spot something in me, she spent hours convincing me that acting wasn't emasculating, or degrading, or . . . until Mrs. Ackerley, see, I'd just been muckin' about. Before that, it was all . . . bullshit."

Unaccustomed to the word, he has inserted it gingerly, but never mind that, he is mutating again. It is uncanny: As he talks, other men, of other times, literally come and go in his speech and manner, quickly, like hurried guests. These transformations are unrelated to ordinary shifts of mood and tone: Each character is precisely defined. He will begin some paragraph as, say, a literate urban cynic, a moon colonist, and in a few sentences he is a Victorian tough slouching on the East India docks. Soon he reclines, smoking languorously, a flaccid Jacobean. Doubtless this explains his screen presence: The *characters* he plays become men through whom others pass. Apparently the conversions are spontaneous; asked about them, he has the question minutely explained, considers it through half a Rothmans, and remarks that, no, he's not aware of this. He may then smile to himself, you cannot quite tell.

". . . So I did summer repertory on the Isle of Wight," he continues. "Mrs. Ackerley helped me get the job, I arrived with all my parts memorized because no one had told me there'd be rehearsals, I honestly believed that professionals just got up an', y'know, *did* it." He found his fellow performers less than exceptional. In the fall, he set out for London on a second-class train coach, to take the town; instead, the Royal Shakespeare Company at Stratford took him, in several ways, at least according to Malcolm. The RSC is thought of by young British actors as a kind of knighthood; what Malcolm says of it is, "England's great ensemble troupe, what a joke! It's an arse-creepin' hierarchy, totally non-creative, but then, the public's easily fooled, in'nt? Christ, I'd hear 'em ask for *Romeo* tickets, an' the bloody thing's sold out so they request seats for *Juliet* instead. True! Management ignored the young players, herded us twelve to a dressing room like fucking cattle, which I would point out to them loudly and often. I think they were pleased when I quit. Did finally *meet* our director, Peter Hall, the day I said good-bye."

It hasn't been wry or ironic, this, it's angry, he's luminous-pale, and at the same time curiously distracted, as if he were really remembering another, older bitterness, perhaps one from the times he's loath to recall. The intensity of it must have colored his audition for *If. . .,* in 1968, a stormy improvisation which caused Lindsay Anderson, who'd never heard of him or seen his work, to cast him on the spot. Which brings one back to *O Lucky Man:* Surprisingly, a version of this audition, his beginning, is the basis for the *end* of a film that apparently is autobiographical. "The *first* thing you see in the picture," Malcolm explains rapidly, projecting his voice over the tape of the score, "is this Brazilian coffee plantation, and one of the workers, the peasant slave-laborers, is havin' 'is hands chopped off for stealing. *Then* there's the title and credits. . . ." The story proper starts with Malcolm, as a boy named Mick, in Liverpool training as a coffee salesman. His striking smile, which is referred to in the script as "the smile of success," is promptly noted by his superiors, and when there's a lucky vacancy in the sales staff he jumps to fill it. An atomic-research lab he services blows up behind him, miraculously he avoids horrible road accidents in which police neglect the dying to estimate the damage. When he visits a church, a buxom vicar's wife breast-feeds him. On the way to London and advancement, another research lab attempts to kidnap him for a sinister experiment. In the city he uses a rich industrialist's daughter to meet the rich industrialist, smiles, and is successful, then is unjustly sent to prison. Shabby and cowed by smiling, he emerges from the lockup to find a man wearing a sandwich-board advertisement for a young man who wants to become "a star." Hundreds wait in a great audition hall, but the "director" spots Mick instantly, calls him up, and asks him to smile. "I can't smile if there's nothing to smile about," Mick replies angrily, and the director hits him smartly on the head with a script. He smiles. The director embraces

186

him, stardom is his. A huge celebration begins immediately, there's music and dancing, Mick and all the other characters from the picture whirl smiling through the room. Mick is smiling the broadest.

Strange: Mick, of course, was the name of the character Malcolm played in *If . . .* , and then there's the coffee-selling thing. The sinister experiment is reminiscent of the Ludovico treatment in *A Clockwork Orange,* and there are other little *If. . .* and *Clockwork* references sprinkled through the script. Strangest of all, the star-making "director" is played by Lindsay Anderson himself. Curious, that at twenty-nine Malcolm should want to do the sort of film usually inspired by the failed life of its star—Judy Garland's *A Star Is Born,* even Marilyn Monroe's *The Misfits.* This notion startles him. "But it's not *really* my life, exactly. It's surreal, the whole picture's almost a fantasy. Hmmm. It grew from what's happened to *all* of us: Lindsay, David, myself, it's truly a collaboration." Silence. "And it's actually *Lindsay*'s picture, y'know, I couldn't do it without him." Silence. "I have few friends, but that's all right: If you won't suffer fools, you're lonely. I have only one friend who guides me, whom I must go to when I, hmm, cannot see the forest for the trees. That friend is Lindsay." Silence. "We didn't have an end for the scenario at first, and Lindsay said, 'Well, what happened to *you?*' What happened, of course, was that I auditioned for *him. . . .*"

We're gently interrupted by a lovely dark flower of a girl entering from the kitchen with a tray of cheeses, biscuits, tea and wine. She's Margot Bennett, formerly an actress, formerly the wife of Keir Dullea, and a New Yorker who's lived with Malcolm three years. "In this neighborhood," she says later, when we're alone, "we don't exactly broadcast that we aren't married." She's speaking, as she usually does, with a sort of subdued, shining excitement, as though she were slightly high, though, like Malcolm, she's not a drug user. "I mean, Kensington is *not* Chelsea. I don't think Malcolm cares at all what they think, but I'm the one who has to go to the greengrocer's." And she laughs, a light arpeggio. No, they haven't any marriage plans, they're happy as they are. Full stop. Margot, also like Malcolm, is not one to talk about personal matters in either the present or past tense. Over tea, they engage in a spirited argu-

187

ment about women's rights, a familiar one: He's for them, but the movement's leaders are too butch and brash, and what do they want, to dig ditches? Margot contests this, of course, in her warm, pleasant way; it's clear that Malcolm is the man of the house, though he seems to play this role with traditional pipe-smoker benevolence, and, smiling almost privately, Margot concedes to him and the discussion dies naturally, like an old hearth fire. Then it's time to make some reservations for dinner out, and to pick up the cricket whites at the dry cleaner's. There's no further chance, that day, to ask any more about the movie, to wonder at such cynicism in a story by such a lucky man.

It happens that the end of the film is being shot next morning, in the cavernous assembly hall of a hoary public school in Hammersmith. The first setup: Mick, entering the "star" audition. Two hundred young male extras wait on benches. Malcolm has only to come in, bewildered, and sit among them; some have extraordinary faces, others are dressed extraordinarily, there is no special lighting for Malcolm, yet you are compelled somehow to watch him, sitting motionless in this aviary; something incredibly focused in him demands it, a thing undefinable commands, "*You,* you look at *me.*" Weird. He calls up this intensity at will, subdues it when it is not needed: At lunch in the makeshift commissary, he is casual, expansive. Over vile grilled plaice, he entertains a group of visitors who do not know one another well with wry parodies of the crotchets and pretensions of his neighbors in Dorset, where he has bought a six-hundred-year-old mill as a country retreat. "They see themselves as lords 'a the manor, down there, Margot and I went into the public house for lunch and the barman, this *publican,* he's sayin', loudly, for our benefit, 'Wonderful shooting for this time of year, what? Bagged some fine pheasant Thursday. . . .' The *publican* is sayin' this! They'd somehow lost their menu. I said, 'Could y'just tell us what y'got, then?' He says, 'No, we are havin' a menu printed for you now, suh.' And it came in very ornate longhand, with tomato soup written out in *French.* In a country pub!"

Needed for a conference with his director, he leaves his food instantly; back in the assembly hall, there is congenial chaos, for the big final celebration must now be filmed, and it includes not only the extras from the morning but the whole cast from all the earlier scenes, except Sir Ralph Richardson, the rich industrialist, who's away on tour. Malcolm, radiant in a gold suit of success, is exultant, on and off camera. "Did y'see Rachel, did y'see what she was doing?" he asks during a break, stifling a laugh. There have been four takes of Rachel Roberts embracing the triumphant Mick, and it's always her grinning face that's been turned toward the camera. "Good old Rachel! I first didn't catch on t'what she was doin', then on the fifth take I outsmarted her and turned *my* face out. Learned somethin' from her today, I did!" Across the room Miss Roberts is shouting good-humoredly, "Lind-see, Lind-see, you prick, come *here!*" Malcolm is overcome. "She's mad, Rachel is, we had a party, the phonograph broke, Rachel shouts, 'Lind-see, Lind-see, you *prick,* come mend the record player.' He says somethin' like, 'Aw, piss off, Rachel,' whereupon she dashes over and bites him. 'At's right, tries to take a chunk from 'is bloody *arm!*"

Between takes, that is how he is: Sometimes he will go and sit quietly on the sidelines, smoking, and when he does, people tend not to approach him, but more often he will joke with another actor, as though he preferred, in idle moments, to remain animated. Rarely does he discuss an upcoming scene with Anderson; there is almost no communication between them, but you can sense a sort of psychic pact they have made. Anderson seems to direct him quickly and efficiently by thought transference. Though there's a dressing room for Malcolm, he seems never to retire to it, in a break, to assume the lotus position or engage in other preparatory rituals favored by movie stars who've heard about Stanislavsky. When they're ready for him, he simply takes his place; if the shot's serious, he may become very still the instant before he begins, but then you perceive that to him few shots in any movie are to be approached with total sobriety, without a touch of his own pervasive irony. Take a brief bit that's filmed late in the day during which Mick, imprisoned, is served a meal in his cell by a guard. The scene is transitional, there's nothing pointed or comic in it, Malcolm has only to eat; but by then we know of Mick's several insatiable appetites, and Malcolm makes a further point about them by a curious, comic way of gripping his fork, by devouring with his eyes the gray prison food as it's set before him. For such a sequence, he will appear to *break* his concentration a second before the camera turns: Catsup bottle raised, as the hush falls over the crew, he announces waggishly, "See, always make the best use of your props, it was Mrs. Ackerley taught me that."

The seventh day, he still didn't rest. By noon that Sunday he's into his whites, taking practice swings in the middle of his living room. "I'd like to sleep all afternoon, but Harold's countin' on me," he asserts satirically, "though I haven't really played cricket since school." Margot, who has never seen a whole match, wonders how we will know when to cheer. He is horrified. "Oh, good God, you do not cheer!" This is delivered by the sour-mouthed Dorset publican. "Occasionally, *not* often, you might say, softly, 'Good shot,' and clap your hands together once or twice, like this." Laughing, he takes another mighty swing with the new bat he has bought for the day, and holds the pose, one of very aggressive vitality.

"Vitality, of course," those are the first three words Lindsay Anderson says of him, "and intuition, and at this point a marvelous *technical* expertise which I think is still underestimated." Though we're in the bar of the Shaftesbury Hotel, and it is teatime, Lindsay is wearing the blue sweat shirt and windbreaker, his uniform. Diminutive, plump, single, his look is, perpetually, as sardonic as Malcolm's. "I'm feeling *exceptionally* neurotic today," he has announced, sitting and making a moue, but he doesn't appear so. After *This Sporting Life* and *If. . . ,* he returned to the Royal Court Theatre, his preferred milieu, to direct David Storey's *Home.* "But you want to talk about young McDowell, don't you? Well, my dear boy, there is *no* young leading man with his range, or stature, or with his incredible security about *who* he is, haven't you noticed it? God knows where it comes from, but it's *sooo* defined in him. Actors are *monumentally* insecure creatures, not him. The *intelligence* he projects, the élan, yes, the *star* quality, which by the way he does *not* use in life. Hmmm? Yes, I wanted the next film I did to grow from, um, life, all our lives, it's a bit Zen, leaving things to chance that way. Oh, no, *I* don't think it's a cynical story, the boy in it *does,* after all, win. And with Malcolm in it, it's tempered by his great humanity, a certain *morality* he projects,

190

which certainly saved the Kubrick thing, didn't it?" By now we've paid the waiter and Lindsay is moving grandly through the hotel lobby, where guests are raptly watching a dreary BBC comedy series; he does a parody of a horrified collapse at the sight of the tubercular screen, and strolling into Shaftesbury Avenue, continues, ". . . In no sense is he the *anti*-hero, this is why the young respond to him so sharply, they've come to *need* heroes. It's rather what the young Henry Fonda had in *The Grapes of Wrath,* and the early, the *very* early John Wayne. . . ."

Fine, except that all his friends speak identically of him, in professional phrases, as an admiring film reviewer might: forthright, honest, intuitive, and, above all, heroic. No one describes him personally. Listen to his fellow artists, to Margot, even to his mailman, and the quotes cannot be distinguished one from another. (The mailman says, with show-business sagacity, "In a film, he's afraid 'a nothin', in'nt he?") Through a maze of faulty London telephone connections, from economical little wine parties in Hampstead to sit-down dinners in Wembley, one hears, after intense prying, only two potentially negative observances, the first from a demure blonde who explains quietly in a stuffy gin-drinking room that she acted with him a season in the RSC. "I'm not an actress anymore, though," she admits, with a calm, unsuccessful smile. "I couldn't quite stomach the sort of bastards of various sexes who go into the profession. Oh, they can be clever, with their horrible pretend modesty, some know how to hide the monstrous ambition. I never really wanted to get to know Malcolm well. He was . . . superior to the others, I suppose, but good God, that ambition! You could *taste* it!" And into the phone, Sir Ralph Richardson, who's taken the receiver from his secretary and fumbled a bit with it, exclaims in a tiny high voice, like a child answering an adult call, "Yesyesyes, what? Who, oh yes, young McDowell, deardeardear. Hmmmm. To whom am I speaking? Oh. Deardeardear. Well, I think McDowell is an extraordinarily *clever* young man. . . ."

"You talked with Sir Ralph! Oh, super! He's getting on, y'know, he won't be with us forever. What'd he say? Good old Sir Ralph! He had me come into the back of his car, the last day he worked, for champagne and cheese he'd brought special, what a lovely man. 'Do have some wine, dear boy,' he says to me, and 'Deardeardear.'" The imitation, though kind, is superb; we're stretched out on the lawn, under a tree older than the empire, the cricket players not far distant. He's perfectly relaxed, waiting to be called to play, Margot's squatting gracefully near him, seeing to Alex, whose chain she holds, and who is determinedly eating a root of an oak. It's clearly not a moment for further questioning. "Y'know, I'm proud of being British," Malcolm remarks, picking a daisy to dissect. "I like it. The traditions. Y'know, there are seventy-five thousand Americans living in London alone, and yet, if we didn't speak somewhat the same language, the British and the Americans would have precisely *nothing* in common. Except, of course, the things no one admits: that our police, for example, are *just* as sadistic as yours. They are thought benevolent because they smile so prettily for the tourists." He's watching, with vast amusement, Harold Pinter's rigorous sidelines warm-up when a stocky man a bit older than Malcolm approaches. Malcolm, laughing, waves. The man is Terry Rigby, renowned throughout the British Isles for his role in a popular television show about a detective. The real star, Malcolm explains, is his assistant, an unbelievably intelligent German shepherd named Radar. "Ah, you should see the condolence letters," Terry begins without preamble. Malcolm, grinning, nods encouragement. Radar, it seems, has recently passed on, Terry thinks from exhaustion. "Terry hated the bleedin' dog," Malcolm offers, "didn't you, Ter? The dog was always pissin' his leg. We saw your picture in the papers, you at Radar's funeral lookin' quite disconsolate."

"His bleedin' fans, they now send me poems, even songs," Terry says, and sings, "'Dear old pal, I'm sorry that you're gone/Dear old pal, I'll try to carry on.' Composed by a gentleman in Middlesex, oh, Christ."

When Terry moves away, Malcolm says, "I lived with Terry when we were both strugglin', in this decrepit house in Camberwell Green, in the East End. There were a dozen other people residin' there too. Terry always was a bit eccentric, he still keeps his telephone in the icebox. Anyway, in those days he owned one suit, which he never changed. We were drinkin' in a pub and he says to me, 'Ah, flower, I don't know why but I don't make out well with the birds.' I said, 'Come with me,' an' took him to this very posh shop in Jermyn Street. The clerk said, with a sneer, 'Mayihelpyousuh?' I told him my friend would like to see some colognes. 'Ofcoursesuh,' an' he brought out these bottles at five quid each, an' Terry barks, 'What's this, five quid for some bleedin' puff juice?' Then I said, 'We'd like some undershorts, size forty-two.' Terry was obese then. All they had in forty-two was something with huge red stripes, and Terry says, 'Oh hell, flower, I take a bird home, and get m'clothes off, an' she takes a look at these bleedin' *stripes*. . . .'" During this Terry has returned; perhaps sensing that the story is being told, he keeps his distance. One notes the odd, unsmiling way he is watching Malcolm, who, of course, does not do television.

"Somebody, a journalist, wrote that I had eyes like Steve McQueen, and *that's* in the picture, too: Sir James, the industrialist, says that to Mick, 'You've got eyes like Steve McQueen!'" We're in the studio again, after Monday's shooting, and he's turning a glass of Chablis in his hands. He knows that I'm going to ask again about *O Lucky Man,* he's tired, and he's resisting the interview, rather the way he did in New York when one asked gingerly, aware of his attitude toward "journalistic" questions, what his ordinary non-working day is like. Grimace. "I have no hobbies. I get up at ten. I then get my paper. I then read it. I then talk on the phone, business calls. I then take Alex for a long walk in the park. I then read, scripts and so on. Margot and I then go out, to little restaurants where no one cares about actors." Pause; as if penitent, he adds, "I do like to walk through department stores, I enjoy demonstrations of things, such as knives which peel tomatoes and carrots simultaneously, or those women who demonstrate wigs in Harrods, I find that endlessly fascinatin'." Now one wonders if he can still wander anonymously through Harrods. Frown. "It has changed, whole groups gather. I don't particularly enjoy it, it has, for me, no *meaning.*"

The phone has rung, it's Stanley Kubrick, asking him to go to still another film festival for another *Clockwork* award. Malcolm can't, he's working; the subject of Kubrick, however, actually loosens him, as it once made him wary; the manic little smile materializes, his eyes dilate. Kubrick has recently written him a long, convoluted letter touched here and there on the page, as if by tears, with oblique references to regrets and differences

193

between them. "An' I'm tellin' you the truth, I don't know what Stanley's talking about here." A grin, he shakes his head. "I've discovered something: that I'm really very fond of Stanley, in a love-hate way. There's only one of him, there's no technician like him." Technician, not artist? "He's a genius, but his humor's black as charcoal. I wonder about his . . . *humanity.* That's what Lindsay has." But, judging from *O Lucky Man,* a rather coal-black humor, too. "*No,* you must see what he's filmed, you can't tell at *all* from the script! He's no sentimentalist, but there is a poetry to his style, and a kind of love. And trust, in *me,* because the boy in this movie must be *very* sincere, the audience *must* believe in him, in his naïveté, and as Lindsay well knows, I'm no longer naïve. Seen too much, I have. Alex, in *Clockwork,* he was a rogue, always havin' the world on, that was easy for me to play, but *this. . . .*"

Isn't the sincerity, the honesty, what directors rely on him to project? The garden is dark and he stares out the long window; the question hasn't pleased him. "I can only tell you what *I* know I am, and do. I'm a realist. I sensed very early that you can expect nothing from life, that it owes you not a farthing, fate drops you someplace an' you an' I could as well have been pickin' coffee beans in Brazil as sittin' in Kensington. The world'll screw you blind if you let it, an' I do *not* think that a movie that says that is cynical, it's just truthful. What *else* do you see around you, in the world as it is, right now, in *our* moment, in *this* decade?" His passion here has charged the air in the room, as if with ions. "It's a joke, my friend, and what I do, on the screen, is go for the meaning through comedy, a gesture, a look, an attitude, because it's all fucking hilarious to me, this planet is. *And it had fucking well better be a giggle, my friend, or we'd not survive it!*" Alex has come to his chair, he pauses to rub the dog's ears. "If, as you say, youth responds to what I do, that's why it is: They know, now, that there's nothing left but to laugh. I wish they had *not* realized that: What do we have now but a sort of modern-day *No, No, Nanette?*" Again, he shakes his head. "There's a line in *Clockwork Orange,* in the Anthony Burgess *novel,* I've said it over and over: 'You're the only man in this sore and sick community that can save you from yourself.' *You've* got to. And acting, being a movie, um, personality, you start to believe in your public self, and then you are *unsavable,* and that's why I'm going to quit it." As if surprised, the dog stares upward. "Oh, yes, I'll direct soon, that's the real film art. You *didn't* suppose I was going to keep on acting, did you? My God, if you're semi-intelligent, semi-coherent, you cannot, without turning into some monstrous animal. . . ." Alex, not monstrous, offers his nose and Malcolm studies his panting clown face made foolish with love, as it was that Sunday when he leaped cooperatively across the cricket pitch, distracting the opposing team and enabling Malcolm to bat successfully and score the needed point, a development which really surprised no one, certainly not the dog or his master.

15.

Fellini: Unknown Planets to Populate

"I BECOME hysterical," Fellini is saying, not hysterical-ly. He has just flown from Italy to New York via Hollywood, to promote the first major film he has made in nearly five years, *Fellini Satyricon,* loosely based on Petronius Arbiter's Latin classic about the New Morality of Nero's Rome, and he dislikes flying, New York and Hollywood, not necessarily in that order. Moreover, United Artists, the picture's distributor, has put him in a suite in the Plaza, which has not turned out to be his favorite hotel. The pearl and peach velvet living room is inexplicably cold, and Fellini glares around with displeasure, as if to spot some icy phantom who has not checked out. He loathes cold. He also loathes noise, and the phones ring perpetually— "Young ladies, wishing to be in his movies," explains Mario, his gentle, smiling secretary, bounding into the bedroom to grab another receiver. Below, drills gouge the pavement. The door buzzer sounds, a startling rasp. "Is this possible?" Fellini asks. "Such a bell, just to announce somebody? I become hysterical!"

But the forty-nine-year-old director, revered in Rome as *Il Maestro* and *Il Poeta,* is really too good-humored to carry off the role of temperamental legend; seeming to sense that, he grins his familiar *mafioso* grin, gulps his late-morning coffee, and loosens his conservative tie. The real problem, he explains, is fatigue, caused mostly by Hollywood journalists, who asked him myriad witless questions about the new picture. "Meaning," he says, making a curious snorting noise. "Always meaning! When someone says, 'What do you mean, in this picture?' it shows he is a prisoner of many conceptual, intellectual, sentimental . . . *chains.* Without his meanings, he feels un-

197

protected. When watching *Satyricon,* the audience must fight as never before their . . . prejudice? Is that how you say it?" Proud of his English, he has dismissed the interpreter hired for his visit; clearly, he does not want to be prompted. One waits.

"No, preconception! They must fight preconceptions about movies having to tell them a story with a start, a development, an end; preconceptions about historical pictures; preconceptions about myself, personally, because they know that before, Fellini always tells them some story. This is not an historical picture, a Cecil B. DeMille picture. It is not even a *Fellini* picture, in the sense of *La Strada* or *Cabiria* or even *La Dolce Vita.* They ask me *why* I make it. How do I know? Because, as a little boy, in Rimini, my papa took me to my first film, and it had Roman gladiators in it? Because for thirty years I have enjoyed Petronius, and now the moment comes right? I cannot answer. When I start 'Satyricon,' I was in the dark. How shall I film this story? Then, suddenly, I realize we don't know one damn thing for sure about Rome thousands of years ago. It is one big *nebulosa,* full of myth, fairy tale, Cecil B. DeMille information. Now I am excited, because I know that the picture will be a trip in the dark, a descent by submarine, a science-fiction, a psychedelic picture! I know that I want no help from books, from archeology, and I feel better. A voyage into total obscurity! An unknown planet for me to populate! And this was good: Only the old are puzzled by it. The very young people, in France, in Italy, where it is very successful, they simply accept it intuitively. They *understand.*"

He draws emphatically upon an imaginary cigarette, or tiny pipe. "Even the young ones *not* smoking, not with drugs, they grasp the picture, they feel the picture, eat the picture, breathe it, without asking, 'What does it mean?' This film, I don't want to sound presumptuous, but it is a very good test just to choose friends with, a test if people are free or not. The young kids, they pass the test."

Then we are to take *Satyricon* literally at its face value, to view it as, say, several hundred thousand spliced-together color slides? Isn't there something more to it, some . . . meaning? I prepare to feel old; but, surprisingly, Fellini shakes his graying head and says, as if it had just occurred to him, "No, there *is* more, I think—the similarity between our world and this socie-

198

ty of Rome, arbited by Petronius. Christ was not yet a threat to them, but, at the same time, a certain psychological era was finished. The pagan myth was dying, and they were awaiting something new. You must realize: in this epoch, an ordinary Roman man goes with his wife and little children to Colosseum, buys tickets for the big festival, sits and applauds all day the killing of thousands of gladiators, blood everywhere. This was commonplace, they felt no guilt about it. Then appears something unbelievable, mysterious: a man who said, 'Love your neighbor like yourself.' Terrific! A new myth! Well, we are the same. Today, we are finished with the Christian myth, and await a new one. Maybe the myth is LSD? And the new Christ comes to us in this form? Anyway, there is analogy in *Satyricon.* It shows pre-Christian time; we live in *post*-Christian time. . . ."

All the phones ring at once, drowning him out. Mario leaps over the thick carpet from one to another, grabbing at them as if catching flies, muttering in apologetic Italian. *Il Maestro* shakes his head, tight-lipped, and starts to get up. I reseat him as quickly as possible with a weighty question, Fellini vs. religion: the fake miracle in *La Dolce Vita,* Cabiria's unsuccessful visit to the shrine, the martyr play in *Juliet of the Spirits,* and the quasi-divinity in *Satyricon,* an albino hermaphrodite oracle who resembles the Christ child, and is kidnapped and carried across the desert in a sequence that looks suspiciously like the flight into Egypt. Any analogies there? He laughs softly.

"Well, you see—to put these things in films, truly, it is not conscious with me, I do not think of it as I do it. I am not very rational. Oh, yes, rational about *how* I make a scene, because to make a picture, you know, requires great rationality, like to put Apollo on the moon. But *why* I put things in? I do not know. It is simply my vision, how life is. Without rationality. When I start a picture, I always have a script—it has been printed that I do not, that I improvise—but I change it every day, I put in what occurs to me that day, out of my imagination. You start on a voyage, you know where you will end up, but not what will occur along the way, you want to be surprised. I surprise myself. I am not conscious that I make some comment about religion; at the same time, I know that I am prisoner of 2,000 years of the

Catholic Church. All Italians are. I do not mean to scorn religion; perhaps all I say is, "We have always needed religion, we have not the strength to do without it.' And where it has been needed, the atmosphere, the symbols, are always the same. In pagan era, there is a shrine, like Lourdes, a child prophet, the *need* for a miracle. And we keep on having that need, though miracles and religions disappoint us. I think I like to examine that; but not consciously."

This time, Mario grabs the pause, to remind Fellini that they have an important luncheon to attend. Fellini grimaces, and sighs. His wife, Giulietta Masina, hurries from the bedroom in a coat of dark fur, and confers in rapid, hushed Italian with the secretary. Off-screen, Masina's huge lost eyes are doubly compelling. Fellini watches me watching her, and, perhaps annoyed at my divided attention, says firmly, "You wonder why I did not use famous actors in *Satyricon?*"

"Uh, yes, I had wondered about that." Masina smiles briefly toward us, bows, and hurries out of the suite.

"It was done purposefully, because I want people to look at the picture without help of a star to guide them." But hadn't he once announced he would ask Mae West, Groucho Marx and Michael J. Pollard to do the leads? "Ah, but I did *not* ask them, because I realize that if I put in some well-known actor, the audience identifies with him and his past roles. Remember, I want to create a world on film in which there are human beings who love, hate, make war, and yet are totally strange to us. So that we have the suspicion that maybe all we know about war, about love, about life, is not absolute after all. For *Satyricon,* I do not even look for actors with strong charisma; just interesting faces. I pick the boys who play the leading parts only because they have the beautiful face, but not too masculine, too sensual. So they have homosexual relationship in the story, so what? I wish here to undramatize sex, to show that sex is not such a big problem, as Christianity has made it. Sex is only the lure of the sexes; sex is just sex. The boys in the film are very good-looking, they make love together, but with detachment, elegance. One of the actors in these roles is American, two British. Why? Their faces are right. So they don't speak a word of Italian, it made no difference. We dub for them, make subtitles. I do not wish the audience to know what anyone is saying anyway. Most of the time, while we shoot, *I* don't know what they are saying. An unknown country must have an unknown language!"

Mario hovers again, this time behind my chair. "Excuse, he must attend luncheon . . . a news magazine . . . you can come back in the afternoon, yes?"

Fellini says, "What? News magazine? What will they ask? Am I to answer with things that make big news?"

At three, the scene in the suite is exactly as it was in the morning, except that Fellini looks incredibly tired. His eyes are shadowed and deeply lined, and he rubs his temples. I ask about the lunch, and he makes a gargoyle face. "Terrible, stu-pid." Did he say anything newsworthy? "Ah, I say different things all the time to writers, not to be uncooperative, only to seem not so dumb, always repeating myself. I am not so serious, you know. I think my talent is the joke, but with a straight face." Gingerly, I bring up his past: his quite ordinary provincial boyhood, his early jobs as sketch-writer and cartoonist, his apprenticeship with Roberto Rossellini as scenario writer for *Open City* and *Paisan,* his first international success with *I Vitelloni* in 1953. He yawns. The past is the past, why discuss it? In fact, the only two things which now seem to interest him at all are *Hair,* which he has just seen in Los Angeles ("Magnificent!"), and The Electric Circus. "We have just been there, last night, and I was amazed: The young people, kids, they recognize me physically! I did not know I was popular here like a movie actor! They speak to me very respectfully, it was very touching, very moving."

How would he like to direct the film version of *Hair?* "Ah, yes, but there is the old problem. America fascinates me, I would like to do movie here, but I would have to study your country first, for a long time. I cannot make a picture without knowing exactly who wears this shirt, that tie, a moustache. I must know intimately everything I put in a shot. Perhaps some-day. . . ."

But they are still drilling down in the street, and he listens a moment to that, shaking his head, as if the prospect was unlikely. What does he plan next, then? What of *Love Duet,* for which he is to direct one half, Ingmar Bergman the other? "No, we don't do that now. Bergman becomes unavailable, so we cancel. When I first sign to make my part of *Spirits of the Dead,* Bergman and Buñuel were to make other parts. Good, I thought. Then they withdraw, and I want to withdraw as well, for with Vadim, it will not be as . . . artistic, but I have started, so I finish. I do not care to see it. I go very rarely to cinema. It is somehow distracting to me. I have two new ideas, one for my wife, one not, but it is too soon to talk of them."

Before the enormous success of *La Dolce Vita,* Fellini always complained to the press about the difficulty of finding backers for his films. These days, apparently, money is no problem. "It comes, you know?" he says, waving his hand gently. "I, myself, am no millionaire. Perhaps I could be. American producers have offered me great sums. But if I accept, I think maybe the picture I make would be wrong. I might try too hard to communicate with the audience, I might explain too much, and destroy the real nature of what I have to say. You must first be faithful to this . . . creature in your mind. If your creature is a monster, you must be true to the monster. So producers say, 'But audiences don't like a monster.' I say, 'But I can't make a monster congenial.' If it is time to talk about monsters, you do so, you do not tame them for audience. You do not know *why* they come to you, or when. If I try to have idea for film, I have none. But when I am just driving my car home, perhaps, then ideas come without knocking."

The Fellinis live in Fregene, a seaside resort half an hour from Rome, in a house that sharply resembles the little temple-like house in *Juliet of the Spirits.* That film concerned a marriage—Guilietta Masina as the troubled, haunted wife of a career-minded philanderer—that may or may not sharply resemble Fellini's marriage. People have been asking him about it for five years, and for five years he has only smiled, enigmatically. "Ah, but everything the artist does is somehow about himself, yes? The woman, Juliet, is not *precisely* my wife, the marriage is not *precisely* my marriage. All art is autobiographical; the pearl is the oyster's autobiography."

Then what about the stories one hears in Rome, about his offscreen relationships with his actresses, especially one particularly temperamental blonde?

"What is this? I have no trouble with her. I have no trouble with actresses, no temperament. Everyone in my films is encouraged to discuss the work with me, make suggestions."

That, I remark, was not exactly the question. He grins, like a benevolent gangster. "My dear friend, if there were truth to this gossip, do you truly think I would tell you?"

Mario tiptoes over the pearly rug, turning on lamps and offering scotch. Fellini decides he doesn't want a drink; neither does he want to stop talking, as long as he doesn't have to answer questions. "The drugs," he says abruptly, after a silence, "I have asked myself, with the young people, why the drugs? Well, the drugs put you in contact with something rich and terrifying: with mystery. So there is a philosophical reason for them. The young, they don't want any more to read our books, learn our philosophy, and they are right. They try to have personal, individual contact with mystery, and this is truly heroic, because it is dangerous, what they are doing. I do not mean the possible physical effects. I mean to face the mystery, without protection of the old ideas of my generation, the old religions. Remove these, and the impact of reality is—terrific! Still, it is necessary now, because the old ways have been tried and have failed. They have produced a society of neurotics, of criminals, of suicides, of egotists, of the big brains—intellectuals who talk and talk about the experience but cannot live it, can no longer feel. The young, they just love, and feel. And if there is a new cinema, pictures such as *2001* and, yes, *Satyricon,* it is for them."

He would go on, but the photographer has arrived. With a great show of resignation, Fellini straightens his tie and starts to rise; then he turns, and whispers, "So, Tom, what do you say, you want to take some LSD today?" He actually looks and sounds quite earnest; but the photographer is directing him into the strong light, and the suite is suddenly full of people, and noise, and in fifteen minutes the afternoon is over. One never quite perceives whether or not he was serious.

16.

Robert Redford, Who Likes Fighters

WHAT you remember best about Redford from movies and plays is the ingenuous smile—perfect uncapped teeth, eyes which crinkle amiably—and so when he achieves a similar smile at 7:30 A.M. in the Mark Hopkins Hotel coffee shop, a dreary room done in cerise vinyl, and about as comfortable as a red leather convertible seat on a July afternoon, you relax and smile back: Obviously he is going to be easy to talk to. Then, when he has smiled at the waitress, warmly enough to cook his order of eggs right there at the table, you say some nice things about *Butch Cassidy and the Sundance Kid,* and ask if he isn't pleased to have done the picture, partly because of what it will mean to his professional future. Since 1961, when he first starred on Broadway in *Sunday in New York,* he has been cast mostly as callow semi-juveniles; won't the role of Sundance, a tough, taciturn, decidedly virile outlaw, convince Hollywood and Broadway once and for all that he is, at thirty-two, a grown-up leading man at last?

Long pause. He puts on his mirrored sunglasses, which render him eyeless, like one of the malevolent children in *Village of the Damned.*

"How do you mean, exactly?"

"Uh, well, the Sundance Kid is actually a new image for. . . ."

"*'Image?'* That word isn't in my vocabulary. I do a part because I feel something for it, not because it builds an image. You sound pretty much like a Hollywood flack with that 'image.'"

I study my reflection in the mirrors; it is not reassuring.

205

Then he smiles again, and I decide to restrain myself from pointing out that I find meticulous word-choosing difficult until after nine. There is a long day ahead. Besides, I have been reading about him, and he does have a point: for ten years, he has fought the entertainment industry's labeling and packaging process. He asked to play the homosexual husband of *Inside Daisy Clover* when most ambitious Hollywood comers were running from the role as if it were a dropped option; was offered a lead in *The Chase* but requested instead the minor part of the convict because he believed in it; refused to be in *Blue* because the final script was atrocious, although he was contractually committed to the picture, desperately needed money, and was threatened with a lawsuit if he didn't show up for work; was offered *The Graduate* and finally tested for it to prove he was *wrong* for Benjamin Braddock; made *Tell Them Willie Boy Is Here* for once blacklisted writer Abraham Polonsky; gambled money and reputation on *Downhill Racer,* a film of his own that most movie magnates thought too risky, and even refused to jump at the chance to be in *Butch Cassidy and the Sundance Kid,* a Paul Newman film, and, therefore, a sure bonanza no matter what its reviews.

"Everybody tried to hop on the *Butch Cassidy* band wagon," he is saying, "and that's not my style." We have conversed gingerly through breakfast and are speeding now in a chauffeured car toward a motorcycle racetrack in San Rafael, where *Little Fauss and Big Halsy* will soon begin its last shooting day. "Fox wanted a super-big name to star opposite Newman. Fine; that left me out. Then William Goldman, who wrote it, asked me to read the script. I refused. Suppose I liked it? Who needs the disappointment? Then my agent called saying it was imperative for me to read it, to see which of the two roles I'd be interested in. I still didn't want to, but when I finally did, I liked it—*both* roles. Then George Roy Hill, the director, called, we got together, and he said, 'I want you in the picture and I'm going to the mat for you.' Great. Except that Newman hadn't decided which part he wanted to play. So we got together for dinner. I'd never met him. We talked about car-racing, uh, where we liked to live, everything but the film. I don't think either of us enjoys talking about movies very much. And we didn't really need to, because right away there seemed to be this tacit understanding that I would make the picture, and that he would play Butch and I would play Sundance. The lovely thing was that this rapport carried over into the work. We never had to say to each other, 'Would Butch do this, would Sundance do that?' We just *did* it."

And George Roy Hill? "Oh, I had a long talk with George about the work, but I don't like to discuss roles, intellectualize them. There's too much *analyzing* in this business. Hill is a very strong guy, he had a very definite idea of what he wanted the movie to be. It defies labeling, you know? Paul describes it best—'an adult fairy tale.' Now, Paul likes to discuss, and Hill will let you disagree with him, as long as you can support your argument. If you can't, you're gonna get your head chopped off. They were constantly into it, and they both have this habit of pointing with their index fingers when they argue, and during this one major, uh, discussion, they were both pointing and their fingers crossed, like locked swords. Hilarious. Everybody broke up. But I like that; I mean, I like fighters."

He talks on about the making of *Butch Cassidy*, laughing gently at the memories, until the car swings off the highway and up a dirt road to the racetrack; then, as we get out, he becomes, quite suddenly, another Robert Redford altogether. The film company has set itself up next to the track, where a number of real-life motorcycle racers are preparing for the day's first event, but the two factions do not mingle. The movie people tinker with their equipment—they will be shooting the actual races for background footage—and ignore the cyclists, who tinker with their engines. Redford, swaggering now, swearing, moves easily between the two camps, talking camera angles one moment, cam shafts the next; he may be an actor, but he also races his own bike on his own time, and he's not letting himself forget it. Told he won't be needed for the filming for some time, he cheers, and joins the cyclists. Eventually, he motions to me with his head, and I go and sit with him on a low concrete wall near the starting line, and ask him about the picture.

"It's the story of this racing circuit, of people who would hock their mothers to get a shiny new bike. About the American compulsion to win, which fascinates me. I'm Halsy, Mike Pollard is Fauss, two guys who race but are neither winners nor losers, just somewhere between, which, in America, is nowhere."

The starting gun is fired, and twenty large motorcycles thun-

der past us ten inches from our feet. When I indicate that I
would enjoy moving back a bit, he frowns, not so much because
I am a coward, but because he would like me to be caught up, as
he is, in the danger of the sport. When he has reluctantly led
the way to safety, one attempts to speak his language.

"What kind of, uh, bike do you have?"

"A two-fifty."

"A two-fifty what?"

"Yamaha." He watches the race excitedly, although the fastest cyclists have now completed the course and caught up with
the slowest, and it is impossible to tell exactly who is winning;
then he says, abruptly, "I grew up around this kind of thing.
Bikes, hot rods. I hung with a pretty rough crowd in high
school."

But at that moment the race ends in metallic cacophony, and
he does not really continue until much later, after we have returned to the city, and he has stretched out on the bed in his hotel room and dealt very tactfully and gently with a fan who has
found out where he is staying and talked the desk into putting
the call through. Again, his manner has altered: He smiles often, speaking quietly about his high school days in Van Nuys,
California. As a student, he was a good quarterback; nights, in a
leather jacket, he raced rods, fought in the streets, and sometimes broke into Bel Air mansions. ("We never stole anything
much, we just did it for kicks. As a generation, we were bored.
Not like today's kids, who are doing beautiful things. We had
no clear image of ourselves.") In 1955, he entered the University of Colorado ("on a baseball scholarship, and my majors were
mountain climbing, hunting and skiing"), but dropped out in
his sophomore year, grabbed a freighter and spent thirteen
months bumming around Europe trying to be a painter. With
the $200 he made from a show of his canvases in Florence, he
came home to New York, enrolled in Pratt, and began studying
at the American Academy of Dramatic Arts, because acting
looked like a way to make enough money to go on painting.

"I'd never been in a play in my life. Acting seemed ludicrous
to me, but people kept telling me I could do it. I hated the
Academy until one day in movement class, when we had put
choreography to a poem. I was damned if I was going to. But
the teacher kept calling on me, and I finally got up without
even thinking and went right into *The Raven,* the only poem I

knew by heart, and I just *went wild!* I used the entire room, I was all over it, doing flips and twists, running out into the hall, grabbing people out of their chairs. I got to the end and the teacher said, 'Fine, now do it again.' And I did it again! I was suddenly so free I could do *anything!*"

The same thing happened the next year, when he auditioned for a walk-on in *Tall Story.* All they wanted was somebody who looked like an athlete; Redford auditoned by dribbing a basketball so fiercely he was cast on the spot. A scant four years later, he found himself the star of *Barefoot in the Park,* but seems to recall the *Tall Story* audition with more pleasure. Long Broadway runs are nice for the money men, disastrous for the actor-as-artist. Asked about his feud with his *Barefoot* co-star, Elizabeth Ashley, his mouth tightens and his eyes once more uncrinkle.

"Nope, you're not going to get me to knock other actors. I've been fortunate with the girls I've worked with—Jane Fonda, Natalie Wood, Katharine Ross. All talented. Ashley is a good performer. Notice I use the word 'performer.' She gives the audience what it wants. I don't work that way. Look, why don't you ask who *helped* me?"

The list includes, besides George Roy Hill, and Garson Kanin and Ruth Gordon, who fought for him in the play *Sunday in New York,* a man named Charles Bluhdorn. In 1966, after making *This Property Is Condemned,* Redford, much in demand, abruptly took off for another year abroad ("I was bored and dissatisfied and I needed time to read and think"). The film of *Barefoot* brought him back, but the only thing that really excited him was a picture about skiing called *Downhill Racer,* which he had conceived himself. The studio boys weren't interested, but he got to Bluhdorn, president of Gulf & Western, which owns Paramount, and spent a frantic fifteen minutes acting out the script. The executive told him to go and prove himself, and Redford instantly headed for the Olympic ski competitions in Grenoble, France, to shoot backgrounds.

"I play one of the leads, and I'm pretty good on skis, but we *had* to shoot the actual Olympic skiers because those few men are the only ones in the world who can race that downhill course authentically. You're skiing eighty miles an hour; one false move and good-bye, Charley. I wanted to show Paramount I could get the footage without spending a lot, so I got the writer, the photographer and some ski-bum assistants over to Grenoble on my own. We were all holed up in one room in this dive by the river. And the French weren't letting people film the Olympics, so we had to use disguises to get by the guards. Like, the photographer was pretty well known, so I fixed him up in a hairpiece and a false nose, so he could get out on the slopes with his camera. He loved it. The ski bums shot a lot of footage too, but they couldn't get by the officials, so they swiped a sign from a refreshment vendor, put it in their car window, and got through that way. Every night we met at the room to see who was still alive. But we came back with 20,000 feet of film."

Downhill Racer opens Thursday. After that, Redford retires for the winter, with his wife of eleven years and his two young sons, to the house he built literally with his own hands in the Utah wilderness. I have been warned that he does not like to talk about the house because he has already been asked about it too often by reporters.

"I'm not going to ask you about your house, because. . . ."

"Good, because I've already talked about it too often."

"Fine, because houses don't interest me very much."

"Good. It's a private thing. It's home. Originally, we only had two acres, but I'm trying to fight these developers who are raping the land, and when I heard they were moving into Utah, I bought 2,400 more acres which I've turned into a ski resort. It's named Sundance. It's not for tourists, it's for people who care for the land. I build buildings around trees before I'll cut the trees down. The house that we live in, I built myself, with the help of just one man, a Hopi Indian. He's a genuine craftsman. It was a pleasure, watching him join two pieces of wood with real skill and care."

He talks on for some time about the house; then hearing himself, he suddenly laughs. I laugh, too. Shortly thereafter I leave, and in the elevator I run into one of the film's assistants, a very young man in bell-bottoms and long bangs. I ask him what he thinks of Redford.

"Well, he's like a rugged individualist. Which is a very fifties-type trip. But he *means* it, man. He's . . . I don't know the word."

How about tough? Concurring, he grins, cynically.

17.

Lauren Bacall: Don't Call Her Bogey's Baby

FOR eight nerve-shredding weeks, Lauren Bacall has been trying out her first musical, *Applause,* nightly belting a dozen songs in her big applejack-brandy alto and swooping through complex dances with such campy insouciance that in Detroit houses full of taciturn auto magnates forget all about Bette Davis and *All About Eve,* on which the show is based, and end up at curtain calls cheering as if the Tigers had just won the pennant. But in a few days, she will have to make New York forget Davis, too. And in a few hours, she will have to learn a whole new final scene. And room service is late with her breakfast. And none of it fazes her in the least. She stalks the hotel suite like a ferret after a garter snake, her long legs aggressive in tweed pants, shaking her long hair, which is the color of fresh celery, swearing amiably, trying not to smoke.

Clearly, she's exhilarated, flying high, and she talks nonstop. She sounds tough; but the growl is chastened by her unmistakable intelligence, her boundless good humor, her great, grudging good will. Twenty-five years ago, the Warner flacks thought up her professional name, but she is still Betty Perske of the Bronx to anybody who has known her more than ten minutes, and she isn't about to let you forget that.

"Listen," she begins, folding herself into a velvet sofa, "do me a favor, do *not* give me that old thing about 'Tell me the story of your life,' or 'How was it you were discovered?' or 'How did you first meet Bogey?' Because I will upchuck, right here. I mean, who *cares* anymore, what does it *matter?* Warner Brothers, blah, blah, blah, aren't people *sick* of it? *I* am! I simply refuse to go into that crap again. Read one of the bios in the programs if

211

you want to know. They're all wrong anyway. And listen, will you please tell me, *why* is one's age brought up every four lines of everything that's written? Would you explain that to me? These bios say I was born in 1924. Well, that's wrong, I was born in 1934. You just put that in: that my bios have been wrong until now."

If that's the case, she would have made *To Have and Have Not,* the first Bogart-Bacall film, in which, fresh from Julia Richman High School and two Broadway flops, she became a star overnight, when she was approximately ten. One does not point this out, however, because Bacall is already laughing, a long triumphant roar at her own joke. For an instant, Tallulah lives. "I'll tell you what *does* interest me: that this show has begun a whole new cycle in my life. No, it's more than a cycle; it's literally a second life. Very weird, uncanny. It's as though the last twenty-five years never happened. I mean, I lived one complete life that had a beginning, a middle and an end, and has nothing whatever to do with my life now. First there was my career, which began well, I had great impact, and then nothing but obstacles, never the best parts at the best times. Jack Warner convinced me very early that I was no good, worthless, rotten to the core. He was terrific at that. I learned one thing from him: to keep myself covered at all times. Even then, I knew I'd somehow be sold down the river, which I was; that they would never have one goddamn bit of respect for me as an actress, a talent, a potential, whatever, and of course I was right. I was a commodity, a piece of meat. What I learned about acting, I learned from Mr. Bogart. I learned from a master, and that, God knows, has stood me in very good stead."

She shoots a challenging look across the coffee table. I have been warned that she no longer answers any questions about the man to whom she was married in 1945, and who died prematurely of cancer twelve years later. "I think I've damn well earned the right to be judged on my own, is all," she says evenly. "That's not sacrilege. I loved Bogey very much, we had a marvelous life, but that life has been over for thirteen years, and it's time I was allowed a life of my own, to be judged and thought of as a person, as *me*. Then, just a few days ago, there's Earl Wilson, writing a column about Bogart's 'Baby.' Jesus! I mean, is it *ever* going to stop? Bogey had true greatness, as a human being, that's why, for him, there's no generation gap, marvelous, fine, but *Christ,* what have I lived on for, if I can't have something that's mine? Even when I'm out with a *man,* people come up and start talking about Humphrey Bogart! I do *not* understand this! Don't they see there's another man there? How can people *be* so insensitive?"

Angrily, she grabs a cigarette pack, shakes out the contents, then grins. "What the hell, I *have* been good, no smoking 'til after the show, and so far, no voice trouble." She raps the wood table hard enough to upset a few knickknacks, accepts a light. "Anyway, with this show, I will hopefully be given that great gift at last—freedom. It doesn't seem very much to ask, somehow."

Mention of *Applause* instantly relaxes her. She is smiling again, speaking almost girlishly, and looks abruptly as though she *had* been born in 1934. "For the first time, I'm working at full functioning capacity. The part came along at precisely the moment I was best able to cope with it, fully able to understand it. I feel so *damn* right on that stage! I think I'm finally fulfilling the promise I showed and then never realized. It's the perfect marriage of—everything. Of course, I *may* have an identity crisis here; the part of Margo Channing just *might* blow my brains out some night, there's so much of me in her, and some of it is, shall we say, a little nervous-making? No, I don't think about the movie any more. Certainly *All About Eve* is a classic film, but our script is updated, refocused; it's really about a woman's insecurities, and Christ, that's always timely!

"Now there's *another* weird thing about this show: the movie. From the time I was fifteen, I had one heroine, Bette Davis. She was everything to me, I literally worshiped that woman. And now, that I should be playing a part that she played, and was so marvelous in—I tell you, it is *too* peculiar. They haven't got me an understudy yet. They must think I'm Man Mountain Dean. Well, that's all right, because nobody's *gonna* get this part away from me! Over my dead body they'll get it!"

Then if the show hits, will she stay indefinitely? After two years in *Cactus Flower,* she swore she'd never let herself in for another long Broadway run. Too exhausting. And boring. "Well, I've got a year contract, and the right to do it in London.

And in California!" She twists the large mouth into a perfect mask of victorious irony. "How d'ya like *that?* As for getting bored, I don't have the chance. That first act is an hour and a half and I don't see the inside of my dressing room 'til intermission. This is real gut time, the sheer physical exertion is incredible, it's like giving twelve quarts of blood per diem, but I am *still* wide awake at midnight, even on matinee days!

"Listen, how do you like my singing, it didn't turn you off, did it? I've been working with a voice coach since *Cactus Flower.* There's still *another* coincidence—I started out wanting the theater, not pictures, and I wanted to do musicals! You know, at parties, somebody was playing, and there I was for the night, knew every old song, but I sang softly, terrified somebody'd listen. So now I'm the Beverly Sills of Broadway, right? Hah! I should be so lucky! I think I've always been better suited to the stage, though I *like* doing films, does that surprise you? I like the life, the hours. Sure, I'd do another, if it was something other than garbage. . . ."

She points a slim finger straight as a ruler at the color TV across the room. "I will *not* have my work coming back on that goddamn box to haunt me! I've got enough on that box to haunt me as it is!" Another lost battle with the cigarettes. "And I will not do a film or anything else unless I can work with the caliber of people I'm working with now. Every person connected with this show—God, such marvelous people, aside from their talent. The one thing I dread is that somebody will leave, after we come into New York, and they get great individual notices and new offers. I try not to think about that, honestly. We are all so . . . together! I tell you, the spirit here is unbelievable."

This is actually true. Though *Applause* is a bible of footlight bitchery, the atmosphere behind the scenes at the Fisher Theater in Detroit is about as malevolent as *Life with Mother.* Betty Comden and Adolph Green, who wrote the script, are two of Bacall's oldest friends, and Ron Field, who directed, obviously worships her. Young Penny Fuller, a deliciously evil Eve Harrington on stage, has developed an offstage relationship with the star that is right out of *My Sister Eileen,* and the singers and dancers call her "Den Mother."

Towering over it all, literally and figuratively, is Betty Perske, who nurtured the camaraderie in the first place. She even likes her producers, Joe Kipness and Larry Kasha, "because, goddamn it, they're human beings, they have broken their necks to give me care, protection, and, most of all, interest. And I am stunned by this, after my experience in *Cactus Flower*. Oh, what the hell, David Merrick is a shit. The only work problem I have ever had was with that man. He hates actors. It bugs him that he needs them. His theory is, 'You'll always work for me, if I have something you want to do.' And my answer is, '*Not* necessarily.' God, two years in his play without missing a performance and he never said 'Thank you,' or 'Drop dead,' or anything. I do *not* want to be pandered to! But after you have put out so damn much of yourself, you'd at least like to *see* your employer occasionally.

"It's a big joke, you know: You're an actor, you only work three hours a night, what a cushy deal! But what you have put into those three hours is incredible; the amount of *you* that you give so the two thousand people who pay to see you go out satisfied. And I'll tell you something, I don't know about this business of walking through a show. I don't understand it. I don't know how it's done. So if you *do* work hard—well, hell, I don't want to socialize with David Merrick, but just an occasional smile, a pat on the back, and if not, then *the hell* with it, who needs it? I would rather work where there is a gemutlich feeling, a warmth, a coziness. I can't stand fighting during rehearsals, screaming, yelling, scenes. Oh, I can fight if I have to, believe me—but then I can't work."

During this, a waiter has brought breakfast, and Bacall has managed to clear a place for the tray, tip generously, and consume half a plate of eggs and sausages with only five small breath-pauses. She has also briefly discussed Adlai Stevenson, whom she considers the second greatest man of our time, and Bobby Kennedy, whom she considers the greatest ("When he went, I went, I will never recover from that, never"), dissected the sixties ("The crappiest decade in history, all our best men murdered, what's fascinating about it?"), dismissed pot and nudity and ground a firm heel into Washington. "I once seriously thought of living there, it's where everything that affects all our lives happens. But right now, baby, it's a wasteland. Hell no, I don't get asked there now, and if I did, I wouldn't go, not in this life or the next. I mean, there's nothing to discuss, right?

"But I like the country feeling of life around Washington; I like the idea of land. No, I don't own any, because I can't afford it. As soon as I meet my prince charming, he'll take me away to the country. Until then, kid, if I don't work, I don't eat. I'm not rich, and never will be, and I don't give a damn. Things, I don't need; I've had enough things. When I was younger, I thought, 'If I could just have this, buy that!' Then I could, and I went crazy, bought ninety of everything, and never used any of it, just let it all lay there. God, I have wasted so much money in my life, thrown away so much dough, and for what? I worked my ass off for every cent of it, and what have I got to show? My apartment in the Dakota. That's it. Except the kids, of course. God, have I been lucky there! You want to see them?"

She bounds into the bedroom as if her children waited there, comes back with three snapshots in silver frames. "I take these everywhere. Never go away without my babies. Here's my beautiful boy, my Bogart boy, Stephen, he's twenty, and this is Leslie, she's seventeen, also Bogey's. You'll look far to find a face as pretty as that. And this is Sam, my little mouse. He's eight. Katie Hepburn's his godmother, and godmothers don't come any better, right? Fantastic bunch of kids."

She puts the pictures carefully out of harm's way and sits down abruptly. For the first time in an hour, she looks distant, distracted. "Stephen got married this year," she says quietly, "to a darling girl. I thought he was a little young; but Christ almighty, why not? There's so much crap in the world, if you find something good, I don't care what it is, then absolutely have it! My daughter's going to college in the fall, so now I'll only have the little one with me. God! It is so terrifying, how life repeats itself! I am now bringing up my *third* child without a father! Oh, I don't mean Sam is really fatherless. But for all intents and purposes, he doesn't have a father who's in the same place for any length of time. Because of the nature of his work. . . ."

Sam's father is Jason Robards, whom his mother divorced last September after eight years of marriage. Asked about this, gently, her eyes narrow, but she smiles, very mischievously. "Hah! I *thought* you were gonna get around to that kind of question! Well, my dear fellow, there is nothing to say about *that* except that it's over. *Period.* Now, will you tell me why these interviews have to be full of gossip? Would you explain that? I mean, who *cares* about that trash? Is that what really matters, what makes a person?" She is on her feet, grabbing her suede duffel coat and a battered script; already she is minutes late for rehearsal.

"What matters," she suddenly announces at the door, "is to live your life. To press on and live your life, and that goes for me, *and* you, and . . . and your goddamn cat, if you've got one!" Then she's gone down the hall to the elevator and to the theater, presumably to live hers.

18.

David Merrick: Hello, Rasputin

INTERVIEWING David Merrick is not really difficult once you get past the preliminaries, which consist of (a) a pleasant, leisurely series of calls to his press people, who are gracious and expansive, and present, eventually, a sort of bartering system, a list of subjects permitted versus subjects forbidden: (the latter include the place and year of his birth, his parents, adolescence, education, college days, law degree, law practice, beginnings on Broadway, first marriage, second marriage, children, addresses, hobbies, eccentricities, dreams, disillusionments, aspirations and politics, and the former include *Hello, Dolly!*), and

(b) the reiteration, by Merrick himself, on whatever agreement has been reached. In his blood-colored office above the St. James Theater, he stands at semiattention beside his antique desk, Rasputin risen from the river. He offers his hand like a well-dealt card and says, "Hello." The things he is loath to discuss are sternly catalogued. "I always lie about them anyway," he adds, as if serving a subpoena, "they're boring, they've been printed so many times." But not with much accuracy, apparently. Grimace, silence, blackout.

Leave aside this dour opening, leave aside the famous epithets—"Typhoid David," "The Abominable Showman"—which were undoubtedly begun not by rival producers but by Merrick himself, because the image sold tickets. A fact remains: At least a third of his sixty-three productions in sixteen years—*Epitaph for George Dillon,* for instance, Menotti's *Maria Golovin, Luther, Becket*—have made New York more tolerable than it would have been without them, and at least half of all his shows, the

219

comedies, the cotton-candy musicals included, have been well worth the staggering price of going outside one's apartment for a whole evening. Really, do his crotchets matter to the theatergoer who wouldn't have seen *Look Back in Anger* if Merrick had listened to the mavens who told him the play would never make it on Broadway? At a time when it seems most foolish, he has remained doggedly true to his almost boyish vision of theater, a glamorous abstract contained within a few dirty Manhattan blocks, and has done more by himself to convey this vision to Keokuk, and so on, than anyone from George M. Cohan to the inventor of orange drink.

He motions toward the red sofa, sits in a straight chair—there is something peculiar about his eyes, the look of essentially mournful persons—starts to unbutton his black suit, thinks better of it. He smiles. This Wednesday, when the matinee curtain falls, *Hello Dolly!* will have played its 2,718th performance, thereby becoming the longest-running Broadway musical in the mind of man. Six years ago, in this same office, he suggested making a musical of *The Matchmaker* to Michael Stewart, who'd written the script of *Carnival* for him. Stewart smiled. Three weeks later, Jerry Herman, a friend of Stewart's, entered the crimson room carrying five song-sheets, one of which contained a big second-act number to be sung by the leading lady while descending a staircase.

"When he left," Merrick says, without marked animation, "I called my general manager and told him, 'I've just found the, uh, greatest composer-lyricist the world has ever known.'" Herman had gone home to write the rest of the score, but was instantly stymied. So was Merrick: Nobody else seemed inordinately interested in *Dolly.* Jerome Robbins didn't want to direct it, neither did Hal Prince. "Hal wrote me a letter that ended with, 'and if you do produce it, for God's sake get rid of that terrible title song!'" Gower Champion wasn't overwhelmed by the idea either, until Merrick offered him practically a partnership. Ethel Merman, Mary Martin and Lucille Ball didn't want to play the title role.

"Then I asked Carol Channing if she'd audition. Carol said, 'Why, SURE.'" He has done a brief, subdued Channing imitation. The first New York run-through was "a disaster," and things didn't go much better in Detroit. Gower, Carol and Jerry Herman stayed up all night, just like in plays about plays out-of-town, and though it was rumored that Merrick wanted to close the show, he denies it. "I had doubts, grave doubts, but they disappeared when we opened in Washington." The notices were raves; Washington is also the place that the notion of a black *Dolly* occurred to him, but he didn't consider it again until many months later, after Channing had departed the St. James Theater and the series of former-film-star leads had begun to run down like a thrift-shop clock.

"Pearl Bailey kept it a secret for eighteen months, which must be a record for an actress keeping her mouth shut. Pearl's company was supposed to be just a road company; I knew it was going to come to New York, and Pearl knew, but nobody else did. One Thursday night, the audience here came expecting to see—who was it, Betty Grable?—and there was Pearl, and they cheered for half an hour. Well, in this business, you gain one thing, lose another. When Ethel Merman finally took over, Pearl was still on the road, in Houston, and one of their critics wrote that he'd been to New York, and that Ethel was the best Dolly of all, and Pearl didn't play the next town. Oh, I haven't got any kicks coming, I *did* have her for two and a half years."

Under extreme pressure, Merrick will admit that he would have made a good director, but decided early on that the action was in producing, which begins, in his case, with conceiving a package. He spends months, sometimes years, thinking out the concept, then presents it to a director, and avoids the early rehearsals, "not just because they're dull, which they are, but to leave the creative people totally free to, uh, do their thing." Eventually, he comes around, to function in "an editorial capacity. When the show and director are right, I don't have to interfere, and even when they aren't quite, I involve myself much less than other producers, some of whom *have* to keep demonstrating their authority. By keeping myself *un*involved, right up to the last moment, I can stay objective about what we have, and sometimes, I'm the only one who is."

He has relaxed some, and seems to want to loosen his gray tie, but doesn't. I ask about the gimmicks—the night he placed the nude statue of the belly dancer from *Fanny,* his first show, on an empty pedestal in the Poet's Corner in Central Park, the time he hired pickets to walk in front of *Flower Drum Song* with signs reading *"The World of Suzie Wong* Is New York's Only Authentic Oriental Show"—but you get the feeling that he has gone beyond such marvelous old-fashioned stunts. "*Dolly* built so much momentum from the start, I wouldn't want to cheapen it that way."

We listen for a moment to the rich hum of his air-conditioner. Everybody knows about Merrick's promotional genius, but lots of people don't quite realize the incredible mileage he has gotten from cul-de-sacs. In 1964, he offered "Hello, Lyndon!" to the Democratic convention, was firmly rejected, and recorded the song anyway, awaiting a typical Merrick windfall. Then Barry Goldwater called him to say he was going to use a song titled "Hello, Barry!" Eureka! Merrick not only shot off a wire stating he would sue for $10 million, but phoned newscaster Nancy Dickerson, who phoned Chet and David, who told the story on the evening news, which Johnson was watching. When he called, Merrick sent the record to the White House. "I *wasn't* responsible for them playing the song every five minutes during the convention," he claims. Neither had he anything to do with the London club called Dolly's, or the playing of the title song at Kennedy airport as Pope Paul deplaned.

But the Vietnam incident was definitely his. He'd easily sold the State Department on the idea of sending Mary Martin's *Dolly* to Japan and Russia, but, at the very moment of departure, the USSR canceled the engagement, blaming our involvement in the Far East. Reporters were waiting for Merrick in Tokyo, the first stop; art, he told them, should transcend politics, and that, during his flight, he had decided to take the company to Vietnam instead, to entertain the troops. There was the slight problem of Washington's total ignorance of his plan, and of the necessary permission to enter a war zone. Merrick simply rang up the White House again.

"Some of the actors didn't want to go—political reasons, or maybe they were just afraid. At the time, Bob Hope had been there once, I think, but no one else. It turned out splendidly, though I never did feel that Ambassador Lodge or General Westmoreland cared very much for the idea. . . ."

As for the future of *Dolly,* Merrick is philosophical. His objective was to out-run *My Fair Lady*. He had once asked Mae West to saunter down the red staircase ("I visited her and got the full treatment, she entered in a gold peignoir and draped herself on a white sofa"), and though she declined, he may ask her again, when Merman leaves, and there is always the possibility of a drag version—though he doesn't talk about it, he is well aware of the show's large homosexual claque—with George Burns as Vandergelder to Jack Benny's matchmaker ("I called Jack, and he said, 'I know why you asked me, it's the way I walk'").

Either way, it seems now to matter little to him, nor does the movie. After he sold the rights to 20th Century-Fox, he let them know he'd be interested in producing the film for them with the original star and director. Fox scoffed. Merrick, along with the authors and backers, has a healthy percentage of the movie's profits, and himself owns more than 200,000 shares of Fox, and has recently played "a sort of Ralph Nader role" at stockholder meetings, chiding Zanuck *père et fils* for the extraordinary cost of getting Streisand to the Harmonia Gardens. "They spent twenty-six million, probably five million on the 'Parade' number alone, I could have made it for a quarter of that. Barbra did valiantly with a part she was basically miscast in, but the picture won't make a profit. I suspect that Fox now wishes they'd done it my way."

There is no animosity in his voice; and when the subject of those who speak ill of him—Lauren Bacall, for example—is introduced, the benign expression doesn't even waver. "What about the, uh, euphoric comments?" he asks. True: A lot of Broadway people neither employed by nor afraid of him, like Steve Sondheim, or even competitors like Hal Prince, seem to enjoy and respect him. "As for Betty Bacall," he begins, almost purring, "I *like* her. I don't much care about her attitude toward me. For Betty, every night of *Cactus Flower* was opening night. But very early, I saw that she is a professional malcontent. All actors, in their childlike way, would like the producer to show up constantly. Well, I have *lots* of shows to see to scattered around the country, playing abroad. After a while, I simply stopped going backstage, because every time I did, Betty would start complaining—about Barry Nelsen, the other actors, the stagehands, everything.

"It got so unpleasant that I *did* pick a fight, so that I wouldn't *have* to go back, and eventually, Abe Burrows, the director, had to do the same thing. After opening night, Betty was suddenly a big stage star, which she hadn't been before. It was no secret that I wanted her for the play and had to force her past the director, and that she owed as much to *Cactus Flower* as it owed her. The real trouble was that she felt she'd been foxed. I'd asked her for a full two-year contract. She already considered herself a star, and wanted ten percent of the gross, a star's salary, in addition to a fourteen-week out to make a film. I said, 'All right, but then I'll only pay you seven and a half per cent.' She chose that, the picture-option contract, which finally cost her, I think, $125,000. Because no picture turned up—which was exactly what I was gambling on."

And the critics? "Hah! They can say any damn thing they please about us, so I've always felt I have the same privilege. Now, as you know, we are surrounded today by mediocrity— everything is mediocre, from the phones to the plays. I've asked critics, separately, 'Do you think there are any masterpieces around that the theater's neglecting?' They've all said no, and I've replied, 'Then I think you fellas are going to *have* to praise the higher grade of mediocrity, which may find an audience, and bring in the tourists, and make enough money that we can afford to produce the occasional good, noncommercial play. If you don't, there won't be any Broadway at all. I mean that, and I think I've begun to make my point. Walter Kerr was always a marvelous critic, but too tough; he has mellowed now. At first, Clive Barnes, like all new critics, went to every opening night looking for a masterpiece, but he finally relaxed, developed into a superb critic, and I won't take that back when he pans some new show of mine. The television men, I can't bear. Newspaper writers usually have some background in drama, TV people just move up, from Lord knows where. Martin Gottfried of *Women's Wear Daily* would be a problem if he wrote for a publication with any power. Right now, he's trying to call attention to himself, to get a better job, and if he does, he'll settle down too. As for John Simon, I'd throw him out of my shows if I knew what he looked like. He is—beyond comment."

Of course there's nothing to Merrick's periodic announcements that he's abandoning the theater—this year, he's already planning the musical of *Some Like It Hot* and possibly *Home* and

The Contractor, which he just saw in London and has in mind for The David Merrick Foundation, which uses profits from big hits to present the longshots. Still, he seems genuinely worried about Broadway, "The best creative people are snapped up by the movies now. There are just three men who account for sixty percent of all the shows—Hal Prince, Neil Simon and myself. Neil, you know, has a nominal producer, Saint Subber, but for all practical purposes he produces his own plays. And all three of us are turning to films because there just isn't enough action in New York any more, we just aren't getting the audiences. The real threat, though, is that we've lost the young people— they don't even attend *Off* Broadway—and it isn't ticket prices, because there are plenty of balcony seats for what they spend to go to a movie. The kids went to *Hair* and I've gotten them on occasion: for *Marat/Sade, Child's Play,* and, oddly, *Stop the World.* Mostly, though, they just aren't interested. The writers and directors who speak to them are working in films."

Then how about a Merrick show specifically aimed at the youth market? "That's exactly what I'm looking for. I do *not* want to go on producing for theater-party organizers and elderly tourists, but it's largely what I'm doing. I'm constantly reading scripts and considering ideas with kids in mind." He frowns, considering. "The producer of *Hair* the director, the writers were all well over thirty. I find that ironic. And hopeful."

When I get up to leave, Merrick rises promptly, looking somewhat relieved. "Uh . . . now really, what *would* you have asked me, anyway, about my background?" He smiles, almost impishly. "I was born . . . November 4, 1954, the night *Fanny* opened on Broadway." Pause. "So that makes me a Sagittarius."

Most astrologers would say that he is, therefore, a Scorpio, one of the people who always win somehow, and if you further research the sign in an astrology book, it does, in Merrick's case, seem to be much more fitting.

19.

Kris Kristofferson's Talking Blues

IN Peru, one kept a daily journal; now Kristofferson bends grinning over its pages, on which, in the winter of '70, Andes mud spilled and dried like blood spots. "Hell," he offers rurally, "wouldn't surprise me none you said it *was* blood." One had gone there to write about the making, or rather, wresting from the soil, of Dennis Hopper's *The Last Movie;* Kris, totally unknown then, was doing the film's score. Rain hung over the Andes like an apathetic fate; we were unanimously weakened and distracted by the paranoia and diarrhea induced by Hopper's inferior coke and an oppressive intuition we shared, about a movie whose title would turn out inadvertently ironical. Yet now Kris happily basks in the journal's glum notes as though they were yearbook inscriptions, or baby pictures:

> Hopper attracts, or surrounds himself with, two types: troubled, abrasive specters and gentle heroes holding to concepts of pleasantness and goodness. The latter includes a composer named Kris, with a *K* . . . though he was a Rhodes scholar at Oxford, his speech is Brownsville bowling alley. Amid the cabin-fever hostility here, he takes elaborate pains to placate, to not challenge; he appears to sleepwalk hung over through some good dream, yet yesterday, when the horses rented for the movie panicked on the set, K. stepped instantly from us cowering bystanders to a wild-eyed black mare . . . before he calmed her, she'd stepped on his hand.

"Man, I didn't even think when I grabbed that bridle," and he laughs down at the page. "I didn't know shit about horses: If

I'd thought I'd never 'a done it." He's lit another brown Bull Durham cigarette; he more or less chain-smokes, further mottling the cream walls of Rita Coolidge's house, a dim, warm, overstuffed cottage on the wrong side of the Hollywood freeway. Until now, we haven't really talked since the Peruvian debacle, when the idea of him as music celebrity or movie star was as remote as canonization. "But you gotta understand, Tom, the whole trip down there, it was my first time near *anything* that bizarre. Hell, I was straight outa Nashville with shit on my boots." His voice is as it was then, scratching warmly from a rusty-iron larynx, his smile is the same, and yet not—darker, or it occurs less easily, less often, except when he thinks about Peru:

> . . . dawn, Monday. With a lady photographer and a foxy actress named, incredibly, Poupee Bocar, K. & I sneak aboard the People's Train for a day at Machu Picchu. (Dennis hates even short-term defections and probably has the railroad station watched.) K.'s hand still bandaged from horse incident; he insists, though, in carrying along his guitar. Ten miles into the mountains, the train, which smells of llamas, malfunctions; instantly Kris herds us off and over the muddy ties in antic procession to the luxurious tourist train, paused ahead for its Retired Shriners, or whatever, to snap Polaroids. Funky, unshaven, we are not welcome among the barbered burghers, but K. of course charms us on. . . . The whole trip home, very stoned, Kris plays and sings songs he's written: "Sunday Mornin' Comin' Down," "Help Me Make It Through the Night," and one about Dennis called "The Pilgrim." All lovely songs but humorous. . . . He's had almost no success peddling them; why does it seem, sadly, that he won't? Because there's about him the good, gentle loser? . . . Good lines in a song about Bobby McGee (Bobby a girl? Ask K.) "Feelin' near as faded as my jeans," "Freedom's just another word for nothing left to lose," etc. . . .

About there, his laugh becomes a cough and he shakes his head as if it hurt. After a moment, one mentions Joplin; after another, he says, "Jesus, I don't like talkin' about her. It's like grave-robbin'. Yeh, I lived with Janis awhile. Met her because—remember how we partied, in Peru, the night I got the telegram

228

from Johnny Cash, askin' me to come on his show soon as I was finished? My first break, an' all. Johnny really hyped my songs after that, I got my first gig at the Bitter End in New York, an' one night there I fell in with Mickey Newbury an' Bobby Neuwirth, he used t'be Dylan's road manager, and Michael J. Pollard, and all these *freaks*. And after this one all-night jam session, Bobby says, 'Hey, let's fly out to the coast and visit Janis.' I used my last cash for the plane. She was in this house in Mill Valley then, and my first impression was, 'This chick is in *very* good shape!' She'd kicked heroin, wasn't even letting her old connections on the place. Oh, she bitched a lot 'cause this doctor wouldn't prescribe her methadone, but she was working out with her band every day, really gettin' it off; she was like Sugar Ray Robinson working out! But Janis . . . she felt she had to be number one, she lived under this paranoid threat that somebody else'd step in and be the big girl, and she'd just become a plain chick nobody wanted. Sad: All this crap you read about her, it's like 'Who Killed Norma Jean?' and it's bullshit. I mean, nobody in this business is very stable, else we wouldn't all be up on stages making asses 'a ourselves."

The grin's the old one. "Oh, there was a lotta drinkin' an' high boogyin' there at Janis'. I never did intend t'stay, but Bobby Neuwirth took off and he had the car. I kept fixin' to leave every day, but it was like Peru: I'd never known anybody like Janis before, it was all new to me. She'd say, 'Shit, pretty soon you're gonna be gypsyin' down the road, to go be a star.' Maybe if I hadn't 'a left . . . she used to get depressed and say, 'If things don't get better next year, I'm gonna off myself.' I didn't believe her, I'd say, 'Aw, Janis, that's just Capricorn trick number 37,' trying to cheer her up. I always figured people could be talked outa offing themselves. And I finally did gypsy off, to Nashville, to cut my first album. From there, I had to go to England for the Isle of Wight concert; Jimi Hendrix was in it, too, an' right after it, Jimi died. Soon as I came back I did the Monterey Folk Festival, and the day it was over, somebody called to say Janis was dead. Wow, it was *very* heavy for a long time after that. I thought, 'Who gives a shit, you devote your life to entertaining people who, in the end, depress you so much you off yourself; that's a killer outfit. . . .'"

From Monterey he made a sort of pilgrimage, tracking her

ghost, south to LA to John Cooke, Joplin's manager. It eluded him ("I'll never know if her dyin' was just a freaky accident"), but during that visit he was cast in his first film, *Cisco Pike,* quite by accident, as he later explains. "I wasn't hot to be in movies, but after Janis, I was very confused about the music trip. So much pain t'put yourself through! I was performing all the time by then, but everything I made I spent on the road, bein' miserable. The movie looked like it'd be a day at the beach; it wasn't. That Christmas, 1970, I did my first Carnegie Hall gig and went from it right up to Woodstock; it was New Year's Eve, the town was covered with snow. At a party, somebody said, 'Hey Kris, you gotta hear this,' and he put on a tape of Janis singing 'Me and Bobby McGee.' Jesus! *I had absolutely no idea she'd recorded it!*"

Exactly at "The town was covered with snow," at that perfect-ly wrong moment, one's new tape recorder begins humming protests. If you tape interviews with celebrities, you must con-ceal your machine's crotchets at any cost, including fake epilep-tic seizure or even, in extreme crisis, interrupting your subject, lest he perceive that his thoughts, usually dredged from the somberest levels of Reich, Janov, Reuben, L. Ron Hubbard and *How to Be Your Own Best Friend,* be lost. Kristofferson studies the recorder as if its rudeness had restored his own good hu-mor, "Rose Mary Woods is lurkin' somewheres," he announces. "Think we can fix it?" And he manipulates and strokes it, successfully. "Know what that really was? This used to be John Garfield's house, and we've had tapes erased for no reason, whole bands of new records won't play. But I swear, John's mostly a friendly dude: The other night his movie *Body and Soul* was on TV and the feelin' in this room was so *good. . . .*"

Except, he adds, pouring a Tia Maria, except he wonders if he could just say all that again, about Joplin, now the machine's OK. "I do want that quoted right, Tom, because everybody's exploitin' the hell outa Janis." Painstakingly, he repeats. ". . . so I sat there in Woodstock and listened to that tape all night, I-dunno-how-many times. The next mornin', my sister in California called to say my dad died. It was a fairly traumatic New Year's. I'd also had walking pneumonia for something like four months without knowing it. Took three weeks off, went

230

back on the road, and been on the road ever since." Grin. "And that's the whole story."

Not quite. In Peru, for instance, one night he had stretched out on the sagging bed of his hotel room, quietly smoking and talking almost until dawn about growing up with a father who was an Air Force major, a career military man who did not cotton to the idea of his eldest son as country musician. "Oh, yeh, well there was that conflict," he offers now, not pleased with the subject, "but this Thanksgiving Rita and I went down home, to San Mateo, and everybody there now is truly bein' extra nice, my dad's gone, so why knock 'em?" Except . . . "Like I told you, when I was a kid, nobody else in the house *ever* listened to country music, and now my mother's the biggest country-rock freak in the state; she and Karen, my sister, call all the stations and request my songs, they disguise their voices. So I don't wanta nail 'em now. Sure, my father tried to program me for an Army career, but I don't think he *really* thought he could, 'cause he saw that all that *ever* interested me, 'sides football, was Hank Williams records. I still got boxes of those old seventy-eights stored somewheres; in those days, the fifties, kids listened to *nothin'* but Johnnie Ray and Patti Page, I was a total weirdo. The first song I wrote was a Hank Williams rip-off called, I think, 'I Hate Your Ugly Face,' I was eleven, I told my dad I wanted to be a writer, not a *song*writer, I knew he pictured writers as wearing elbow patches and smoking pipes, not smoking funny stuff in Nashville. At home they always said, 'Now, Craig,' he's my younger brother, 'Craig will make money 'cause he cares, and Kris won't make any 'cause he just doesn't.' Well, they were right. I never did care. Still don't."

Oh. He sees that reaction in your eyes. Hastily, "I mean it was never a matter of money: I never thought of *selling* songs, profit wasn't the motive. They were just the only way I could express some kind of . . . suffering. Shit, no, separation. I always felt separate. In high school, I wanted to be a big football star, more than a songwriter, maybe for the same reason; tried to get football scholarships to both Yale and Dartmouth, no way, and for Stanford, you had to weigh, like, two-fifty just t'get into a uniform, so I went to Pomona. Played, yeh, but I busted my head and cartilage in my knee. I was the worst ROTC platoon commander in the history of the school, never could give a guy a demerit. But my grades were real good, got that Rhodes scholarship, even got my picture in *Sports Illustrated* for sports, and, man, I went off to Oxford a *star*. Hah! An' quickly found out what a fucked-up little wimp I was, damn!"

Unexpectedly, he slaps his knee. "Those British, shit, peel off layers 'a bullshit instantly! I'd organized a rugby team at Pomona, but at Oxford they wouldn't even let me try out for the team. They maintained an American couldn't know shit from rugby. Nothing much is gonna impress those British! I never did wanta pick up any British accent. They all called me Yank, so I just kept on talkin' more like I always had. . . ."

Like Hank Williams. He laughs, tentatively. Well, after all he did grow up in the West, he points out, first in Texas, then San Mateo, California. But through his Grand Ole Opry inflection constantly surfaces, like ice floes, the precision of Academe. "Yeh, okay. So I'm an oral schizophrenic. That's what I felt in England. I got an okay with them English athletes, it was the sherry-party guys that drove me bananas; they truly gave me t'understand I had shit on my boots. An' I had gotten *heavy* inta literature over there. William Blake had just opened *doors* for me. I'd even started writin' a novel. . . ."

But at one of the sherry parties, he respectfully told Nevill Coghill, the world's foremost Chaucer translator and don of Cambridge dons, how Blake's "The Mental Traveller" ought really to be read. "He was like this big expert, they'd given me another year on my dissertation, but after that I was officially taken off Blake." He went home to California for Christmas, "and I never did go back. See, there was this girl at home, I'd gone with her in high school. Fran Beer, as in 'beer.' We thought we could solve each other's problems, we, uh, got married, she got pregnant, my novel I'd finished got rejected, and I was suddenly stuck, totally, with the breadwinner role. Tom, I really figured right then, good-bye to writing. Joined the Air Force, shit, I remember drivin' onto the military base the first day, it was like driving into hell; like driving into San Francisco when I was a kid used to scare the devil outa me, all those boxy houses squeezed against one another. If you was really bad, you got stuck inta one 'a those places."

Oddly, for years he stuck to those places, through the burnt-

232

orange carpet-and-drape inferno of furnished apartments in military towns, largely drunk and unproductive. "I touched a bottom, I hadn't written a song in years, when I was smashed it seemed clear, I would never write one, nor a novel, nor much of anything, so I drank more. It was very rough, especially on my wife: When you're not doing what y'think you should in life, you take it out on your old lady, or whoever. One weekend leave, I just got crazy; instead of going to Fran I got on a plane for Nashville, still in uniform. It was my first time there, everybody called me 'Captain.' "

He wangled a meeting with Johnny Cash. "I was determined to meet him; there was no way in hell that I wouldn't have. Johnny's got an instinct 'bout pickin' people who are going to make it." After that leave he was to go to West Point to teach, "but in Nashville, the life had come back into me. Went home and quit the Air Force for good, which scared hell outa Fran: All she'd ever seen 'a the music business was this funky band I had while I was stationed in Germany; we played the worst kinda dives, but she came with me back to Nashville anyways. I rented this fifty-dollar-a-month cold-water flat, a tenement." Smiling, as if nostalgic, he adds, "I still got that apartment. There's an old lady lives next door, her husband died and she came over cryin' and asked me not to move, 'cause she was afraid some hippie freak'd move in. So I just keep payin' the rent; there's a young guy livin' there who's trying to get into the music business. . . ."

Still talking, he goes to open a fresh Tia Maria bottle. Two black mongrel cats and the one luxurious white Angora have assembled at the front door, expectant; they bow courteously when Rita Coolidge comes in, her eight-month pregnancy obscured by shopping bags. "I went to see the house," she tells Kris, with a smile like his. There's a serene, womanly, humorous grace about her; she has the cheekbones and the onyx hair of a Cherokee, but there's a stolid, Celtic richness in the pale, good skin, the lips. Kris stretches and half-bows, like the cats, who follow them to the kitchen.

". . . and that house, it's just ten times better than anything else I saw!" Kris has explained they want to move, and that Rita's been house-hunting, in the hills and canyons above Malibu Beach. "It's got three acres, a great orchard, a pool, three bedrooms and this huge fieldstone fireplace in the living room. It's just so peaceful up there on that hill!" Her speech, like his, is rural. "A nice older couple live there now, they really love the place, but they want to travel. They said today they think that *we* ought to have it."

"Oh, really?" His reading is unexpectedly urbane. "You tell the accountant that."

"Well, what they meant was," and she's smiling, "they thought we'd be happy livin' there."

When she goes in to cook supper, Kris offers, "Jesus, I never owned no house before! It's like buyin' a ball and chain, but you can't bring up a baby in motel rooms. When he hears the price of this place, the accountant will shit. Yeh, I can afford it, it's just very heavy, settlin' down, becoming a father again. Baby's due next month; last night I had t'go again with Rita to her natural-childbirth class. I felt like we were Dick Van Dyke and Mary Tyler Moore—just like a TV show, there were these *representative* couples. One black, one Jewish, one Chicano, one straight, and us, the freaks. The Mexican guy said, 'I got seven sisters, I don't know there *was* another way to have a baby.'" Rita, he adds, will have the child in a hospital, "but I'm not too cool in hospitals, had some bad times in 'em. My first wife—our daughter was born first, she was fine, but our son, he was born with his esophagus and trachea attached, a *bad* time. Ran up about a $10,000 hospital bill, I was making $200 a month working as a janitor at Columbia Records in Nashville. I tell ya, it's weird now, headlining on the same bill with guys you used to empty ashtrays for, tryin' to pitch 'em your songs on the side. It was the only job I could get.

"Then we had a little dispute 'bout wages and I went down the road to work at the Tally Ho Tavern, sweepin' up. And all this time, I'm getting letters from my folks with these significant clippings from the hometown paper, saying so-and-so won a Silver Star and little Harry Greenfield just got elected president 'a the United Nations. Shit, though, once you get right down there on the bottom, totally broke and an embarrassment to your loved ones, and it still hasn't killed you, suddenly, it's all easier: nothin' left t'lose, y'know? Luckily, I was *not* a good enough performer to work as the singer in the Holiday Inn, or like that, so I didn't get molded into bein' that kinda entertain-

234

er—though believe me, I'd 'a jumped at it, 'cause *nobody* wanted my songs! I just kept tellin' myself that in country music, nobody makes it fast, but that once you do, it's a lot more stable: Guys like Webb Pierce and Ernest Tubb are still makin' records twenty years after their first hit. . . ."

But didn't his songs actually satirize Pierce, Tubb and the whole country-and-western tradition? Besides, he was trying to sell them in the mid-sixties, when long-haired renegades were still pariahs in straight, patriotic Nashville, still phantoms of the Grand Ole Opry. "Well, yeh, that's sorta true." Silence. One has noted before that he doesn't like putting down Nashville, conversationally, nor is he anxious to analyze his work at any length. "The songs are . . . well, I dunno what they are. I think they're pretty easy to understand." This last has sounded defensive; then, apologetically, "They can start out a little obscure, before I polish 'em, like this one here I'm gonna record tomorrow night, it's brand new and *not* finished." He takes a guitar from the corner of the fireplace, and sings, hoarsely smoke-cured, a song from the album he's just recording:

> Shandy was somebody's daughter
> Driving to something insane
> They busted her crossin' the border
> Swift as a sniff 'a cocaine
> All she could pay was attention
> So all they could take was her time
> Proving an ounce of possession
> Ain't worth a piece of your mind

The next verse is something about Martin locked in a gold-handled bathroom, wiping the mask of the man in the mirror who really is Billy the Kid. "Damn, it needs work! What I do is, just keep tightening the images, making them specific when they ain't, until, hopefully, *I* understand what it's about." He strums and sings until Rita puts a chicken sandwich in front of him.

Then he has to go work with his band. The next afternoon, one talks with his record producer, David Anderle, who says, "The new album is called *Spooky Lady's Sideshow* and in it Kris has stretched himself in a totally new direction. I mean, the last album, *Jesus Was a Capricorn*, was a gold record and the single from it, "Why Me, Lord?" was a runaway hit and Kris could have just turned out more of the same, but the range in *Spooky Lady* is fantastic: from pure country to a totally new sound. . . ." Then, driving back to their house, the radio, in a fifteen-minute space, plays two of his songs. In the traffic lines, one idly strings together lines of his lyrics; clearly, what all the songs so far have been about is that, for us all, things have already been as good as they will ever get. A chronic nostalgia. A story about him told to me by Peter Rachtman, manager of John Stewart and Flash Cadillac, surfaces: "I was in a restaurant in Vegas with Karen Black—this was just after they'd finished *Cisco Pike*—we were talking about Kris, and a guy from the next table came over and said, 'You talking about *Kristofferson?*' Turned out the guy was in his class at Pomona, he asked whatever happened to him. I told him, a movie about to come out and so on, he didn't seem to understand that Kris was just about to make it. He shook his head sadly, and said, "We always thought he'd do something big. He was president of his freshman class, sophomore class, *every* class; of the debating team, the writing club, the football team, baseball. Kris was the most respected, best-liked boy that school ever saw. Kris Kristofferson could have been president of the country right then, if he'd run. But there always was something . . . *else* about him, nice as he was. A . . . sadness. In a funny way, I wasn't surprised we didn't hear of him again."

One has intended to coerce him into a discussion of the songs right away, this afternoon, but he is occupied, at the top of the steep little drive, patiently smiling at a sullen, pudgy girl in an Avis blazer who's come to replace his faulty rented Plymouth. ". . . No, ma'am, I dunno what's wrong with it, except it keeps stoppin'. My mechanical knowledge is nil." Dutifully, he looks under the hood, as she writes on a pad. "Now, it might be the starter," he offers, gesturing vaguely at the dark metallic tangle, "wherever that is. Hmm? No, it's with a *k*, and two *f*s . . . no, both of them is *o*s . . . no, see the first also starts with a *k*." A mechanic arrives to take the sedan away and replace it with an identical one; the girl leaves with a brief, suspicious smile, as if she doubted the transaction. When we're inside before the fireplace, I ask if he thinks she recognized him. This startles him visibly. "Jesus, I dunno. I have no idea. I

. . . don't think about that shit, honestly, it don't occur to me."

Oh. I tell him my thinking about the songs. "Hey, yeh, nobody ever said it like that before, quite. I'm sorry, but once I finish writing, Tom, the umbilical cord's cut. I . . . know my limits as a performer, but not yet as a songwriter. Bein' on the road rips my throat up, but I couldn't write without it, I really get it off workin' with my band; they are so good it stretches me musically, so that when I get home, I can write 'cause I been with them. A good song, I think, has gotta be bought on the most immediate, the simplest level 'a the words, just what they mean. Funny, they get changed by artists when you first get 'em recorded. *Everybody* fuckin' changes your lyrics 'cause they assume you don't know what you're doin' yet. Like in 'Bobby McGee,' Janis, on that tape, she changed an important line, it was supposed t'be, 'Them windshield wipers slappin' time/and Bobby clappin' hands we finally sang up ever song that driver knew.' See, I had a sorta inner rhyme worked out there, but she changed it, I dunno why. Now, 'Feelin' near as faded as my jeans,' I'm proud 'a that one, because you *think* you heard it before, but it was *not* used before in country music; it was maybe the first time that New Orleans was rhymed with somethin' other than 'Cajun queens.' Most listeners never analyze that shit, I get letters that just say, 'Hey, you're singin' what I'm thinkin'.' I can dig that. Then you open *Rolling Stone* an' some critic'll say, 'What'd he really mean by "Help Me Make It Through the Night"?' and shit, I thought the message of that number was pretty up front! Or they accuse me of being on a Jesus trip, they refuse t'see that I'm just being humorous. That really hurts, you can sell a zillion records and one bad review still riles you. I got totally ripped apart by *Rolling Stone* for the *Border Lord* album; the reviewer hated everything about me. If I'd had a dog he'd 'a hated the dog. I don't do songs from that album anymore; the first album I made, it got great notices except for one which said my work was all pitying. Shit, sad about mankind, maybe, that's just inevitable."

And nothing alleviates it? "No, not too often; you should know that. Take just an ordinary dude, though, noncreative, he's lost his old lady, and that's all he is, a loser. A writer, though, he uses that loss, like a whore uses, but he can write it an' get a good feeling from that. Maybe not as good as the feeling he got with his old lady, but he's still better off than the guy who can't write at all. Even though he'll always hurt more."

All yesterday, all this afternoon, the yellow telephone on the floor has rung every twenty minutes or so; he points, a finger at it now, as it rings again. "I'd just let the service get it, but I think that's one 'a the band, and I gotta talk to him. 'Cuse me." Rita says from the kitchen door, "We're gonna be eatin' supper pretty soon." It's her way of extending an invitation. Kris says into the phone, "Hey, Donnie," and walks, talking, to the bedroom. Rita comes in and sits, her hands folded placidly on the swollen stomach under her apron. "It's just great," she says of her pregnancy, when asked, "I get some heartburn, but otherwise no morning sickness, nothin'. I can hardly wait! Doctor says it sounds like a boy; there's a test you can take to tell, but I don't want to: Why not be surprised? I don't want any drugs while I'm in labor, the baby can come out drugged if you do. How can mothers go through all the shit of being pregnant and then be doped through the end of the trip?" Rita comes from Tennessee, it turns out, her father was a Baptist preacher. "I started singin' in church when I was two, I've been doin' it ever since, but I never planned on makin' it a career. I sang on weekends to pay my way through college, just so's I could get through art school and teach. But after I graduated, I couldn't find a job, so I started singing to pay for a master's degree. Thought I'd work a year; at the end of it, I was hooked."

She started the year singing radio spots for Pepper-Tanner, "It's Memphis's biggest jingle factory." Her sight-reading got her studio work. "Then Pepper-Tanner signed me to a contract to cut a single, they'd started their own new label. I cut the song, then decided to come to LA— by the time I got here, the song, "Turn Around and Love Me,' had become this surprise hit, they played it all through that summer. I never went back to Memphis." She toured with Joe Cocker, cut an album, played the minor clubs, but of course it was her alliance with Kris that established her name.

"Sure, we've had our falling-outs," she says easily, gesturing toward the bedroom, "we've split up. It's *very* hard, in this business, to stay peaceful—the competition, for one thing. In a way, we're all competin' with each other professionally; we're all accustomed to fightin', bein' stubborn, 'cause you gotta do both to

238

make it in music. And there's the strain of bein' on the road. But we got it together now; I think Kris is a lot more settled. He's got a place t'go every night, some roots, and that's given him a lot more confidence in his music: He's really writin' an playin' well. He used t'let people make all these demands on him, and he's learned to say no. He can blame it on me now; he can say, 'I can't, I gotta take the old lady home.' He used t'be out every night; now we go out maybe once every six months, t'one 'a these Hollywood-type parties, and every time we do, all the way home we're sayin' how glad we were t'leave early. Over the holidays, there was one, up at Robert Altman's house—he and his wife are really fine, but I was talking to a few 'a these big movie people, an' somebody bumped my elbow and I spilled a glass 'a wine on the front of my dress. They *froze*. I turned around t'find something to wipe it with; and when I turned back, everybody had gone, everybody! That, to me, is a Hollywood party."

Her laugh's rich, a good clear arpeggio. I ask about the first time she met Kris, and she laughs again, quietly. "I remember . . . I couldn't get over his face. The colors: that brown hair, the pitch-black beard with those gray hairs in it and those incredible deep-set blue eyes. I didn't wanta keep staring at him, but I couldn't help it. I couldn't get over how *different* he looked. And how good-looking. Then you talk to him, and he's sort of . . . fumbly-warm." She goes to the kitchen, and, after he has come in and sat down again, she sets before us on the long coffee table a substantial meatloaf, light fresh corn and salad. Eating, we speak of the smoking of funny stuff, a proper dinner-table subject as it is of common interest. Kris offers, "I think ladies roll smokes better than guys do."

"Yeh, for the same reason they cook better," Rita says, her black eyes ironically wide, "cause they're the ones who've gotta do it." Kris laughs extensively; when she takes the empty plates away, he watches with canine affection, catches himself being watched. "She's really far out. Did she say how we met? I'd just broke up with this girl, felt really funky; I was in an airport— we're *all always* in airports—on the way to Nashville to do my first interview with *Life* magazine, and her manager recognized me. I was in *no* mood t'deal with anybody, but hell, when people recognize you, you *gotta* deal, it's one 'a the prices you pay. He introduced Rita, she looked . . . well, like she looks: somethin' else. On the plane, they saved a seat for me. There was this thing about her: She *listens*. She was gettin' off in Memphis to work with her band, fixin' t'go on the road, an' I just got off with her, never did do the *Life* interview. My next booking was up in Edmonton, so was hers, 'cept somehow hers got canceled, an' I said, why not go on with me? That's two years ago, we been bookin' out together ever since."

He didn't exactly divorce his first wife, he adds, until just last summer. "Fran and I are friends, I see the kids whenever I can. She was really fine about the settlement, she coulda asked for half 'a everything I got, which is I-don't-know-how-much. Yeh, a lot," and he grimaces, "but you gotta remember, for years there I didn't make shit and didn't even know it! Down there in Peru, Dennis paid me expenses and a little salary and I thought, *Wow, this is as good as it gets!* I told that to my piano player, Donnie Frits—he was in Durango with me, he did a bit part in *Pat Garrett and Billy the Kid*—an' he said, 'Kris, it just keeps on gettin' better!' A year ago, I didn't know who Sam Peckinpah was and this New Year's I'm goin' to his house!"

Until now, he's barely referred to his movies, and one hasn't pressed, sensing that this new crown rests heavily. Now one offers that on screen, especially in *Blume in Love*, he projects a strong, old-fashioned blend of sexuality and niceness, rather as Gable did; that Gable was so referred because his sexuality was good-humored, it didn't challenge other males; that those of either sex who wished to ball him trusted him as well; that the Kristofferson presence is similar. He listens, understandably alarmed, and grins, Gable-like. "Hell, thank you. But I just fell into the acting. Down in Peru I thought I'd like to learn to *direct* a movie, but acting? It didn't interest me then, and I sure as hell ain't no Laurence Olivier now, nor will I be. Jesus, these guys who really study for it, they must figure, who the fuck is this, some shot-kicker they hauled off the Troubadour stage. . . ."

It was about that simple: After his big Troubadour debut, myriad agents and managers called and he was, abruptly, on lots of guest lists. At a party at Jack Nicholson's, Fred Roos, the young casting director of *Five Easy Pieces*, asked if he'd like to audition for *Two Lane Blacktop*. "I was stoned that night, I said, 'Sure,' and the next day all I could remember was, I had this appoint-

240

ment at Columbia, only I thought it was Columbia Records. Got to the office, I was *wasted*, it was right outa a Kafka novel. The guy said did I know anything about cars—*Two Lane Blacktop* was about cars, only nobody told me that—I said, 'Can't even change a tire,' and got up and left." He didn't get the part, but they offered him *Cisco Pike* anyway. "I'd never even been in no school play, but I read the script and I could identify with this cat, this dope dealer. People said, 'Don't do it, take acting lessons first! But it seemed t'me that acting must be just understanding a character, and then being just as honest as you can possibly be. I shoulda been scared, but then I shoulda been scared the first time on that Troubadour stage and I wasn't. *Cisco Pike* wasn't all that good, but it led me to *Billy the Kid.* . . ."

Peckinpah's machismo, his romance with the rugged and rough-hewn had always attracted Kris, and he'd jumped at the chance to play Billy, but now the subject of the movie visibly unsettles him. It was, as he puts it, no day at the beach; apparently, Peckinpah's Durango was almost as schizophrenic as Hopper's Peru. Not only that, but it was Kris who talked Dylan into his acting debut. "I called him; he said, 'But if I do it, then they *got* me, on *film*.' I said, 'Hell, Bobby, they already got you on records, come on, we'll have a ball.' We didn't, but I think Bobby, at least, came off pretty good in the picture. I *don't* want t'give you the impression I'm one of Bobby's best friends, that I know him all that well. Hell, *nobody* knows Bobby that well. He's . . . a dozen different people. A genius, I guess. I sure know he digs pickin'. . . ."

Unexpectedly, he's restless, as if suddenly too aware of being interviewed, and gets up to wander around the room, cracking his knuckles. Quick, Kris, before we lose you: Did the role in *Blume in Love* look as good on paper as it turned out to be? Frown. "I can't read a script that way, just for my part, I've got to dig the whole story. Jesus, I see these actors come in with just their lines learned, like it was a union dig, they don't care shit for the rest of it, that's *gotta* be wrong. *Blume in Love* seemed t'me like it had lotsa levels, lotsa colors; Paul Mazursky, the director, he told me to just be natural, be myself, which I think is a good way 'a directing me—he even had me wear my own

241

clothes, y'know? Except in this new one I'm gonna make in Tucson. Name of it's *Alice Doesn't Live Here Anymore*. This young dude who's directing it, Martin Scorsese, wants me to do some *real* acting, if I gotta play a sort of tough, self-made complex man. Oh, I had t'do some acting in *Blume in Love*, as it turned out: Rita and I had split, I was up all night wonderin' about her, and I was supposed to be this cool dude who don't give a damn! I used to be like that, but no more. I mean, now I got . . . responsibilities."

The rubbery, urban word is awkward in his mouth. When troubled, he tends to hunch forward and growl sotto voce as if through smoked ham. "Aw, shit, I guess I got no complaints. It's just, you get to this point, you become so fucking *vulnerable*." Earlier he's remarked that even if we'd been sitting here all afternoon blowing dope, he'd no longer want that kind of thing printed about himself, so one assumes he means that sort of vulnerability—most celebrities believe that narcotics officers doggedly scan everything from *Atlantic Monthly* to *Crawdaddy*, for clues—but no. "No, I mean, I've now seen all these famous actors and big rock people bein' so paranoid 'a the slightest competition, an' heard 'em bitch endlessly about payin' big taxes and havin' to sign autographs. Well, I think you got a responsibility to *not* be that way. I'll tell y'when I felt put-upon: when I was a janitor. Hell, I can rent a car now, I can go wherever I want on this earth, I send all my kids to college on just a few songs. Two years ago a Vegas hotel said, *maybe* they'd hire me if I'd get into some schmucky rock-star costume; now they want me anytime on my terms; and you can*not* tell me I'm in worse shape 'cause I got big taxes and responsibilities." Grin, and he shakes his head comically. "I *do* feel like a shithead signin' autographs, they always ask when you're hurryin' to a plane carryin' three bags and a guitar, but if you don't sign, you feel like *more* of a shithead. . . ."

Rita's come in to listen; he's late for his recording session now, but clearly he wants to keep on. As he studies his hands, it occurs to you that they're good, but not young. Uncannily, as he does, he completes your unspoken sentence. "Shit, I already feel old: Time presses. Well, I'm thirty-seven. Old friends call you and you don't have time for 'em no more 'cause you got this plane to catch and that accountant to meet, and you end up see-in' alotta people you don't give shit for. I just got this long letter from Johnny Cash, which he wrote 'cause we ain't *talked* in two years. People who wouldn't walk across the street to shake your hand before, they run up and nail you; you *gotta* become selfish. They come backstage everywhere, with songs, could I listen for five minutes? Jesus, I just been performing, I'm wast-ed, I ask 'em for a tape to take home. 'But it's only two songs!' An' it's the only two the guy's ever written, and they're awful, and you shouldn't give him false hope. But if you don't lis-ten . . . you can miss some good shit, I first heard John Prine that way. I said nicely t' this one guy, 'Well, there's all these songwriters in Nashville, you could go hang out with 'em and learn.' He grabbed me and shouted, 'Learn! Just how many song hits *you* had?'"

Huge laugh. "You *gotta* laugh, or it'd get you. It's just that *all* of it's started to take me too far away from what I really am: a writer. For instance, this acting, I dunno. I told Peckinpah, I think the first thing you need to be a good actor is a prefontal lobotomy. You *can't* question your own importance. In no way am I gonna let acting take me away from the music business, and *if* I go on doing it, I want it to be for directors like Peckin-pah or Paul Mazursky—except nobody can go on bein' that lucky. I got alotta scripts, yeh, after *Blume*, but I'm always on the road, and I don't think I *hear* about the good movies till it's too late. Maybe you gotta hang out with the people who make 'em."

One thought he'd started doing that, having noted his pres-ence at the Reynolds Wrap Byzantium known as the Cannes Film Festival, and in Hollywood on outings with Streisand. He's not amused. "Well, *you* oughta know, that's the bullshit printed in papers." He did take Rita to Cannes—purposely, he pro-nounces the *s*—because the *Blume in Love* people invited him and paid the way, and they'd never seen the Riviera. "We even went to a couple 'a those movie-star parties there. It was comi-cal."

"Comical," Rita adds, and they laugh, looking at each other.

"And Barbra—that was embarrassin', in print, I really looked like Kristofferson, star-fucker, and all that happened was her manager brought her backstage at the Troubadour to meet me, and we talked, got along good, so we got together a few times after that. One night we went on a double date with this big agent. It was just to a movie, but when we got to the theater, the agent charged outa the car and up to the manager, shoutin' 'Streisand's here! I don't want any fuss, just give us tickets!' A regular drill sergeant. But Barbra struck me as too intelligent to surround herself with people she doesn't at least trust—because it's *gotta* cross her mind that everybody's out t'sccrew her. I'll tell ya, it crosses mine."

This thought, crossing, gets him smartly to his feet, and we're off with guitar down the hill to record. His driving is workmanlike, without relish. "That girl, from Avis . . . see, now you got me wonderin', did she know me, or didn't she, damn!" He doesn't turn on the radio. When I ask, gingerly, who he thinks "You're So Vain" is about, he is seen, by the dash-lights, to grin. "I heard it was about Warren Beatty." Apparently he was ready for the question. "I sure don't think it's me, I never had a Lear jet or went to Nova Scotia. I like Carly, and James, man, he was *everybody's* darling until he got on the cover of *Time*, when they all wrote he was an Establishment tool, corrupted by the industry. . . . Jesus, *I* don't see all this corruption, rock stars getting free dope, I never even got a *joint* from anybody free. Maybe you gotta ask. When I do a concert, there's some Cokes and beers and maybe a bottle backstage; shit, I'm glad to have that, I remember when I had t'bring my own." At Santa Monica Boulevard, he points: "See that corner, that's where I got busted. During my first Troubadour gig, I was making a turn late at night and a cop stopped me 'cause he thought he'd busted me before. I had this little bottle of Binaca. He said, 'What's that?'; I said, 'Oh, I shoot up Binaca.' Bang, hands behind me, handcuffs, and I spent the night in jail. Next day the cop apologized—turned out he'd recognized me from TV."

While he parks, I repeat something told to me that morning by a Warner's publicist: that in Cannes Kris had taken the time, though late for his plane, to return the car provided for him to the publicist's hotel, and to leave a thank-you note on the front seat. "A movie star did that!" the publicist had whispered, as if describing Kohoutek. Kris considers this as he kills the engine. "Hmm. Well, it can't be that big a deal. You mean in movies, nobody ever says thanks for anythin'?"

Soft pastel spots are the only lights in the little recording studio. Through the glass of the control booth, it seems an opulent rosy tank in which fluid magnifies sound, an aquarium of musicians for an underwater ballet; Kris's backup band, four tranquil, clear-eyed country or mountain boys with faces like old pictures of rebel soldiers, cease tuning up, cheerfully deferring to his arrival. "Hey, man!" etcetera. While they practice and retune, Kris sends out for a Tia Maria fifth and wanders smiling around the control room, a Bull Durham now permanently attached to his lower lip. Through the bullet-colored velvet of smoke, he consults his sound engineer. ". . . yeh, I could see puttin' a rhythm or a twelve on it, then goin' out there with the vocals, that'd be nice." Clearly, here, in this ambience, he is less somnambulistic, more vital and concentrated. In a month, one will visit, by chance, the Tucson location shooting of *Alice Doesn't Live Here Anymore*, and observe, with surprise, a Kristofferson too determinedly vital, too concentrated on nurturing, off-camera, a public self, which emerges hard-edged, metallic, because he's too smart not to suspect himself for nurturing a public self in the first place. But here, in this ambience, where he is not yet treated as a movie star, he is still tranquil. "Well, hell, let's cut this turkey," he finally announces, exiting into the tiny solist's booth, the pink tank-within-the-tank. Enclosed behind glass, he begins a new lyric, quite believable, about a lonely musician.

20.

Geraldo Saves

SOMETHING is wrong. He is demonstrably intelligent, conspicuously honest, scrupulously benevolent, and something is wrong, something in his aura is minutely, perilously tilted off axis, but what? It is arcane, independent of his private, and especially his public, presence, which is impressive: Geraldo Rivera has never made a movie, yet no movie star has ever collected so emotional a following. In New York he is already beyond legend: when he walks a Manhattan street, it is as if George M. Cohan had really been Puerto Rican and the statue of him in Times Square had been given life: Cabdrivers pull over to him when he has not hailed them, hoods, pushers, matrons with Korvettes bags, all manner of devious types mellow at the sight of him. At stoplights, their dilemmas are ceaselessly aired; he untangles these Gordian knots patiently, by hand, missing several WALK signs. Who has been so extensively loved and remained so accessible to his lovers, with the possible exception of Mayor Jimmy Walker? But something's wrong.

This is not it, but we begin badly, in the summer of '73, a taut start to a year of meetings. On the phone, the voice is unmistakable, the sibilant second tenor of ABC's *Eyewitness News (Good Night America,* his own nighttime ninety minutes with which ABC intends him to replace the diminishing Dick Cavett, is not yet quite a reality). "I don't want to do those anymore," he has said, not rudely: One has requested an interview. Okay, let's forget it. *"But . . .* we could meet, I might be interested. If you're serious." Oh? "If you want to examine me seriously. Everything that's written, it reads like I go around all day kissing girls' nipples."

Weird: Except for one brief, silly bit about him at the back of *New York* magazine, his press has been, if not enlightening, generally respectful and awed. Only a few writers have ever observed him at, or rather under, the ABC news building on West Sixty-sixth Street, penetrated his old offices, actually a bustling, partitioned basement cluttered with letters from well-wishers and supplicators, pictures of Geraldo, candy bars, empty Coke cans and deli bags, all manner of other memorabilia, and usually, it turns out, with half a dozen supporting players. This day, though, he waits alone, feet on his piled desk. You are instantly struck by the presence: the familiar black Charlemagne hair, the ginger mustache, the sense of cleanness, as though he showered hourly. The clothes are those in which he broadcasts, twenty-dollar faded jeans, whimsical shirts that cost much more, denim high-heel shoes. Often he is seen in his T-shirt imprinted WORKING CLASS HERO, but not today.

Stronger than the presence is the feeling of accessibility: A moment of trivial exchange and you bluntly ask about the rumor—no, accepted fact—that, for starters, he intends to be New York's first Puerto Rican mayor; his manner encourages such directness, though not his answer. "I have, um, *no* political ambitions that are totally defined, that's that, man." Such statements he delivers in selected italics. "The problem is, no one in media can comprehend my ambitions, they just can't, *won't* conceive, anymore, of somebody working hard *not* for themselves, somebody just wanting *to do good.* God. Cynical times. Look, *New York* magazine, *The Village Voice,* or, yes, *Esquire* are run by smart-ass cynics who do *not* reflect the community, who are *not the people.* They can't damage my credibility, though, because the vast majority of *the people* they believe in me." He is gesturing gently, perpetually, with his right hand, as he does on the news. "Let's assume that I'm using my position to become an elected politician. *So what?* It's pretty clear, isn't it, from what I've already done publicly, who I would defend, who I'd fight? That I'd be a strong radical-liberal, is that *bad?* That I have never done *any* of this for personal gain? That I happen to know powerful politicians and beautiful stars socially, but from seven A.M. till sometimes midnight I work my ass off? These smart cynics, man, what would they *have* me be?"

Finis, for now: He becomes restless talking about himself, or listening, for more than five minutes. Today he is saved by his schedule, and abruptly we are outside in his pastel VW convertible with its New York press plates ("Bill Beutel gets parking privileges in a garage. I've never asked") bouncing above the speed limit south to Manhattan's hellhole jail, The Tombs; Abbie Hoffman has been arrested for cocaine possession, his bail is $202,000. "I'm *not* an Abbie Hoffman supporter, no way," Geraldo asserts shrilly over the traffic, running a red light, "but bail for that charge I *know* is always much less; they're victimizing him." Behind us, the camera crew's car is trying to keep pace, without success. (It is unnecessary to ask him how his network feels about these little sorties into potentially controversial territory; they make ABC highly nervous, but he's given free rein because, if ordered to cover too many fashion shows, he could be lost to another channel, and it's his presence and controversialism that account for *Eyewitness News'* high Nielsens, not the program's tittering, Orpheum-Circuit ambience.)

Downtown he parks illegally on the curb by the prison, and moves confidently, with the expression of pleasant alertness he always wears in public, past a group of blacks grinning and nodding at him on the jail steps, inside to demand an interview with Abbie. The officer in charge stammers; few celebrities visit The Tombs. Unfortunately, regulations state the prisoner will have to be asked if he wants to be on TV. "I'll be back," Geraldo warns politely, and races, literally, on foot, to the courtrooms where bail records are kept. He is right: Bails in similar cases have been a fraction of Abbie's. Tight-lipped, he strides to the jail to find a note from the prisoner: A TV interview, Abbie feels, would be "unfair to the other prisoners." The note is crumpled without comment. It's nearly visiting hour, and outside a long line waits for entrance. At its end, Mrs. Abbie Hoffman, a slim, worried brunette, readily agrees to talk, and Geraldo's camera and sound men, idling at the curb, move in. Wet-eyed, Mrs. Hoffman asserts that the charge is of course unfair and so is the bail and since Abbie has given away every cent to further the Revolution, she urges his friends everywhere to send bail money. Geraldo's impatience, or boredom, is not evident on camera; the film is given to a yawning motorcycle courier to be rushed back to ABC for editing and the evening news. Geraldo drives even faster back uptown, remarking testily, "See, so many of these stories you go out on, they're nothing, they have no real *meaning.*" An Elton John concert, for example—hysterical fans behind police barriers, Elton murmuring genially into Geraldo's hand mike—or the Hell's Angels' boat ride up the Hudson, or the transgressions of oil companies, which everybody else covered too. "But listen, I'm supposed to be reporting on *something,* and you just don't happen on a Willowbrook every week. . . ."

It was Willowbrook that made him famous, of course, so famous that Random House published a book he wrote about it. When it happened, early in 1972, he'd been at ABC a year and a half and, except for a brief bit about drug addiction in East Harlem, had mostly covered fashion shows and similar "meaningless" events. He begins *Willowbrook: A Report on How It Is and Why It Doesn't Have to Be That Way* with: "Being a television reporter in New York is like being a builder of snowmen. . . . A tremendous amount of time and energy is spent filming and putting together a story. The piece flashes onto several million TV screens. Then, like the melting snowman . . . it is gone. And whether the story was meaningful . . . life in the Big Town goes on. Because it is so hard to change the world, I have to settle for more mundane satisfactions such as money, fan mail, and awards. Of the three, winning awards is most important because it means prestige, credibility and above all, the freedom to pick and choose assignments. Without this freedom, a newsman remains faceless . . . with it, a newsman acquires an identity he can control and build upon."

No, the tone of this is not meant to sound satirical, however it may read: He is deadly serious. The day, he explains, is Wednesday, January 5; he is at home, which was then Avenue C, the grim Lower East Side; he'd just reported an old man who lived in his car because urban renewal had demolished his tenement. As the snowmen melted, he received a call from a radical young doctor, Michael Wilkins, whom he'd met two years before when he was still a storefront lawyer. Dr. Wilkins told him that he'd just been fired from Willowbrook State School, a local home for the mentally retarded, because he'd been trying to improve the vile facility. Would *Eyewitness News,* meaning Geraldo, do a story?

It did not instantly strike Geraldo as his sort of hot item; he said he'd think about it. ABC wasn't enthusiastic either, which sparked Geraldo's enthusiasm; he called Wilkins that day to say yes, and the doctor said that Willowbrook's buildings were all locked, but he had a master key. "In the building where I worked," he added, "most of the kids are naked and they lie in their own shit." That very afternoon, Geraldo and his film crew met Wilkins at a diner near the institution, and together they drove without obstruction to the side door of Wilkins' former building, number six. "Mike opened the outer door," the book states, not mentioning a key; no one was in sight to stop them. Things inside were actually worse than the doctor had intimated: One child was drinking leisurely from a filthy toilet bowl. For five minutes the crew filmed, and they all left. Back at the diner, a motorcycle courier was waiting.

Even before he reached the station, according to Geraldo, everybody'd heard they'd got a "dynamite" story, and that night *Eyewitness News* gave Willowbrook seven minutes rather than the average two-and-a-half maximum. In the next twenty-four hours, the station received almost a thousand calls about it— that many people don't bother calling a TV station that fast about some local news item—and Geraldo, literally overnight, advanced from what one of his staff calls "ABC's resident spik" to celebrity status. But at Willowbrook, he still asserts, he cried, because the place had finally defined for him his purpose. It had also defined for both him and his network what such a story could do for a so-far obscure reporter. The next night he was permitted to do the first Willowbrook follow-up, a rerun of the footage shown the previous evening, a report of all the phone calls, and Geraldo's slightly histrionic conclusion. "We're not going to let this story die," he assured viewers somewhat tearfully. "We're going back to Willowbrook . . . again. And look at these horrible wards . . . again. And show them to you . . . again and again and again. Until somebody changes them."

After the show, he writes, he cried. Again. Willowbrook had become his idée fixe. In all, he reported from there a dozen times, and though ABC became tired of running his *Marat-Sade* material every night at dinnertime, Geraldo insisted and they did not balk. After all, everybody was watching. Parents of the retarded began rallying noisily at the hospital, confronting the perpetually silent Dr. Jack Hammond, Willowbrook's director;

great bundles of clothing were sent by ABC watchers. Hammond did publicly allow that if Willowbrook were to be improved, the state must stop slashing the Department of Mental Health budget; Geraldo flew to Albany to confront, with his cameraman, the entire state legislature, which led Governor Rockefeller to channel another twenty million into retarded care. "Willowbrook will now be able to hire three hundred new employees," Geraldo reported grimly, "or about six hundred less than it needs."

"At a party back then," he says now over a Ginger Man hamburger gobbled minutes before his entrance on the evening news, "Senator Javits came up to me and asked why, since other stations had started reporting Willowbrook, Channel Seven was getting all the credit? I said, because of me; that I was first, that I *refused* to give New York State credit for doing *anything* right because the good it did was *nothing* compared to the bad. He said wasn't I taking too much power into my own hands? I told him I was better qualified to decide right and wrong than a lot of the sons of bitches, including politicians, with vested interests, and as for giving anybody equal time, I wouldn't. I quoted Edward R. Murrow. 'Some stories don't have another side.' "

His side and his face were spread across the country, during '72, via *Life* and *Newsweek,* which covered not Willowbrook but Geraldo covering Willowbrook; everybody everywhere talked about him; for whatever motive, he kept the issue open, long after he, not the institution, had become the issue. ABC rushed together a big special titled *Willowbrook: The Last Great Disgrace,* starring Geraldo. Awards poured in, Dick Cavett gave him and mental retardation a whole ninety minutes. The Javitses had him to dinner, George Plimpton had him to parties, Elaine cleared tables for him, never again would he be stymied seeking a cab in a snowstorm—all of which he found amusing, but irrelevant. Noting that ABC's news-building basement was unused, he asked if he could have an office down there; suddenly the network found the area crowded not so much with Geraldo as with a network-paid staff already busy on phones recruiting volunteers for a project Geraldo had devised and named "One-to-One." That was what institutionalized retarded people lacked, he had deduced, one-to-one care, some notion of what a

252

human relationship might be. By summer it was set: One-to-One day, during which thousands of the mentally deficient were bused into Central Park; every one of them was met by a normal volunteer, games were played, as best they could be. That night, Geraldo took over Madison Square Garden for a benefit concert by John Lennon and Yoko, Roberta Flack, Stevie Wonder and Sha-Na-Na. Tickets weren't cheap; nearly half a million dollars was raised. Each year since, the park event has become more ambitious; the last concert starred John Denver, Judy Collins, Peter, Paul and Mary, Richie Havens, Kris Kristofferson and Sly Stone. The staff does the rudimentary telephoning, then Geraldo takes the receiver. "Hi, John, this is Geraldo Rivera." Pause. "I want to ask a favor, man. . . ."

In such situations, he is very verbal; in his cave under ABC, he is actually not. The talking is done by the staff, while he covers assignments, or sits about, abstracted, trying to think of some new story with the relevance of Willowbrook. In an adjoining room, a dozen teen-age girls, volunteers who come in after school, are folding One-to-One things into envelopes, or addressing dozens of cards with a picture of Geraldo on the front and a printed message on the back:

I hope you won't mind this brief note—my schedule is so busy these days . . . I deeply appreciate all your warm wishes. It's so encouraging to learn that there are friends behind my work . . . especially when the world is not particularly optimistic. But working together, I'm sure we can help to make life a little brighter for so many who need our strength. . . . Love and Peace.

Working, the little volunteer girls prattle incessantly, giggling; when he passes through their room, they instantly fall silent, as if some wire connecting them had shorted, and twenty-four amazed eyes attempt to meet his. He will nod, half smiling, in their direction.

It's no longer because of Channel 7 activities alone that the world writes Geraldo: To ABC's further disgruntlement, he volunteered to conduct a continuing program on public Channel 13 called *Help* (advertised with subway placards with his picture), during which he referred the troubled to Legal Aid or a similar agency, and it was local Channel 9 which got all the publicity when he used it for two One-to-One telethons, the last of which raised, in its brief seven hours, an incredible $650,000 (as compared to, say, Easter Seals, which in twenty hours on TV raised half that sum). Out in the vast glumness of the five boroughs, and beyond, they are clearly no longer intrigued by his celebrity, or legend, or even his early-projected sexuality (he is now, on camera, purposefully asexual, in the classic manner of ascetics, or heroes). He has become their savior, and it is the same with his office staff. Its five mature, permanent members, when questioned privately, speak of him with amazing similarity, but then they are themselves amazingly similar, former teachers, journalists, social workers who found their professions disillusioning as they, too, wished to alter the world fast. They came to him, he didn't seek them out. Two have been with him ever since One-to-One's inception and don't want to leave. Though unshakably serious when speaking of him, they tend toward high animation outside the office, as when we all go to lunch near the news building. In restaurants with groups, Geraldo tends automatically to sit at the head of the table or the center of the booth, as if this spot was reserved by tacit agreement: His associates surround him, chattering, interrupting one another good-humoredly. Half smiling, half listening, he examines distant, invisible horizons, though he clearly enjoys their presence, requires it. He is never alone by design, and dislikes being so. When addressed directly, he half turns. "I was in a restaurant the other night," one of the female assistants informs him abruptly, "and there were these three jock types near me and they were discussing you. They said, 'That Geraldo, he looks like he swings both ways sexually, maybe more the *other* way.' I got up and stepped over and said, 'Uh, excuse me, gentlemen, but I happen to know Geraldo Rivera and what you're saying is definitely inaccurate.'" Nodding, smiling, Geraldo offers, "Must have been that thing two summers ago, when the Sixth Police Precinct challenged the Mattachine Society to a baseball game, and both teams asked me to pitch. They both figured I was halfway between the police and the gay activists." Pause; when he laughs, it strikes you how rarely he does. "I think I said once publicly that I had this sort of dream, to have been like a ballet star, Balanchine's principal dancer, like that, I guess that didn't help either. What the hell, my feeling is, let them perpetuate any myths they want to, you know? I *do* have the worst voice on television."

Implicit in his confidence here is his conviction that he is somehow untouchable. "Gossip can't really hurt me, neither can the press. My life's been threatened more times than . . . like, when I report drug things, the big syndicate pushers call to tell me I've got an hour to live, but I'm here. I have this strange *belief* that I cannot really be harmed." At least not seriously, he adds. Back in the office after lunch, limping a bit, he mentions a sore knee from a rough touch-football game. Immediately, the whole staff (though not the volunteer girls, who aren't encouraged to enter the main office) kneels, directing that he roll up his pant leg. An Ace bandage is magically produced, sixteen hands alternately administer to him. During this, he frowns ceilingward. "God, last night, I was limping up my stairs and it hit me: I've *got* to do something about the *physically* handicapped. Jeez, the trouble it must be to climb *one* step." But the idea seems somehow to depress him.

Alone with him again in his partitioned space, one attempts to trace the source of his obsessiveness. Asked to describe his past, he looks even glummer and begins a familiar litany: born thirty-one years ago in a place most people never see, the Williamsburg section of Brooklyn. "My dad's Puerto Rican, my mom's Jewish. They met in a cafeteria where he washed dishes and she tended counter. Her folks were so appalled at the idea of a Puerto Rican son-in-law, they died soon after the marriage, literally of shame." Memories of grade school are vague: He was a poor student, and besides, when he was a teen-ager his family moved out to the humbler part of Babylon, Long Island, where his father worked in the kitchen of Republic Aviation. "My folks are still out there; Mom's got all my awards, about a hundred of them, on one wall. But my father, God, what was done to him *still* pisses me off: the racist bastards he had to work for. He was valedictorian of his high-school class in Puerto Rico, and the best job he ever got here was in a kitchen. My only other strong memory is of my Bar Mitzvah. All my Puerto Rican cousins came, they kept taking off the yarmulkes and putting them over their hearts. . . ."

Emerging from high school directionless, he accomplished, with astounding speed, study at the Bronx Maritime College, service in the Merchant Marine, the selling of clothing on both coasts ("I *seriously* intended to become an industry baron") and a degree from the University of Arizona. "It was the only school that'd take me. *What a screw-up.* I wore madras shorts and used a different name—no, *never* Jerry Rivers, where do these things *start?* Jeez. I mean, the 'Jerry,' they call me that around here for short, you've heard them, I don't ask for it, I *don't* 'use' it. This is important, I want it clear: It does say 'Riv-i-era' on, like, my school enrollments, because my mother thought it sounded more, oh, European, and when I left home my father said, 'Use the spelling, be Italian, Spanish, *anything* but Puerto Rican.' In Arizona I was officially Gerald Riv-i-era, which *sickens* me now! God, the *most* shameful thing I have ever done! I was old enough to make a choice! Jesus, I don't even want to talk about it."

College did provide an Army deferment ("I thought, 'If I get sent to Vietnam, I'll never be *anybody*'"). By graduation, his social consciousness had materialized, and he hurried back east, bound for Africa to aid the starving, only to be apprehended by the FBI because he'd neglected to tell the draft board his whereabouts. "But they still wanted to draft me, that's why I entered Brooklyn Law School, another deferment." To his surprise, he enjoyed law, his grades were excellent, he used his real name, "and got treated for the first time as a Puerto Rican person, got recognized ethnically, it was terrific. Lived in this hovel on Avenue C, thirty-three dollars a month, got involved in block associations, as soon as I got my diploma I started representing neighbors in court. I'd say, 'Your Honor, I know Jose Garcia's turf because I live there, can you blame him for stealing a typewriter? At least he's kicked hard drugs.' And it *worked!*" The Young Lords, a Puerto Rican street gang who'd progressed from mugging to organizing slum day-care centers and raising New York's Puerto Rican ethnic consciousness, were then heavily publicized, and Geraldo became their attorney. For the first time he was publicized himself, but was not content. "It wasn't challenging enough, I knew the gang thing, I'd established one when I was a kid, The Corner Boys; but the whole storefront lawyer bit, I realized I couldn't change the world defending gangs and poverty cases. Besides, all I ever earned in law was maybe three months' rent."

Through his Young Lords connection he met CBS newswoman Gloria Rojas, then the only Puerto Rican on big-time TV news; she told Geraldo she'd heard ABC was looking for one, too. Without even auditioning him, the network sent him to Columbia's Graduate School of Journalism, and in September, 1970, he quietly debuted on *Eyewitness News.* Not realizing what they had hired, ABC assigned him to the coverage of society parties. In five months, at one of these, he met Edith Vonnegut, Kurt Vonnegut Jr.'s daughter, whom Geraldo calls "Pie." They moved in together that night, and in ten months or so decided to get married.

Relating this, he is markedly bored: One hand explores the opulent rings on the fingers of the other, a wall clock is consulted. Curious, that a man so clearly self-cherishing so dislikes discussing himself in any terms except, what? His goals, which he abruptly reverts to. "I dunno, they want me to try *Good Night America* on a regular basis. I did a couple of shows called that for their 'Wide World of Entertainment' spot, eleven-thirty at night till one, a sort of young, very aware, hip video magazine, a *serious* talk show. I want to *educate* them, about draft-dodger amnesty, Harlem, urban poverty, our inhumane drug laws, victimless crimes like homosexuality, VD, the shopping-bag ladies—homeless old women you see on the street with their *life* in a shopping bag. They've got to be *helped,* and I can make America *aware* of them. But to do it, I first have to change television." A depressed sigh, then he pounds, or slaps, his desk. "Okay, good! That is going to be *Good Night America*'s mission!"

One leaves him as vaguely depressed, or mystified, as he has seemed. *What is wrong?* What is so sharply unsettling about his Zhivagoesque missions and goals? For the present, there is no answer, except this: that his ambience is depressing if you are not of it; that if you are not demonstrably committed to "change," if you are not, in plainest terms, a doer of good, then you don't belong near him, there is directed toward you the faintest, most subtle disapproval, as vague as the shadows cast by the basement's ceiling fluorescents, but discernible. The

257

sense of tilt persists, like the tiny, multiple discrepancies in Shirley Jackson's Hill House, where every angle of every room varies minutely from every other angle, to create finally an enormous, pervasive distortion.

You rather doubt that meeting his wife will clarify much, but she cheerfully agrees to it, if one doesn't mind waiting until late: Geraldo has said that she's a gifted artist and also works as assistant to fashion designer Giorgio di Sant'Angelo, and he's currently preparing a fashion show. She hops from a cab in front of their West Village brownstone one late autumn evening—they stayed on Avenue C their first year together, and are moving again, uptown to a high rise near ABC—and hurries, smiling, resplendent in the wet night, up the hallway stairs. She is delicate, exquisite, Lee Remick at twenty-five; watching her dart around their home, you think of a word now anachronistic except in the writings of Eugenia Sheppard: vivacious. The apartment is a tiny duplex, at least their bedroom is up a narrow stairway; the slanting ceiling over the bed is covered with one of her works, a funny, touching cartoon portrait of her and her husband, both with feathery wings, floating whimsically nude through cumulus cloud banks. The drawings on the downstairs walls are startling, mothers with bird wings, infants with piglet ears. They are impossible to ignore, but so is she. When Geraldo is mentioned, she says, "He . . . changes. Very changeable. We met when I'd been in New York one day, after two years in the West Indies where my brother has a goat farm. My father took me to this bizarre party, and there was Geraldo. I knew no one, I'd grown up on Cape Cod, knew *nothing.* I didn't know where Avenue C was; I was the one who finally said let's move, Avenue C is *highly* scary!"

The laugh is a continuum, like punctuation. "I don't think Geraldo's complicated about his work, or mysterious: He wants to save the world, it is that simple. His projects are . . . lovely. I'm glad there *is* somebody to do them. I don't get involved with them because I have my own life." Abruptly, her slightly nasal, antic voice is earnest. "See, I'm just not dependent. We understood each other immediately: he can't paint but he loves my painting, I'm no good in front of crowds or being a big powerful star, so it works *very* well. I wouldn't ever work for him, I never go to his office. The, uh, people that hang around there," and she laughs, knowing you know she means the girls, "he doesn't want me to know them, it's good that I don't. If I worried over every girl who fawns on Geraldo, I wouldn't get any sleep."

Something passes behind her eyes, a question, as if she suspected this was not what you wanted to hear. "Some of the things written about Geraldo, they disturb me: It's so easy to see him on an enormous ego trip, it's *truly* not just that. Some moods he's in, sure, he can seem a maniac. He does worry incessantly about the *next* thing in his life; I think he will never be satisfied. His philosophy, to do good, it's so he won't feel bad when he dies. He sees himself dying young, did he tell you? He and Kurt have these great debates, about . . . life."

She says nothing of her father's writing, perhaps because Geraldo has unexpectedly entered, talking. At home he smiles easily. Pie asks if he's eaten. "Yeah, a rotten chicken sandwich off a lunch wagon, I'm hungry." He calls a Village restaurant. "Hi, this is Geraldo Rivera. Could I come for dinner with some people? Oh, you are? Thank you anyway, I appreciate it." Hanging up he explains, "Shit, they're really booked. So much for stardom."

"Luchow's?" Pie suggests.

"I dunno. It's too Teutonic there." He is not joking.

"A *little* Teutonic doesn't hurt."

"I don't like even a little. Let's go to Max's."

"Jeez-Louise," Pie remarks satirically.

He has been anxious to show off one of the new retarded homes that One-to-One has established around New York—there are half a dozen now, many more planned. The home is in the Chelsea district of Manhattan. ". . . You'll see," he says, "that *this* is what it *ought* to be, *going* to be, for every handicapped person!" The converted brownstone is tidier, outside, than the mud-colored structures pressing its sides; within there's a pleasant, well-appointed lounging/dining room where the thirty-odd residents are just finishing dinner. They greet Geraldo shyly, with infinite wonder; several women and young men instantly suspend their meal at his entrance. They appear, for a moment, to be like any well-groomed, casually dressed supper party—but they appear to be dining on, what? A listing ship. Except for the three social workers who supervise the premises, no one quite moves or coordinates normally, no one is quite the correct . . . shape. Their demeanors are unsure yet exaggerated, their smiles and speech curious. Idiotically, sadly, one is frightened; Geraldo makes introductions. "Jane, Richard, Irwin, this is my friend. . . ." Their timidity and delight are overwhelming as they attempt to shake hands. The supervisors offer a tour of the building. "No," Geraldo says, "let Irwin show him around," and one follows a short, thirtyish man with the peculiar eyes, the smile, upstairs to view three floors of rooms with baths which are Spartan but freshly painted and scrubbed. On bedside tables are their possessions, objects a child of ten might prize. "I made this," Irwin explains laboriously, holding out a small, oddly shaped ceramic.."The teacher said it was good." One praises it; he stares, his eyes unbearable with the knowledge of his abnormality.

Downstairs, about to leave, Geraldo asks Irwin about his new job, sweeping up in a hamburger house. "And he's got a girl friend now, too, don't you, Irwin? They took a ride on the Staten Island ferry, didn't you?" The man, or boy, blushes, but grins and nods with surprising conviction.

In the cab, we say little; back beneath ABC, he explains that a retarded IQ may be zero; that zero to thirty isn't much better than zero; that the home's residents' IQ's are between thirty and sixty, or that of a very young child; that they won't get better. "But they can live reasonably normal lives, they can work in, like, maintenance; ABC has used them. Legally, they can still be paid subminimal wages, and I'm going to change that. Equal pay for equal work!"

One barely listens. Suddenly it's obvious: His ultimate goal, his mission accomplished, is really *Irwin's girl friend.* You interrupt him with those three words, and he stares, not pleased. "Yeah? What about her? Don't the retarded have as much right to fool around as you and me?"

No, decidedly not. He stares again. It's clear, even to a layman, that parents with IQ's of sixty aren't remotely prepared to raise offspring, assuming their *children* are normal; many geneticists are convinced retardation's hereditary. He speaks evenly, his eyes are grim. "*Wrong.* Most of it's not hereditary.

And most retarded couples don't have children. In that house you saw, most of the women are told about birth control." They're expected to remember when to take a pill, to take it at all? *"I believe they have the absolute right to make love if they want to!"* Has it ever occurred to him to expend his energy and power in furthering birth control for them? It can be determined medically, early in pregnancy, if a child will be subnormal; how about urging those mothers to abort? In fact, how about a law requiring it? He is shocked. "If I were, like, governor or President, I would mandate that every pregnant woman have that test, and that if it's negative, the mother and father are fully informed and may *choose* to abort. Period. There is *no way* the federal government should force it." Why? Without a law, the door's left open for more of these pathetic creatures. "Listen," and he is very emotional now, "the state can *never* intervene that grossly! It would be controlling life and death! If *I* could make that decision in every case in the world, I'd trust myself to do it, but the *state?* It's barbaric; it is *pure fascism!* Also, it's just . . . *not moral."*

William Shockley, he adds, is to blame for this sort of fascistic theorizing. ("Shockley, Christ, everybody's listening to him and he's not even a biologist, he's a physicist, a lousy inventor, and a *schmuck!* He is . . . the dirt under my feet, he is a skunk!") He elaborates on this until news time; it turns out to be our last exchange in New York, though one repeats it to a young eastern geneticist, who laughs sourly. *"Sure,* some serious types of retardation are hereditary, but if *any* baby's going to be born a blob, that fetus should be aborted, by law. As for Shockley, *all* he's *ever* said is that blacks make lower IQ scores than whites and that *one* explanation *might* be a genetic inferiority. Geraldo's state-control-fascism bit, Jesus, so dumb! The state controls us anyway. That's just that weary old liberal shibboleth."

For the next few months, one sees him only on *Good Night America,* which succeeds eminently in the Nielsen ratings. Geraldo's clothing and conduct are young, hip and aware; it is the first time the whole nation is treated to his smile, rarely seen on the news, now perpetual. Pronounced informality, if not giddiness, is striven for: Surprise visitors such as his parents and his father-in-law are always being introduced from the audience. Their comments are brief, as are his on drugs, amnesty and Ce-

261

sar Chavez. Most of the show is devoted to young, hip, aware and very famous performers who sing or otherwise entertain, and then converse about their philosophies, which turn out to be very similar, not only to each other's but to the host's. On 1974's final show, for example, he introduces Shirley Mac-Laine, who explains why she's decided to forsake politics for a return to the screen and her new nightclub act—it's her need for people, to relate to them, to share love with them—and John Denver, who sings from his albums and then speaks of the Colorado Rockies, clean air, and the importance of our universal need for love, and to relate. At least there are no Alpo commercials.

We speak for the last time in Los Angeles, at the Malibu Beach retreat of the manager he has acquired, Jerry Weintraub, who sees to the business matters of John Denver, among other headliners. Geraldo is alone on the deck of the big house, moodily observing the dull, expansive Pacific forty yards in front of him. He's come west for the weekend with a dual purpose: to meet ABC's Hollywood brass ("They wanted to see I wasn't just a flaming, uh, uncontrollable youth") and to report upon Folsom prison, in that order. Though the sun has blessed and burned him, he is testy, defensive. "I'm, uh, *very* excited about *Good Night America*'s potential: The network's talking about doing the show every other week in 1975, they're *very* excited about public response. Look, there's a limit to what you can do on the budget they've been giving me, *that's* been the problem: only twenty-five thousand a show, and for network TV you need a thousand a *minute*. We've had to limit location shooting—like drugs, VD, we had to do those in the studio, *very* limited, but the network VIP's out here are *very* happy, so is New York, they're already talking about, like a sixty-thousand-dollar budget for a Harlem story alone. It's a start, and if we do two shows a month, *if* I get popular enough. . . ."

In the relentless sun, he seems momentarily disoriented. "I *swear* to you, I won't lose sight of my goals." Silence. "A lot of people love me for my, uh, charitable involvement, so what if it *is* self-aggrandizing, does that mean I should stop it? Jeez. Look, right here and now I want to expose all the skeletons in my closet to you, because I want the public record *straight*. First, I was married once before—when I was in school in Arizona. Everybody I knew was getting married, it lasted a year, I haven't seen the girl since, no children, no problems, but *I want it in the public record.* I don't want to appear to hide *anything.* This image of mine as a spotless white kight is basically true, but I *am* human. Look, ever since the resignation I *constantly* hear I'm running for President. Maybe my thinking about that's changed; maybe I could be talked into it. But I am *thirty-one,* at *forty-five* I will be a young man, I'm just flexing my muscles, just beginning to reach twenty million people a show, it would be a . . . *cop-out,* now, to abandon television."

He is on his feet, still exposing skeletons. "Another thing I want clear in print is my Israeli war coverage. There was a big rumor that I faked it, started by another *Eyewitness* newsman, don't try to find out who. I *asked* to cover it, I've always felt, oh, guilty about not going to Vietnam, and I've got *reckless* courage in any physical danger. Also, Israel was the hottest story in the world. So I'm there with my cameraman, in occupied Syria, Hill 1102, I think, as close as we could get, the fighting was *one* kilometer away, and we're driving back into Israel, crossing the Daughters of Jacob Bridge, and suddenly Syrian artillery shells start dropping right *on* us! We jump out, literally dodging them, my cameraman films every second. The film's sent immediately to ABC over the satellite, *everybody* looked at it and saw it could *not* have been faked. But this other newsman calls every publication in town to say it was, and I had to deny that absurdity to every editor in the East: Christ, that *anybody* would *think* I was *less than brave!* I took that newsman down to the basement and I beat him like I haven't beat anybody in, oh, maybe five years, gave him two black eyes, he fell, and I kicked him, screaming 'I will kill you right now!' I mean, my *greatest* strength, my *honesty,* was in question! At stake was my *credibility!*"

He is trembling, which he was never prone to. Then Mr. and Mrs. John Denver and their new baby arrive in a limousine to talk to Weintraub, and one goes to watch Geraldo play tennis at the Malibu Colony's private courts. Players include ABC's West Coast president and a delicate blond friend of his who turns out to be another Billie Jean King. While she sits out a set, one asks her to rate the form of the four men still playing. She mentions Geraldo last.

"He has enormous energy," she offers tentatively, studying him, crouched for first serve, through her amber glasses. "And concentration. He's played a lot. Physically strong. But notice, he's losing. There's something wrong with his game. I can't put my finger on it."

21.

David Carradine, Who Doesn't Own a Television

"SO *he tells the* Times *he grows his smoke in his yard!*" Before hissing that, sotto voce, the ever-young associate producer of television, costumed in long sculptured buckwheat hair, ginger beard and Bill Blass, has cast dilated eyes about the Beverly Hills Hotel pool and placed a hand over his margarita glass, as if to muffle it, and now he pings its rim with a nail, for emphasis. *"The* Times, *he tells this, dig it!"* We've pulled two Colombian joints to ash on the way here in his buckwheat Mercedes; he has told the elderly waiter, bent in service but California-tanned, like an old tarnished spoon, that he prefers sea salt on the margarita rim, *sea salt,* and has gotten sea salt because he's known to leave a fifteen-dollar cash tip on a thirty-dollar Master Charge tab. And now, after three drinks and another surreptitious joint passed under the table, short-winded now in the Pleistocene rain-forest air by the heated pool, his drug-informed machismo has dampened and blurred. "Babe," he begins now, instead of "man," gesturing loosely, "Listen, babe, I mean Hopper and Fonda already *did* rebellion, it's very 1968, snorting coke on the Cavett show and so on, also, it's extremely *dumb,* when you are living in a fucking police state and your dealer's probably a double agent, and you tell the *Times you grow your smoke!* I mean, ABC is *shitting,* they've got a junkie in prime time. They never dreamed *Kung Fu* would make it and now they are stuck with this hippie superstar, they keep saying to him, uh, David, couldn't you, uh, emulate Richard Thomas a bit more in your, uh, public behavior, and they put him on the Cavett show which he does very stoned, Cavett starts sweating, then David's girl friend comes out, Barbara Hershey? Only she changed it to Barbara Seagull—you heard?—because a dead bird balled her or something, and she brings out the baby, which they have named Free, I mean, thank you Grace Slick. Cavett turns paler. Free starts bawling and Barbara, on camera, opens her sweater and whips one out and nurses him, *on camera!* Instant cut to Cavett, who has turned green and says, "Uh, I believe we have just witnessed a television first. . . ."

Through his steamed smoked glasses, he studies the bright amphibians in the hotel pool. "And they do this free-spirit number with a great show of childlike conviction, you know? I mean, you *almost* believe it."

That is the sort of smog-yellow whisper you hear now within the viscera of the television industry (one more doggedly mean-spirited than movies, if that's possible) about *Kung Fu*'s triumph and David Carradine's sudden media canonization, unless you talk to ABC, where everyone is very jubilant about what is one of TV's two or three great historic freak successes, like *Laugh-In* or *Sesame Street*. Well, apprehensively jubilant, especially when one requests an interview with David in the name of *Rolling Stone*. A great clearing of throats occurs among PR people at the other ends of phone lines; there is industrious shuffling of papers followed by helpful suggestions from Hollywood Panic Referral: Actually, you'll have to call Morty on that, and Morty refers you to Gordon, who explains that *that* sort of thing is ordinarily batted over into Dave's court, or you could call Sheldon. "Um, Shelly's extension is. . . ." What Shelly says is, "Oh, *right*. Except . . ." And you can feel him mentally flipping the Panic Referral card wheel and then gripping the Fabergé egg on his desk because his was the last card. "Hmmm, *Rolling Stone*. Actually, that would have to be discussed . . . their orientation is so . . . actually, David lives quite simply up there in Laurel Canyon, close to the soil, a simple cat, you dig? Not precisely a talker, knowhatimean. I don't think you'll get much. You, um, you aren't going to print anything about him growing marijuana . . . ?"

"*Why don't you just call him up?*" Impatient while the network discusses, one seeks out a Canyon resident nearly as legendary in Laurel as Carradine himself, an aspiring young actor-writer and bona fide mystic oracle named Michael Pelto, who looks like James Dean at twenty if Dean had had hair like Julie Christie, and who sometimes works for David in the team of erratic, flamboyant actor-writer-carpenters whom one has observed all spring hammering moodily about the blackened rafters of the weird old half-burned house David has bought on the peak of Laurel's highest hill. "Why, his number's right there in the book," Michael, gently bucolic, offers. "Why sure, just dial it, he likes to stay in touch with the people." Oh. What the ever-young producer says of that, when told is, "Beautiful! Perfect, babe! A *listed number!*"

David's telephone conversations tend to be desultory: "Yeh, man, uh, Saturday . . . no, come Sunday . . . we'll, uh, rap." His voice is cat-purr, smoke-cured. Sunday comes darkly, a November in Vermont misplaced; in Southern California a day without sun affects one like blindness; it heightens the auditory sense, one imagines hearing portentous crackings in the earth's crust. It is with misgiving that one ascends, through aggressive weeds, the seventy-eight broken wooden steps to the crumbling wood farmhouse, the richest home in Appalachia, which David occupies until the burned house is repaired. The old Dutch door contains a hand-lettered notice, don't LET BLUEBIRD OUT, SHE'S IN HEAT, and is answered by, besides Bluebird, the spaniel, Barbara Seagull, rurally beautiful, stoically smiling in an old sweater unbuttoned for feeding Free, who seems to nurse perpetually. Barbara murmurs welcoming things—at David's, things seem to be murmured, rather than spoken, or exclaimed—and saunters under the dusty living room's hand-hewn beams (by David), past its furnishings (one baby grand, one mattress), to the only other room, a little chamber containing a suggestion of an Oriental mat and David, squatting coolie-fashion in pants like toolshop rags and a hairy tan wool shirt with a brass chauffeur's identification button, 1950 CHAUFFEUR 29796. Cradling his guitar, he grins in the vicinity of the visitor, nodding: No gaucheries like handshakes are needed in this bower. Barbara and the baby fold themselves down beside him, Free drooling cheerfully onto pink footie pajamas, listening raptly as David strums and hums over his instrument, leaning into it almost double as if to warm it, and then sings the title song of an independent movie he's just produced and directed, starring himself and Barbara: "You and me . . . that's how it's gonna be . . . from now on. . . . 'Cause that's the name of this song." He sings to Barbara though he doesn't look at her. He sounds like Woody Guthrie.

Eventually one tries, in a pause, to introduce the idea of rudimentary conversation; he does not reject or resist this, he ignores it, grinning, strumming, nodding, humming, eventually going into the living room to consult with the actor-carpenters who seem always to be entering and exiting leisurely under the dimming skylight, men in honest earth clothing, sometimes with women in home-woven pioneer garments and granny glasses. Murmuring consultations among the men are held, multiple architectural concerns are sketched, money is mentioned. David considers: "There's, like, money in the Burnt-Out House account. . . ." His antic homemade pipe, a fantastic brass carburetor which he assembled himself from opulent, antique parts is passed, and he brings it to us in the bedroom, softly bobbing his large head like a Macy's parade balloon, blinking his curious puffy eyes, a benevolent serpent. After more guitar, lulled by the exceptional pipe, he begins to talk about the evolution of this enigma, this abrupt legend, *Kung Fu,* an old script dragged from the dustbin at Warner's (which produces the series for ABC) about this half-Chinese, half-American orphan boy named Kwai Chang Caine who's brought up by Buddhist monks in a Shaolin temple in China and taught the ancient Oriental art ("science" says the Warner's press release) of personal combat called Kung Fu (you can almost hear the yawns at Warner's programming conference tables). Young Caine kills by mistake a prince of the Imperial House and is exiled to America with a price on his head, where he roams the gold-rush West disinterested in gold, championing the downtrodden and almost never smiling. (Yawn, belch.) Mysteriously, perhaps magically, Jerry Thorpe, a young producer hired by Warner's television to develop new projects, talked, or cajoled or mesmerized the studio into making what turned out to be an excellent pilot film of the script. Gingerly, it was shown, the response was also excellent. By the time the series had been on a year, Warner's was buying up and distributing cheapie Kung Fu movies on the order of *Deep Thrust* which the Orient was turning out faster than transistor radios.

". . . So my head was shaved," David is explaining, "a few days *before* I heard anything about this script. Far out. But it wasn't anything mystical. Like, I'd played an Indian in a movie and my hair was stripped of color for it and dyed black, and then I did this picture with Barbara called *Boxcar Bertha* and my hair was all fucked up for that, so I thought the only way I'd ever get it back to normal was to shave it. Barbara did it herself with this . . . razor. Then I got the *Kung Fu* script, far out. Except I never thought it'd ever really get on TV, this Chinese Western. I went to see them anyway, and this producer, Jerry Thorpe, he drives up to Warner's in this chocolate brown Continental, and he is in chocolate brown and is carrying a chocolate brown briefcase, a real studio type, a company man, and I thought, 'This man is Satan! The Devil!' Dig it?"

His ham hands trace little karate chops in the air, for emphasis. "So they look at me, these company men, my bald head and all, and they want me for the part, but after the meeting I heard that one of 'em said, 'But look, he's a dope fiend.' Far out! The next time I went over there to talk to them, I wasn't really high, but I pretended to be *wasted*, like I was on smack or something, which I don't take. I went in this executive office and lay down on the brown leather sofa, groaning. And they *still* hired me. . . ."

The guitar again, more smoke. "You and me . . ." he sings, sweetly, simply, to Barbara. Abruptly, the sun comes out, to set, to remind us of where we really are, not in Woody Guthrie's mountain cabin, but in Hollywood, a place created by a phenomenon undreamed of through all the centuries until this one. In the late twenties, when talkies were introduced, Metro-Goldwyn-Mayer, in one of the first great personal publicity campaigns, the first modern stary-hype, determined whether or not Garbo could talk on the screen, found that she could and then quickly put her into semiretirement. For more than a year, they took ads: GARBO WILL TALK, then GARBO TALKS IN HER NEXT PICTURE, then GARBO TALKS! Everywhere they lined up to hear this wonder. Who are you, when you are this, more attended than Delphic oracles? Yet stars of television are even more closely attended. Who are you, then, if you are this man, gently strumming in the mountain dusk? Not simple, not what you would wish to be, or appear; impossible. *Carradine talks!*

269

Which, surprisingly, he is doing again, unprompted: "Uh, they asked me at the studio if I knew anything about, you know, karate, judo, the martial arts, Kung Fu combat. I told them, 'Not a fucking thing,' and I still don't. After I signed and the show got started, they tried to get some local Kung Fu experts, and there are lots of them everywhere now, to come and help us but they refused, they thought we were just some commercial rip-off bullshit. Kung Fu people are very dedicated, very serious. So, like, it's all faked, man, the fight scenes, they're, like, choreographed. I mean, I am a dancer. . . ."

Barbara goes to answer the phone, then beckons to David; oddly, it's a twelve-year-old Massachusetts boy who has gotten the number from information. David grins into the receiver at this unknown worshiper: *"Hey, man . . ."* Eventually the boy asks him if the Kung Fu fights are real or faked. "Yuh, well, lots of people ask that. . . ." Gently, tactfully, David is honest. We're all in the living room now, except Barbara, who's brewing fresh coffee in the tiny adjacent kitchen, murmuring sometimes from her cluttered woman's island to the larger peninsula of males—the rough-hewn mountain men, the actor-carpenters, bluntly lit with a dim bulb as if by kerosene lamp or camp fire, waiting upon David's next words, or thought, without appearing to wait. They are, one perceives, exactly the sort of crusty entourage that used to attend Dennis Hopper when, at the end of the sixties, he was revered as the new media savior. In fact, it is the *same* entourage: One recognizes here, through the greenish smoke screen, at least one of the actor-carpenter apostles who used to attend so closely to Dennis' Socratic dialogues over *pisco* in Peruvian bars while he attempted to wrest a new art form, his disastrous *The Last Movie,* from the old Inca soil.

Carradine talks. The next time he does, it is down the hill in the real world, in the Warners executive lunchroom. Most series actors, even the stars, don't eat here, but David enters guilelessly, shoeless, as he was four minutes before in the back lot, on the *Kung Fu* set, the Western Town of Movies, with its polyethylene General Store and Styrofoam Blacksmith Shop, lovingly painted by the last fine-arts craftsmen, the studio set decorators, to resemble rough-hewn wood. One has watched the last setup of the morning, a sequence to be shown weeks later, the familiar *Kung Fu* Street Confrontation: Squinting inscrutably, Caine faces rustlers, or robbers or railroad barons mounted on studio horses. One of them tells David they know it was a chink who took the gold shipment and simultaneously raped Miss Ainsley. To which David, as Caine, replies that they ought to give the railroad workers shorter hours. The meanest baron, this week's cameo player, dismounts in a flash and offers Caine a fat fist, from which he first withdraws, with dignity. When threatened further, he flips the antagonist over his shoulder with his index fingers like a spent roach, having observed, as usual, the teachings of the Shaolin temple: Avoid before confront, maim before kill, humility, patience, peace.

Cut. Okay, people, short lunch, next setup at one, needed at one sharp are Mister Carradine, Mister . . . Laughing, the actors drop character instantly, like disengaged marionettes; except David, who seems to shake off Caine gently, to segue slowly from his character's austerity to his own looser self, like someone smiling on slow-motion film. It's been clear, watching him on the set, clearer, somehow than it ever is on television: The contemplative, highly formalized way he moves and speaks when playing Caine is meant satirically, a wry deadpan comment on the preposterousness of the story and his role. "Oh, yeah," he says when I mention this, laughing, nodding, jumping over the jammed door of his old scarred topless Lancia convertible, to rush us through the back lot streets of ersatz old New York and rural America, to the dining room and hastily ordered scrambled eggs and coffee, of which he seems to drink about two dozen cups a day. Over the food, I try again about the humor in his performance; this time he considers, chewing, then nods with great animation.

"You see that? That's far out, man. Good. I've tried to keep it very, you know, subtle. Maybe it's too subdued, because I don't think audiences dig it. I dunno . . . I think they'll get more used to it next season, partly because *I'm* getting more into it." Incredibly, he's speaking with great urgency, he is almost vivacious, as though he had left his mountain self back in the canyon cabin. "I *want* them to see the humor, but I'm still very serious about the part. Somebody said, when I told him the fights were faked, he said, 'Oh, then it's all just acting.' *Just* acting?

Man, to me, acting is life, I don't differentiate between acting and living. I want to live Caine, I want him to grow with me, and me with him: Like, just on a physical level, the wardrobe department had me wearing shoes, and right in the beginning I just took them off and left them off. I realized that Caine wouldn't *need* shoes and wouldn't wear them. And I'm just letting my hair grow, haven't cut it since we started and I'm not going to, I had to fight them on that and I won. See, I want Caine to be affected by this new culture he's thrust into, the American thing . . . maybe it begins to amuse him, this crazy country, maybe he becomes less rigid, this new world gradually, very subtly, lightens him. . . ."

As in a speeded-up film clip, he finishes the eggs and we're back in the Lancia. It's hardly the moment to make him examine himself as a presence who magically enters, every week at an appointed time (as God once entered minds and hearts Sunday mornings), the millions of dimmed living rooms, to glide in liquid earth tones and pastels across the mind of the suburban Republic. Instead, for now, one merely asks whether he cares about the Emmy award (for which he'd been nominated), and whether he intends something so earthbound as getting into a tux and attending the ceremonies. The questions seem to disturb him; again he assumes the demeanor of the mountain man. "Uh, like . . . well, I dig the ceremonies, the, uh, pomp . . . I dig those things. But what I thought I'd do, I'll send in my place, like, the lowliest *Kung Fu* employee, like the guy who runs the coffee wagon. You dig that? Farrr out."

This guilelessness, this bumpkin ambience, though apparently genuine, is puzzling. It's like trying to accept the Nashville homilies of Kris Kristofferson once you know that he was educated at Oxford and was a Rhodes scholar. You wonder how David could have functioned at length within the sophisticated aura of, for instance, the New York stage? What minute fraction of *Kung Fu*'s vast audience realizes that before he abruptly materialized before them as Kwai Chang Caine, he had, among other things, played Laertes to his father's Hamlet and starred on Broadway? Kwai Chang Caine, on *Broadway,* jaded Byzantium, where opulent homosexual philosophies are purveyed six nights, two matinees to suspicious expense-account burghers nodding sleepily into the orange drink? Yet in 1965 they were lining up to see him as the Inca chief in *The Royal Hunt of the Sun.* "Uh, it was far out," he says of it. "No, man, I *liked* Broadway, that was a great thing, doing this big role in this big play every night." And what led up to the play hadn't exactly been a trip in an honest truck on a country road. His father, John, was a stage and movie star who spent a lot of time touring, marrying and divorcing; by puberty, David had been to six private academies on both coasts and one reform school for playing hooky from all the others. (This was in the early fifties; he's now thirty-seven, an odd age for the hero of a young viewing audience which previously canonized David Cassidy.) He went to San Francisco State to study music, "But, like, in the student cafeteria the musicians all had their tables and the drama students had theirs and I just naturally gravitated to the theater kids, I dug them." They did not necessarily mention to him, it would be uncool, that nights they stayed up to watch his father in movies on *The Late Show.*

"Oh, I guess, like, I wouldn't have gone into acting if my Dad hadn't been into it, he *kind of* influenced me. We always got on okay, sometimes he seemed like a god to me, sometimes . . . less, but, man, like, he was the *first* hippie, he had hair down his back in the forties. He lives on his boat now, down at the marina. He can be really conservative, like, I don't think he approved of Barbara and me living together and having the baby and all, but he's come around, I think now *he'd* like to live like us. My mom lives in San Francisco now, she's remarried and like she *really* digs us, I think I got my uh, idea of freedom from her. See, my dad . . . I idolized him when I was young, then I saw that I was mimicking him, doing his style, I freaked out." The freak-out apparently occurred after the drop-out: He left Oakland to start acting in little theaters all over Northern California, mostly doing classics and Shakespeare as his father had done. He also recited poetry in sincere fifties coffeehouses, sold sewing machines and encyclopedias door to door, and became one of the original San Francisco beatniks.

He was busted and subsequently drafted; the grass charge was thrown out of court, but the Army was more persistent. He spent two years at Fort Eustis, Virginia, most of it in the brig after various courts-martial, three in two years. "For, hmm, like, you know, *nothing,* man, like in the Army they bust you if your shoelaces aren't tied. No, I kinda enjoyed it: I got these very good, very well-tailored uniforms, really *trim;* except I was always court-martialed so I never got any insignias or like that on them, I didn't even make PFC, so the result was my uniform was very bare, like an officer's; guys would salute thinking that's what I was. Dig it?" The only thing about military life that seemed to interest him, besides the uniforms, was the talent contests the Army put on. "I made the finals in one show," he explains, obviously proud of this. "I did the, uh, soliloquy from *Richard II.* Huh: Then I lost first place to some guy who twirled batons. . . ."

After the discharge, which was actually honorable, he did a lot more little theater work and a good deal of television, including a year on *Wagon Train,* and some movie parts, nothing spectacular, and the Broadway thing, and an off-Broadway play called *The Transgressor Rides Again* in which he played a character who may or may not have been Christ. Opening night, he was stoned and fell, onstage, off a chair in an uncontrollable laughing fit. The critics were not amused and the show closed. Another off-Broadway musical, *The Ballad of Johnny Pot,* about a Johnny Appleseed character who crosses the country seed-sowing, he dropped out on the day before opening night. During this period, he threw a cue ball through the stained-glass window of the Players Club in Manhattan after a slight disagreement with his father over the way *Hamlet* should be performed. What he says of it all is, "Yeh, I fucked up a lot. I really liked acting, I respected the profession and all, but I kept making the . . . wrong choices. Like, *The Royal Hunt of the Sun* was this big Broadway hit and I left it after only six months to do the lead in this TV series, *Shane.* Based on the old movie, you know? Only I tried to make Shane this sort of offbeat, slightly comic hero, sort of a folk-rock hero, and I guess TV wasn't ready for that in the sixties, the series bombed." The industry then punished him by casting him mostly as villains, in dreary movies like *Heaven with a Gun,* which starred Glenn Ford (*Glenn Ford?*) and featured Barbara Hershey, who had not yet encountered the doomed winged creature who would cause her to change her name.

Cheerfully she explains it, the matter of the bird. We're sitting again on the bedroom mat, the child attached to her as usual like a hungry Siamese twin. Again, it's Sunday; in the early afternoon, David has played the guitar a bit and smoked a bit and then abruptly driven me, in his 1958 Packard convertible (which, like the Lancia, is usually topless) across the hill to inspect the Burnt-Out House. Workmen have finished gutting the downstairs, which, David explains, will become one large room: He does not much cotton to walls. Upstairs their bedroom, David's, Barbara's and Free's, faces the sunrise, hugely windowed, a room cosmically floating. He remarks, surveying the canyon floor 2000 feet below, "The, uh, sun's up here. We don't get enough sun at the other place, with that hill behind it. I wanted to get right up on top, into the sun. But . . . hmmm . . . buying a house and fixing it up, that's like an experiment. I started this place when I was really, like, content for the first time . . . Barbara had just had the baby . . . so we'll move in, maybe in a few more months, whenever, um, we all get around to finishing it up. Then, hmm, after that, I somehow don't expect I'll stay here very long. I dunno . . . I feel. . . ." Silence. He leaves the statement Pinteresque.

When we go back, some carpenters come and he must talk to them; Barbara and I go into the bedroom, we don't bring any grass. "No, I never really cared for drugs," she says, sitting, "Oh, I tried them all at different points, but they're really not my trip. I never liked smoking cigarettes, so I don't really enjoy grass, and now, with the baby, I wouldn't anyway." She speaks briskly, smiling often, although she has begun by remarking, easily, that she loathes the idea of doing interviews and that David has urged her to do them anyway; he feels it's important for them both, now that they're making their own movies and so on. Even the most continuous contemporary bit player has learned never to say anything remotely like that to a reporter, press agents having explained about the nasty New Journalism, and instructed clients to involve themselves with writers, to "relate" on a "personal level," to make the lonely, underpaid son-of-a-bitch feel wanted and needed. That Barbara either doesn't know that or doesn't care is distinctly exhilarating. Also, she is darkly beautiful, pleasant to watch and listen to, never mind the words, yet . . . what? There's an odd remove about her, one seems to listen to her over wide distances, long empty beaches, deep shadowed canyons. Except that she is not blond, she seems the ultimate Southern California girl, vague, amber-gold.

She was in fact born in Anaheim; her father is editor of the *Racing Form.* She always fantasized about being a famous actress, "I'd act out all the characters in the Disney movies." Before she'd finished at Hollywood High, she'd been hired to play the ingenue in the TV series *The McMasters* (which, like *The Waltons,* presented the vicissitudes of a pioneer family in such a way as to seem not dissimilar to those of your average Covina time-study man). When she met David, their first day together on the set of *Heaven with a Gun,* "It was just instantaneous between us. We've been with each other since that day. We don't think marriage is very important. He is very straightforward, very . . . beautiful. We both have this idea that we want to become . . . like *gods.*"

Oh? "It's very hard to explain, it sounds strange, conceited. But all it is, really, is living . . . fully. David says, you know, like trying not to concern yourself with things that are less than cosmic, as so many people do. We would both like when acting to play only heroes—because to do that well you must become heroic. I guess, hmm, David and I don't really live much like other people. Like, we never go out to parties here, we never get asked; they know we wouldn't come. Sometimes we do go out, like we went to the ballet, to see Nureyev. It was strange, I didn't realize that you're not supposed to bring babies to the ballet. Free cried a lot during the performance, I had to go and stand at the back with him. . . ."

She regards the drooling baby with infinite love. "It was so great when Free was being born. David was here with me, he got dressed in animal skins and all his Indian jewelry, and he played the piano and the guitar and hung by the rafters up there, to relax. Hmm? Oh, yes, I had Free right here in the house. I'd decided not to have a doctor, but after I was in labor a while I chickened out and we called one. It was a wild night. Mostly, I was sitting up in that rocking chair. Gravity helps pull the baby down, and out . . . it's much easier than lying down, I mean, if you can imagine taking a shit lying down. We, uh, had planned to eat the placenta. Animals do that, it's incredibly

276

nourishing. But after we looked at it, we decided instead to put it in the ground and plant this fig tree on it, and when the tree grows, Free can eat the figs grown from his own placenta. You know? And the tree is really doing fine. . . ."

Right, one says. Silence. Uh, about the name? "Well, I'd always sort of wanted to change it, then, while I was making *Last Summer,* did you see it? I was this very disturbed girl who befriends this seagull and when it turns on her, she kills it. Well, the bird I worked with was very special, I could feel her spirit, I felt very close to her. And the crew used to call me 'Barbara Seagull.' But in this one scene, I had to throw her into the air, to make her fly, and we had to keep reshooting, and I could tell she was very tired; and when the shot was right, Frank Perry, the director, came up to me and told me that on the last throw, the bird had broken her neck. And right then, *I felt her spirit enter my body.* I didn't tell anybody for a long time. I finally knew I had to change my name, and did it legally. Oh, yes, I did read *Jonathan Livingston Seagull,* but that really had nothing to do with my trip. Except it was a nice book, you know? Now, I have these great flying dreams, I really *soar.* I went to Holland to make this movie and when I got there, I told them about the name and they were sort of upset, they wanted to use Hershey because it was known, but I was firm. . . ."

The planet turns; Free listens with amazed eyes to the muttering from the living room, which is now dim and dotted with the tips of lighted joints, like circling fireflies. David reenters, beams at Barbara and softly plays another song he's composing for another movie they're going to do. They're planning lots of movies, whether or not they ever get distributors for them. One has, by then, seen parts of a very rough cut of *You and Me,* which seems to deal exhaustively (and, to a great extent, silently) with a long trip taken by a biker and a little boy on a high-powered chopper. The specters of Hopper and Fonda seem to lurk about its gentle Kodachrome edges; it is somewhat allegorical David intimates, its meaning is not easily perceived. "It's sort of part biker picture, part Walt Disney and, um, part its own thing. The next one is, like about this guy who repairs merry-go-rounds, but what it's *really* about is . . . well, it can't be explained, you have to see it. Directing is this new, *incredible* trip for me . . . like, to me, a movie is a Declaration of Independence, a statement of freedom. And freedom, man, I guess you've noticed, freedom is my *big* thing. If you make a movie that is truly personal, without compromise, it'll be commercial, too, I know that. Now, Fellini . . . they told him his trip wouldn't be commercial and *he* didn't listen. . . . "

One asks him about movies he's liked and disliked; the subject doesn't much stimulate him. ". . . Like, *McCabe and Mrs. Miller,* I didn't like that, it was shot, so much of it, out of focus and I go to a movie to *see* it." He thought *What's Up, Doc?* hilarious and seems startled when I tell him it was, like all of Peter Bogdanovich's work, loveless, condescending and totally devoid of humor. "Well, I really laughed . . . I don't think *any* of these guys, like Bogdanovich, or Robert Altman or Frank Perry, are really trying to say anything. They haven't *got* any statements to make, you know?"

He examines the lighted roach he holds, then calmly swallows it. "The thing about me is . . . it isn't sensible to write about me unless you take me seriously, because I am really a, hmmm, serious thing. I am, uh, actually having a definite effect upon, at least, the youth of the United States and, potentially, the world. Far out. What everybody's watching, you dig, on *Kung Fu,* is me—somebody who is spiritually seeking, somebody who's taken four or five *hundred* acid trips, who's used LSD as a tool, to gain knowledge, to, um, find truth. Hmm? No, I'd feel weird, as a cultural hero, telling all the kids who watch me to drop acid because some people do become basket cases on it; but I could tell 'em that I myself see no reason to fear anything that happens within my own head. I *want* to know, that's my trip, I am like Che Guevara, except I'm doing it in a TV series. That's extraordinary, you don't find people like that doing a TV series. Truth? Well, one way to it is striving constantly not to lie ever, under any circumstance, for any purpose, *ever.* The truth is like, um, a desert, all white sand, and one lie is a dark stain on the sand, visible for miles. . . ."

He pursues that metaphor for perhaps several minutes, or more, it is hard to tell. ". . . and Barbara, the first night we balled, she said, 'Look, let's not ever lie to each other.' Wow, the idea shocked me. I mean, it's one thing not to lie, but not lie to a woman? Impossible!" He so rarely smiles that when he does it is like an unexpected benediction. One does not much interrupt him here, except to nod encouragement, sensing that such monologues are, for him, rare, and somewhat difficult, and will not bear repeating. "But acid . . . I dunno, it's just not doing for me what it used to do. Like, I haven't had an hallucination in, oh, I don't know how long. I'm getting impatient: Like, if it's really true that there is reincarnation, and that we are all just recycling over and over till we get it right, well, I want to reflect my era and get going on to the next: I feel a *responsibility* to do that. I will do it through *truth,* which I have been working on for years and I'm now, uh, almost one hundred percent truthful. Like, once I used to even steal, shoplift. I don't now."

One is tempted to remark here that honesty is more viable with a $100,000-a-year television contract; one does not remark it. "So, uh, but my last heavy acid trip—well, tripping, I always go into this very heavy self-examination thing, like this medical examiner comes and shows me through the interior of me. Some places, I'm, like all patched together with bandages and see grayness and decay, and ask the examiner, *What the fuck is that?* I gotta examine that! And he would let me. But this last trip, we were walking through this corridor inside me and there was a door and he said, 'You're not allowed in there, man,' and I said, *'I gotta see,'* and I reached for the doorknob and it *disappeared!* Dig it? And I knew right then that that psychedelic experience was never gonna be quite enough to break all the barriers. Seewhatimean? And I knew, too, that you can't break 'em with systems—psychoanalysis, religion, scientology—because they're all, uh, below the spiritual problem I'm researching. Because they *exist.* I mean, when an idea's written down, it becomes forever stationary, locked in. If it isn't, it can, uh, always continue to expand, like the universe. Knowhatimean?"

Definitely, David, you needn't elaborate. "Still . . . I don't know, I don't think I want to do this series much longer," he offers suddenly, "I mean, there's this enormous distance between me and, uh, the *structure*. The studio gave me the job because they knew I was right for the part: Caine is untouched by the *structure,* so am I, I seek what Caine seeks. You dig? Listen, man, those studio guys all take dope, only they do speed and sniff their coke, they will *not* take psychedelics because they *know* that LSD could break down their *structure,* their system, it's a fucking monkey wrench in their stability. So they just seek escape, not knowledge. They *know* their structure's doomed, like the Third Reich. This Jerry Thorpe, the producer—he's like Kit Carson who the president hires to communicate with me, Geronimo; he is the connection between Me and Them, except he is also Them. You dig? He deals with the universe in a totally personalized way, the universe is as *he* sees it in *his* head. He is like a black magician, but with no magic power at all. Like, from the beginning, all he cared about *Kung Fu* was that it would succeed, get ratings, make money, he cared nothing for its spiritual values. Now, when the scripts are wrong, or bad or untrue to the spiritual values, I have *got* to fight him. Them. The company men. And they are all black magicians, there is maybe one other person involved with the show, besides myself, whom I sense is totally white. Well, shit, what can you expect? Thorpe, man, all of them, after all they work in *television. . . .*"

Smiling, he sneers. Silence. During this afternoon, looking around the house, it's occurred to me what's missing: a television set. I ask about that, but he's tuning the guitar and the question is distracting.

"Hmmmm? Oh . . . yeh. Well, like, I had one once, but I gave it away. Watching television is poisonous. Pollutes the consciousness. Did you see that movie *Play It As It Lays?* That actor in it who balls the girl, only beforehand they have to sit and watch him on his TV show? If you start taking yourself too seriously, that's what you become."

22.

1966: When There Was Still Splendor in the Grass

ONE may as well begin with Claude M., who is twenty-eight, who lives in a new, centrally air-conditioned building near Second Avenue in the Seventies, whose three-room apartment is furnished in a pleasant, solid fashion, not at all camp or exhibitionistic. Claude M. runs a tight ship: He keeps the apartment tidy, makes his bed weekday mornings, and so on; and yet, when you visit him, he does not run around emptying ashtrays, figuratively or literally. When he has you to dinner, he does not serve beef *Bourguignonne,* nor does he make a thing about what he has cooked. He has a very solid job, in Market Research. Claude finds this field stimulating. In a few more years, he will marry and move out, having achieved just the right series of promotions. He does a normal amount of sucking up to his superiors, but he is also quite likable, and capable, in an unspectacular way. He has no major confusions. His clothes are right. His teeth are naturally good, and well taken care of.

On a recent Saturday, Claude M. awoke about eleven from an untroubled sleep and got up. We will skip, for the sake of suspense, what occupied the next ten minutes of his morning.

At 11:10, Claude turned on his bedroom television and got back into bed to watch whatever the screen offered. What it offered was *Space Adventure Theatre,* a regular Saturday morning film feature. In this particular installment, Rocky Jones, captain of the ersatz-looking space ship X-V2, along with Winkey (the comic-juvenile copilot), Vena (the space lady) and little Bobby (an articulate child of the rocket age), were all strapped into their contour space chairs, because they were being pulled down onto the surface of an alien planet by a strange magnetic force.

"We are being pulled down onto the surface of an alien planet by a strange magnetic force," Rocky said with some agitation.

"Oh, wo-ow," Claude exclaimed, delighted. Promptly—though to Claude it seemed to take about half an hour—the X-V2 was forced to land on a very supercharged, electricity-fraught satellite, over which terrific, oversized lightning bolts crack every fifteen or twenty seconds and giant balls of electric fire constantly rain.

"It turned out," Claude M. explained to a friend on the phone an hour later, "that in this particular galaxy, or whatever, everything is electric, man. Everything! And two planets are at war. An electric war! But one planet has developed a special weapon—supersonic music. You hear this electric music and it drives you mad. Like Ulysses and the sirens, as little Bobby points out. He has been reading about Ulysses. No, man, not Joyce! He was reading *The Odyssey*! Oh, wow, it's too complicated! I'm getting completely hung up in this, aren't I? Constant lightning and thunder, and supersonic music! I was seeing this in color, I swear, and, baby, it wasn't *in* color. . . ."

To clarify what may seem to some of you out there a singular little scene, a distinctly suspect dialogue, I need only fill in that ten-minute period before Claude turned on his television. Claude, of course, turned on himself. No, he was decidedly not tripping on LSD. Claude wouldn't think of trying acid. He has read, in *Life, Time, Harper's, The East Village Other* and *The Reader's Digest* that the effects of LSD are unpredictable. Neither would he dream of taking heroin, cocaine or opium. If a doctor offered him morphine, he would hesitate. The names of these drugs have, for Claude, a worrisome, negative connotation, like "syphilis" or "Black Mass."

No, from behind the three volumes of Mencken's *The American Language* in his bookcase, he extracted, this Saturday morning, a little empty Anacin container—empty, that is, of its original contents, full now of a very high-grade clean green marijuana. From the same hiding place, he took a little packet of "roll-your-own" cigarette papers. (At one of the several Manhattan tobacconists that stock them, he sometimes says, with only the faintest trace of self-consciousness, "I use them to clean my contact lenses.") Deftly he licked one of the papers—he is a past master, having been turned on about a year now—opened the Anacin bottle, and tapped out a neat, accurate quarter-inch of pot along the length of what will become, in a moment, a joint.

Joint? Pot? The third time Claude got high alone, it seemed to him a very interesting little project to look up the origin and evolution of these words. He turned first to Mencken, got thoroughly hung up in the Mencken style, and somehow never concluded the quest. Since then, he has learned, from occasional casual research, from literate acquaintances, from television panel shows, from *The Marihuana Papers*, and so on, that hemp, from which pot is derived, has been thriving possibly since prehistory; that it was grown on George Washington's Virginia estate and that he, among other late celebrities, is thought, by some forward-looking historians, to have smoked it; that it was not made illegal in this country until 1937; that from 1937 until now, the number of U.S. potheads has probably quintupled; that although it is smuggled in daily from Mexico and the Orient, the best stuff originates in Cuba, where it is hung up to dry, sprayed with alcohol, baked in ovens, and crumbled up for export; that in the now-notorious 1944 LaGuardia Report, scientists stated that they found the stuff to be not only nonaddictive, but physically and mentally harmless to all except certain hardcore psychotics and those ready to freak out at any moment anyway.

And so Claude M. is perfectly confident about his little indulgence, for he is positive that he suffers from no psychoses. He simply enjoys that blurring of depth perceptions, that added soupçon of suggestibility, that rounding off of inhibition's sharp corners which pot affords him. He does not drink much, by the way. He smokes about a pack a day of civilian cigarettes. He never upsets the Anacin container when turning on, because he quickly learned to replace the cap before striking the match. After his first inhale, his coordinations seem to—not so much dissolve as tilt, at a ten- or fifteen-degree angle, and then one can so easily make a cautious yet slightly false move and upset the bottle, and it is perfect hell to have to gather up spilled pot from the carpet, especially if it is nice and clean. Claude's supply, like his carpet, is always very clean. It is clean when he receives it—quite finely ground, including only about twelve of the plant's original seeds and stems. It is never cut down with oregano (which it resembles), like the pot purchased by teeny-boppers on Village street corners Saturday nights. A close friend of Claude's—the daughter of a Beekman Place psychiatrist—gets it from a girl she went to Bennington with, who gets it from a diplomatic attaché she was living with, who gets the very best during his frequent trips to Central America and brings it back in his attaché case, wrapped neatly in American aluminum foil.

Though it is clean, Claude always cleans it again, so it is superfine. He works the whole "nickel bag" (approximately the contents of a standard bar jigger, for five dollars) through an ordinary kitchen strainer; the remaining seeds and stems he grinds by pressing them with the bowl of a spoon against the side of a coffee cup and then mixes the result in with the finely sifted original. There is little chance now of the bad, nervous, irritable, rather paranoid high one risks with the stuff unclean.

Though the squares among Claude's alert young East Side neighbors—the non-turned-on—will reach the laundry, and Gristede's that Saturday, perhaps a bit earlier than he will, they will accomplish no more. Claude will, just as surely, drop off the sheets, and later select some steaks, celery, some Gruyère cheese, instant oatmeal, and so on, with the same assurance. Except that as Claude makes his way to the laundry, he will slow down and marvel at the colors of the traffic lights, and of the sky, which, he imagines, no one else in Manhattan has noticed that day. Not that anything he says to the laundryman will be wrong, exactly, or noticeable; it will only be, to him, tilted, and too gratuitous, and will sound, in retrospect, slightly hysterical. In the grocery, it will take forever—as did the descent of the X-V2—to decide which is the best veining in a steak. He will read the pitch on the back covers of cereal boxes and get hung up in the lettering and the bright colors.

Friday night, Claude turned on quietly with a small group of congenial close friends who live on lower Fifth Avenue (the only really acceptable Village address, as far as he is concerned). Saturday evening, he will attend an uptown cocktail party, with a date, possibly Judy C., who is bright, who teaches

284

at an exclusive Manhattan girls' school, who studies Russian at night at the New School, whose brownstone apartment is noticeably unkempt (the prerogative of girls of Judy's class who grew up in a household with at least one in service). Judy also has her own remote connection: The dealer is about three times removed from the customer. Like Claude, she prefers to keep the seller-buyer relationship isolated. When she first turned on, she used a little pipe, with a piece of screen in the bottom of the bowl, to improve the draw, but lately she has worked out a quiet little high of her own. She rolls out about a half-inch of tobacco from each cigarette in a pack of filtered Camels, fills the empty space with grass, and inhales right through the filter. A couple of these restrained joints Saturday noon, and she can complete a sink of dishes, the vacuuming, and the windows in less than an hour with an enormous, virtuous sense of efficiency.

One could go on with these case studies, chronicling the envied young broker whose charming wife is such an accomplished, gracious hostess. Euphoric would describe her more accurately, because they always get slightly high before parties; in fact, they turn on three or four nights a week, over martinis, before dinner, as it seems to heighten one's sense of taste. Or one could examine the popular media rep from Larchmont, whose wife worries about his knowing their dealer firsthand. (For this reason, the exchange is made lunchtimes in the men's washroom of an expensive midtown restaurant—green for green—practically under the nose of the see-nothing attendant.) Or we might study the pert executive secretary who gets it from her fiancé in Queens and resells it to a handful of old friends at the office for a modest but increasingly substantial profit. Note that neither Claude M. nor Judy C. nor anyone here described is in the least otherwise colorful. They bear no relation to the 1958, or Jack Kerouac-type, pothead; to those intense, humorless, life-students who evolved with the beat syndrome, whose descendants now reside near the Bowery, or the Haight-Ashbury district of San Francisco, or at Berkeley—persons who think jazz important, who are suspicious of affectation, of the Broadway musical, of collections of Beatrice Lillie recordings. Neither have I included apple-cheeked teens—we are already too crashingly aware of their attachment to the narcotic—or top fashion models, theater people, courtesans, people with private jets, and other golden, jaded types who, as everyone knows, have been dope fiends since before Tutankhamen.

No, the new upwardly-mobile marijuana users are worldly in a nice, comfortable way. They do not ask back for drinks people who are intense about relationships, truth games, or pushing forward the frontiers of human experience. Like Claude, they are suspicious of the more publicized escapes, mostly because of the kind of people the press associates with them. Heroin, to them, is something indulged in by rather grubby, manqué persons who live on the West Side; it is not so much scary as déclassé. The same is true of LSD: The wrong people got hold of it too quickly, that trying West Coast gang. Besides, one reads that, under its influence, people walk through upper-story plate glass windows and hurl themselves under the BMT, and that kind of behavior is hardly going to do anything for anyone's career. Neither, for that matter, does alcohol: Liquor plays hell with one's timing, and one's face, and has, moreover, become the fundamental of parties given by, and jokes told by, the union-electrician set who live in Forest Hills.

For Claude M., the single most compelling aspect of pot is its . . . cachet. To tilt a few degrees beyond the already pill-stuffed masses is to be Contemporary. To squint into the eyes of a fellow head and giggle is to share the new, educated hip. This clubby atmosphere is not a fantasy: Pot does create its own cachet. One may go to an ordinary cocktail party, drink only orange juice and sustain some sense of belonging. It is virtually impossible, however, to remain at a gathering at which all present are smoking marijuana and not get the vague feeling that everyone else in the world has discovered the right expressway while you still grope along a service road. Everyone else is sitting benignly, passing the joint around; something flamboyant and highly styled—perhaps even the best of The Mamas and The Papas—is heard in stereo. After a euphoric silence, someone says:

"You know, I can see that music in color."

"I know what you mean."

"Not if you're not experiencing it. I can close my eyes and see note combinations—chords—bouncing along a staff. With the musical signature and all. Like the Terry Toons cartoon thing. And every note is a different color! I can see the words too. If I want, I see a little pingpong ball bouncing along over them, like in the old sing-along short subjects. —Oh, I'm getting all hung up in this!"

Laughter all around; a silence.

"There are so many *levels* to this music!"

"Look: See this ashtray? It's big and heavy, right? Well, it's heavy because this entire planet is attached to the bottom of it. It has attached itself to the earth. And if I pick it up—which I am going to do—the table it's on will rise with it, and the floor, and this building, and the entire earth will move a few degrees out of orbit!"

"Oh, wo-ow! Oh, man, don't touch it! Don't pick it up!" they exclaim, quite seriously.

"You'll screw up the entire galaxy!"

Obviously, one must be high to enjoy this argot, these fanciful little inanities which have nothing whatever to do with mind expansion. Look at the faces around this room: The expressions are gentle, the facial muscles slightly slack, the eyes half-closed, almost puffy. No one here is attempting to discover some ultimate plateau of total honesty. No, everyone is simply drawing a little pastel curtain upon the difficulty of finding a taxi in the rain; of working at a job which is, though cushy, hardly the fulfillment of one's visionary years back at Yale; of having to relate to the race problem; of the possibility of having to live with the same wife, or husband, year in, year out. One can forget these things, and imagine oneself on an island in Maine at the age of sixteen. It is a sunny late afternoon and you have four hours to get ready for the big July dance at the Tennis Club. Or it is 1915 and at the Strand in Hoboken, the headlining act is drunk, and you go on instead, and are bathed in applause. . . .

Of course, the next morning it will be raining, and you will have to find a cab. You will not be in Maine. Unless, like Judy C., you light a discreet, filtered joint before leaving for the office, and inhale it with your orange juice. Then Maine is but a gentle inch or so from Madison Avenue.

"The teenyboppers," said one of Claude M.'s living-room-full of pot-smoking guests, "you know what they turn on with?

287

They bake the scrapings from the insides of banana skins and roll them in joints. This is supposed to produce a substitute pot-high."

"What teenybopper is *that* tight up for grass?"

"My little brother knows more dealers than *I* do!"

"Ha-ha," remarked a thoroughly stoned fashion copywriter sitting on the carpet near Claude's chair.

"You know, you always laugh very verbally," said an accountant from across the room. "You invariably say 'ha-ha' when you laugh. You are the Ha-Ha Girl."

"Wow! What a great title for a musical—*The Ha-Ha Girl!*"

"Right: The heroine is a poor laborer on a vast Caribbean Ha-Ha plantation! Every morning at dawn she goes out into the Ha-Ha fields to help reap the Ha-Ha Harvest!"

"It'll run for years! There'll be a movie sequel: *The Daughter of Ha-Ha Girl!*"

"*Thoroughly Modern Ha-Ha Girl!*"

"*The Ha-Ha Girl Goes Junior League!*"

The laughter is general, silly, sweet and blissful. As further cadenzas are improvised, Claude lights a fresh joint and hands it to the girl seated next to him, beginning it on its trip around the room. Pot always renders Claude magnanimous; it is, to him, a giving, a sharing thing. He enjoys turning his friends on, but none need depend upon his largess, for they all have the phone number of someone such as Allen, one of the city's myriad reliable marijuana dealers.

Allen—that is definitely not his name—is twenty-seven. After four years at Harvard Business School and a brief, somewhat disoriented stint at a downtown brokerage firm ("The streets around Wall are too narrow; I developed claustrophobia"), he found himself in the role of the modern pot peddler. In his J. Press jacket and white shirt from Brooks, he looks—rather like Claude M., actually, except that while Claude is older, Allen is mellowed; his face has not retained those pockets of baby fat peculiar to American lifelong man-boy. He is cool, though not at all in the self-conscious, early-fifties sense of the word. He is personable and straightforward—yet if his name were indeed Allen, no one with the slightest intuition would think of calling him "Al."

"The grass traffic," he explained with quiet irony, "has become a vast underground industry. Unbelievable! It has its own mores, its own intricate economics. I deal in terms of ounces for Claude and his crowd only as a favor. It's easier to store an ounce—roughly half the contents of a water glass—in a small apartment, and the possession charge in New York State is only a misdemeanor if you're busted with less than an ounce. But the principal part of my business is by the pound. I sell to other dealers, who break my pounds down into ounces and nickel and dime bags—five- and ten-dollar lots. There are four to six nickel bags in an ounce, depending how generous a count you give. I make less than my dealer-customers do. Well, figure it out: I'm able to get hold of good boo for as little as $50 a pound. I resell it to another dealer for, say, $160 to $200. If that seems like quite a mark up, remember that the going rate per ounce in New York is $20. If my customer resells by the ounce, he's grossing $320, for a $160 profit. If he breaks it down into nickel bags, at $5 per bag, theoretically he's at junior-executive salary level. And why don't I deal in small quantities? Because if you're selling ounces, you've got to know, say, twenty regular customers; by nickel bag, you've got to know dozens. Not only do you have to spend all day setting up exchanges, cabbing all over the city, and so on, but the risk is enormous. Too many people involved, too many chances to get busted. I have maybe a dozen dealer customers—several post-graduate students, for instance, who are paying for PhD's with their profits. Medical students, they tell me, account for most of their sales. The secretary to the president of one of the biggest firms in the country makes as much from dealing my grass as she does from her job. Most of her customers are right inside her organization. They include her boss. The typing-pool girl with a nickel-bag sideline operation is now a common thing, everywhere, by the way. And one of the city's top psychiatrists buys from me regularly, by the pound. He doesn't resell; just entertains extensively. It's mostly for his social-register guests. He is by far my most paranoid consumer—obsessed with the idea that his phone is tapped. I've told him it isn't. It's easy to hear a tap, interference and so on—but he insists that when I call, I say something like, "I've got a load of fresh vegetables for you." The fuzz—police—are naturally a threat, but at least there are no hang-ups with hoods. There's no gangster control of grass, because there are no really gargantuan profits in it. Not the kind there are with heroin pushing. I've never met a pot dealer who also handles narcotics. Pills, yes—amphetamine, barbiturates, some mescaline, hash, of course. You'd be surprised how many tea-heads don't know that both hashish and pot come from the same plant. Hash is more expensive, harder to come by, but I'm getting more and more requests for it. Not many for acid—LSD and the others—not in any quantity. It's big on campuses, but still very much a West Coast thing. My conservative eastern seaboard customers won't touch it yet, but give it about three more years. I predict that it will be an industry unto itself by 1970.

"Anyway, 'horse'—heroin—is strictly the domain of the shiny-suited, pinky-ringed pushers. So are morphine and opium and cocaine. Nice young heads practically faint if you even suggest those things. Incidentally, it is a grave faux pas to call a pot peddler a pusher. Dirty word! Very déclassé. Thank God they are separate gigs; it keeps the grass traffic nice and cordial, no unpleasantness. Oh, I've gotten burned a couple of times—trusted a pot source, put up the money, and never received what I paid for. A couple of months ago, somebody I work with occasionally got word of a really exceptional shipment available at $100 a kilo—kilogram, about two and a quarter pounds. We were to come to The —— Hotel, in the Village, to pick it up, but then we heard through other sources that this particular exchange was possibly not legitimate. My partner borrowed a 'piece'—revolver—and we checked into the hotel too. We would have gotten burned without the piece and a little one-upmanship."

He laughed softly. "This argot—burned, busted, piece, nickel bag—evolved as a code to fake out the fuzz. It's part of the lighter side of the work. Grownup cops and robbers. Why do we play? Because we don't like the idea of the office routine; because the profits are tax free; because we are our own bosses. That's part of it, but I wonder if the real motivation isn't the intrigue, the underworld aspect. I am concerned about breaking the law only because of what happens when you get caught. But then, who does worry about the law in any other sense anymore? Who grows up with any real sense of lawbreaking as a moral issue? I don't know anyone, and I had a nice, comfortable, upper-middle-class adolescence. So did most of the dealers I know, even the ones who deal in a bigger way, the dealers who supply me. Most of them are California-based. They make a great many crosscountry trips. What's that airline commercial—"for professional travelers"? Some of my sources make fifty trips a year, West Coast to East and back. They purchase up to a hundred pounds of boo, and carry it from LA or Frisco to New York in their luggage. No problem. Most of them fly first-class. If they get busted, well, their fathers usually have good lawyers; with the right defense, a first offender usually gets a suspended sentence. Ask any dealer. You know, you ought to talk now to a small-quantity peddler. That's a different scene entirely. Time-consuming, and so on, but colorful. The ounce and nickel-bag man is usually very gregarious. He makes most deliveries right to the door, meets a lot of kicky people. Things happen to him. He's always getting asked to parties, dinners. It's a social-contact occupation. Here, call this number. Ask for Martin. Not Marty, Martin. . . ."

On the phone, Martin was cordial, but concerned. "I'm sorry, but I can't take you on my delivery rounds. I'd like to. I hope you understand. No respectable dealer could do that. Allen told me that's what you wanted, so I broached the subject with my customers. They didn't take to the idea at all. Too many of them have too much to lose. Not that you would. . . ."

"I understand."

"And I can't afford to lose my customers. But listen: Saturday, if you like, I'll stay home. Saturday is a big delivery day, but I'll say I'm waiting for a shipment, which is partly true. I'm almost always waiting for a shipment. I'll have them come to my place. You come too, stay all afternoon if you want to. As far as they're concerned, you'll just be a sympathetic friend. They'll stay, some of them, and talk, if I encourage it."

Martin's apartment is in an indifferent-looking building in Turtle Bay. Its interior is not indifferent. The bay-windowed living room is painted a soft red, the parquet floor is white. Aubrey Beardsley prints, handsomely framed, cover one wall. The furniture is contemporary and good; in a corner there is a century plant on a stand. White shutters are closed against the strong spring sunlight, and though the room is very dim, Martin wears yellow tinted glasses. He is also in his middle twenties, and the face behind the glasses is untroubled. He wears an army shirt and Levi's and smokes a thin, tipped cigar.

"Sit down. Welcome. You're early. I've never gotten anywhere early in my life, that I can remember. Would you like Indian tea? To drink, I mean. It's a good thing you could get here today, because I'm liquidating the business in a very short time. I'm an actor; did Allen tell you? Well, I heard this morning that I'm definitely set for the juvenile lead in a summer package of this musical. The only thing left is for the director to okay me, and I sign the contract. The show's supposed to come to Broadway in the fall. So good-bye to the grass business! I've been in and out of it since I was eighteen. It paid for more than half of my education, and that was before it had become a major campus attraction. I was ahead of my time—no pun intended. This enormous use of boo by the nice, middle-class student began in earnest, I would say, in the early sixties. If I were dealing now, in college—man, it would be the equivalent of a full-tuition scholarship! Still, I'll be glad to get out of it. I suppose Allen told you the small dealer makes big profits. He's exaggerating. Oh, *he* gives me a fair enough count, but what you get from most pound dealers—uncleaned—has a way of breaking down into a lot fewer good nickel bags than it should. And customers have a way of coming and going. It's a restless generation; they take off for a year in Europe, California, you name it. They find other connections they think are better. Also, unless you're really able to be ruthless, you end up giving away as much as you sell. It's a loving thing, you know? The whole grass syndrome. You turn on yourself, you are happy, your friends drop in, you want them to be happy, you turn them on, they bring new people around—you've got to be heartless, and who needs that? Many small dealers end up making enough to live and pay for their own—supply. I almost said 'habit,' which would be very inaccurate. Pot is absolutely nonaddictive, I can definitely vouch for that. . . ."

Footsteps are heard in the hall outside. "Damn! Somebody left the lobby door open again!" Martin moves with somewhat elaborate stealth to the peephole in his door, and after careful scrutiny, opens it to Claire, a brisk, healthy blonde in a Burberry raincoat.

"Martin, baby!" she exclaims with affection, pulling off her scarf. "I'm in a terrific rush. I'm having my hair cut in twenty minutes, then I'm meeting Jeanie and some friends of hers, guess where! The Palm Court at the Plaza! Is that a camp? We are going to light up, right there in strolling-violinsville. Even if the waiters suspect, who's going to say anything? I've been going there since I was twelve, for God's sake!"

Martin steps to a bookcase and extracts a copy of Daniel Blum's big book, *Great Stars of the American Stage.* A large hollow has been cut in its pages; from this, he takes one of several aluminum foil packets.

"An ounce, right?" Claire says. "No, of course I don't want to examine it. Have you ever done me wrong? Here: five, ten, fifteen, twenty, nice new bills just for you, lovey. I'd like to turn on here with you and your friend, but must toddle. Oh, listen, Martin, can I give a very, *very* close and old friend your number? I can vouch for her; absolutely to be trusted. Thanks, dear. Oh yes, I've settled what I told you: I'm taking a house with Jeanie at Easthampton for July and August, and you have a standing invitation, if you aren't playing in stock. Call you next week, love. . . ."

"She is totally sincere, by the way," Martin said, securing the door with both a bolt and a chain arrangement. "Last summer, I wasn't working, practically lived at her house at Fire Island, rent free. At Christmas, she took me for the weekend to her parents' place in Short Hills. What a layout! Can you figure her background? That's simple, in her case—Miss Porter's, Smith, Europe, and now she works at a very responsible job at a nonprofit outfit. Makes no money, but takes a cab to the office every morning. I know her well, and I swear there's not one thing complicated or confused about her. Straight people—the non-turned-on—always look for something maladjusted about a head. Ridiculous. Say, how about sharing a joint from my private stash? Sorry, I forgot. You're working. But you don't mind if I do?"

From within *Great Stars,* Martin produced a joint, lit it, inhaled, held the smoke in, swallowing it. "This particular grass is something else. Acapulco gold, Allen's latest shipment. Heads are fond of blaming bad highs—headaches, depression, paranoia—on what they're smoking. 'Poor quality grass,' they'll say. I don't agree, unless they're talking about the coarse local stuff,

293

the kind that grows wild along the Jersey turnpike. I don't think the boo is at fault. It's the mood you're in when you're turning on. There are different tastes, naturally, varying strengths, colors. The names slay me—besides Acapulco gold and Panama red, I know of maybe a dozen more, and new ones keep turning up; California brilliant, Kansas standard, African rust, Guatemalan chartreuse. Every month a new name, new customers. You heard Claire? 'A very close old friend wants to call'? Claire's for real, but that's the standard pitch. You'd never dream so many people would have so many old, close friends turning up out of the blue to turn on."

He relit his joint. "Why? Why the grass obsession? I'm not a sociologist but look at this century. I mean, look how many dippies the bluenoses produced with Prohibition. It made drunks of thousands who'd never have gotten interested if the law hadn't said they shouldn't. As soon as pot was outlawed—in 1937—the same thing happened. Well, not as fast; in the forties, everybody was busy with the big war. No time to blow grass. And there was this innocent, childlike sort of belief going on in America. The masses still believed we were fighting the war to end wars. Middle-class ideas were still potent, including the idea that drugs, besides being vaguely unclean, stifle the old U.S. concept of onward-and-upward. Then the fifties—wow! What a draggy decade! Korea, Eisenhower, McCarthy! Claire and her kind were growing up watching their elders gulping booze. The only vital thing going seemed to be the beat movement, the folk musicians and poets, all identified closely with grass. The old ideas began to look, to the young, like tired radishes in a gone-to-seed Victory garden, or something. Wow, I'm getting hung up here! Very literary! What I'm trying to say is that Claire, Allen, all of them, are just as disaffiliated as those renegade acid heads in California, but the traditions of their class are very strong with them. They don't want to grub around in communal apartments in San Francisco. And so pot is their baby—their answer to the world of Mother Bell, which is *their* world. You know what I mean? The idea is to sit in an office with a carpet and bleed Mother Corporation of your fifteen thou a year, at the same time turning on right under her big eyes. It's the poetic justice of the sixties. . . .

"As for legalizing grass—in some ways it would be idyllic. People would be gentler with one another. They would stop competing so fiercely for taxis, tables at restaurants. They would smile at one another in the streets. Man, consider the freeways of America! Benign! That aura of competition driving would disappear. Speed limits might become obsolete: People would idle along about thirty mph, digging the scenery, the pulse of the engine. You tend to be very cautious driving when you're high; it is not nearly as dangerous as driving while sauced. And the draft problem! If all those reluctant recruits knew they were going to get a daily pot ration along with the franks and beans, or whatever they eat, there'd be no more draft-card burning. If regular pot smoking gained worldwide acceptance, who knows, maybe there'd be no need for armies. Nice thought, at least. As for the drawbacks: well, part of the kick of the pot syndrome is that feeling of being a naughty child, functioning on a level the squares know not. If everyone were turning on openly in the New Haven and Hartford club cars, pot would lose a lot of its new privilege-class status. And of course it would bankrupt small businessmen like me."

The doorbell rang, two shorts, one long. "Good, the downstairs door's closed again. That's my customer signal." He pressed the buzzer. "You know, something occurs to me: Pot, hash and acid are nonverbal things. How do you describe a pot high? An acid trip—it's impossible. With both of them, your sense of time is distorted, your sense of—urgency practically disappears. If the use of head drugs keeps spreading like it's been spreading, among the Brooks Brothers set, what's going to happen, eventually, to the corporate structures? Those are action careers, verbal jobs. With a world full of young heads, where is Mother Corporation going to find the bright-eyed VPs? It's something to think about."

The next customer turned out to be an advertising executive, or so Martin claimed after he left. He said little, seemed highly nervous, asked to examine his purchase, bought three ounces, and exited as quickly as possible. "You'd think I was dealing in hot emeralds or something," Martin remarked with mild annoyance as he rebolted the door. Within twenty minutes, three more guests arrived together: a tall, very smart and aggressive woman in her mid-thirties, a man slightly older, and a very striking girl in an off-white pants suit. The woman paid for the supply, promptly opened it, and, seating herself, proceeded to fill a small, graceful jade-green pipe with pot. They all had a smoke. When they left, Martin said, "The guy and the older girl are with——" (he named a top fashion magazine.) "He used to be a lush, smokes now instead. Many drinkers become vipers to kick the alcohol habit. The girl is a model. Grass is very popular with people who want to preserve their looks; it has no damaging effects, internal or external, and you know what demon rum can do along those lines. Between the three of them, they're good for an average of one dinner or party per week. It's become very much the thing to have your dealer in to meet your friends; very status. Sometimes I wear a square dark business suit, which seems to shake them up. Did you dig the pipe? It's from one of the headshops downtown. These little viper boutiques are springing up all over the country. They feature a complete line of accouterments for the modern boo-blower: all kinds of pipes, from thirty-cent corn cobs to forty-dollar imported hookahs—water pipes—and wild little roach pipes for making the most of that final bit of the joint without burning your fingers. Trip equipment, too, for the acidhead. Everything but the vital ingredient that you can't sell in stores. In a couple of years, headshops may become as lucrative as dealing. And safer. What can the fuzz do? Arrest you for selling smoking supplies?"

During the next hour or so, half a dozen more customers called. Some stayed; a little party developed. Pipes were passed. Martin served Indian tea, to drink.

"Did you hear that up in Connecticut, or somewhere like that, kids turn on by smoking through a rotten pepper?"

"Smoking *what* through a rotten pepper?"

"Civilian cigarettes."

"You mean like a green pepper, that you stuff?"

"A *rotten* green pepper that you stuff."

The room is silent, contemplating the image of the teenager and the square greengrocer; it is, for obscure reasons, sublimely funny. During the laughter, Martin, who has been studying a copy of *The Marihuana Papers* which one of the guests has brought him as a present, stands, steps forward and says, "Listen to this, about the hemp plant. 'George Washington raised it at Mount Vernon. Once, during one of his many extended absences, Washington was reported to have expressed the wistful hope that he would be able to return to his plantation in time for the September hemp harvest.'"

"Oh, wow!"

"And remember, man: He *couldn't* tell a lie."

23.

Princess Leda's Castle in the Air

ON Santa Monica Boulevard in West Hollywood, the manager of the Happyshop (frozen delicacies, prescriptions filled, choice wines and liquors) has hurried the Mexican sweep-up boys through closing time (good boys, really, they wear gold crosses outside their aprons), has changed quickly into his blue suit and Sacred Heart tie clasp and is now traveling fast in his Toyota because Friday night sabbath at the Chapel of Jesus Christ of the True Believers begins in eight minutes and if he is very late there won't even be standing room. The chapel, the second floor of a poodle-grooming salon, used to be adequate enough, but this year the congregation has burgeoned, inexplicably. To everyone's horror, these newest True Believers wear neither blue suits nor tiepins, nor, indeed, ties, but flowered semitransparent shirts and curley pageboys; on the other hand, they do display the largest, most baroque crucifixes in the entire congregation and can quote from memory almost the entire Book of Revelations, a chapel favorite. Moreover, they set out *on foot* after the service, into the Inferno, which is Sunset Boulevard, where, it is said, they stride up and down most of the night brandishing their Bibles and shouting, "Stamp out Satan!" and "Death to the demon-worshipers!" in the very faces of the demon-worshipers themselves. The rest of the True Believers, of course, drive straight home with locked doors, and get inside with dispatch, barked at by their own guard dogs, because up in the Hollywood Hills, and in Benedict, Laurel and Topanga Canyons, the Satanists, warlocks and devil brides are just rubbing the sleep from their eyes, rising from their coffins, and dropping their wake-up acid caps.

299

Though the murder of Sharon Tate affected Los Angeles profoundly, that terror decidedly did not manifest itself full-bloomed at dawn (as certain deadly herbs are said to do) the morning the bodies were found. The Happyshop and Kuick-Karwash managers had begun noting, perhaps two full years ago, a new and even more sobering offspring of the drug culture; they had just become grudgingly accustomed to the bearded, barefoot boy-girl and the wistful, ironed-hair girl-boy, when in came a far more worrisome sort of hippie, in hand-made seventeenth-century breeches, or in gold-painted eyes and rare white peacock feathers; persons with assured mocking laughter and lightly commanding airs, who requested not Gallo port but obscure, foreign champagnes, or who drove up to the car wash not in serviceable, dented Impalas but antique silver Packards with black satin window curtains. They seemed easily able to pay, but it was this *thing* about them: a frightening, fancy malevolence. Then the papers began implying that marijuana, that witches' weed, scourge of the decade, was considered by many to be not only harmless but boring; that the affluent up in the hills have taken to drinking cups full of acid instead, certain chemical combinations which afford them special knowledge of Satan and the Black Arts, and that decent Christians everywhere were now prey to these new sorcerers in Bentleys and feathers, who could apparently cast spells upon you if you shortchanged or otherwise annoyed them.

The flower children, of course, have more sophisticated information, but their reaction to the new Hollywood is markedly similar. Lonny, a Bible salesman whom one meets Sunday morning on the Strip, and who carries a half-dozen black plastic Old Testaments and wears a gold cross embossed with symbols of Catholicism ("No, man, I'm not Catholic, never was, but I know a lot of *Jews* out here who are blessing themselves pretty regularly these days"), is one of the few persons now residing within the Los Angeles County limits who does not claim to have once been a guest at the Tate-Sebring-Folger-Frykowski establishment. "But I've been around that scene, man, cats who have *given themselves up to the Lord Satan.* If you sense an evil here, you are right, and I'll tell you what it is: too many people turned on to acid. If you make a habit of tripping—well, acid is so spiritual, so, uh, metaphysical, that you are going to be forced into making a choice, between opting for good, staying on a goodness or Christian trip, and tripping with the Lord Satan. That's the whole heavy thing about too many people turned on to acid: to most of them, the devil just looks groovier. Acid is incredible—I've been on one hundred and seventy-two trips now—but it shouldn't be available to everybody and anybody."

If the California evil is just a matter of drugs, then why is he wearing the cross? He considers. "Acid does expand the mind. I believe in powers you can't explain. And if these sick Hollywood heads *are* into these powers—well, I want some protection. It freaks them to see a cross—if they're wearing a cross upside down. Suppose they *are* into black magic, weaving of spells? They can't touch you, wearing the mark of the Lord Jesus."

He asks if I might be interested in purchasing a Bible. I ask if he knows of a local woman, the Princess, Princess Leda Amun Ra.

"Oh, wow. *Her.* Take care, man. Wear a cross. . . ."

One sees her first dancing a salute to Satan in the Climax. An enormous private nightclub on La Cienega Boulevard, it is mecca for young persons with visible wealth but invisible sources of income, Hollywood's anonymous seekers-after-lasciviousness (as opposed to patrons of The Factory, who are movie stars and tourists). Climax members lie about on velveteen divans solemnly viewing antique vampire films, or making convulsive movements before the twenty-foot Satan's head, its foolish eyes painted with Day-Glo. The ambience is so conscientiously wanton that, after twenty minutes, one prepares to leave. Then she materializes, dancing alone, as is her habit. One first supposes that she has been hired by the management to lend some credibility to the place; amid so much papier-mâché debauchery, she is overwhelmingly authentic. Her body is covered with black feathers, which seem to grow from her chalk-white skin; her bare breasts are loosely held with gold fishnet. Her hair is blacker than the feathers; her huge mad eyes are ringed with black smudges of sleeplessness, but bright as if lit from behind with bulbs. Her dance is a definition of lust. She is Salome undulating with the severed head. She is the Eumenides, and Theda Bara; she is totally magnificent.

My companion, a native, knows of her; yes, everyone knows of her. In subterranean Hollywood, she is the acid goddess, the Princess Leda Amun Ra, a legend, supposedly a witch. She lives in a sort of castle somewhere in the hills. Her chariot is said to be a golden Jaguar. Possibly she is thirty, but in daylight looks twenty-one. The young man sitting at the table near her, the Prince Valiant in red tights and swashbuckler boots, with a sword in a scabbard at his hip, and a dueling shirt open to expose his carefully defined pectoral muscles, is her King, the young King of her mythic world. One of the tales that surround him is that he owns a gold Jaguar, with a television set on its dashboard, so that he may view old movies as he drives. Supposedly, he is an astrologist who commands thousand-dollar fees for a basic reading. No one has the vaguest idea where they come from, or what their real names are; in a city which avoids last names, they do not even have first ones. They are simply the Princess and the King; their titles are undisputed.

One asks a waiter to ask her to join our table for a soda (the Climax serves no liquor). He approaches her tremulously and waits; when she is ready, she listens to him, then stares over at us and whispers to him briefly. He reports that, instead, she would like us to join her at her castle for a little post-midnight gathering; nothing spectacular, apparently, it is only Tuesday and "she says to tell you she has been in, uh, a heavy trance since Saturday noon and is a little tired. To get there, she said, you go up La Cienega and. . . ." By the time my native guide has understood the directions, shouted over the music, the King's table is empty, and both he and the Princess have vanished.

The castle is actually a sort of mosque, white stone, not really large; but it is so perfectly placed upon its hill that it appears to float above Hollywood, tenuously anchored: a house in the Casbah as it is imagined by persons who have read about, but not actually visited Tangier. The narrow windows are covered by rococo shutters, hand-carved. There is no moat, but there is a high cement wall and an iron gate. Behind the house is a dank, foul-smelling garden, choked with untended tropical trees, guarded by a stone Satan's head, with moss hanging from jowls and eye sockets.

Our knock is unanswered; we try the knob, which is unlocked. Facing us in the vaulted foyer, lit with a dim amber spot, a round dais, on which wait five tall wooden dolls, dressed in shrouds; their skin looks decayed, their eyes alert. To the right, a long medieval dining room; beyond it, a circular alcove, containing another dais. This one supports a four-foot wooden coffin. In it, resting uneasily on the remains of rotting hyacinths, a doll looking like an infant corpse of, perhaps, a four-year-old of indeterminate sex. Its face is shockingly convulsed; the little teeth have bitten the lower lip almost in two, drawing blood apparently long-dried. It wears a plain linen nightgown and a tiny, blood-spattered nightcap, with embroidered frills.

Turning sharply away, one notices a young man who has apparently been standing behind us, in the alcove entrance, for some time. His white crepe jumpsuit is unzipped from the neck to the fly, to expose a shadow of pubic hair. On his hairless chest is tattooed, in red, TRANSPLANT THIS HEART. His smile is oddly fixed, as though he had slapped it there hours ago, in the morning, and then forgotten it, like a piece of tissue on a shaving cut.

"Welcome," he says gently, exposing broken teeth. "Welcome to the temple." There is something curiously insinuating in his pleasant voice, an unspoken threat. "The Princess is preparing herself, she will be down to receive you soon. There is no smoking of cigarettes in the temple." Obligingly, he reaches out and takes the cigarette I have lit; it disappears, apparently into his sleeve. "Otherwise, you are at liberty. Go here, go there, go everywhere. Go out, come back; the doors of the temple are never locked."

Never? "Why would a god need to lock her doors?" We move into the living room, where the music seems to be loudest: *Daphnis and Chloe,* from multiple, unseen speakers. Above a sofa of genuine tiger skins, a huge red damask canopy hovers like an apathetic fate. A long, low table holds perhaps fifty lighted candles, attached to the table's surface by a sea of melted wax. In the huge fireplace, gas flames char but never quite consume a large toy replica of a Jaguar sedan. A dusty love seat is occupied by another doll, a plaster gentlewoman in silks and a Regency wig, one stiff, pale hand raised to her bleeding mouth. Near the waxy table, a ponderous damask throne; the King half-reclines on it, his eyes dilated, distant.

The other guests—there are at least a dozen—move through the rooms as if halfheartedly rehearsing a choreographic pattern that has not been made quite clear to them: a tall, pathetically thin girl, nearly nude, with a helmet of milkweed-pod hair; a dark lovely girl who chatters incessantly to herself; a black boy in green leather pants, who wears two chains, one holding a silver pentagram, or magus medallion, the other holding a silver crucifix on which an agonized Christ hangs nailed upside down. They eye the newcomers, strangers to the temple, with interest; and when I wander into the dining room, they follow silently, and surround me in a stifling little triangle. They all smile. The black boy has a perfect silver star for a left front molar.

"You have the time, man?" asks the blond girl, grabbing one's wrist to see if there is a watch.

"You must be a Capricorn, because your eyebrows fluff out at the ends," the dark girl says suddenly.

"You a native of *Chicago,* man?" says the colored boy loudly, grinning. "Well, whether you are or you ain't, we *are going to do a number on you.*"

"Number, number!" they all shout. "Listen carefully!" They speak simultaneously, thus:

—"The hands of your watch say twelve and two, the little hand on the former, the big one on the latter, the second hands is sweeping past six, now tell me, quick, without looking, *what's the time?*"

—"The eyebrows of Capricorn always fluff out, the nature of Capricorn tends to cop out, but you're safe if your rising sign's Leo or Cancer. Come on, man, tell me your rising sign!"

—"You come from Chi, where my mama did washing, and was often beat up by snotty ofays. *Do you deny whipping my mother?*"

Somehow, they contrive to come to the ends of their separate speeches at the same moment, and stand glaring, silently demanding their answers. Of course it is ridiculous. One attempts a casual smile. Perhaps it is their physical presence that is so unnerving. We have backed up into the alcove, against the dais with the coffin.

"Try just answering the questions one at a time, beginning with the first, progressing to the last," the Negro demands, leaning close. Then they begin to laugh, uncontrollably, on and on. The laughter does not help. Feigning laughter, one wedges between them, with difficulty—they do not budge—and through the dining room into the hall. Somewhere beyond the top of the central stairway, a rich contralto voice is singing wordlessly. The King is halfway up the stairs; one follows him, into the Princess' bedchamber.

It cannot be happening, it cannot be taking place. The boudoir, painted predominantly black, is large, but the bed is almost too large for it—wide as two YWCA rooms side by side, canopied in black bombazine. In the bed, the Princess Leda Amun Ra, doe naked, her skin dusted with pumice, or volcanic ash. She lies on her back, her legs splayed. Her thighs are firm as a girl's. Between her thighs is a full-grown black swan, its neck arched like a cobra's, its yellow eyes fixed, amazed. It makes one harsh, comic noise, like an echo from a rain forest.

"*I will conceive,*" the Princess shouts, heaving joyously. Half a dozen people have come into the room by now. No one else makes a sound. No one laughs; no one even smiles.

"Swan or no swan, these people, man are *dangerous.*" The girl, a singer of some note, asks not to be identified, "Because I am not about to make enemies in that crowd." We are eating salads in The Source, a health-food bar on the Strip, which, like the temple, forbids smoking. The restaurant is crowded, and she speaks softly, glancing around to see who is listening. "I've studied the occult in depth, as a hobby. I suspect Leda's power is spelled L-S-D. At the same time—well, don't quote me so I could be identified. I know the scene at the temple. I don't go there anymore, at least not alone."

But nobody has actually been . . . *hurt* there, have they?

She smiles, somewhat patronizingly, and says it, the expected: "*Nobody had actually been hurt at Sharon Tate's.* Listen, man, I could tell you about another place. This party, about eight months ago, where you were greeted at the door with a glass of their special hallucinogenic formula: acids and a pinch of strychnine. Rat poison. Makes the trip very physical. You went in and there were three altars. On two of them, these boys were tied with leather thongs. They were sobbing. These two faggots dressed as nuns—one had a *goatee*—were beating them with big

305

black rosaries. On the middle altar there was a very young girl. This guy wearing a goat's head had crushed a live frog on her privates. When I came in, he had just cut a little cross on her stomach; not deep, but the party had just started. I don't know how deep the cuts got, because, man, I split from there like Wonder Woman. Okay, that was one California party, and I've been to them all. Very few heads are that messed up. *So far.* But that's where it's all going. Of *course* it's acid. First you're Christ, then you're Lord of the Underworld. Ken Kesey finally saw what would happen as a result of daily tripping. Even Leary has begun to dig it. . . ."

I asked why she thinks demons seem to abound in California, and not in New York, where just as much acid is available.

"Maybe it's the San Andreas fault. Maybe it's the goddamned sun, always hanging in there, like somebody reading over your shoulder." She laughs, trying to swallow a chunk of avocado, and gestures with her fork. "New York is a together place. You've got to take care of business, or get out. People come here purposely to freak. They do things here they'd never have dreamed of back in St. Paul or somewhere. They come with the idea that it's one long Malibu Beach. They find out that what it is is one big freeway smashup, and they can't get it together. This is Leisureland, they're supposed to be grooving, and they just keep looking for new ways to groove, until. . . ."

When the waitress had left the check, she says, "You want another scary thought? Well, LA's major export is style: life-styles. It's very good at developing externals and getting the rest of the country interested in them. What's happening here today, that's what will be very big in Manhattan in, say, eighteen months. Scary."

Does she know anyone whom she believes to be a bona fide witch? She laughs. "Sure, a couple, but they loathe publicity. And they're about as sinister as Donald Duck. They've always been here. They're nice, harmless people who got disillusioned with churches and started reading the *Book of the Dead* at home. And *none* of them are heads! They get their kicks from pre-scribed ritual—spreading rings of salt, and like that. Acid freaks make up their own rituals as they go along. That's their danger."

306

But if I *must* meet a magus; okay, she does know somebody who knows Samson De Brier, believed to be a powerful warlock. Four phone calls, and an appointment is made. It turns out that his home is quite close to Leda's; and while it is much smaller, it is nearly as remarkable, but in a significantly different way: The temple is a monument to California's new directions; the sanctuary of Samson De Brier is a gentle junkyard, a repository of rotting portiers, chipped gilt frames. Regency ball gowns on wooden dress dummies, disintegrating first editions stacked on floors, tables and love seats; of dusty whorehouse mirrors; of gold-plated peacocks with zircon wings; of photographs of Gide, who was Samson's closest companion; of death masks, including one of James Dean, with rouged cheeks and lips, as if it had been executed by a mediocre undertaker; and of Samson De Brier himself, sometimes indistinguishable from his surroundings, a tiny, tremulous man of perhaps seventy-five, swathed in black, with gray bangs and wet, vulnerable eyes.

"See here," he says cordially, rummaging in a box of tintypes. "Here I am in Paris, with Anaïs Nin. Isn't that a remarkable likeness?"

Yes, it is. Could you explain, at all, about your powers?

"Um. I suppose you want to look at talismans, and amulets. No *serious* witch would discuss those things to strangers."

Do you use talismans and amulets?

"Um, I became aware of my powers at a very early age. I was about twelve." How did you become aware of them?

"Ummmm. Powers are dissipated if they are defined or made public. But I have always used my powers as a force of good. There are both good and evil witches. . . ."

But don't the words "witch" and "warlock" imply the worship of Satan, the denial of Christ? And if Satan is an evil force. . . .

"I don't recognize the difference between good and evil. Here, let me show you this: a cigarette holder that belonged to Valentino. See the lovely red lacquer and the serpent curling around it?"

You're acquainted with the Princess Leda Amun. . . .

"Oh, Lord! You're seeing *her*? Well, I mean, I wouldn't want to be quoted as saying anything against her. I admire her . . . daring. But you see, you've got to understand the difference between true witches, and people who take drugs. For instance, *the murder.* No serious witch could have done such a thing as that. . . ."

The Beverly Hills policeman dissents. He is not over thirty; he has the nose, hair and jaw of Edward Kennedy. His eyes are subtly, perpetually frightened. As he talks, he bites incessantly at his thumbnail. I have begun by asking him only about a possible increase in crimes of special or elaborate violence, but he isn't fooled. "Friend, I can state this as a fact, and you can quote me, this used to be a nice town, Los Angeles, and then you had this influx of Satanist dope fiends, and now you don't like to go out alone anymore."

I was speaking to him several weeks before arrests were made in the Tate case, and the policeman said, "When they find the killer, they'll find him to be a doper and a hellhound. They're one and the same thing. What the eastern papers are calling our witches, they're our drug takers. There was a case back in May, this fellow, a *war veteran,* he'd built himself this cross out of planks, and then leaned it on a telephone pole and chained himself to it, and he had stayed there for days. . . . Now, picture it—the mess he made. Lord almighty. Of course, *he* was questioned." Questioned? "About *the murder!*" Why, exactly?

"*Dope,* friend. People like him are always on dope, and if he done that to himself, what might he've done to *her.* . . .

Her. To most of southern California, she is now simply Sharon (as to Wilkes Barre, Mary Jo Kopechne is just plain Mary Jo). Like all martyrs, her talent was an excellence at dying. Dead, she is meaningful, serviceable to all, the first bona fide martyr to the evils of the New Hollywood (as opposed to Marilyn and Judy, martyrs to the old).

"Sharon," says Leda, "will eventually speak to me of the terror." I have come to the castle in the afternoon, to talk to her alone. One somehow expects to find her singular house less singular by day, but that is not the case. It still has the look of something imagined during a high fever. Inside, where the sun never penetrates, the melting candles, still lit, continue to ooze across the tabletop and the Princess waits on the throne, wrapped in white peacock feathers, her long hair secured by a silver uraeus, the sacred serpent of Egyptian divinities. Her eyes are still formidable, but her lovely face is ashen, and she is clawing furiously at her onyx rings. There is unrest in the temple. A cataclysm has occured. The black swan has died.

Of exhaustion?

Actually, one says nothing, and waits. "The bird was not sacrificed," she announces, as if issuing a decree, "though I must soon sacrifice a black swan. I have already sacrificed a peacock. The flesh, feathers and blood of the peacock are sacred to me."

Any particular reason? She glares. "Because I am Leda, Leda Amun Ra, and these are my sacred relics." Well, uh, how, exactly, was the peacock sacrificed? She smiles distantly, ignoring the question. One longs to light a cigarette. Instead, one asks about the significance of her names, the first Greek, the last two Egyptian. Again she smiles, and tilts her head regally. Then what about the name on her birth certificate? One means, to whom is the telephone bill addressed?

"I have no telephone bill, because I have no telephone. When I wish to communicate with a disciple, I summon him by thought. I have no birth certificate. I was reborn here, in this temple, two years ago, by *your* measurement of time. Reborn!"

And did this rebirth have any connection with drugs? She is silent, somber; then, very abruptly, she throws back her head and guffaws, a rich, coarse, comfortable laugh, and says as if delivering a ribald punch line, "*What else, baby?* Would you *believe,* darling, that three years ago the Princess Leda was a *homemaker?* A Clairol-blonded housefrau? A blonde who wasn't having any *fun?*" Grinning, she winks broadly. I am unable to wink, and no other response seems adequate. Where did she live as a housefrau? She only laughs again; but her inflection, when not regal, or ribald, is solid, educated Middle America, that of a thoughtful, protected girl, the daughter of an Indiana scholar.

She is drinking from a silver cup: "My private hallucinatory formula. I cannot reveal it. Yes, dear, I drop acid daily. I prayed for a special formula of drugs to be brought to me, to further open my mind, and within fourteen hours, a boy—uh, this Hollywood dealer—arrived with it at the door of my temple." I ask again about her names. She seems momentarily puzzled. "My soul . . . came to me, and entered me in the form of a swan. In a previous manifestation, you see, *I was Leda!* My legend has lived on, through the ages. But first, before all other things, I was—*am*—Amun Ra, the sun god, the god of Thebes. What you see sitting here before you is simply Amun Ra in his present mortal form. I have taken many forms in many ages. I have been both perfect male and perfect female. I have reason to believe that I was a high priest in Atlantis. In a later manifestation, I was Sarah Bernhardt. The book about me, by that woman, what's her name, Cornelia Skinner—*full of misrepresentations!* But in the beginning, I was the sun god. I have only recently understood that the sun takes energy from *man*, and transmits it to the moon. The moon then refines it and gives it back."

She glances toward the hall and claps her hands, adding, as if parenthetically, "I was also Nephthys, sister of Isis and Osiris. During that manifestation, I learned the ancient Egyptian recipe for alligator beer." A corpulent Negro boy with a silver dog's leash around his neck steps quickly in to the throne and kneels to kiss her bare, rather soiled left foot. He whispers to her, then retreats rapidly. The Princess' eyes darken. "The swan's grave is not yet properly dug. My slave recalls me from other lives; from the eighteenth Egyptian dynasty, when I ruled Thebes." A sudden, coarse, familiar laugh. "I turned him onto acid. He lives in a dungeon under the house and eats raw chuck steak." Then, with cool dignity: "But I'm considering selling him. He persists in thinking of me as his social equal, and of course I can not accept that. There is so little sense of . . . *propriety* these days. I have also considered human sacrifice. I feel more and more, each day, that it is somehow *required* of me, to consummate my rebirth."

Have you considered the legal repercussions?

She twists the onyx ring, annoyed. "Listen, I don't think I'm getting through to you, baby! You *must* understand! I am totally evolved spiritually! Why, baby, should I fear the law? I mean, *how can the fuzz hassle a god?*"

She is on her feet, pacing, sipping from her goblet. "This town is full of stenographers and file clerks trying to call up spirits. The fashionable one this year is Sharon, naturally. *Those stupid assholes!* I am the manifestation of a deity; I am able both to capture and to receive souls. No, I can't explain how, because

310

I don't know myself. But I swear to you, the morning that Sharon died, I got up early, which I never do, and I began rolling on the floor, screaming in pain. Wolf teeth biting into my guts! Sharon had been here just once, while alive, brought here, incidentally, by the worst degenerate homicidal homosexual in the county. She was very sweet and gentle, though; she followed me around this house all evening, and she said, over and over, *I swear,* 'I'm going to come back here in another life, I'm going to, I know it!' And she has been here constantly since her death. She is not strong enough yet to speak, but I am transmitting strength to her. She is not at rest. Soon she will speak. Sebring's been here too. Whenever he came, the room turned icy cold. I sent his soul on to . . . to Tom Jones. No, I don't know him, but he's beautiful, and I sense that he is together enough to receive it, and to *deal.* . . ."

Isn't sending and receiving souls a witchlike power?

She laughs richly and begins to dance. "Godlike power! A godlike power!" The fire is lit, and she undulates toward it, as if to receive its soul. When she notices me staring at the flaming model car, she suddenly says, "I have a son. Quite young. He comes here sometimes to play. I never see my husband now, and will tell you nothing about him. Except that he *drinks!* The young must be saved from such persons. I will emerge as their new spiritual leader. More and more, the young are drawn here to the temple. I will lead an army of flower children against the *true* American savage: *the white, Anglo-Saxon Christian,* with a cross in one hand and a whip in the other! We will crush him with mind power! Once, the young were led by Mr. Timothy Leary. They thought of him as a pope. *Some pope!* A plastic messiah, misuser of sacred chemicals. I give acid to persons who have never dropped it without telling them. I think of this as the administering of Holy Communion. . . ."

The photographer arrives to take pictures of her, but it is late in the afternoon; stoned, flying, she announces abruptly that she has an appointment to pick up her new swan, and since her slave is busy burying the old one, could we just run her down in the car to get it! It is not far, in Arcadia; no, baby, not the Grecian province, the *suburb,* just down by the Santa Anita racetrack. This sounds reasonable enough. After an hour of wandering on and off freeways, during which the Princess, riding in state in the rear, recounts a convoluted acid dream and goes in and out of three trances, we park by the Arcadia arboretum, a Los Angeles county wildlife preserve: acres of ominous, primeval flora surrounding a rancid lake.

"Well, uh, Leda, this is a public park. You bought a swan from a public park?"

"Leda will have her swan!" She is already out of the car, trailing white feathers, sweeping past the security guards at the entrance gate, carrying her enormous carpetbag. She walks briskly—we double-time, to keep up—through gardens self-consciously arranged to simulate the dawn of time, to the edge of the lake, where wooden placards caution against the feeding or touching of the swans. A dozen blond California children, supervised by mothers with tired, penciled eyes, throw scraps of cookies into the water. Without hesitation, Leda cuts through them, elbowing a little boy in a Dodgers cap; dips gracefully; holds out her ivory arms; and lifts a fine black bird from the dirty water.

"What is she doing to that swan?" The mother, very young and quite pretty, pulls her boys from the lake's edge. A park guide, lecturing to a bored tour group, stops dead in midsentence. "Officer," the young mother calls to him, "they are *torturing* that swan!"

"I am Leda!" Leda says, struggling with the bird.

"I'm Frank," says an old gentleman, tipping his straw hat in an obscene vaudevillian parody.

"I will conceive by this bird!"

"They're, uh, making a TV commercial," the guide announces, but the crowd refuses to move on. Frank is especially difficult. Leda gets up, suddenly brisk and businesslike. "Go back to the car," she whispers, cradling the swan in her arms. "Go on! We've got to get rid of this crowd. Just go, leave the rest to me, I'll be there in a minute, *go!*" We walk grimly to the parking lot; the photographer starts the engine. There she is at the gate, sooner than expected, sailing past the guards. Her carpetbag now bulges hideously.

"Leda has her swan," she shouts. As we pull very rapidly out of the parking lot, onto the rush-hour freeway, she produces an acid cap, tosses it into the air, catches in her mouth, and unzips the bag. The bird's black neck rises like a charmed snake. A

312

highway patrolman, passing on a motorcycle, glances into the car, then stares. We listen for the siren. Inexplicably, he overtakes us and disappears into the traffic lines. Leda's raucous laugh shatters the tense silence.

"Re*lax*, baby! We are super cool! Remember: Can a dumb cop hassle a goddess?"

Hours later: Saturday midnight. The same boy in the same white crepe jumpsuit makes the same menacing greeting. "No smoking . . . no drinking of alcohol. . . ." Neither Leda, nor the swan, nor the shades of Sharon and Jay are in sight, but most of underground Hollywood is. Evidently Leda has already made Holy Communion available. The choreography is by de Sade, the costumes by Bosch, as usual. Various trios and quartets gyrate lewdly. Four people abuse a wide-eyed girl with soft, insistent questions. The King relaxes on the throne, smiling, splendidly aloof. His presence is a relief; one senses that he is the only member of the company who has somehow remained untainted by this frenetic pursuit of evil.

I ask where Leda is. He grins amiably. "Don't know, man." We have never really talked before; he does not sound especially regal, but he does sound sane. He rises, adjusting his red fur-trimmed cape, tossing his hair back into place determinedly, a stud horse shaking its mane. The music, Stravinsky, seems to annoy him; we go out the front door, and sit on the crumbling stone steps.

King what? I ask abruptly.

He smiles into the darkness. "Amun Ra."

Why?

"Because Leda says so." His tone is gently ironic. It turns out that his given name is Garrison; that he comes from "the West"; that he is an actor who has actually acted, occasionally, bit parts; that he owns a horse which he rides every morning at dawn. He was married, and has a son whom he sees often. He had short hair and a nondescript job until he dropped acid. He believes in acid; it is his faith. He is vague about specifics, especially his astrological endeavors. Yes, he *did* read charts—meticulously, by studying the planets through a telescope. But wouldn't one have to be an astronomer to do that? Yeh, that's right: Well, he rarely does readings nowadays, anyway. "It's part of the past, man. You gotta move on, you know?"

To what? "Whatever, man. You just gotta groove. You just do your thing, every day, whatever your thing is, that day. . . ."

One understands. He is the King of the new Hollywood. He is today's Gable, or Bogart. Let the physicists at the Rand think tank in Santa Monica hassle themselves about tomorrow.

And Leda: Is she really a sorceress? He does not hesitate. "Leda does have powers, man. I know that for a fact. She *can* capture souls. I'm not putting you on. She has tried to capture mine." He smiles. "But you see, man, I have powers too. Maybe she's stronger than me. And maybe she isn't. . . ."

Soon the King rises and wanders off through the dark foliage, his cape billowing. From within the temple one hears Leda's remarkable contralto, soaring over Stravinsky in a formless, wordless dirge. She is alone in the dining room, white-robed, her white skin almost transparent, her eyes enormous. Still singing, she searches through a chest near the coffin. It takes her some time to find what she is looking for: a heavy carving knife with a tarnished blade and plain wood handle. Then, with the knife in her hand, she strides ceremoniously through the central hall to the back garden door, and stops there, studying the scene beyond the terrace. In the pool, her new swan glides triumphant. Near it is a stone bench. Tied to the bench with what looks like telephone cable, a boy of perhaps twenty, with christlike hair, beard and eyes, naked except for a loincloth and a crown of braided rose stems. He is not struggling but he looks somewhat apprehensive. His forehead bleeds slightly where the thorns have scratched it.

The Princess stands in the doorway, expressionless. Revelers from the temple dance slowly around the boy, improvising what they suppose to be mystic-sounding chants. Evidently, they are waiting.

Leda looks up at the moon, as if consulting it. Then, abruptly, she laughs, her wild, unruly, liberated-housefrau laugh. Everyone stops dancing. She drops the knife to her feet, slams the garden door, and runs back through the temple and up the stairs, giggling, and sobbing.

Outside, her disciples pause, more or less at a loss. Somebody starts to untie the Christ-boy. One perceives the evening is drawing to a close, the temple will be still until tomorrow, the first night of the full moon.

314

24.

Boone:
What a Friend He Has in Jesus

. . . whatsoever ye shall ask in prayer, believing, ye shall receive.

—Matthew 21:22

*Hi, kids, it's me, Jesus. Look what I'm wearing on my wrist. It's a
wristwatch with a five-color picture of me on the dial and hands attached to a crimson heart. . . .*

—Radio commercial, 1971

CLEARLY, they want to touch him. The sermon is over,
the last hymn has been sung, God has not yet arrived, but Pat
Boone stands before them and they want to touch his hands.
He has journeyed some fifty miles from Beverly Hills to the
patio of Calvary Chapel, a Jesus Movement church in Santa
Ana, and they press to him gratefully, hundreds of them, quiv-
ering with Pentecostal fervor, like Judy Garland's fans approaching the stage during "Over the Rainbow." And he moves
through them amicably, as Christ entered Jerusalem, although
he has come not upon an ass but in a black Rolls-Royce convertible. "Howdy," he is saying to them, and "Praise the Lord,"
shaking hands in both of his, smiling with a sort of vegetable
magnetism, speaking gently as he did to reassure the virginal
Shirley Jones in *April Love.* They are all too young for adequate
car insurance, their skins are troubled, they do not eat enough,
the air in the patio is mildly tainted with the smell of hair not recently shampooed; somewhat awed, they inspect his pressed
double-knit slacks, crepe body-shirt and white Guccis, his cat-
green eyes clear as if anointed with Visine, his Bel Air golf-

315

course suntan, his neat, anachronistic sculptured haircut. They do not understand that he defined the youth of the fifties; no one of those sweet, depleted nuclear children ever saw *April Love,* or did the box step in suburban rumpus rooms to " Love Letters in the Sand," forty-five revolutions per minute, or heard "Ain't That a Shame" through the radios of cars with fender skirts. White buck shoes they know not. That he has just made a comeback via the new, salable Christianity (after an eclipse during the rise of rock, dope and secularism) interests them only because they have heard he appears on prime-time television to further their cause. The word has passed among them: He is a Christian leader, and they are watching for a leader with Messianic qualities. Besides, he is a very ingenuous-looking thirty-seven, and so fits their conception of both God the Father and God the Son.

"I read your book, Pat. I saw your movie. They changed my life. I don't shoot speed anymore." The boy is dressed in Jesus couture: white tunic, white ducks.

"Bless you, brother!"

"We didn't have the bread to buy your book, Pat, so we went to a bookstore every day and read it there."

"Praise God!"

A tall, strenuously beatified girl plucks at his sleeve saying, "Oh, Mr. Boone, you're full of the Lord! I read in your book about your marriage being a bummer because you hadn't found the Lord, so I made my old man read it because he was sniffing coke and being very godless, and now. . . ."

Pat attempts to listen with compassion, but his other sleeve is being plucked by the Reverend "Chuck" Smith, minister of Calvary Chapel, to whom attention must be paid. A banal-looking middle-aged man given to sensible haircuts, blue suits, narrow ties and a dentured, Dale Carnegie grin, is an acknowledged neo-Christian phenomenon: Nightly the Jesus children fill his church beyond capacity, and when you've heard him preach you see why. Like great film personalities, he exudes something uncannily accessible. This is no sonorous Billy Graham, no virtuoso faith healer. Literate, ecumenical, he stands pleasantly before them interpreting the Scripture as a sort of supernatural *Whole Earth Catalog,* invoking an image of Jesus as a combined wise parent, lenient professor, storefront lawyer and sensitive football coach. In the pulpit, at least, he seems eminently sane, and it would be kindest to leave him in it, but Pat has suggested a personal confrontation.

"This is the writer from *Esquire*," he announces when Chuck has joined us. The Reverend, accustomed to meeting the press, smiles professionally, but a youth beside him, who precisely resembles the effete, Aryan Christs of Sunday schoolroom portraits, sniffs intently, as if to detect the odor of sulfur, and says, "That magazine named the Campus Crusade for Christ as one of ten movements not to follow. They named us in front of the Weathermen and Gay Liberation." He steps forward belligerently, and one is spirited away by Pat and Chuck to the safety of a nearby House of Pies, where, even before his first forkful of fresh peach, the Reverend says, enigmatically, "Two dozen drivers have reported it."

"Gives you goose bumps," Pat exclaims. It turns out that certain California motorists have reported stopping for a young hitchhiker with Biblical hair who rides for a while in silence, asserts "Christ is coming soon," and disappears. "Just literally vanishes from the car seat," Pat concludes, wide-eyed. "If it really happened—and it could have—it's a definite sign."

"Makes you think of the Rapture," Chuck adds, turning to me. "We learn much about the Rapture in the First Corinthians, and in Philippians. Very soon now, in a split second, all those who have been truly baptized in the Holy Spirit will disappear." He snaps his fingers. "*Disappear* from the face of the earth. Cars on freeways will suddenly be empty! Members of families will vanish from dinner tables into thin air! They will be transported to paradise, which the Bible describes as a wondrous place beyond our comprehension, hence the word Rapture. The Bible has prophesied everything in history, the Bible has *never been wrong.* . . ."

Pie eaters at neighboring tables have turned to listen; one of them, a fat, barefoot girl in crumbling bells and a T-shirt with "Have A Nice Forever" written on the chest, lunges from her chair to Chuck's side. "Oh yes, isn't it *wunnerful?*" she shouts. Startled, he drops his fork. "Excuse me, Reverend, excuse me, Mr. Boone, but I heard you. Praise God! My name's Charlene, I have been to the chapel five nights in a row. Reverend, when may we expect the Rapture?"

317

"In this decade, Charlene, or the beginning of the next at the latest, that is what the Bible says."

"Oh, joy!" She has been beckoning behind her, and is joined by a giggling woman in pedal pushers. "This is my mother. She used to drink, now she is commited to Jesus."

"*Are you really Pat Boone?*" mother says, wavering above him like a serenaded cobra.

"Yes, this movement is far, far more than a fad," Pat begins. We are halted in homeward traffic, the huge Rolls a brontosaurus in cowering lines of Mavericks and Larks. Their occupants, enclosed behind safety glass like the bodies of saints, recognize him and gesticulate soundlessly. "Yes, all the Jesus kids believe in the Rapture. They have no reason to question it, because the Bible promises it. Soon, thousands, millions more will find hope in Biblical promises; the Scripture predicts dramatic mass conversions before Christ's final coming." Impulsively, he shoves a tape cartridge into the deck on the dashboard. "I always have the Scripture with me." From multiple speakers, a basso declaims the Book of Genesis. "When I go jogging, I always carry a little tape machine with the Bible on cassettes. The other day I was jogging past Lucille Ball's house, and she was out front and I went over. She said, 'You listening to the baseball game, Pat?' I said, 'No, Lucy, I'm listening to the word of God.' She looked at me kind of funny, but she took the earphone and listened too, and then asked me some really serious questions. You see? God speaks to anyone who'll listen."

Compassionate smile. "I guess this is a lot for you to take in all at once." When we met, only an hour before the evening's trip, he quickly ascertained that I am not only unsaved, but unacquainted with the finer points of Biblical prophecy. "Let me explain about the Rapture, and what's in store for us all here on earth in the next few years. It'll blow your mind."

The mind-blower, put simply, though new-Christians never put anything simply, is rooted in both the Old and New Testament clairvoyance of Christ and the lesser prophets, who asserted, some two thousand years before the fact, that Israel would rise and prosper again; and that when it did, humanity should prepare for the Apocalypse. The rest of the world, they said, would then be plagued with famine, overcrowding and

318

ecological malaise, and would be forced to unite, for survival, under a world government and one omnipotent ruler who will promise peace. Forget it: This leader is the anti-Christ, and will precipitate a time of awful tribulation. Russia and China, for instance, will invade Israel; the ensuing strife will escalate to involve everybody else in the final great war, the dreaded Armageddon. Here, Christ returns to earth, stops the fighting and casts off the planet all who did not acknowledge Him early on; which apparently means that everyone who's left gets cast off, for the Bible further predicts that before the last big battle, all who have witnessed for Jesus will be whisked away to heaven to wait rapturously until the blood stops flowing and it's convenient to descend again.

". . . and of course there are hundreds of Biblical references to these events." Would he name some? "Sure. Let's see: Christ himself said—you'll find this in Matthew 24, Verses 32 to 34—that as soon as the branch of the fig tree becomes tender and puts forth its leaves, you know that summer is near. Well, do you know what the national symbol of Israel is? The fig tree! Also in Matthew, Jesus told us that when the fig tree blossoms, the generation then alive will also see all the other prophecies fulfilled, and His second coming. And Israel became a nation again on May 14, 1948; and a generation in Biblical terms is about forty years. *You* add it up; doesn't it give you goose bumps? Man, the countdown has begun! I think it's fascinating that when I heard the theme song from the movie *Exodus,* something stirred in me and I went to the piano and the words to the tune just came to me!"

And he sings: "'This land is mine . . . this lovely land is. . . .' Sure, I wrote those. Now, why? It's a mystery. I'm *not* Jewish. The one-world government, that's in Daniel, chapter seven: the beast with ten horns, which many Bible scholars believe represents the ten-nation confederacy of Europe that's already shaping up. Look at the Common Market. Even Arnold Toynbee, the, ah, famous historian, predicted a one-world government in 1970, and he's not even a Christian. The anti-Christ is described in Revelations 13: a beast like a leopard with the feet of a bear and the mouth of a lion. . . . Ezekiel 38 and 39 state that Israel will be invaded by an enemy from 'the uppermost north,' and that's where Russia is located, they're sending

319

arms to the Arabs right *now*. . . . China will wipe out Russia at the start of the Armageddon: Revelations refers to the conquering 'Kings of the East'. . . . You oughta read Hal Lindsey's *The Late Great Planet Earth*; it's fascinating."

And what Biblical book describes the Rapture? "Well, of course the word itself is not in the Scripture, it's simply one we've come to use. Paul, in First Thessalonians 4, speaks of true Christians going to meet God in the air, the clouds. . . ."

When we reach Sunset Boulevard; he is silent for a while, negotiating the heavy traffic. . . . "in the air, the clouds." One recalls the pale, vacant, vulnerable moon-faces in the Chapel courtyard, an army of disoriented child crusaders whose minds were blown up and popped like midway balloons before the soft part of the skull had hardened; who wearied quickly of hedonism, for which they had little talent in the first place; who feared death too early yet found reasons to welcome it. Presto: comes a dignified, learned, pious man bearing an ancient, revered book that tells of an ultimate trip, one not available from dealers; of a space shot to a perfect Walden, an ecologically balanced Emerald City benevolently ruled by a long-haired despot who once suffered ridicule from his elders, as they have. To join His commune, one need only grow organically, without the further addition of harmful chemicals. Suppose the promises in the book are somewhat vaguely worded, rather fey and hoary and, actually, open to infinite interpretation. Who has the stamina left to question them?

"I still have a copy of my book at home, I think," Pat says abruptly. "I'm always giving them away. I'll stop and get it for you before I drop you. It's called *A New Song*. It'll explain some of the changes I've been through." He adds, perhaps pointedly, that it has helped a lot of lost people.

One stays up most of the night reading it, though not quite for the reasons Pat would suppose. As an unconscious self-caricature it is embarrassing; as an autobiography of a good man doggedly loyal to a difficult wife, it is almost touching. One has met Shirley Boone just before the Santa Ana trip, over a dinner of organic barley, organic cabbage, organic Chinese vegetables and organic peach shortcake served by placid blacks in the dining room of the Boone's enormous, vaguely French-provincial manor house on Beverly Drive. Although her con-

320

versation is animated, one notes instantly something curious around and between the eyes of this attractive, personable woman in modish hair and an orange pantsuit: something constricted, wary, self-cherishing.

Even this doesn't prepare one for the Shirley Boone of *A New Song;* nothing could. The book starts routinely enough. Pat allows right off that the Boones of Donelson, Tennessee, were direct descendants of the legendary Daniel, just as poor but not so mobile; that Mr. Boone was "a gentle man" who relied on the Bible and got up at five-thirty every morning to read it; that Mrs. Boone, more pragmatic, relied on an old sewing-machine belt with which to intimidate Pat, his brother and two sisters; that he sang to Rosemary, their cow, while milking her. At ten, he was singing Saturday matinees at the Belle Meade movie theater in Nashville for a salary of banana splits. The audience threw popcorn at him. Neither were the Kiwanis and Lions clubs very attentive when he performed at their banquets. In high school, he was offered a job as vocalist with a Nashville band, and the family prayed together, asking God if he ought to enter show business. God handed down a negative there, but did acquiesce about letting Pat sing and play his ukulele on local radio, and by the time he'd finished a year at Nashville's Lipscomb College, he'd won a talent contest that offered a trip to New York and a spot on *Ted Mack's Amateur Hour,* which he won three weeks in a row. He wasn't a star yet, of course, but he kept on praying. Then in the summer of '54 he returned to Manhattan, won both the Ted Mack and Arthur Godfrey shows in the same week, got a recording contract, and by the end of 1955 could be heard on national jukeboxes doing "Ain't That a Shame" and "Two Hearts," both of which sold more than a million copies. After transferring to Columbia (from which he eventually graduated Phi Beta Kappa and magna cum laude), he talked himself onto the Godfrey show as a regular; by 1960, when he left the East to settle forever in Beverly Hills, he'd earned ten more gold records, became a movie star via *Bernadine, Mardi Gras* and, of course, *April Love,* and spent three years as host of *Pat Boone's Chevy Show* on television. All over the world, boys in wide pants were purposefully smudging their new white bucks and studying ukulele chords.

". . . so we eloped on a beautiful fall afternoon in 1953." He

321

and Shirley Foley, daughter of the famous country singer Red Foley, went to the same high school: "I was attracted by Shirley's gaiety, although she certainly wasn't frivolous . . . she lived the way she thought God wanted her to. She was my kind of gal." Despite the gaiety, Shirley was, if possible, even more religious than Pat. She didn't care much for the idea of his singing publicly for money, but he promised her that he would keep on preaching and praying (in New York they seemed to spend most of their leisure time at the Manhattan Church of Christ), turn down TV offers if the show were sponsored by a cigarette manufacturer, and continue asking "our friends from the entertainment industry to join us in our little worship services." Not many of these friends accepted the invitations, however; and by the time they moved to California, Shirley was too busy supervising their four infant daughters to see to Pat's spiritual well-being. Pat was suddenly too busy going to Hollywood cocktail parties to see to it either. "I would go to a party on Saturday night," he writes, "and be out until two or three in the morning. During these hours I would engage in a lot of ribald, suggestive conversation with many people including young women."

And obviously loving it. A movie personality who knew the Boones well at the time says, "Pat was a swinger. Everybody tried to get Shirley to loosen up and swing with him, but she just cried and prayed." Actually, Pat affirms this in his book. At least he explains that Shirley's conversation, even when they'd gone to bed, ran thus: "'Pat, you know we aren't studying the Bible, we're not praying, we're not talking to anybody about the Lord.'" Or, by dawn's early light, "'Pat, when are we going to start reading and studying the Bible as a family?'" Otherwise, she weeps nonstop over the elusiveness of the Holy Spirit, not to mention the elusiveness of her husband, who, during an especially trying night, had left Shirley asleep and gone downstairs with the thought of leaving for good. (The weeping had its own effect. When Buddy Adler, then head of production at 20th Century-Fox, offered him the title role in *The St. Bernard Story*, he insisted that the following words appear at the start of the movie: "Mr. Boone wishes to state that as a member of the Church of Christ, he does not necessarily endorse all the practices or doctrine depicted in the film. . . ." Told this, Adler supposedly used several more words that couldn't then be put in any film, but agreed. Still, Shirley and Pat prayed together about the advisability of making a Catholic picture and, after hearing God's opinion, called Adler back to say no.)

For about fifty more pages, Pat parties and Shirley prays and weeps, and finds herself so disgusted with her husband that she is unable to touch him. Nevertheless she becomes pregnant, but, because of the "mixed-up spiritual climate in our home," prays "for God to take this baby," and miscarries in her fifth month. Pat, meanwhile, buys a basketball team called the Oakland Oaks, which quickly runs him into two million dollars' debt. Here, money becomes a vital motif: A wealthy businessman named George Otis befriends the worried Boones and tells Shirley (Pat's away on tour) that he, too, was a reprobate and debtor until he found Christ; that she should go right upstairs and pray directly to Jesus, who would solve their difficulties, especially the financial ones. She does so and finds perfect Pentecostal love, which she later describes to Pat like this:

"'All I wanted was more of Jesus. Whatever it took I was willing.'" She prayed, "'Jesus, I need You—and only You. I need Your Spirit to fill me. I want You to *baptize me in Your Holy Spirit.*'" And when, as Pat puts it, Jesus "met her," she finally achieved release. "It seemed that 'rivers of living water' were flowing from her, washing her clean."

Now that Shirley's eyes, at least, are dry, Pat, panting after a similar experience, consults a millionaire Christer who "showed me that God and business are inseparable." Together with what the author describes as a group of "dynamic Christian businessmen," they pray out by the swimming pool; two days later a stranger, dynamic though not Christian, buys the Oakland Oaks for two million. Pat then finds Jesus, though he refrains from describing the experience in detail, and sings a new song, or songs, Jesus songs: The record industry, perceiving that God's in the Top Ten, has already obtained spiritual music from George Harrison and Gladys Knight and The Pips, so why shouldn't Pat Boone, who really *is* religious, turn a little profit too?

The book, Pat allows, hasn't done too badly either. We're sitting on a ten-foot sofa in a handsome room at the back of the house; a huge disc of a work table, several sofas and easy chairs, a stereo and video-tape player and a billiard table do not crowd it. Glass walls reflect the clipped green lawns and a pool bluer and wider than the Beverly Hills sky. "But I have no say in what the publisher does," he asserts, adding that he prefers I ring up his editor at Creation House in Carol Stream, Illinois, to determine how the book has sold (almost 200,000 copies since it was published in August, 1970), then yawns and glances toward the closed doors to the living room, where his daughters are rehearsing a song. Two years ago, when Jesus began his comeback, Pat initiated his own by adding Shirley and the girls to his moribund club and concert act. Since the revival of wholesome entertainment, or nostalgic treacle, depending on your point of view, The Pat Boone Family is in great demand.

"The night we were on TV with Flip Wilson, the show got a forty-nine-percent share of the Nielsen," Shirley states. Pat has been called to the phone, and she has wandered into what she refers to as "The Family Room" to keep me company. "You didn't see us with Flip? Well, we have a print of it." Expertly, she flips switches on the video-tape console, and the girls flicker across the screen singing "Bless the Beasts and Children" in close harmony, like The Chordettes. "We've had some letters about those necklines of theirs," she mutters, concerned: The girls' dresses are cut in very demure V's. "I suppose they aren't quite the right image. But we don't have time for new costumes now, we have a week of one-night stands coming up and a concert at the Hollywood Bowl, and a TV special from Ford's Theatre in Washington, and. . . ."

Pat reenters, and Shirley shows him a new fall she has bought to wear onstage. "Do you think it's the right image, for a mother?" she asks, hurrying toward the kitchen where their cook is calling her. "I *like* it," Pat says, grinning. "Funny how a buncha curls turn a guy on. Something so *feminine* about 'em. I kinda feel sorry for unfeminine women, for these liberationists. A family to do for, a home, that makes a woman happiest. Actually the Bible has something to say about that. Want me to look it up?"

No, one would prefer to talk about the book again; specifically about his share of its royalties, and his fees for records and concerts, and the financial aspects of his movie, *The Cross and*

324

the Switchblade, which is based on the best-selling autobiography of David Wilkerson, a small-town minister who goes, at God's urging, to the Puerto Rican ghettos of Manhattan to instill junkies with the Spirit of Jesus. "Well, my agents, manager, and accountants have been begging me to cool it on this 'Jesus thing' for a couple of years now. They're sure I'm committing suicide professionally—they may be right. Financially, it's been a sacrifice. But I'm not concerned with any of that. I do contribute a certain portion of my income to God." Churches like Calvary Chapel, he explains, and enterprises such as *The Hollywood Free Paper,* an aggressive biweekly Jesus tract with a million circulation, are almost entirely supported by donors, which include Pat and dynamic businessmen. "But otherwise, I feel that my finances ought to be strictly between me and God. I've worked out a private arrangement with Him on that matter. Jesus commands that in Matthew 6. Now, *The Cross and the Switchblade* has only grossed six million so far, but a major distributor is interested; and my agent says that all the big studios are now *clamoring* for family entertainment movies. That's a switch, isn't it? But I'm not trying to see into my future—I committed that to God sometime ago."

Terrific. But does he really feel, as a devout Christian, that it is right to make money from the Lord? Wasn't Christ's example one of austerity and material sacrifice? The question does not give him pause; at least the changes in his tone, the agitations of certain facial muscles, are so nearly imperceptible that they may be imagined. "Yes, that's a good area for discussion. You see, modern Christians do not actually *own* the things they own. The way it's put in the Bible—I'm paraphrasing now—is that once you have committed your life to Jesus, then everything you possess really belongs to Him. This house, my Rolls-Royce, Shirley's Cadillac, our clothes, everything belongs to the Lord. I realize that masses of people are in need; but would it do any real good if I gave all this away, would it really change anything? No, the emphasis among wealthy Christians today is, Jesus, it's Your bank account, Your Rolls-Royce, You show us what to do with these things, we are just Your *stewards.* We'll give it away or try to manage and direct it—as You lead."

He sighs, pleased with his explanation. "Man, I pity those who are using the name of the Lord only for their personal gain; they aren't Christians, they couldn't be, and God will deal with them. Sometimes good things happen, though unintentionally. *Jesus Christ Superstar,* even though it denies the divinity of Jesus and is done strictly for dollars, has had a side effect of causing many young people to think about Our Lord—for the first time! But I'd prefer to see Christians making the money; men whose lives and purse strings are in the hands of Jesus. He takes care of those who are *sincerely* spreading His word. In my recording session yesterday, the audio system suddenly and unexplainably broke down, so the musicians, engineers and I just gathered together in the control booth and we prayed, asking God if He wanted us to go on or not. Five minutes later, the system was functioning perfectly! A miracle? Well, why not? God works 'em every day. The Jesus kids know this, it's why they've been turned off by organized religion, because it denies the supernatural working of God today. The Jesus kids understand the wonderful proposition God offers them, exchanging His abilities for theirs! Incredible swap, isn't it?"

Apparently the young Negroes haven't yet found out about it, though; does he know why there was not one among the thousands at Calvary Chapel? "Yes, that's a good point. Blacks aren't excluded, they're welcomed—but they may not realize it yet. *Regrettably.* It's just that the thinking young blacks have been put off by what they've seen in black churches: preachers who whip crowds into religious frenzies and then have two or three women on the side. Like a certain prominent ex-Congressman who preaches Sundays, then takes off to the islands with his mistress. Black kids see the hypocrisy in this, and they probably think the Jesus Movement is more of the same, but they'll come around. We want them to." Pause; then carefully, "I'm often asked if I'd let my daughters marry Negroes. I don't think it's likely; I wouldn't prevent it, but I would encourage them to count the cost. I know the girls would want to pray about such a decision. I'm certain *any* guy they'd choose would be a good Christian. So then, maybe color wouldn't matter quite as much." Another pause. "I have been praying to be used by God in some way to draw all good men together—black, white, red, yellow. Why, when good white people and good black people get to *know* each other, color becomes such an *inconsequential* thing. . . ."

326

"Christers! Man, they hate blacks! Scratch the surface of any Jesus freak and you find a middle-class white supremacist pig, I don't care if he's seventeen or seventy!" This from a Los Angeles Black Panther, and his party's not the only angry group. In fact, since all neo-Christians vociferously oppose drinking, smoking, discotheque dancing, card-playing, gambling, suggestive movies, suggestive books, suggestive thoughts, homosexuality, heterosexuality before the wedding, all drugs, all established religions, doctors, psychiatrists, Communists, revolutionaries, liberated females, and staying up late Saturday nights, they have, in the space of a year, managed to offend almost everyone in the country that they haven't converted. Even suburban parents who once searched fearfully under the boxer shorts in bureau drawers for traces of green or white powder now blanch at the sight of a concealed King James, for it probably means that some resident minor will soon drop out to hit the road selling not grass but the Gospel. Even the police are restive: Jesus freaks advocate the freeing of condemned murderers in order to effect their rehabilitation through Christ, and are constantly asserting that Charlie Manson could become a useful citizen if freed in the custody of an evangelist.

"I'll tell you how they'd like to baptize *all* of us," says Michael L., a bright young California physicist, when I invite him to go with me to one of Reverend Chuck Smith's public baptisms. "In very deep water for about half an hour." But when we arrive at the beach at Corona Del Mar, a scrubbed seaside community just south of Calvary Chapel, it appears that he has been an alarmist. The thousands of young Christians on the buff-colored cliffs and the white sand below hold candles and Bibles, some are singing, there is nothing threatening here. Patiently, dozens of baptismal candidates wait at the edge of the water; Chuck Smith, in sweat shirt, chinos and smile, leads one after another of them out to a depth of three feet, murmurs something. "I believe that Jesus Christ is the Son of God," the penitent exclaims joyously, and is submerged for a moment, and then led back to shore to be embraced by those already dunked. We've watched this ritual perhaps three times when a cheerful-looking boy of about eighteen in Levi shorts and Medusa hair steps up to us.

"Beautiful, brothers! You couldn't stay away, you were com-

327

pelled to come here, God brought you, Jesus sent you, praise Jesus! Go down to the water, brothers, let Chuck Smith immerse you in holy water, cleanse yourself of those sins! *Give yourself up!*"

A group to our left that has been chanting, "Gimme a J, Gimme an E, Gimme an S,"stops to listen. One of them, a slim blonde girl with feverish eyes, says intently, "It's their first time here," and she and the others move toward us with resolute expressions.

"When did you first feel the need of Jesus?" the boy continues, louder. "You are abandoned, given up to Satan, smoking weed, fornicating! Oh, brothers, go down to the holy water. . . ." We turn toward the parking lot, but they all follow. The boy is reciting, "'The wicked shall be cast into hell, I will utterly pluck up and destroy them *saith the Lord!*'"

On the road home, Michael said, "They *sense* who's with them and who isn't, and they do not *like* who isn't. This, *this* is scary: Any madman with a good speaking voice and a new Bible translation can *possess* their heads; and if he says death to sinners, we're going to have another Inquisition, or a Salem, Massachusetts. God, the horrors that have been done in the name of God! Give them a few years. That sign of theirs, the arm raised up, the pointed finger, how far is that from *Sieg Heil?* 'One Way'—Hitler said that too."

Another half mile and he says, "Listen, if you're going to write about this, don't use my real name."

> If there is found among you . . . a man or woman who does what is evil in the sight of the Lord . . . then you shall inquire diligently, and if it is true . . . then you shall bring forth to your gates that man or woman . . . and you shall stone that man or woman to death. . . . So you shall purge the evil from the midst of you.
>
> —Deuteronomy 17:2-7

"Yes, well some of the kids do get a little carried away," Pat says genially when told of the evening at the beach. "To them, see, it is a war—an actual war between good and evil, as described by Paul in Ephesians six: We war against spirits without bodies—put on God's armor." We're sitting in the Family Room

328

again, he holds a copy of William Peter Blatty's *The Exorcist*. Of the genre of fiction written with one eye on the *Variety* film grosses, it concerns a child possessed by a demon. "I had my daughters read this. I think everyone ought to read it. Because of course I have *seen* these things."

Can he mean actual demoniac possession? Yes, emphatically. "Satan is very real, the Bible identifies him many times. Demons are very real. Wherever Jesus went there was *tremendous* demoniac activity, and because he is with us today, we're entering a time of much, ah, higher octane power of the devil. Witchcraft is practiced by millions of Americans, it is a real *menace*. In Spokane, Washington, *four hundred* priests were just ordained in the church of Satan! The Catholics only got a handful of new priests in that area last year. Back in the hills near San Jose there are Satanist communes where cannibalism is practiced; somehow they get orphan babies and sacrifice them to the devil and actually *eat the hearts of the corpses*. Up in San Francisco, the U.S. Navy actually sent a color guard to stand at attention while Anton LaVey, head of that satanic church up there, consigned the soul of this young sailor to the devil. Satan works everywhere today: Those who burn draft records, bomb banks, they're all fitting into the devil's master plan. Charles Manson, Angela Davis, George Jackson, Jerry Rubin, the Berrigans—*all* who use violent or illegal means even in a worthy cause—are being inflamed and used by Satan. Man, it happened to the Apostle Peter in Matthew 16! I hate war, but the Bible says we *must* respect those we put in authority . . . the Russians are possessed, their space program is now *stalked* with tragedy, and since Frank Borman read the Genesis record of creation to the world that Christmas Eve, we have jumped *dramatically* ahead. . . ."

A man about Pat's age, similarly tanned, trim and clear-eyed, similarly done up in temperate mod, has come into the room and sat listening. At the Boone house, entrances and exits seem to be made on cue: the first afternoon when Pat was extolling cures through faith, he was interrupted briefly by a young friend of one of his daughters. "This boy," Pat said, introducing him, "had chronic asthma and an *indescribable* cough, didn't you, Chip? And then he found Jesus and now his asthma is gone and he's recording some of the songs he writes for RCA

Records." Today, the new arrival turns out to be Albie Pearson, a center fielder with the California Angels during the sixties, who forsook sports to preach the Word, and whose specialty seems to be demons and their expulsion. He waits, coiled; when Pat pauses for breath, he springs.

"Fiends from hell, now they can possess a baby at *birth*," he begins. His tone is congenial, civilized. "The way to deal with demons, though, is not exorcism, but with God's word. Now, the true sign of demoniac possession is abnormality. Any kind of *abnormality*. The Catholics, and I'm not knockin' 'em, they believe that baptism saves babies from demons. *Not a chance.* The Bible says that a child may be baptized only after the age of reason; only then can he be saved from abnormality. Asylums are full of people called schizophrenics, who could easily be cured with the spirit of Jesus. And alcoholics. . . ."

"Gluttons," Pat offers.

"Yeh, and cigarette smokers." Albie leans close, begins tapping me on the knee. "Would you like to be rid of the demon that's telling you to smoke that cigarette? Just declare yourself for the Lord!" Like a pigeon from his sleeve, a Bible appears in his hand and he starts reading aloud very rapidly. One is struck with the notion that this is all an elaborate joke, a put-on, but it is not: Both these men claim huge followings among an ascendant generation, they are both deadly serious. "'. . . God gave them up unto vile affections, for even their women did change the natural use into that which is against nature; and likewise also the men, leaving the natural use of the woman, burned in their lust one toward another, men with men working that which is unseemly.' Now, the demon of homosexuality—"

"It sure is a possession, all right," Pat says, clicking his tongue twice.

"Right, I have dealt with hundreds of people bound demoniacally to the homosexual spirit of sodomy, and I've only had two deliverances from it in all my years of ministry."

Here, Pat cuts in helpfully with the story of the decidedly possessed young minister who started having illicit relations with the small boys in his parish, then with a friend's son, then with his own son, age seven. "He and a deviate friend even *switched* sons," Pat adds evenly. But when exposed to a dynamic Christian businessman, he promptly renounced these dark

330

pleasures. This is followed by the account of the lesbian school-teacher whom Pat instructed to fast for three days and nights and read chapters six, seven and eight of Romans. "'It's a prescription,' I told her, 'that God will honor.' And she was miraculously transformed and now sings in church. She sent me some tapes of her songs and I carry them with me in the car, and play 'em whenever I feel a little glum."

"Praise God," Albie remarks. "Psychiatrists couldn't cure her."

"They can't cure the demoniac possession of drug addiction, either. Up at the University of California at Berkeley, Dr. Hardin Jones did a six-year series of studies on marijuana and proved that it affects the nerve seat area in the brain from which both sexual and spiritual impulses spring. Now, this explains why so many religions have taken on orgiastic aspects in the past; how priests could take virgins and deflower them in front of the worshipers—in the name of religion! The brain *will* allow the association."

Albie says, "I have had success delivering youngsters from the alien demoniac spirit of dope; one evening I delivered this girl from *three* demoniac spirits. . . ." Upstaged, Pat breaks in. "My parents told me about a wonderful thing that happened in my hometown recently. There's a young Christian group there called the Twenty-third Psalm Ministry, and they try to get people off drugs through Jesus. There was a local kid whose mind was so blown by LSD that doctors thought he'd become a permanent schizophrenic, but the Twenty-third Psalm people asked him to come to them for a few days. Now, what they did was, they put him into a dark closet and locked the door, and twenty-four hours a day somebody stood outside that closet and prayed and read the Scriptures to him and commanded the demon to leave this boy. In a day or so, he was beating on the door and screaming in a very strange voice and begging them to please let him go, he screamed that he'd never bother them again if they'd just let him out. But they didn't give up, they fasted, prayed and focused the power of God on his demon; the third day, he wept and wept. Then they let him out. He was very quiet, the crazy, abnormal side of him had disappeared. The last I heard, he was a changed, restored guy. I wasn't there, Tom, I didn't see it; but if it sounds strange or bizarre, read Matthew 8 through 17, especially 17:21. God hasn't changed—*or* the devil!"

Praise the Lord, Albie says. They both sit silently, contemplating this miracle.

Then Albie leaves, and Pat sees him out. One of the girls—Laury, a fourteen-year-old—wanders in looking sleepy. A black Angora cat is idling on the pool table. Laury fingers the eight ball, then rolls it sharply at the cat's legs. "I'm so *tired,*" she says, apparently to the cat. "We were out on the road all week, and now we have to go again. Riding in a bus, a different town every night. And *we've* got just as much homework as the *other* girls in school. You can't study on a bus."

One asks her, gently, if Christianity means a great deal to her. She turns, understandably startled, then stares with a certain shrewdness. "Yes," she says without expression. "Mother came to the school and now a lot of the kids pray. It means a great deal to us."

She yawns. Cherry, the eldest girl, enters briskly and turns on the stereo, which plays a tape of a new song, a hard-rock number, innocent but not Christianized, that she and the girls want to put into the act. Pat and Shirley and the rest of the daughters and Pat's manager, a portly cigar smoker, gather to listen. The girls snap their fingers, swaying.

When it's over, the manager says, "Hmmmmmmm."

"I don't think that's for you, girls," Pat says.

"Not the right image," says the manager in a voice that might gently scratch diamonds.

"We'd have to change the words," Shirley suggests. "Make them more suitable."

Cherry, apparently the spokesman for the others, says, not pleasantly, "*Why?* It's not what we've been doing, but who could it possibly offend? Why do we have to stick to that same sweet sound?"

Abruptly, the stranger in their midst is remembered, and they all turn to me at once, smiling tenaciously, like the picture in the ad for their act.

One sees Pat just once more, at ten o'clock Saturday morning on a day transcendentally bright. Beside his swimming pool, sixty or seventy Christians, most of them very young, are gath-

332

ered muttering prayers, waiting for the baptism to begin. He has explained that he often baptizes converts in his pool, "which is heated. The house is on the movie-star maps, and kids come to the door constantly, looking for me. What they're really looking for is Jesus." Usually he performs the ritual himself. Today, two other baptizers have been recruited, a huge Negro and an ex-convict with a prison haircut and infinitely kind eyes. For openers, Pat reads from the Bible, the parable of Philip and the Ethiopian eunuch, a curious choice, though the Negro listens, nodding enthusiastically. Then, as the immersions proceed, I ask him a final question: Will he become a full-time minister himself?

"My main role in life," he says quietly, but with surprising emotion, "has been that of an entertainer. *Up to now.* Paul was a tentmaker, and continued to be one even while he preached. Still: *If* this battle with Satan escalates into something even hotter and wilder and if God tells me I am *needed* in some other capacity. . . ."

But the circle around the water has started to sing. No one announces a hymn, the sound simply begins. Pat says, loudly, "Let's all join hands and praise God!" A woman on the opposite lip of the pool calls, "Praise God!" One steps back, not wanting to intrude upon their prayer; and receives sixty menacing looks; and so takes the hands insistently offered, there is hardly an alternative.

25.

The Violet Millennium, Featuring Total License & the Consequences

DON'T misunderstand, they aren't your traditional Hilton rubes, this Pasadena burgher and the little woman, they have viewed with compassion the Louds and wouldn't be caught dead in New York in madras shorts or cameras on straps like talismans, but this, *this,* it does give them pause and they freeze at the curb like Lot's wives, hit full-face by the nightmare custard pie of it: 10,000 perverts advancing at high noon Sunday down Seventh Avenue in sumptuous mufti; cosmic males in lime platform wedgies, aggressive males with volleyball shoulders holding hands, bearded boys in WAC uniforms, lesbians in waffle stompers, Sweet ORR coveralls and baseball caps, all led triumphant through Manhattan by a dozen gargantuan transvestites, brazen demonic Gorgons in taxi-dancer Lurex gowns, big vinyl wigs like fuchsia or champagne toadstools, and beaded bags which they twirl like batons, the self- · appointed majorettes of this Hieronymus Bosch homecoming. Through bullhorns, they astound the very air with the war cries of illicit sexuality, *"Hey, hey, try it the other way, 2-4-6-8, we don't overpopulate,"* scorning the old deviate anonymity with Shriner parade banners, GAY HOMOPHILES, UNIVERSITY OF, you fill in the blank, almost any school will do, LOVE HAS NO SEX! To Pasadena, of course, incomprehensible, like entering the Rosebowl to find Linda Lovelace crowned queen.

But shocked? Nowhere near, they are a decade beyond shock; they simply do not have handy the correct reaction, and so they glance about among the other spectators for persons like themselves, who recall the planet before it tilted off its axis; that couple there, for example, they appear reasonable, they would not have read Benjamin Spock. And look, *they're* smiling. Hmm, and waving, to that manly blond boy who is, uh, massaging the pectorals of that other manly blond boy, and smiling back at them, just as he did last week from the rostrum, during his high-school commencement, *"Hi, Mom."*

Then they're all swept south, through the gut of heterosexual New York, *"We're number two and we do try harder, out of the closets and into the streets, gimme a G, gimme an A, gimme a Y,"* down into Greenwich Village, Manhattan's gay privates, to settle into Washington Square Park to see Bette Midler in a twenty-two-act show that's going to make Altamont look like a Civil War vets picnic; but first, a moment of silence in front of the gay Gettysburg, a former saloon called The Stonewall Inn, where, only four years ago, on the eve of Independence Day and Judy Garland's funeral, the cops tried to waste them, the gays, and, instead, incredibly, gays wasted the cops. Limp wrist, slap clenched fist. Or, as one astounded officer put it at the time, "You couldn'ta believe it, tactical police called out to handle alotta *fruits.*"

What the police hadn't seen was that some flamboyant homosexual emergence was then about a year overdue. That spring, one had been asked by *Esquire* to examine what seemed to be a great burgeoning of bisexuality: It was then still surprising to see virile-looking males in headbands and tapestry bells holding hands on Manhattan sidewalks, en route, it turned out, to co-ed orgies in lofts. Uptown, Jacqueline Onassis and other (presumably) heterosexual theatergoers gingerly attended *The Boys in the Band,* only to discover that a sodomy play didn't much shock them after all, that the Novocain of permissiveness had already numbed them.

This new moon, though, had its dark face: One found, doing the *Esquire* story, that while Westchester was ready to embrace the idea of perversion, the police aggressively weren't. Unbenevolent patrolmen from Bayside, Queens, who still went to the YMCA to play handball, were loathe to witness the advanced corruption of youth being finished off by a lot of interior decorators; hence, the rampant entrapment of homosexuals by eager vice squaders, who'd pretend, in the dim bars, to consent, and then later, in dimmer apartments, would whip out, instead of what was supposed to be whipped out, a badge.

The public knew little of this, it hadn't exactly been a favorite subject of the Food Fashions Family Furnishings pages. "Gay people, man, were scared shitless," Michael Denmeno, a young humorously hip commercial artist, asserts of the sixties. One met him during the *Esquire* research, when nobody wanted their last names printed. "Now all those dummy gay militants are all over the papers, they're all, like, social workers and assistant instructors. How else'd they get their names in print? They tried to get all of us to stay out of the bars because bars are run by straight oppressors, lots of luck: Bars'll always be the homo's country club. What's a typical gay? Every small town's restless freak, the high-school Hedda Gabler, into getting high, getting it on in the big city, lights, music, life is a cabaret. Dope loosened fags up in the sixties even more than it did straights, it was great watching gays, uh, greening up those apologetic, rabbity faces with long hair and beards, getting into funky clothes and buying strobes; but fags still drink more than turned-on straights, because, frankly, forgetting all this gay-is-proud bullshit, it's a rough life—a really ironic name for it, 'gay'—rougher than straight, even less permanent if that's still possible. It did used to be worse, getting back to bars, because the leg you pressed during the second Schlitz could always be a pig's. Alotta people, including me, *liked* it that way, it was underground, there was *intrigue*, like there once was about weed. The Mafia ran the gay joints, having noticed that fags had lots of money to spend, so there was, invariably, this Newark hood in a pinky ring guarding the door, like Fricka at the cave, and it was 'Joe sent us,' very Zelda Fitzgerald. Inside there were signs, FACE THE BAR, no shit, and of course most gays are just masochistic enough to dig that, being disciplined by Daddy, by the godfather. You'd see the fuzz strolling out of places to squad cars counting the cash payoffs, and if any bar protested, they were busted the next Saturday night, dozens of squealing fairies into the paddy wagons. Nobody much ever complained about it. . . ."

Of course he means prior to the great pariah uprising, the Revolt at The Stonewall Inn, now fabled in legend and song. Immediately following it, the meeting halls of every liberal Manhattan church, and even a couple of temples, were SRO every night of the week, for some new gay-activist group or other, ranting about the sodomy laws and the conservatism of Big Mama, The Mattachine Society. But no one really believed, in 1969, that anything specific would ever come of all this. "They'll have a few more meetings," Michael asserted, "and shout a lot, whee, this week, we're the Christopher Street Seven. It's just camp. Queens are basically too dizzy to organize." So one finished one's *Esquire* piece and returned to one's usual writing; the big papers, though, began to note that wherever lawmakers convened, in City Hall or Albany or Gracie Mansion, they were being confronted and sat-in upon by gaggles of vociferous deviates shouting about the sodomy statues. *Uh, Mr. Mayor, they're here again, in the outer office. The, uh, fags.* Groan. Soon, though, alert young politicans sensed what the Stonewall manager had sensed instantly, and began figuring methods to court the votes of these curious new groups—the Gay Liberation Front, Gay Activist Alliance, Radicalesbians, even a splinter faction called, incredibly, "Homosexuals Intransigent!" or, for short, HI!—without simultaneously alienating Pasadena burghers.

In late June, 1970, just a year after the advent of what would eventually be called, in story and song, "the Stonewall Nation," a few hundred homosexuals assembled on a Sunday morning in the Village, tentatively, not even certain why they'd come, or that anybody else would, and walked together up Sixth Avenue into Central Park, where their leaders turned around to find that a couple of thousand more, including countless heterosexuals, had joined them on the way, and that everyone was nodding and smiling and ready now to cavort about on the grass, to celebrate. What? Oh, Sunday, the untroubled sky, the possibility of ignoring, until dusk, the endless gray tangle of urban concerns. *Um, it's called a gay-in now, Mr. Mayor. Uh, G-A-Y, hyphen, and an "in." No, sir, they don't meet in churches anymore, this Gay Activist Alliance seems to have purchased an old firehouse, no, it was NOT city property. It might really be a good idea, sir, if you'd see them, we've had word that Johnny Carson's going to . . .*

Eventually, everyone did, except the Young Christians, who pointed out that, according to the Bible, the only book to outsell *Gone with the Wind*, sodomites were going to hell; the national mood, however, was distinctly not in the Jesus camp. Gay militancy could be credited with it, or held responsible, depending on your viewpoint: For a mere five dollars, the Warhol *Oeuvre* or Wakefield Poole's *Boys in the Sand* or *Get That Sailor* could be seen at the corner flick as readily as, for a nickel, you once watched Mary Pickford, and the big film studios, who used to spend about as much buying up gay stars' police department yellow sheets as they did on movies, now gently set about persuading big names to play, say, Tschaikovsky, Rimbaud or heroes of the works of Mann. *(No, sweetheart, not Newman, not McQueen, they're not ready yet, try somebody English first, there it's already legal.)* Jagger finally quit wearing a jock strap, Edgar Winter put on a diamond choker and Revlon tangerine, Bowie Perma-Lashed, Lou Reed sang about street drags. *Whee, in the streets!*

Super-straight trade rags like *Variety* started speculating about what Paul Simon really meant he was doing with Julio down by the schoolyard, and who Don McLean's Vincent and Elton's Daniel really were, and started really thinking through the lyrics of "Ventura Highway" and "If You Meet a Boy/That You Like a Lot" as sung by Cher. Even television was no longer apprehensive of creating young heroes like David Cassidy and Richard Thomas without asking them to, well, try and move a little more purposefully. On serious panel programs, gay politicals were suddenly experiencing the raised consciousness of being heard by forty million people and asked for autographs at the stage door. The networks even encouraged the regular booking of certain celebrity guests such as Truman Capote and Rex Reed, formerly considered distinctly too *tapette* for River City, Iowa; and previously obscure writers like Merle Miller, and Kate Millet, who'd sensed (again, like the Stonewall hood; or as did Gloria Steinem when first hearing of Women's Lib) that the creative artist with a Pound Ridge house is the creative artist who keeps abreast of the times, were practically lining up at the NBC elevators, ready to expose themselves.

So that this curious, whimsical, rather touching phenomenon that began by chance on an antic Village street, and was later guilelessly marched uptown into the sun, had acquired lighting by Kleig, and an ass perpetually kissed by the media, including, now, all major newspapers, who had noticed with alarm that there were suddenly more gay journals on newsstands than most cities had dailies. The Los Angeles *Advocate* had been around since September '67 imagining itself a gay-rights crusader; what everyone bought the *Advocate* for was the sex ads in the back: *Big sissy baby boy, 23, wants spankings, diapers changed.* By late '68 permissiveness had spawned *Screw*, which, three years later, spawned *Gay*, both of which everybody bought for the sex ads. By '72, there were nearly a hundred other homosexual magazines, papers, newsletters and paperback guides available in the U.S. called, variously, *David, Effeminist, Data-Boy*, etc. Squeamish queens always bought them from blind news dealers. Large establishment papers, intimidated by homosexual militancy, felt it their civic duty to hire the new gay activist journalists (who, until gay activism, had not composed anything more complex than Bloomingdale's shopping lists) to report upon, say, the notorious gay bank caper of 1972, in which scenario a homosexual robbed a Brooklyn bank and held everybody hostage at gunpoint while he explained to the press that he was doing it to obtain a sex-change operation for his lover. (When he told the attendant cops he was hungry, they quickly sent out for a pizza.) It had, by then, also occurred to opportunists on both coasts that since gay bars were now more or less legal, they all just might like to advertise in slick little magazines devoted to rave reviews of the drinks, food and atmospheres of all ad-takers. Available on newsstands and in the bars themselves for about a dollar, *Michael's Thing* and *Where It's At*, for example, are fearlessly devoted to the editorial concept of stroking the advertisers; they even include gossip columns which socially lionize gay bartenders. *Was that the ever handsome Ronnie of the Maroon Macaw at Fire Island tête à tête with beautiful Freddie of the Puce Pelican?*

Of course the gay preachers began hawking their gay churches in the homophile press; straight clergy noted high attendance records of gay services and started showing up at GAA confrontations. At the University of Minnesota, (*Minnesota?*) a young man who had attempted to legally marry his male lover campaigned for and won the senior class presidency with a poster of himself in chinos, sweater and women's high-heeled pumps. TV presented the Louds presenting Lance, who quickly became a star fully as talented and interesting as Holly Woodlawn. At the Dallas convention of the American Librarian's Association, the biggest attraction was the "Kiss a Homosexual" booth. And in high schools everywhere, the popular choice for the senior class play was a revival of the classic everyone had so enjoyed reading in English III, *The Boys in the Band.*

"I don't go to the Firehouse meetings anymore." Arthur Bell sighs, and quickly smiles, ironically. Diminutive, wistful, thirtyish, Arthur was one of the gay liberation founders. He had been a book publicist; his involvement in the movement led him to quit his job and begin a career writing about gay liberation for the *Village Voice.* "It was so exhilarating once, this revolution, everyone was so dedicated, and dressed, you know, in radical chic. It became *sexually* exciting." We're drinking in the back room of Julius, the only gay bar where the jukebox competes with televised Mets games. "The idea of it all, and of the parade, was to show what individual freedom might be, then GAA began creating stars, in order to vote on key issues you had to fuck your way to the top. All these Bloomingdale's shoe clerks became celebrities. Now all they talk about at the Firehouse is money. . . ."

And though that's exaggerated, the GAA meetings now aren't exactly charged with patriot ardor. The 300 folding chairs, Thursday nights, are always full; behind the speakers' table a huge purple banner instructs HOLD HANDS. If much talk does concern finances, even more is devoted to the puffing or panning of city council members, depending on whether or not they were present the last time Intro 475, a bill to end homosexual discrimination drafted by GAA lawyers, was voted on. (When it is, there is always, mysteriously, a high council absenteeism.) Actually, gay activists seem ill-disposed to most politicians at all times, not to mention most psychiatrists, the Pope, the media, the Mafia and David Reuben. The lesbian feminist contingent suspects, in addition, all males on general principle, and wields a heavy hand during Nomenclature Sessions, which deal exhaustively with the pressing problems of substituting, for "Chairman" or "Chairwoman," the word "Chairperson" and whether "homosexuality" or "sexual dysfunction" would be a more accurate word for your shrink to use about you, and though, while "boy" and "girl" are sexist, "man" and "woman"

341

are nonspecific, it's necessary to substitute "genital" male or female because, these days, with drags starring in movies, who really knows?

"For that, I gave up *Kung Fu*?" Michael demands that night as we walk north from the Firehouse to Sheridan Square. "Jesus H. Christ, what's happened to them? Hasn't anybody told them? None of us really care very much anymore about straight people's laws, apparently even *straight* people don't. Who cares what the fucking analysts think, man, who cares who sucks what? Lie back and enjoy it."

Naturally, Dr. Bruce Voeller dissents. The Gay Activist Alliance president, he's a young longhair PhD currently on leave from the Rockefeller University faculty to propagate the gay faith, and permanently on leave from the Oregon small town where he was born and from his wife and two children. ("I always had homosexual feelings but did what society taught me, got married, had kids, then I went to a GAA meeting, it brought me out of the closet forever.") At Rockefeller he was paid professor's salary; now, GAA picks up at least part of the tab, and he has, with two partners, opened a somewhat recherché restaurant in Soho, the new mecca for informed Pasadena tourists who've already done the Village. Fiercely dedicated, ascetically handsome in the manner of Sunday school portraits of the Aryan Christ, Bruce maintains, "People do not realize that gay aliens are thrown out of this country if they're discovered. They come down to the Firehouse all the time. We try to find some sympathetic, um, gay woman to marry them, if it's a man, and vice versa, that way they can stay. We've gotten constant calls from gay people who've been turned down by the taxi licensing commission, gay teachers are incessantly getting fired. . . ."

Not that you'd suspect it, visiting a contemporary high school as one does with Bruce: The GAA, he explains, now has, besides lawyers and press representatives, an active speakers' bureau, which is constantly called, incredibly, by public high schools, including a mid-Manhattan high where, that Friday, on the last day of the term, the sun through the open windows suspends eraser dust in freeze-frame as Dr. Bruce and a balding professor, a studious-looking black man and two truculent dykes, wearing always, in their minds, gym costumes, address four large morning classes, like scouting corporate recruiters, on the glories of being queer. The student body is maybe sixty percent black. Outside the door of the first class, a gleeful black boy asks, "Hey, in here, for the fairy society?" There are more surreptitious giggles, but what strikes you immediately is the dignity of these kids, their sad sobriety, their courtesy, their dogged attention, as Voeller and the others, seated in front of them, drone on, about their "sexual pride," until Voeller submits, "All we're talking about here, is, uh, our preference in plumbing."

Oh, right, ha ha, what else is new? After the silence, another black boy asks, his peripheral vision on his classmates, "Uh, how did you people get funny?" He has not been to the nomenclature meetings, but "funny" is meant to be tactful here, and obviously his question is sincere.

Funny? The panel collectively swells, like aroused puffer fish. "How'd you get to be straight?" the largest of the lesbians fires back, dealing the question like a fresh tarot card, the Hanged Man. The students don't ask many more questions after that; later, when I describe the morning to a fifteen-year-old, so far straight, he offers, "Well, it musta been the teacher that asked the gay people in there, teachers, they still make a big deal about sex stuff. Son-of-a-bitch. I met some gay people, they don't bother anybody." And abruptly, he slaps his knee, like a country singer, or his approximation of one. "You tellin' me they go around to school assemblies like a fucking debating team, telling about what they do balling? That seems very uncool to me, man. They think they're gonna get the governor's offical stamp of approval? My sister, man, she's fourteen. She just got knocked up for the second time, *she* ain't gay, but my old man still knocked her down some stairs. There's always gonna be somebody who don't care for how you ball, man. Change the laws about weed, it won't change anything. Somebody will still be uptight. Black people still can't live lots of places and they *already* changed those laws. So fuck it, just live where it's cool, just be cool, just dig it. . . ."

So much for the bigotries of nuclear children. Unless, of course, you talk to the nuclear hustler, the ghosts of the Haight or St. Mark's Place who work the midtown hotels or the expensive East Fifties, folded into doorways like discarded florists' boxes, waiting for johns, or "chickenhawks" from whom they extract from $5 to $50 or more "a hit," as a coughing teenager puts it, a runaway and addict who hasn't much to say and couldn't if he did, who hustles to buy dope and seems not especially homosexual, or even asexual, or sexual at all. "I don't care what a john wants to do with me, man, or wants done. Fuckit. I care about that score, and his bread is going to buy it. He will always come across. I dunno, I don't much like fags. But I never think about shit like that." The third street hustler, or chickenhawk prey one interviews, is, surprisingly (and one tends to believe him), a young pianist studying for a concert career, bright, intelligent, not a hard-drug user, a student of one of the famous Eastern piano coaches, whom he couldn't.afford without "moonlighting." He likes to talk about his work, "I'm gay so it isn't that much of a hassle, you know, you're in service, so whatever they want. I make up dreams about who is really doing it to me, sometimes I talk to the hookers, girls, they're funny, they say the same thing, it sure beats typing. . . ."

You can talk to the chicken easily; chickenhawks, the Uncle Toms of the old homosexuality, you don't exactly interview by calling their PR men, as you do movie stars, or gay activists. In fact, the only way it's possible is to stand around pretending to be part of the merchandise, and when they learn you're not, they aren't pleased, or articulate. Eventually I speak with two: a middle-aged out-of-town businessman (he won't say what business) in a seersucker suit, a gold wedding band and rimless bifocals shielding wet, alarmed eyes; and, oddly, a friendly, middle-aged airline pilot, the only one of the two who really talks. He's married, "got, uh, two fine boys." When he's laid over in cities, this, he says, is his diversion, "I mean, I don't like going to movies. And the, uh, lady streetwalkers look kind of, hmm, *unclean*, do you know?"

And he smiles virtuously, his eyes flicking over the genital male streetwalkers sauntering near the East Fifties corner we're standing on. "Gay what? Oh, those political people, they're ruining everything. Parades, indeed. Next, they'll want to legalize prostitution. I don't mind paying for what I want; I can afford it. It's all very impersonal. I never see the same trick twice. I don't ask what they do with their earnings, I've never been robbed or had trouble with these boys, though it happens, I guess. No, I hate the bars, all that pretense, that time wasted, you have to *talk*. Besides, I'm opposed to the use of alcohol. . . ."

The new Christopher Street Liberation Day Committee wouldn't agree, at least they're not opposed to the use of bars, in more ways than one. The 1973 chairperson, John Paul Hudson, pale, gentle, over thirty, was a night club review actor-singer until (a) the revolution came, and (b) bookings did not. Like so many gay activists, he has been moved by gay activism to take up the gay activist pen: He is the author of a column in Gay and two gay guide books, sort of deviate Michelins. He addresses all homosexual genital males as "Brother," and speaks of Gay Lib with reverent sonorous emotion (which, you feel, is controlled with difficulty, as if he were an old soldier seeing again the flag raised over Iwo Jima); and he is solemnly indignant with those, like Arthur Bell, who maintain that gay bars are running Liberation Day just to goose up business. Not at all, John Paul opines; Gays need bars, bars need business, gay singers need showcases, bars need singers to bring in more business and so they charge more to present the performers to make more money to give to the Liberation Day Committee to build a stage to provde the singers with the proper showcase to. . . .

"To get a talent agent," Arthur Bell would snap. "The middle class and the bars control everything now, it's so *incredibly* commercial, the parade was to celebrate a new, free gay life-style. This is back to the old oppression, except now gay bars are run by gays, so the oppressed are oppressing the oppressed."

But Arthur does sound, well, rather earthbound if you really tour New York bars as they are now: greened places with swampfire lighting, opulent music and neatly inferred sexuality which heighten's one's temperature a degree, like a dog's; places which challenge even the most Byzantine of the bars attracting the straight unattached, where similar energies seem somehow to have crystallized, become subject to gravitational pull. Maybe the gay places aren't Mafia-managed anymore, but syndicate types do still lurk around. I ask one of these, the manager of a sumptuous uptown gay restaurant, how he felt about

345

contributing toward the Liberation Day treasury (all the other barkeeps have expressed ecstasy at the very thought). About as garrulous as the chickenhawks, he remarks, blinking rapidly, "Yuh, well, I always treated the boys right, anything for da boys, y'know?" And he sighs, his fisheyes distant with the memory of a more comprehensible time, when you paid off the cops, not the gays.

". . . just study the eyes, now, in gay places," John Paul directs, his own clouding at the thought, "the *fear* is gone, not so much of laws, but of, um, relating one-to-one. The, uh, hetero-imitative thing's broken down. Brother looks at brother, not just as a sex object, but, um, in terms of one-to-one relationships. Strangers smile at strangers. Now, I happen to like cruising Central Park, and even there, whereas, once, in the dark, a hand first went to your *cock*—I use the word in my books, that's what it *is*—well, now, often as not, someone *kisses* me first. . . ."

He and the committee don't *really* suppose that Mayor Lindsay is *really* going to chopper in for the rally, but who can tell? It's the big final major meeting of the committee on the first day of the big Gay Pride Week, which the big parade and rally and rock show will culminate, and already, everybody's *wasted* with fatigue. One diminutive lesbian committeeperson, a stolid little Weimaraner of a girl, who deals counterfeit subway tokens that really work, seven for one dollar, sighs, and gesturing toward another diminutive lesbian, complains, "On top of all the work this week, I've been going for artificial insemination. My, um, lover and I decided we want a child." She yawns, as does everyone, but they're flying, too: Nine months of labor, delivery's at hand! Rumors abound: *A gay 747, from London! Buses from Boston and Philly and LA, so many hundreds to be billeted, Columbia offers a dorm! At the rally, Debbie Reynolds will speak, Barbra will sing! Bette will perform, Midler and Davis!* But a hush pervades the assembled committeepersons, partly because the meeting is being held in the chapel of the Episcopalian Church of the Holy Apostles, in Chelsea, which features, according to its circulars, a "gay ministry" reminding you that "Jesus was your First Lover." Another reason for the tense quiet is that nobody's got enough money, at this eleventh hour, to pay for the bullhorns and walkie-talkies and autos needed to supervise all the marchers, and certainly not enough to pay for building a large outdoor Woodstock-type stage and amplification system, but fiddle-dee-dee, certain rich deviate celebrities are going to kick in anonymously at the last moment. No need for knitted brows, they crack the Erase.

Chairperson John Paul appears collected and stoical, quietly suffering a fellow-committeeperson's brief stamping outburst ("Everyone *else* here has permitted themselves the *luxury* of a tantrum!") and placating a transvestite committeeperson. (It's rumored that if any drag queens appear on the rally stage, the lesbian feminists will trash the place, as they feel drag's insulting to women, and that the gay genital-male leather-jacket-and-boots contingent will also riot, because they feel drag's insulting to men.) But everyone agrees about the bars and the baths, how splendidly they've all come through with contributions: The rally's rock band, for instance, has been donated by Steve Ostrow, never mind that he wants to sing, in his pavement drill baritone, one of his awful operetta ballads. Even without music he's a homophile celebrity, the entrepreneur of the notorious Continental Baths, opulent deviate pleasure palace (genital males only) and night club (genital females invited, if you don't ask what's happening in the steam room and don't mind watching a show among a lot of genital males clad only in towels), the historic spot where Miss M first became Divine by following the pragmatic example of Streisand, who got *her* first following singing in gay bars. Of course neither Miss S nor M works the gay circuit anymore, finding more receptive audiences and slightly larger fees now in Vegas, but there are a lot of new, eager kids singing in the new cabarets, *they* don't seem anxious to split the scene just to work some homophobic dump like Caesar's Palace. They care for the *cause;* don't they?

"An evening spent with Hannah down upon your knees/is like eating baked Alaska in your BVDs!" It's the punch line of a classic blues song called "Hard Hearted Hannah, the Vamp of Savannah," and it's just now rending the brick walls of Brothers and Sisters, a midtown gay cabaret and bar that's been lending its back room and stage every Wednesday night since May for a Liberation Day show, proceeds ($2 a head) given to the committee. With drinks a buck and a quarter as usual, these evenings,

SRO, are also charitable toward Dave Vangen, the owner, one of the new friendly, eager young non-Mafia gay-saloonkeepers; but what the hell, it's a warm, wooded, denlike place, his, a lot funkier and more welcoming than status discotheques, such as the Hippopotamus; and clearly, Dave does believe in the concept of casual places where new Streisands and Midlers can germinate. It's not like he's becoming Howard Hughes here. On benefit nights, you can sometimes catch a young singer with something like potential; otherwise, what you've got is political singers, a political cabaret, touted as the first since Germany in the twenties, when Weill and Brecht were musically nudging the Nazis. For this ambience, credit GAA, because it's where most of the new bar singers came from, the little Friday night stage down at the Firehouse. Like Topsy, and GAA itself, the modest little amateur entertainment just growed and growed: And this Friday, Gay Pride Friday ("The gay *Good Friday*," an activist solemnly explains, "because Sunday we rise again") the Firehouse will be got up in red to resemble Liza Minnelli's Berlin, with blond waiters and a Joel Greyish MC, and, sadly, the usual Firehouse talent, which does not yet present much of a threat to that of the professional gay cabaret circuit, which, in turn, doesn't yet threaten Midler. Uptown, on the gay bistro stages, her ambling, throw-away satire is widely mimicked without success. Two fine young black blues belters, Dawn Hampton and Alaina Reed don't do Midler but haven't quite been embraced by this audience, possibly because the homosexual liberation movement is acutely aware that its origins and most of its members are white and distinctly middle-class. The genital male performers are of two stripes: young old-order stylists with Visined eyes and unswervably smiling deliveries of songs like "Maybe This Time" (gay males who still sing "she" loves me instead of the liberated "he" incur the wrath of activists), and scruffy adenoidal guitarists in semi-pageboys who do homemade ballads about the world being a better place after the passage of Intro 475.

There are exceptions: There's Chris Robison (once of Elephant's Memory, pre-Lennon) who resembles, in a perfectly masculine way, a younger Julie Christie; who says of his days traveling with groups, "The *only* rock people I could say for sure were straight, were, let's see, hmm, John Denver," and who seems able to write and sing about sex apolitically, with a certain elliptical, straight-faced irony. A plain Rumanian boy he's balled becomes "My Gypsy Frog." Probably his least subtle piece, "I'm Looking for a Boy Tonight," is being given cautious play by the more adventurous New York FM stations. (Ahmet Ertegun, et al. are about to explore the commercial possibilities of forthright, clear-eyed boys singing folk-rock ballads about fellatio, but just now, during the payola debacle, they're giving the gay singers a don't-call-us.)

". . . there was Hannah pouring water on a drowning man." And there is Sally Eaton, the girl who sang "Carbon Monoxide" in *Hair* in a voice like a Maserati exhaust, and now saunters down the middle aisle of Brothers and Sisters to this great, surprising barrelhouse overture by her accompanist, Cliff Gresham; she looks too fragile to make the step up onto the stage, a pale vanilla cream in a shedding boa and an old top hat, but she makes it and then sidles around for a while, smiling, as if she knew the only really good new joke and isn't telling, and then sings, old blues, in a ripe applejack brandy alto, straight out, daring you not to find the entire history of the civilized world hilarious.

"We don't *know* when Miss Eaton'll be going onstage, we can't give that information," one of the committeepeople snaps when asked the order of the rally's twenty-two acts. It's the big Sunday morning, the parade-and-rally morning, the Resurrection, clearly God is living and letting live: The weather's perfect, but the chairpeople slightly haggard. It's been run, run, run all week to emergency finance meetings and leaflettings and the Mattachine's party to celebrate the opening of its new library of gay books donated by a deceased merchant seaman ("That's spelled seaman, *not* the other way," a Mattachine chairperson asserts, making a moue). The benefits and cabarets and gay-activist poetry readings, the parade marshal training groups, the special performances of *Coming Out,* a sort of staged reading of almost everything written about homosexuality since, as one audience member puts it, "the first bone was smoked." There's barely been time to get to the openings of *Tubstrip,* a new off-Broadway play set in a gay steambath, or *The Faggot,* the latest musical by New York's most famous singing clergyman, the Reverend Al Carmines. And all the gay buses, planes and trains have arrived, to disgorge flamboyant visitors who've crashed on everyone's floors, especially all three floors of the Firehouse. The Atlas Construction Company of Long Island has been up all night constructing the stage under Washington Square's Triumphal Arch. (It's said that the playwright Arthur Laurents finally came through with the cash.) For the more devout marchers, however, it was early to bed, alone, if necessary, to be on time for the prayer service and hymn-sing at the parade assembly point at 11 A.M. *"We humbly ask God to bless this gay day. . . ."*

Did the goddamn thing start yet? It's a voice from central police control, heterosexual, crackling through the walkie-talkie held by a young patrolman with a beer hangover stationed at noon at the Sixty-first Street south edge of Central Park, the parade's point of origin. "Yeah, just started," he returns, into the box, and groans, loud as a belch. And behind a patrol escort car and a huge violet banner, the street transvestites stalk forward in I. Miller spikes, cheering, cheered on, from behind, by a marching crowd larger, apparently, than the one that heard the Sermon on the Mount. Hundreds of GAY PRIDE balloons begin to jiggle, like sails on a lake, like the pencils of the dozens of reporters, like the Nikons of the AP and the hand-held Arriflexes of all the independent filmmakers who sense here, as they did at Woodstock, and as did the Stonewall manager, a viable life-art. All the gay bars have made signs and banners to carry; if allowed, they would have done floats, like the Rose Parade. The new "macho" transvestitism, called vulgarly "genderfuck," a curious satire of female impersonation—dresses, pumps, full make-up and beards—is represented by, among others, three men in WAC uniforms and big moustaches. So is Lily Tomlin, by a boy dressed as Ernestine, the telephone operator, and Scarlett O'Hara, by a genital male in hoop skirts and a bonnet, and a sign, FRANKLY, MY DEAR, WE DON'T GIVE A DAMN. A grizzled old man at the curb remarks, "Cops lined up from here to the Village, police barricades, the whole *schmeer*. Listen, I don't give a shit if they wanta suck cock, but we gotta pay *taxes* for this."

350

"Sex, anyone?" A big black marching queen invites the watchers. "Join us, join us!" she entreats. *"Out of the closets into the streets!"* And suddenly they obey, dozens of men and women who've followed along sheepishly on the sidewalk. A cheer starts at the front of the line and sweeps to the end, now fifteen blocks behind: Look, a car with a GAY-1 license! Look, a gay horse, wearing, on its bridle, a button that says DYKE! and another demanding, HOW DARE YOU ASSUME I'M HETEROSEXUAL? At Times Square, by the statue of George M. Cohan, who hated fairies, a dykes' marching band in coveralls rips into "Give My Regards to Broadway," and the spectators break up, sensing that they witness here the ultimate American comedy, beyond Albee, beyond Ringling and Barnum. The silly season is upon us: *Yes, Yes, Nanette!*

Of course the Con Ed workers in hard hats standing grimly slew-footed at a midtown curb aren't smiling. "Sickies. Man, there sure are a lotta screwed up people in the world." Thank you, Bayside, Queens; they aren't shouting, though, and their little protest is lost in the band noise. A straight group denouncing abortion has arranged itself behind a young man dressed as Christ (assuming He'd have worn an Azuma bedspread), an actual-size barnwood cross on his shoulder, standing immobile: The kid-you-abort-might-be-Jesus. Sorry, J.C., it's not your day. At Thirty-fourth Street, a young Negro in a Lacoste shirt mutters, *"If I had a bomb I'd blow their fuckin' asses off, look at that black fairy, man, he ain't creditin' his race."* But even he's dumbstruck by the gay veterans of Vietnam and the gay ministry of the Church of the Holy Apostles, beaming in their ceremonial surplices and robes, carrying above them, like Saint Joan's sword, an ornate crucifix. They've been preceded by a man carrying a six-year-old girl wearing a GAY PRIDE button, preceded by a Parents of Gays group, and a small, sprightly granny in a little flowered dress and a sign, I'M PROUD OF MY GAY SON. At the curb, a shapeless matron from the putty-colored tenements in the side streets demands of a grim cop, "Whadisdis, some social workers?"

"Gay people."

"Huh?"

"Homos."

She picks at her thumbnail urgently. *"Carrying a goddamn cross?"*

The Village simply waits: Downtown people wouldn't dream of getting up early enough on Sunday to go uptown in order to walk back down. Locals are lounging around the streets in smoked glasses and clever denim ensembles, passing flag-paper joints, being ironical. "But this parade, it's the losers' ball," says my former Columbia classmate, "the triumph of psychological fascism, of total mediocrity. The pool-attendant mentality. Why don't they go march in Indiana, or somewhere it'd make sense? This, man, is where acid ended up: These people still think it's very racy to drop acid." Here he is silenced by a silence: The marchers, led by John Paul Hudson, in severe macho black and boots, have entered Christopher Street triumphantly and now pause mute for one minute at the old Stonewall, in tribute. Well, ten seconds, anyway: Everyone's itching to get to Washington Square now, where, to the irritation of the committee, a whole Woodstock hillside awaits, already lazing in the sun under a pleasant canopy of greenish smoke. Angrily, some chairperson shouts, *"Gimme a G, Gimme an A . . . ."*

"Oh, gimme a joint already!" That's Larry Ziegler, one of the new gay press writers. A twenty-seven-year-old LA native, "scion," as he puts it, deadpan, "of a Jewish bakery supplier," he came to New York to stage manage and direct. His show-business column in *Where It's At* came about casually ("Somebody just asked me, I'd never written anything") and he looks upon his job, not to mention all aspects of the new, big-time gay lib, with pleasing camp-irony. Pointing now from the press section at the elephantine stage, he throws up his hands. "Who'd 'a thunk it?" he demands satirically, like Pokey in *The Group*, watching the dozens of rally marshals in lavender armbands being officious. "Listen, when is Debbie Reynolds' limo arriving? I hear Reverend Al Carmines is entering on a moon, like Angela in *Mame*. Someone said they're flying in Garland's casket, and we can all sing along. . . ." Joining us, Arthur Bell offers, "Next year, there'll be at least five groups doing separate protest parades, they'll all collide at the Stonewall for another riot. All the politicians—Bella Abzug, Carter Burden, Badillo—

they're sending wires. They couldn't happen to join us today. Again."

Then we're blasted by a sound system that easily reaches Pittsburgh, and the speeches start. *"We have learned to ENJOY our diversity."* Yeah, right on, sing 'em all and we'll stay all night. Start the music, somebody get Bette! The MC announces that "a four-year-old woman is lost, will her parents . . ." and then he's eclipsed by the big backstage screeching title-bout, not on the entertainment program: The genital-male transvestites, the original Stonewall riot instigators, are clustered shrieking in torn gowns and disintegrating pancake at the edge of the stage, from which they're being barred by a cordon of weight-lifting lesbian marshals and hefty bartender committeepersons. *"Bullshit," they maintain. "Just fuckin' bullshit up there; we started the first fuckin' Stonewall riot. Let us speak to the people in behalf of our gay sisters who are in prison!"* Their leader, a genital male named Sylvia Rivera, muscular, blond-streaked, a gargoyle in an unraveling gold jumpsuit, demands to plead for STAR (Street Transvestites Action Revolutionaries) and Miss Bambi Lamour, a compatriot at present incarcerated unjustly of course down in the Tombs. Sobbing, clawing, irrational ("Too much Sunshine in her breakfast Bloody Mary," another drag queen laments) Sylvia leaps, in a furious Nureyev parody, onto the stage, where instantly a big dyke deals her a lightning right hook and it starts. Stonewall revisited, contentious mobs swaying against one another in the lunatic slow-motion of riots. The police, ubiquitous, tightlipped, don't intervene: *For Chrissake, fellas, let 'em tear each other's balls off, we looked bad enough in the papers four years ago.*

Oh, poor Sylvia will ultimately be allowed to speak, and the entertainers will all plug their albums of gay songs and their gay off-Broadway shows and the gay bars where they're booked next; and, like Sylvia, will refuse to relinquish the mike once they've got hold of it; and a massive grim lesbian will sing about twenty-four choruses of "Stonewall Nation," which she wrote herself, apparently under the influence of "Massa's in de Cold, Cold Ground"; and then, just when the day finally does need defining, a scarlet Eldorado pulls up under the arch, the marshals make a human-chain path, and she materializes in her red, shoulder-pad bolero jacket, floppy pants and wedgies, her

353

Puerto-Rican-parody look, and ascends to the stage without need of the stairs. The emcee just manages, "Here she IS BETTE MIDLER," and it occurs, that pulverizing surge, applause that's tangible, hardly heard quite that way since, hmm, well, Woodstock. She just stands there grinning, her hands exploring her pelvic girdle, daring them to stop clapping, this friendly schlepping puffball, and *waits. Sleazy, tacky,* as she puts it. Everybody's standing now. Finally, as if Frenching the mike, "Ummm, thanks, I wanta congratulate you-all on your hmmm, fourth anniversary. Yeah, I been listening to the radio this afternoon; I heard you were beating each other, hmmm, up, down here." They laugh like a clap. "So, hmm, now, we'll singalilsong." SHE'S REALLY GOING TO SING. The slow build, then it's heard in Pittsburgh, what else, *"You Gotta Have Frien-nds!"* If anybody within, literally, a quarter-mile radius was sitting, they aren't now; she isn't singing it quite like she ever did before. She has never before quite had these 100,000 hands clapping, in rhythm, *"Frienn-nnds!"* Until she kisses her hands and runs back out through the human fence to the Eldorado, it has all been, for five minutes, credible.

It goes on, of course, non-credibly, after the stage is struck, through the Village bars, each offering free spaghetti buffets or "Champagne Galas" or quarter beer: One writhes airless through masses of bodies, giddy forcefields. *She came, she sang, that right-on woman.* With the papers, one retires at dawn to read that, even at the moment Midler sang, twenty-nine homosexuals had died in a quick fire in the renowned Upstairs Barn, New Orleans, local home of a gay church and of a cabaret, featuring full-length shows such as *He Done Everybody Wrong,* or *The Deviate's Comeuppance.* It was the worst national fire death toll since 1970, and was apparently set by a patron's jealous lover who surreptitiously distributed gasoline about the stairway and then tossed a match. Next day, in the Village, no one had much to say about it, because, after all, it was too bad but didn't have much to do with anything.

"It was a *gay* bar?" Jessie X, not her real name, asks in the cocktail lounge of an uptown hotel the next afternoon, Monday, about five. "The *Times* said that? I read the *Times,* I must

354

have missed that. . . ." She pats her Collins glass vaguely, as if to soothe it, a young suburban mother in a Halston copy and aviator shades. Her husband, she has allowed, does investment counseling; her son, Raymond, seventeen, didn't get along well in his private school and now lives in a gay commune in Idaho. She has agreed to be interviewed only with an assurance of impenetrable anonymity, "I have *no* intention," she asserts, "of becoming the second Pat Loud. Really. You wonder how she could have done it, turning it all over to media that way, she *looks* bright. Really. Of course, they don't read out there, do they? Maybe if she, this Pat Loud, had been a reader. . . ."

She laughs shortly, Jessie, at odd points in sentences, as if to punctuate them. "It was Raymond's idea that we subscribe to *The New Yorker.* I didn't think anybody read it anymore. Our relationship to Raymond isn't at all troubled. No, I don't know why he's sexually orientated as he is, and I don't think analysts know, all this psychiatry thing, it's really getting passé. You know? During the big drug thing, he was twelve, we had a talk with him and he explained about marijuana not being really harmful in any way. He brought this, uh, gay thing up himself, he started by saying that he, uh, slept around a lot. Only he meant with boys. Well, there are so many *heterosexual* tragedies these days, with girls of course off the pill. His father, though really liberal, freaked out, kind of. So Raymond suggested that he go to one of these gay parents' consciousness-raising groups. He said that in less than seventy years, the planet won't be able to support the life it's producing, and that homosexuality is nature's way of preventing disaster. I said to him that I thought there might be a problem, that if you're homosexual, you just aren't in the mainstream, because the majority of people you meet *aren't*, and that you won't ever really be accepted, and might face a future of great unhappiness. Something like that. He explained, very logically, what was wrong with that thinking. I forget his exact words. . . ."

26.

Liza Minnelli: The Rainbow Ends Here

ONCE she would snap incessantly at her nails. They looked chewed as if by small animals; now they are untroubled and her hands, which would explore one another whenever she talked, rest neatly in the lap of her jeans. Where are the tarantula eyelashes, the chain-smoked Marlboros? Where's the feverish Liza of Vegas cabarets and Plaza suites? She has been replaced, for now, in the cast, by a scrubbed, westernized young matron, the sort of vigorous semirural girl seen tossing Frisbees on the beaches of rustic summer houses like this one, just turned fiery inside by the Malibu sunset. With a little can, she waters the ferns she has bought to place on the table beside the framed pictures of herself on the covers of *Time* and *Newsweek,* to personalize the rented house. She notes that in six days the plants must again be watered; that for supper, the sausage must be defrosted, she does not need her secretary or the housekeeper to remind her. Gently, she speaks of supermarkets and paper towels.

Paper towels? Liza May, who'd order caviar from the deli if the dog's stomach growled? "Oh, yeah, but to run a real household well," she asserts primly, "you gotta figure, um, how to do things fastest and cheapest, so it won't put *tsuris* on your head. I found out that supermarkets are really convenient. Also, they're great equalizers: You're all just women on common ground in there. Oh, sometimes ladies do point, and come up and say hello. Nice." And she laughs, suburbanly. "I was really shocked with myself, yesterday, the cashier didn't know the price of my paper towels, and I said, 'Uh, thirty-nine, they went up,' *I* said that, *me!*" Turning to the glass deck door, she regards the dark, boyish source of all this serenity, quite ordinary in his chinos and parka: the fifty-million-dollar TV baby, Desiderio Alberto Arnaz IV, whose birth in January, 1953, bumped the Eisenhower Inauguration from the headlines, and who, at this moment, is throwing bread scraps to a dozen circling gulls. Not really asking a question, Liza says: "Do you *believe* it!"

Clearly, she does, though she has always seemed to believe implicitly in her immediate circumstances, as do most actors: for them all, really, the life-movie shoots perpetually, each new setup is as convincing as the last. She had believed, too, in her serenity four years before, sitting cross-legged on the new grass in Central Park. Then, though, there was a subtle urgency about her, an undercutting apprehension, and her nails were pathetically ragged. To get acquainted, we'd met to have lunch in the park, both wearing protective glasses, though the sky was dirty cotton; when the sun came out we took the glasses off. She was being coltish, disarming; her movie, *The Sterile Cuckoo,* was still unreleased, but she had begun what you sensed would be a spectacular career. She had already willed it.

Then, as now (though no one near her ever fully acknowledges it) her mother's ghost (Garland was then still alive, or apparently so) passed continually through her body, eyes, inflection, like a hurried guest. She spoke of Garland tentatively: "Dancing, it came first with me, y'know?" She would smile a lot then, as she talked. "Because I sort of grew up at MGM, it was a fantastic playground, I knew every inch of it, all the underground passages to the sound stages. Terrific! And Daddy would let me ride on the camera boom with him. But what I *really* dug was the dance rehearsals: Fred Astaire, Gene Kelly. Uh, my mother. I'd memorize the routines and go home and rehearse them in front of a mirror for literally hours. The singing came much later: When I was a teenager, I used to jam with these musician friends, and one day we rented a studio and recorded three songs, and I gave the record to Mama for her birthday. They were just standards, Harold Arlen, like that, the stuff she sang. She was really, uh, pleased, but . . . I guess everybody thinks she got me started. *Wronnng.* It was *my idea.* She was, like, busy when I was starting. She was getting married again. I had to talk people into giving me work, I waited two years for the part in *Sterile Cuckoo.* When I got it, I sent the

358

script to Mama in London and she called and said, 'But why do you want to play *this*? How could you possibly understand this screwed-up, neurotic girl?'"

Smiling, she tore at a cuticle. "Well, all parents worry about their kids understanding adult sickness. Don't they? I had to say, 'No, Mama, calm down, it's got nothing to do with *you. . . .*"

And she hugged the grizzled head of Ocho, a gray mutt suspicious of the world who growls continually in half-sleep. "I found Ocho in the street when I was singing in San Juan, he was all bones and bloody from fighting, I took him right back to the hotel. Somebody'd castrated him. I think he dreams about his old loves." Then she was up, hurrying to the road to find a cab to go and rehearse *The Ed Sullivan Show*. At the curb, some very young long-hairs asked to take her picture—one carried, oddly, an old scarred Kodak—and she offered a quick, public smile. As I helped her shove Ocho into the taxi she says, "Hey, come up for dinner tonight, just a couple of people—Ocho, come *on*—I cook a mean roast."

So you watched the disappearing cab not subjugated. Neither are the kids with the camera.

"Who's that?" the youngest asks an older girl.

"You know, on television, like that. . . ."

Surprising they'd recognize her at all, she was hardly a youth cult figure; so far, she'd devoted herself to their parents' music, nostalgic treacle and show tunes. She had made her debut on the stage of the Palace, New York, dancing briefly with her mother in one of the first of the continuing Judy Garland Comeback Series, but Mama, occupied with marriages, divorces and breakdowns, wasn't much help professionally. By the time she was twenty-one, Liza had been kicked out of at least one New York hospital for nonpayment of the bill, had slept in the Park and on the steps of the Plaza Fountain, had talked herself into one off-Broadway musical and one Broadway flop, and had served on several of her mother's concert tours as duenna and crying towel. "We traveled with charisma," she said satirically the night her mother died, sitting on the floor of her bedroom talking until dawn, "there were never less than twenty-six pieces of luggage, and I'm talking about *checkable* luggage. The hand stuff, forget it: shopping bags, food bags, medicine bags. I was always in charge of her personal ice bucket, which she *had* to have. It was her firm belief that there would never be anything, ever, in any hotel in the world that she could just order from room service. But I didn't mind, because Mama almost always made it fun. You know? She was *truly* one of the *funniest* people I've ever known! A lot of times we had to sneak out of hotels because she was out of bread, and she would make an incredibly funny game of it. We would put on all the clothes we could, about five layers, and just walk out leaving the rest. Mama'd say, 'Oh, hell, I needed a new wardrobe anyway.' Descending in the elevator, she would assume her very imperious air, she'd whisper, 'No problem, always keep in mind, *I am Judy Garland. . . .*"

She answered the apartment door herself, Liza, that night at dinnertime: she appeared very high, though it turned out she did not drink much and would have nothing to do with drugs. A joint would be passed, she would sometimes take a hit and then recoil from it, coughing. "She won't even take aspirin, luv," her husband, Peter Allen, explained later. "When she was a kid, a doctor told her that Judy could not take more than a couple of Nembutals a day, that more might kill her, but that she had to *believe* she was taking more, so it was up to Liza to empty out most of the capsules and fill them with sugar. I mean, Liza's not the kind of girl you'd even, um, break a popper with, during sex."

"Quick, to the kitchen," Liza said, dashing ahead to a little room full of steaming appliances and the diners: Peter; his younger sister Lynn, the sort of lacquered beauty who wore hot pants to discotheques a full year before anybody else wore them anywhere; an artist friend of Peter's, prettier than Lynn; Kay Thompson, octogenarian eccentric, creator of *Eloise* and Garland's closest friend, in black pants and a toreador hat. James Taylor complained loudly from the stereo, everyone talked at once, there weren't enough chairs for the makeshift dining table in the canopied dining alcove. The first course was a baked potato stuffed with sour cream, caviar and vodka. "Ocho," Liza asserted ironically, "prefers caviar mixed with steak." The pork roast was perfectly cooked. Then, in the living room—contemporary, expensive, genial, navy walls, baby spotlights on good

360

paintings, chairs like massive velvet building blocks, a Lucite sculpture on the baby grand—we sat apart from the others with glasses of Grand Marnier, and she talked again, rapidly, with great animation:

". . . for me, the work's got to come from *here,* not here." She pointed first to her heart, then her head. "It's gotta be instinctive, totally felt. Still, *everything* registers on my face and that's not good. Did you see that small part I did in *Charlie Bubbles?* Well, Albert Finney, really a nice man, but he kept saying, 'Tone it down, luv, do half what you're doing,' and he was right. I could see it myself, on that early TV work: *ghastly.* Shreeek! I had *big* dinners for everybody I could think of, the nights I was on, and serve late and keep everybody at the table and set the clocks back, so that when it came time to watch, we'd missed the program. Look, I fought for the *Sterile Cuckoo* part, but I was scared out of my wits of it, because Pookie Adams *never* shuts up, she is, as written, *miles* larger than life. Somehow it helped me to concentrate on how little she really knew of the real world. When you've been in prison, in your head, for nineteen years, you are frightened of free-side, you say, 'Aw no, it's a bum rap, out there. . . .'"

Out of cigarettes, again, she bummed one. "I just discovered this: that if you are feeling your character fully, there is this point when she steps from *here* into *here.*" With her hands, she moved an invisible Pookie Adams from beside her to inside her. "And it comes when you're least looking . . . terrific! Like, before we started shooting *Cuckoo,* up at Hamilton College, Alan Pakula, the director, got me together with the four college girls who were going to appear as, you, know, the girls in Pookie's dorm, so we could get to know each other, talk about ourselves. The first girl said, 'Well, my mother collects antiques; my father's a minister.' Like that. The next girl started, and I thought, 'Oh, hell, what am *I* gonna say? That I come from this show business family, and my father is a really fine movie director and my mother's really this groovy chick, no matter what you may have read about her.' It would sound so, um, conspicuous. And when it was my turn to talk, suddenly, Pookie Adams moved right in, automatically, I was telling *her* background, no parents, no home, nothing but confusion from the day she was born."

At the piano, Kay Thompson was lining out "Think Pink," which she sang in *Funny Face,* and Liza listened, nodding; you could feel her being pulled into the spotlight, the actual one aimed at the piano bench, and she shifted restlessly. She does not like sustaining any conversation very long, especially when someone else is performing. Her father, she said absently, taught her a lot, about words, how to find the one word in a line that will make an actor think that line, feel it, "and he gave me a wonderful sense of a film as a whole, a kind of director's vision of a script. . . ."

And her mother? She'd gotten up, stopped, and sat again. "Mama's the ultimate actress; there is no division, for her, between life and fantasy. Maybe she's given me my one great acting lesson. I was up for this TV role, on *Ben Casey* I think, the part of this teenager who was pregnant and is in the hospital after her abortion, and I was scared of one scene and took the script to Mama sort of gingerly, and said, you know, 'Mom, help me.' Well, she was in the right mood. We sat down on the floor and she said, 'Now, read me the whole scene, your lines and the doctor's lines, both.' I did. I told her that when the doctor said, 'Did you want this baby?' I was supposed to cry, but somehow I couldn't feel it. Mama said, 'All right, *this* is what you feel: That you should have had this baby, that you loved the father, but he's left you and the baby's gone, and why is this doctor intruding upon you with this question? And you are *not* going to let him see you're vulnerable! You're strong, your teachers told you that, your parents told you, *you* know it, and so you are *not* going to cry, *you're not going to cry!'* She had become the character. Right *then* I cried, and she said, 'Fine, perfect!' And if I've got a method, when acting, that's it: that I'm *not* gonna cry."

Then she went to the piano, Peter played, and she sang, a whole living room concert; but there were many other nights like that one, at home, when she did not want to sing, possibly because she sensed an unmanageable audience: Too often the room was filled with Peter's friends, Lynn's friends, friends of their friends, the Hippopotamus contingent, boys who cut hair, others who should, boys who brought boys, various breeds and sexes. Their humor seemed shrill and obscure; they laughed too often, at random, insinuatingly, private smirks were exchanged. The room did subtly defer to Liza, as any room will to its thoroughbred, whether or not she is hostess, and decidedly, she was hostess. The empty bottles and the deli containers filled the garbage, but, except for the grass that was smoked, no one else ever seemed to bring anything. She never patronized or mocked this little aviary. She never behaved, as someone once said of Julie Andrews, describing her in such a situation, "like a royal personage visiting the poor," but she didn't laugh much either, and increasingly there was a sad apprehensiveness in her expression. One excessive afternoon, she bit so intently at a hanging cuticle that, abruptly, a great gush of blood sprang from the end of her finger and somebody had to be sent back to the deli, for Band-Aids.

A Sunday morning, very early, they got the call in Southampton, Long Island, where the entourage was spending the weekend at somebody's summer place: Mickey Deans, Garland's fifth husband, sobbed through a bad transatlantic connection about pills, too many, accidental. Supposedly, Liza listened calmly, and consoled her young father-in-law. Then they all drove quickly into Manhattan. Liza cried once, in the car, with abandon, and did not cry again for a week, at least when anyone could see her. The rest of New York wept copiously. It had always been said that the *Daily News* and the *Post* kept the headline JUDY TAKES OVERDOSE set in permanent, easily accessible type, and now they could compose addendas and codas: JUDY DEATH ACCIDENTAL? . . . JUDY'S LAST TRIP HOME . . . LAST RAINBOW FOR JUDY . . . THOUSANDS SOB AT JUDY RITES. Radios broadcast dreary, specious Judy anecdotes hourly, television news kept running her "Somewhere Over the Rainbow" sequence from *The Wizard of Oz*. The week was warm even for June, and, in the Village, myriad windows were opened, in the evenings, to stereos playing "Over the Rainbow." Friday, the day of the funeral, mobs completely blocked Madison Avenue around the Frank Campbell Funeral Home, many had slept all night in the street, playing portable phonographs. ". . . If happy little bluebirds fly beyond the rainbow, why oh why can't . . ." They were permitted to file past the open casket all day Thursday, closely watched by guards: It was entirely possible that one among the huge number of the androgynous, rouged persons who used to haul armfuls of roses to her concerts and attempt to touch her hands at the curtain calls would now try to disturb the body, though it lay enclosed behind glass, like the bodies of saints. They were not allowed to pause long at the coffin, so they would get back in line and walk by twice, and, after the chapel doors were closed for the night, they lingered in the street.

"Well, she is happy at last, she was smiling."

"The undertaker did that, her eyes were *anguished*."

"How do you know; they were closed."

"She is too pale. The eyebrows are wrong, the lips are literally *orange*. Listen, she was a make-up expert, she'd never have gone before a camera looking like that. . . ."

They found Liza's apartment building. They had really never tried before; now they needed the reassurance of an immediate transfer of their devotion, from mother to daughter. An instant Judy replacement was sorely required, as Johnson's instant presidency was required in 1963. Sometimes there were dozens of them downstairs, but they were largely quiet when she would descend to get into a limousine or taxi. The doormen didn't let them close to the canopy, so there was no way to try to touch her. They were quiet, too, when the famous, arriving in the city for the funeral, would stop at the apartment to pay respects: Mickey Rooney, Fred Astaire, James Mason, Gene Kelly, Sinatra, each shockingly old in the light, tired and sad, specters from the attic of Dorian Gray. Thursday, Mickey Deans came from London with the casket, stoned and tearful, ready to help, but there were no more arrangements to be made. Kay Thompson, Peter Allen and Liza's press agent, Lois Smith, once publicist for Marilyn Monroe, all helped with the endless details, but it was Liza, pale and rational, who decided, against opposition, that the service would be strictly private; that James Mason would speak at the rites; that the only flowers would be dozens of yellow roses which she would buy herself; that this, while not an hilarious occasion, would neither be one for keening and wailing. Otto Preminger had just begun rehearsing her for the lead in the eventually disastrous *Tell Me That You Love Me, Junie Moon,* and offered to suspend work un-

364

til she felt well. "I told Otto, 'Thanks, but I feel fine, let's get on with it. I can handle the arrangements during breaks.' "

This she explained to the group lurking in her living room, for once subdued. Then, in an effort to cheer them: "You shoulda seen Kay at the funeral home. The usual Kay! We were cracking up. The organist played the music he'd chosen, very solemnly, and when he was finished, in the silence, Kay exclaims, 'perf, darling, absolutely perf!' Like it was a sound stage. . . ."

She laughed, too, that evening in her bedroom, sitting on the white rug, hanging up the white phone. She had called Hollywood to ask Eva Gabor if she could borrow, for a day, the make-up man who had always done Garland for the MGM musicals, so that he might prepare her dead face; had listened intently, said good-bye politely, slammed down the receiver, and laughed.

"Oh, God! Hilarious. Come in and shut the door, I don't want them all trooping in right now. Well, what Eva said was, 'Dahlink, I *need* him, without him I shall look ghastly, and ve shoot tomorrow.' He does her make-up for *Green Acres!*" And she doubles over. "*Green Acres!* Oh, Mama would have found that funnier than anything." But the laughter ended in a cough, from too many cigarettes. "I want to write a book about Mama, you wanta help? Because everybody will be doing it, the husbands, the so-called friends. I want to write what no one will, that my mother was the ultimate comic! That life with her was theater of the absurd. When I was a little kid, she started locking herself in the bathroom, announcing that she was going to OD, and I soon discovered that what she'd done was empty half an aspirin bottle into the john. I once took some big shears and cut through the screen and climbed in, and that's what she'd done. All she wanted was attention! I had to hire the servants when I was twelve. She couldn't, and there was this one chauffeur who was always drunk, but Mama liked him and wouldn't fire him, so there was nobody to take Lorna and Joey to school. I had no notion how to drive, but I taught myself fast. I'd cut my last class to go pick 'em up. To Mama, it was all funny, always. A few years ago, she was on a hospital's critical list, we were gathered at her bedside, expecting the worst. She suddenly sat up, out of a coma, and announced, 'Spyros Skouras choreographs the Rockettes!' And flopped down, to go to sleep and get well. Now, *that* was her crazy humor!"

A sharp exhale through her nose; she isn't even smiling now. "Of course the papers made great *tsouris* when she didn't show up for my first big opening night, off-Broadway in *Best Foot Forward*. Well, at intermission I called her hotel, and she said, sounding uncomfortable, that she'd thought opening was the *next* night, and of course I understood instantly that she didn't come because she didn't want to, um, draw attention away from me. *I* think that was pretty *swell*. I mean, she did come the second night, and cried, and told reporters how proud she was and so on. Oh, God, maybe *I'm* gonna cry now. No . . . no, I'm not. Hey, did I tell you, 'cause I've told it before, about how I was in the ladies' room with her when I was about fourteen, she was washing her hands and this drunk lady came in and started saying, 'Oh, Judy, never forget the rainbow, whatever happens, *never* forget the rainbow,' and Mama said exiting grandly, 'Madam, how *could* I forget the rainbow, I've got rainbows up my ass.' And I had never heard Mom say a word like that before, she was always very discreet in front of us kids, about language. Oh, yeah, she could be a terror. I got used to her tantrums, scenes. Though now I . . . still can't stand to hear anybody yell. I can't stand temperament. Screaming, fighting, I will run from it at *any* cost. I . . . the best, funniest thing she ever said was, 'When I die, my darling, they will lower the flag to half-mast at Cherry Grove. I can see 'em now, standing erect at the meat rack, singing: '*Somewhere, over the. . . .*'"

Saturday, when the service was over and they had taken the body to Ferncliff Cemetery, Liza, Mickey Deans and Peter rented a car and took a long drive, out into rural New Jersey. "At night, driving back on the turnpike," Peter said, "some record of Judy's played on the radio. It was somehow very relaxing. Nobody said anything, nobody changed the station. After it was over, we just talked on, as if we'd never heard it." By then, a number of people, including the press, had begun to state and to imply several unpleasant things about Peter; they were the same people, who, later, pointed triumphantly to what he said to *Time*, about Rex Kramer, the musician Liza had taken up with: "Rex is the exact opposite of me, he hates the city and loves girls."

Tuesday evening, the living room was still more or less full of loungers, tired now, but not quite wanting to let go of the funeral week, to open the window and let out the ghost. No one was speaking at all. The radio played an opulent orchestration of "Sad, Rainy Day."

"Y'know," Peter remarked quietly, to no one, "that is really *quite* a well-written song."

"Yeah," Liza said flatly. "It's the fags' national anthem."

Nobody laughed.

Then she went away to make *Junie Moon;* but one saw her in California, for an afternoon at the end of summer, after she had called, unexpectedly, from her bungalow at the Beverly Hills Hotel, saying, "I *heard* you're in town, super! I am always so *wired* in Hollywood, Christ, I am certain that someday, somebody is gonna yell, 'Okay, it's a wrap, strike the set,' and the place will just, whoosh, disappear! Come right over. I don't know *anybody* here!"

A curious, if not ludicrous assertion, that last, but one went. She seemed haggard, distracted, and blamed that on working with Preminger. "Peter's playing a lounge in Vegas," she offered absently. "He's really been working on his music. He's going to do a record. You know, he *is* talented. He *is* going to make it. Eventually." Then she had wanted to go into the Polo Lounge to drink—unlike her—and rapidly drank several scotches-and-Coke, also unlike her. She did not mention her mother. That fall, *The Sterile Cuckoo* opened, and she was, abruptly, a movie star. The Judy articles had begun to appear everywhere, including a gushing *Look* piece by Mickey Deans. "I have *not* read it," Liza asserted one night back in New York, sitting on her floor, her arm wrapped tightly around Peter's knee. "I have *heard*. But, see, I am lucky enough to have the kind of husband who just won't let me look at that kind of junk."

Oh. "Listen, last night we went out to dinner and afterward we had about forty cents left, but we walked home past the theater where *Cuckoo* is playing, and nobody was on the door so we just walked in, and the usher was beside us in five minutes saying, 'You gotta pay or leave.' So Peter whispered to him, 'Uh, we just wanted to see if anybody was here and how they liked it, y'know,' and pointed to me. No good, we were bounced!" They laughed, too long; one noted how much they touched, how purposefully, when they never had before, as if to reassure themselves. The phone rang constantly, and all the calls were for Liza. By then, of course, everyone wanted her, including all the world's nightclubs, and she seemed to accept every offer. There was always a new act to rehearse. Peter languished, mostly unemployed, in Manhattan, while she traveled, and though we talked, he didn't talk much about his wife. She'd hired a Texas rock group to back her, and it included Rex Kramer; that spring, over a drink, Peter mimicked him, expertly, and not kindly. He didn't have to explain that the marriage was finished. "Rex's relatives live in Arkansas. She goes there with him to pick blackberries, or whatever they pick in Arkansas. Maybe she needs that. She never had any sort of childhood, so maybe she's reverting. He's an incredible noisy hick, maybe she needs that, too. In Arkansas, they don't care about Judy Garland."

Very thoughtfully, for Peter, he added: "They write to Liza now, y'know, all those *straange* people who were obsessed with Judy. I don't think she sees a lot of the mail. She was in New York not long ago, rehearsing, but we hadn't seen each other, and I went to the studio. And I had to wait to see her, two hours: The agents, the lawyers, the press people, the business people, they were all on queue ahead of me. She's a good person, y'know, Liza is, but she is working too hard, for one thing, which she never did before. She can*not* rest. Anyway, I finally got into the dressing room, she turned around, she was in make-up, the eyelashes, y'know, like bugs. She looked frightening, in these white lights, and frightened. I said, 'Now, damn it, I am still your husband and I don't like having to make appointments to see you.' And she started to cry, the make-up ran, she kept saying over and over that *she* was at fault, that *she* was no good for me, that *she* had been a rotten wife. . . .

"Which of course is nonsense, but it is what she *felt at that moment*. She is very much of the moment, isn't she?" Pause. "Did you ever really listen to the record at the Palladium in London, when she introduced Liza first as a grown-up? I was at that concert. Liza was, I think, eighteen. We'd just met. On the record, you can hear the applause when Judy said, 'And now, Miss Liza Minnelli.' It was polite. Then listen to the applause at the end of Liza's first song: incredible, like thunder! Nobody expected it, and I watched to see how Judy would react, and it was weird. Love-hate. She was as startled as anybody, and proud, but she'd never had to share her audience with anybody before. Think of it, sharing that unbelievable devotion! At the curtain call, Judy literally shoved Liza right off into the wings, smiling, of course, as she did sometimes, that big, steely smile."

October, 1971, Las Vegas. Even at Ann-Margret's show they don't set aside their daiquiris, the weekenders in Sy Devore suits, before the star enters. At Liza's, the anticipatory chatter begins with the overture, just as it did at the Garland appearances. The first few bars of "Cabaret" are played—the movie, though finished, is not yet released, but she has already made the song hers—and she charges on, offering love before she has hit stage center, reaching for them, with her energy, as if they were kidnapped children just returned to her. They are amazed, somewhat stunned. They relax a bit, basking, during her new rock medley: She performs it rather than interprets it, she makes it comprehensible to them, persuading them that they, too, can be young. Then, for the first time, she sidles out from the wings, after a break, in black velvet knickers and a white blouse and does "Mammy," starting softly, with a tear, finishing full out down on one knee. They finish on their feet, delighted; never mind that Garland never sang that particular song.

She was no longer staying in the suites provided by the hotels she plays, preferring now to rent houses. The Vegas place, a Holiday Inn without the sign, contained a white candy-box living room of which she later remarked, "This has *got* to be what Shelley Winters' bedroom looks like." But she did not remark it yet, because she was still in bed. Last night, as usual, after her own late show, she caught somebody else's closing, or opening, and there was another party. "Well, it *is* only two in the afternoon," asserted Deanna, her new British secretary, with soft, smiling irony, "She hasn't suddenly turned into an early riser." Deanna, young but unflappable, had seen Liza through the difficult *Cabaret* shooting in Germany, a sort of apprenticeship; at three, she said briskly, "*I* know what'll rouse her," strode to the phonograph and slipped on *Barbra Joan Streisand.* And winked. Sixteen bars or so, and Liza, heavy-lidded and petulant, loped downstairs in jeans and a sweatshirt, embraced us painfully, as if still asleep, and folded herself onto the white sofa. Deanna quickly killed the music and went to get her breakfast, a tumbler of milk.

"Umnuh, Deanna, are we *really* out of Bosco?"

"I can order some in a jiffy."

No answer. Deanna fetched the Marlboros. "So, have you seen Peter? Is he okay?" Against her will, she yawned. "Let's call him later. He's still a very close friend. A good man." She picks a tooth. "Know what I was thinking? That *every* American girl, I don't care who she is, is absolutely brought up, conditioned by this, um, society, to believe that she should expect one thing above all: to get married and ride off into the sunset, right? It's wrong, and silly, but it's true and I was no exception. Now I did make a very *good* choice, a very talented man, one I'd been engaged to for two years, one who was—is—a pal. We were interested in the same things, my mother liked him, we had a very good time together. So we were ready for marriage, right? *Wronnng.* You're married, a guy's career goes well, swell; but the *girl's* dies, and his *doesn't,* and it's *panic* time! I could not believe that anything so dumb could be happening to us, but we were doing *A Star Is Born.* He'd say, 'You never come home anymore to cook supper,' he'd say, 'I'm the man, *I* should be making the money to buy the food to . . . .'"

Again she yawned. In silence, Deanna replaced the milk with a scotch and Coke, and Liza led the way back upstairs to her big bedroom, where dozens of stills from *Cabaret* are spread on the floor. "Aren't the clothes perfect? And the nightclub numbers are truly raunchy, the chorus girls actually grew hair under their arms, at the wrap party we gave 'em gift razors. Sally Bowles was played before as this little lost innocent, and what she is is a tramp, a user, a bitch, and a lotta times you hate her, but by the time she finally sings "Cabaret," at the end, she's learned something, she is finally feeling, suffering, I dig ladies like her; they burn high energy levels. I can play them. It's the kind of energy level you use doing nightclubs: You must start

370

high and stay high, or you lose them. It's hard to hold 'em when they've got a good steak going, no matter who you are, but I'm after their emotions, not their heads. I've tried being aloof and remote, like, um, Barbra, and I'm *nowhere*. I've got to tell 'em. 'Come with me, come *to* me.' And now they're not afraid of touching me. I don't necessarily want that, or encourage it, but they've got to feel *able* to. . . ."

Ocho, cheerful as ever, snarled and headed down toward the kitchen and we followed. Germany, Liza said, was deadly dull, and ominous. "They were very suspicious of this film there because it criticized Nazism. *Yes.* Not everyone, of course, but there's a revival of Nazi, well, interest, at least. Scary. Also, we were shut up in this one dreary hotel and Rex Kramer, who was with me, became, frankly—*uggick*—madly possessive." She sounds, here, like Sally Bowles. "Impossible, and I *knew* he was using me. I suspected that way back in Arkansas. First I thought, 'Oh, *farms* are the good life, the simple life,' only to discover that the good life ain't so simple. A month of it and you gotta say, 'Okay, now out of the overalls, where's the *action?*'"

She found it, in August: Suddenly the papers were sprinkled with items about her vacationing at the Rothschild villa or gambling with a baron. *Liza,* with barons, in villas? "Right!" she shouted, clapping her hands; in the kitchen, Deanna laughs softly. "Wanta know what really happened? I'd finished *Cabaret,* dumped Rex, Deanna went on a holiday. Suddenly, for the first time, I had nowhere to go." She is somber, telling this part. "Got on a plane for Paris. *Alone.* Nearly went berserk. I thought, 'I don't know anybody in Paris,' got a total anxiety attack in mid-flight. At Orly, told the taxi to 'Take me to the, uh, Plaza Athenée,' because it was the only good hotel I could think of. Asked for the manager. Said, 'Uh, I would like a suite, please.' Thought that sounded good. Got in the suite—*crash*—sat there one hour biting my nails. Finally called Kay in New York, she shouted, 'Go *instantly* downstairs and out into the street and shout, "Paris, you are beautiful, and so am I!" And I *did* it, to the doorman's dismay. And it worked, I actually just walked around, *by myself,* and I was breathing again."

Back in the hotel, she called Marisa Berenson, international

371

model, granddaughter of Schiaparelli, "Marisa played the rich Jewish girl in the movie, we became terrific friends. I remembered she might be in town, she said she was just leaving for the Rothschilds', on the Riviera, and I was to come with her. I said, 'Swell,' then hung up and thought, 'Oh God, all my clothes are awful and how do you talk to a Rothschild?' I'd never talked to anybody like that before. Started biting my nails. Went anyway. We arrive at this really lovely, unpretentious house, just nice furniture and fresh flowers everywhere, like anybody's beach house, and Guy de Rothschild asks what I would like to drink. Marisa and I had been sort of giggling anyway, and I said, without thinking about it, 'Oh, just a bit of home-brew.' Get it? Rothschild vineyards? Hah! I thought it was pretty good, but the only one who laughed was this Baron, Alexis de Rede. And after dinner, he asked me out."

The Rothschilds, she added earnestly, turned out to be casual and unaffected. Just folks. "We all laughed all the time. I think that when you're a Rothschild, you don't have to pretend to be *anything* else. Wow, but everybody was so gorgeously dressed, and I looked like Funk City." Here, she is girlish again, the old Liza, sitting in the park. "So I flew back to New York to ask Halston if he'd do me an entire new wardrobe. He said, 'Where are we going to be wearing these clothes?' I said, 'We'll be wearing them to the races and the casinos and receptions in villas.' He said, 'Ahhh,' and did these fabulous ensembles for me, and I flew right back, to Deauville. The Baron was there, and he was super. Wait!" And she bounded back upstairs, and right down with a little blue velvet box. "*Regardez* that, dahling," she demanded satirically, producing a ring of rare woods, gold and diamonds. "Fabulous? It's a friendship ring, we are just friends. *Perfecto!* I'm seeing him again next month, as soon as I finish at Tahoe, where we go after here. No, really, he is very sweet and gentle, this great gentleman, and a good pal, though somewhat formal. Very serious. I'm always saying to him, "Alex-ii, *laugh!*" And I, like, jab him in the ribs or sort of punch him, and he laughs."

During that, Deanna had brought more drinks, and sat down to listen, and laugh, though in a corner, not with us. She glanced significantly at her watch. When she had retreated again, Liza said, tentatively, "Uh, I asked somebody to come by

372

for a drink before I go do the show, I suppose you're going to think it's a little strange. Because it's Jim Bailey. But listen, have you seen him work? I hadn't, and I'd heard that in his act, he was doing, besides Barbra and Mae West and so on, that he was doing an imitation of Mama. This bothered me very much; but he's booked in a lounge here, and I finally decided to go, with *enormous* trepidation, and he's incredible! There is nothing nasty or cheap in it, no put-down. He is a genuine actor. Uh, he *is* Mama, he even sings like her. I was totally speechless with admiration! He *becomes* Mama when he is performing. I even went backstage and congratulated him, and he was really supernice, and so I asked him over because I want to talk to him about how he does it. It's a mystery to me. It's . . . when he is onstage, for me, it's like Mama is alive again. . . ."

He came, of course, and talked and laughed. "I don't actually think about it," Bailey explained, "but while I'm getting into my make-up, and into her dress, and when I put on her wig, I start to sort of move as she did; I smoke like her; I cross my legs; my hands begin to tremble a little, I have a drink. And I start to speak as she did. And by the time I'm on, I'm Judy." Liza listened politely. When he'd gone, she said, subdued, "Mama would have been the first to enjoy what he's doing, the *first*. You know, people that write about us, they're *still* getting a lot of it wrong—about Mama, about me. I've read lately that I'm compulsive about work. Look, I've *had* to work a lot, there were debts when she died, and Lorna and Joey's education, which, as far as I know, wasn't being taken care of by anybody else. Also, I happen to *like* to work. Is that neurotic? If you have a God-given gift, you do not screw it up. It is *not allowed*. I use that phrase often now: I am 'not allowed' a thing if it's going to be detrimental to me. Of course the damn fan magazines also have me hating my father, which is *true* rubbish, because he is my *best* friend in the world—he and Peter are. God, what an exceptional man!

"Know what I figured out that Mama really was? A true schizophrenic: The *definition* of the word. I used to kid her, I'd call her "Queen of the 8:25 Come-backs," because she would be in *total* collapse in her dressing room at 8:20, and the overture would start, and *zap*, she's on her feet, bright-eyed and ready! I'm certain, now, that she did not kill herself. What she did was, she let her guard down for one night, that's all. Did you read Mel Torme's book about her? Hah! Do you know what Mama used to say about Mel Torme, who claims he was this great friend of hers? She said, 'Mel Torme has eggs-Benedict eyes!' Isn't that terrific? I finally looked at Mickey Deans' article, by the way. He has his right to his memories of Mama, but he wrote them for millions of readers, and they aren't accurate. He claimed that in six months of marriage, he had eliminated forty years of pain, and that is total bull. I guarantee you that what Mickey wanted Mama to be, she was, and that what she didn't want him to see, he never saw. I've been in her dressing room when, say, a nice, ordinary straight woman would come in and say, 'Judy, we all just love you!' And Mama would laugh and say, 'Well, *thanks*, that's wonderful, and I feel just *fine*!" And the next minute, a rather, um, effete young man would enter, and take her hand and whisper, 'Oh, Judy . . . ' And her lip would start to tremble and she'd whisper, 'Oh, yes, darling, don't say a thing, I *know*.' I think I told you this, that once I accused her of being full of self-pity, and she turned to me, smiling, and said, 'Don't you understand? Sympathy is my business!' That was her survival. That's what I learned from Mama—survival."

Two nights after that night, backstage, she met, or rather, remet, Desi Arnaz IV. "We'd always known each other," Desi said of this, rather shyly, "our parents were friends, we'd say hello at parties and so on, so I guess it's not exactly love at *first* sight." He'd come in from the Malibu Beach, and Liza was on the phone, so we went back outside to watch the last of the sunset. His smile is his father's, his hands are very young, the nails long and virginal. "I was really depressed that night. Some friends were flying up from LA to see Tony Bennett in Vegas, and asked, at the last minute, if I wanted to go, and he's my favorite singer, so I just said yes, but I was really low at that time. I mean, uh, the whole human predicament had got to me: its absurdities, jealousies, possessiveness. It seemed to me that everybody I'd ever known had had these really incredible opportunities to be dynamite, and that something had happened to them, that they couldn't accept their successes, they'd become, um, heavy-headed. Of course I had been through the whole thing with Patty Duke, a real mess, made much worse than it was by the fan magazines, the publicity was horrendous. . . ."

For years, the pulp press had been indicting him for affairs with older women—at fourteen, he was supposed to be involved with a starlet in her twenties—and while he denies those stories with vigor, it's true that both Patty Duke and Liza are several years older than he is. "Anyway," he said, "that Vegas weekend, I went to Liza's dressing room to say hello with some other people, and, wow, it was just instantaneous. I looked at this girl and thought, 'Well, I want to be with her forever, *forever.*' Right then, there was no doubt in my mind that we were destined to be together for, uh, the rest of our lives. I'd never felt totally secure before, with anybody, I'd never felt so *without fear.* I could see that Liza could . . . handle anything. That we'd been looking for each other for maybe nineteen years and, 'Wow, where have you *been?* We coulda been having a helluva lot of fun all this time!' I felt like we'd both been preparing for each other: We'd had the same kind of life, it's *not* the usual life, and it's hard to find somebody who can share it, who knows what it meant, and she is so strong, so knowledgeable about it! I dunno: could it be true that you have, as a human being, this other half waiting somewhere for you, always? I mean, maybe love is that, finding that. I think about things like that a lot. Liza does, too, except that she doesn't intellectualize them, she just feels them intuitively. Hmm, maybe *that's* the essential difference between men and women, that men always think about all of that, and women just use emotion to get to the same place. But of course that's all just conditioning. . . ."

Slowly, the thought exhausted itself; aware of that, he grinned, hopefully. Then Liza called him back to the house; he had to pack, they were leaving in an hour for a ski tournament up north. Deanna was consulted: When does the limo come for them, what time is the plane? Could Ocho and Liza's two new poodles be taken? Desi wanted them; Liza objected: "Honey, it's our *honeymoon.* We don't want to take the kids!" They then fried some sausage; watching them bumping into each other in the kitchen they seem well-suited physically; each is what the other attracts.

The Oscars are to be given in a week, and I ask about that; Liza's wicked grin. "I have two words to say about the Oscar:

Diana Ross." Big laugh. "I, um, enjoyed her performance, let's leave it at that. You're nominated, sure you want win, but at the same time, you wanta forget about it until the awards night comes, and nobody lets you; they mean well, but they talk about it all the time. They want you to talk about it, promote yourself, and I just don't take to that. If you get it, fine, if not—how else can you *possibly* feel about it? I *will* say, though, that *Cabaret* itself deserves to win. I don't like *every* choice I made in the part, but the movie as a whole is a total breakthrough in filmmaking. You know? Look, I've read that some people, critics, objected to the fact that Sally Bowles sang so well onstage, when she's supposed to be this second-rate performer in this dive, and I don't get that. To me, it was completely believable that Sally would have real talent, but no discipline; that she wasn't really interested in being good, or in a real career, that all she wanted was glamour. It would be fairer if every movie review or critical piece began with the phrase, 'I think that,' or 'In my opinion,' because that's all a review is, one opinion. What is it that qualifies a writer to become a critic? Oh, the press has always been pretty good to me, actually, though that can't be said of *everybody* in this household."

When her direct gaze begins to cloud, it's always subject-changing time. What about her new record album, a rock-pop assemblage that's had less than ecstatic reception? "I chose the songs myself. I'm going to go right on singing too. I love its emotional sweep, the way you can take one emotion and sustain and build it; though it's not too different than, say, what you can do with "Maybe This Time," a standard-type ballad, and maybe my all-time favorite number."

And written for her? She nodded, absently, skipping a beat. "You know, I'm not at all sure I want to work all that much in the future. Because I have recently discovered that there are other things in the world—tennis, skiing, people. It's amazing: Before Desi, I had never wanted to get into the whole Hollywood social-life scene. I always assumed it was totally phoney and *bluughk*. Well, listen: When you play tennis with these people, or ski, or play backgammon, you're all concentrating on something outside yourselves and each other, you're equalized. Everyone's thinking about the game; nobody's thinking of sta-

376

tus and is your latest movie doing better than mine? Sports are a great way of finding out that there are really some *swell* people out here."

Desi, of course, is swellest. "And *now*," she announces, "I suppose I am going to start gushing; but really, he *is* terrifically intelligent, and kind, and funny, we are *always* laughing. And he is so mature for his age; like me, he sort of missed being a kid. He has been working since he was a child; he has *insisted* on making his own spending money since he was a teenager. And he is really turning into a fine actor. We would love to do something together, now, maybe even something musical. To sing, and dance, and act, and live together—who could ask for anything more, as the song says. Yeh, we're looking for a house to buy here. *Sure* we'll get married, because . . . Well, you know me, I'm just not that independent of convention. Like, I think women should be equal and all, but at the same time, I *love* having doors opened for me, I love being feminine. And I *hate* having to go.into a hotel together and there are two different names on the register. And it seems to me that if two people are afraid of committing themselves to a wedding ceremony, a marriage license, then maybe they shouldn't be together in the first place. Also, I adore ceremonies. I'm very sentimental about them. We told this one writer that we'd just made up this private ceremony and said to each other ourselves, on the beach, with candles, and he printed that we did that. I don't think it'd really be enough for me, in the end. I'd never have kids without being married, I just couldn't. *Not* that I want them. Oh, I would love to, when I'm about thirty. I couldn't devote myself to motherhood right now, there is just too much else to do. . . ."

Quiet frown. "Do you think I've changed, since we met?"

"You're older."

"Sure, but I've been . . . consistent. Haven't I? *I* think I've been a pretty clear-cut person. Hah, so funny, one interviewer recently started out by saying he'd heard that I drink a bottle of Grand Marnier *per day!* Hilarious. The point is, they all seem so disappointed that I haven't turned into some kind of jaded, raging monster. They seem to expect me to explain why I *haven't.*" Pointing to the bedroom again, she adds, "Thank *God*

377

that in there is one person in the world I don't have to explain myself to. Because he *knows*. To this man, you see, I do *not* have to *apologize* for being *very good at what I do*."

The day after the Academy Awards, she calls, breathless, from her father's house in Beverly Hills. In the background, multiple conversation: They're having a meeting with the business people for the film they'll do together this summer, wisely waiting until the Oscar was announced to close the deal, but she doesn't say that. What she says is, "Today, I feel a *lot* of faith in the film industry, because last night they gave a truly courageous, experimental movie its proper due." You point out that it wasn't *Cabaret* itself they gave the Oscar to, but she doesn't seem to hear that, someone near her is trying to speak to her. "And, I'm pretty excited about my profession today. Got the statue right here, with the ones Daddy won. Had a whole acceptance speech ready, got up there and could *not* remember a word of it. There's something I wanted to say that I didn't, maybe you could sort of, um, say it for me?"

One waits. "That . . . I am a very *lucky* lady."

That's *all?* "That I'm very lucky to be in a business I love, in an industry that supports me."

Oh, for Christ's sake, come off it. Though you long to say that aloud, you don't. Something's warned you before now: As canny as she can be, at times, there are these other moments, like the ones in the Polo Lounge, when she genuinely cannot hear herself transforming herself into Liza's Public Presence. The camera is turning again, in her head, but now she's living the life-movie without remembering it's a movie, as fake as the real ones. Chillingly, she sounds like her mother in *A Star Is Born,* the vocal tremolo is Vicki Lester, accepting the award for Norman Main.

She goes on a bit, it doesn't play. You interrupt, repeating what another actress at a post-Awards party said, "Liza got the Oscar because this town fucked her mother, and now they're doing their penance."

Prolonged unquiet silence. "Bull. Who said that? Oh, her; well she's a *bit* long-in-the-teeth. The young here, they see me as *me*. Me." The tremolo disintegrates, something febrile and serrated replaces it. "I did *not* like, at the Oscars, what that what's-his-name, Clint Eastwood, said before he gave it to me—that crap about in Hollywood, bloodlines count, and Liza's got the bloodlines. Sally in *Cabaret,* that performance was *mine.* Did you notice what I said accepting it, very pointedly? 'Thank you for giving *me* this award, you've made *me* very happy.'"